THE MURDER OF
WILLIE LINCOLN

❧ A JOHN HAY MYSTERY ❧

The Murder of Willie Lincoln

BURT SOLOMON

A TOM DOHERTY ASSOCIATES BOOK

NEW YORK

THE MURDER OF WILLIE LINCOLN

Copyright © 2017 by Burt Solomon

A Forge Book
Published by Tom Doherty Associates
175 Fifth Avenue
New York, NY 10010

Forge® is a registered trademark of Macmillan Publishing Group, LLC.

ISBN 978-0-7653-8583-3

Printed in the United States of America

To Jack and Nolan,
the next generation

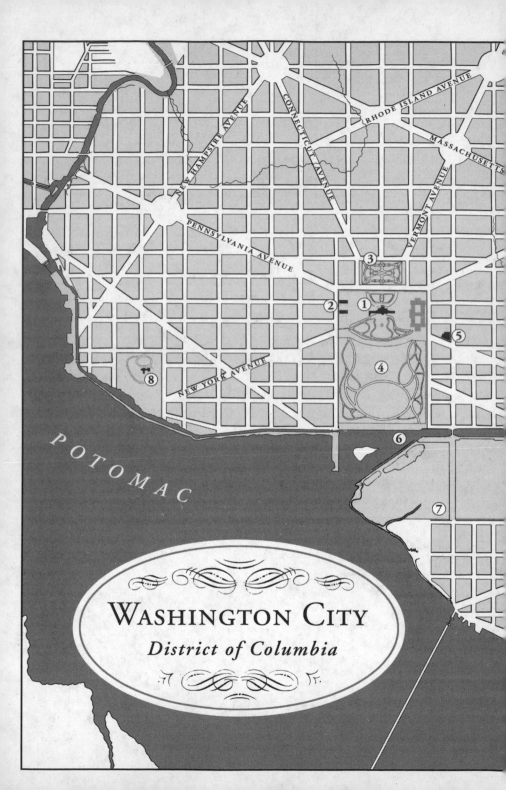

RHODE ISLAND AVENUE

MASSACHUSETTS

NEW HAMPSHIRE AVENUE

CONNECTICUT AVENUE

VERMONT AVENUE

PENNSYLVANIA AVENUE

NEW YORK AVENUE

① ② ③ ④ ⑤ ⑥ ⑦ ⑧

P O T O M A C

WASHINGTON CITY

District of Columbia

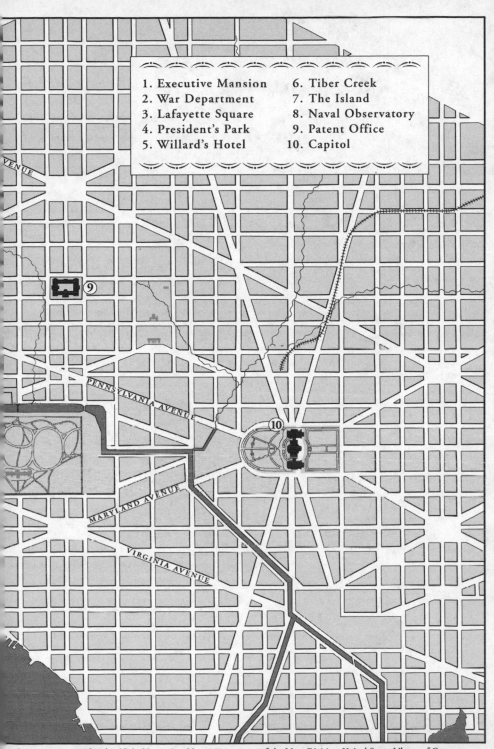

1. Executive Mansion
2. War Department
3. Lafayette Square
4. President's Park
5. Willard's Hotel
6. Tiber Creek
7. The Island
8. Naval Observatory
9. Patent Office
10. Capitol

THE MURDER OF
WILLIE LINCOLN

Chapter One

John Hay strolled to the double doors of the East-room. From his embroidered waistcoat he drew his grandfather's gold pocket watch, with the delicate links in the chain. It was two minutes before ten o'clock. Hay was late, although not as late as he would have liked. President Lincoln's assistant private secretary, just twenty-three years old, cottoned to nightlife of almost any description. But receptions in the Executive Mansion were simply work in a different dress—and for the gentlemen, not so different. Socializing in Washington City, Hay had learned, was not about pleasure.

Just outside the opened doors, the Marine Band played its absurd adaptations of operatic airs, its director having conferred with Madam President about the evening's selections. The butlers hovered in their mulberry uniforms, made to match Mrs. Lincoln's new set of china.

Hay glanced at himself in the gilded French looking glass and, as usual, liked what he saw. He could understand how his countenance might be mistaken for Edgar Allan Poe's—more than one feminine admirer had told him so—before the poet's descent into sweet wine and laudanum. Only, lighter in complexion and a dollop more debonair. His mischievous hazel eyes, the sparse yet raffish mustache, the nut-brown hair pomaded and parted fashionably to the side, the smile that Hay could turn devilish on command—the aesthete in him approved. His dainty chin and scrawny build were hardly his own doing and, therefore, no cause for shame. The same for his peach-blossom face, as innocent as an altar boy's, which served to conceal the machinations within.

The grandest room in the Executive Mansion, the East-room was considered one of the finest (Hay shuddered to think) in Christendom. The high frescoed ceiling and the three glittering chandeliers told of a designer trying too hard. As did the new carpet of Belgian velvet, ocean green and embellished with roses, woven into a single piece, as lush and meticulous as a medieval tapestry—and nearly as expensive. Hay had handled the $2,575 invoice from Carryl and Brother, the Philadelphia merchants who were also responsible for the gaudy new bed in the Prince of Wales Room.

The East-room was less crowded than Hay had expected. He noted with satisfaction that the desperation for invitations among the city's social aristocracy had evidently been unaccompanied by any actual desire to attend. Either that, or the Republicans who had conquered this southern, standoffish city had learned at last the politesse of a late arrival.

At the center of the room, the president and his wife stood back-to-back. They reminded Hay of a telegraph pole by a carousel, an asymmetry of shape that belonged onstage at Christy's minstrels, after the Ethiopian songs and before the burlesque. "The long and the short of it," Lincoln liked to say. Well-wishers stood in a line, concealing all but the apex of Mrs. Lincoln's black-and-white flowered headdress, the crêpe myrtle drooping down. The president's head and shoulders bobbed above the circle of guests, his swallowtail coat hanging on his angular frame, a white kid glove protecting his hand, as he bowed in mechanical greeting: "Good evening, Lord Lyons . . . Senator Sumner, a pleasure . . . General Doubleday, how do you do?" Hay strode in the Lincolns' direction, meaning to relieve whoever was announcing the guests. A tedious duty, but a duty nonetheless.

He passed by Mrs. Lincoln, almost as near as the radius of her hoop skirt. Her face was plump, and her eyes were unnaturally bright—an untamable look. For an instant, Hay caught sight of what the Ancient must have seen in her once, a vivacity that was not exactly beauty but could fool a man into thinking it was. To-night, she was swathed in Mrs. Keckly's simple and elegant gown of a dazzling white satin with flounces of black lace and a train a yard in length and a half yard wide. She showed her bare shoulders and daringly deep décolletage, leaving her milking vessels on display. This is what women do, Hay supposed, when they doubt their looks or worth.

Mary Lincoln swiveled toward Hay as if to shake another hand. When she saw who it was, she flinched. The president, in his magical way, noticed the awkwardness behind his back; turning toward Hay's unspoken inquiry, he shook his head and sent his aide away.

Hay espied Nicolay standing along the back wall, by the liquid refreshments. As Lincoln's private secretary, John George Nicolay was Hay's immediate boss, as well as his roommate upstairs and his dearest friend.

Hay weaved his way between the couples strolling past. The candlelight from the chandeliers and the sconces reflected off the men's silken vests and the ladies' satins and jewels. Hay was careful not to step on the hem of any floor-length gown. He kept his eyes to the carpet so as not to be waylaid. (Faces were not Hay's forte; nor were names, truth be told.) He listened hard to the snatches of chatter he passed through. About the congressional debate over the bill to issue another $100 million in greenbacks as legal tender. About the Senate's two-thirds vote that afternoon to expel Bright of Indiana, an obstinate Democrat, for addressing a letter to Jefferson Davis as the president of the Confederacy—treasonable communication—*before* the war broke out. About the war, the war, the war, always the war. The departure of the Burnside expedition, its flotilla sailing along the Virginia coast, toward the Carolinas. The fifteen hundred Confederates who threw down their arms after the rout at Mill Springs in Kentucky. The Union army's foray into Tennessee. The chessboard of a war that would surely end by springtime. Or by harvest time. Or by Christmas. Or never.

He had nearly reached Nicolay when he heard a voice like the chime of a crystal bell. A scrum of men, young and not so young, concealed its source, but Hay effortlessly pictured Kate Chase's face— the taut ivory skin, the coquettish tilt of her head, the long eyelashes and sinuous neck, her features as delicate as a china doll's, a pout ever poised at the corners of her impertinent mouth. Her round, sweet face that hid the venom beneath. Two manly backs parted, revealing the twenty-one-year-old daughter of the secretary of the Treasury, holding court. Her mauve silk dress, devoid of ornamentation, intensified her violet eyes. Her regal self-possession had excited the jealousies of every lady in Washington City, especially the one whom the correspondent for *The Times* of London had dubbed the *First* Lady.

"Good evening, Mister Hay," Kate Chase said.

He felt himself blush. "A pleasure, as . . ." He hesitated.

"Always," she finished.

He had intended to say *usual*. "As always," he agreed, bowing low, too low, sarcastically low. "And lovely as always. And ever so kind as always, to all who love you."

He glanced around at her worshipers. Hay had dismissed the rumors of her dalliance with a married young industrialist back home, in Ohio. But the thirty-one-year-old governor of Rhode Island posed more of a threat. William Sprague IV was not only a veteran of Bull Run, but his calico-milling millions could pull the presidency within Kate's duplicitous father's grasp; no greater ambition did Salmon—or Kate—Chase harbor. And should the Boy Governor come up lame, by the grace of a wretch's God, there was the dashing young war hero who at present was standing stiffly at her side. Colonel James A. Garfield had a chestful of medals, a colonel-sized build, and an extravagant beard that hid half his face. One wooer was a millionaire, the other a certified warrior. How could a stone-broke civilian compete? She had caught his eye—indeed, every man's eye—at the inauguration, and she had allowed him to accompany her to the odd senator's dinner and to the Hell-cat's Blue Room soirées. She would smile at Hay and lean her cheek in for a peck, or occasionally more, but for the most part kept him literally at arm's length.

"Yes, kind above all," she said. "That is my mission in life. That, and love."

"Ah, love. 'I fear thy kisses, gentle maiden. Thou needest not fear mine,'" Hay recited. "Shelley, as you are doubtless aware."

"I am, sir. But please allow me to assure you that I fear nothing of the sort." There was a tittering all around. "And you, Mister Hay, shall never need fear mine."

A guffaw from Hay's left.

"Then if you will excuse me, my dear Miss Chase, I shall leave you to your many suitors." Hay struggled to hide his exasperation. "My sorrows need to be drowned."

"As you prefer, Mister Hay," she announced to his back. He could imagine her taunting smile. "As always."

Ordinarily, things came easily to Hay. At Brown, he had rarely cracked a book, yet a Phi Beta Kappa key mingled with the ashes on his bedside table upstairs. He was equally adept at friendship; his apparent lack of need for it (which masked his longing) drew other men in. With women, however, everything was different. In his verbal duels with Kate Chase, why did he always finish second? Or possibly he failed to notice when he won. In either case, he kept returning for more. Hay was not the sort of man inclined to cozy up to pain, although he would accept it, or at least tolerate it, for a purpose. His purpose with Kate Chase, of course, was obvious to everyone, even to himself, and so was her advantage, the oldest known. No, not that—well, not only that. It was that he wanted her more than she wanted him—or wanted anyone, best he could tell. This was the source of her power, and not over Hay alone. In a kinder world, the knowledge that other men shared his plight would have eased his pain, but not in this one.

Hay made a beeline for the table in the back. The gigantic Japanese punch bowl was filled to the brim, twenty bottles of champagne mixed in unknowable proportions with rum and arrack. (Hay had seen those invoices, too.) He was scooping the ambrosial liquid into a crystal cup when Nicolay approached with a brotherly smirk.

"And how, may I ask, is the lovely Miss Chase?" he said. A trace of Bavaria, where Nicolay had spent his earliest years, still stiffened his diction. Orphaned at an early age, he had always toiled long hours to get by, and had never bothered to become an American citizen, as Hay alone was aware. Nicolay had no family and no confidants, save for Therena and Hay.

"Miss Chaste, you mean," Hay said.

"I see nothing has changed. Except that you have learned, no doubt, your proper place."

"Not this year," Hay replied with a toss of his head. "Maybe next."

"We can but hope."

The cadaverous Nicolay was ordinarily the least fanciful and the most literal of men—taciturn, methodical, and oh so German. His head was shaped like an inverted teardrop; the V of a receding hairline topped an elongated forehead, deeply set eyes, and emaciated cheeks, then narrowed into a pursed mouth and a scraggly Vandyke. His reputation for seeming sour and aloof to the point of arrogance was not undeserved— and ever useful to a president who hated to turn anyone away. For the perpetual lines of job seekers who snaked up the stairs and into Lincoln's reception room, hoping to gain (as they invariably protested) a scant five minutes of the president's time, it was Nicolay's job to impede them. He had a gift for saying no in the most disagreeable manner. But never to Hay.

"How 'bout this?" said Hay. He leaned his head to the side and started to compose:

> *Ill fares the man who vainly tries*
> *To gaze into a woman's eyes . . .*

Not bad. Then, stalling, Hay gazed at the ceiling, trolling for rhymes in his mind—*ties, fries, sighs, cries* . . . Hmmm.

> *She will keep him* . . . What—locked, sad, torn? . . . *will*
>   *keep him fraught*—yes!—*until he cries . . .*
> *And gains the advantage of her* . . . Hay paused, then
>   grinned. . . . *thighs.*

Hay expected Nicolay to laugh—a rarity—but instead a faraway look entered his doleful blue eyes. He must miss Therena terribly; Nico's fiancée was still in Illinois. That was where Nicolay had labored for Lincoln's long-shot campaign as the journalist-turned-clerk in the Illinois secretary of state's office, which was practically the state's Republican headquarters. After Lincoln was nominated for president, Nicolay became his private secretary and asked Hay, his pal from earlier days, to help out. Hay was reading for the law in his uncle's firm—on the same floor, in the same building, as the Lincoln-Herndon Law Office—and found any diversion desirable. Now, it was Hay who laughed instead.

Then he gestured back toward the Lincolns and said, "No one?" Announcing the guests, he meant; they spoke in shorthand.

"No need." Nicolay had returned to himself. "So sayeth the Ancient. He is on his own to-night." From anyone else, Hay would have suspected sarcasm. But not from Nicolay, whose reverence for Lincoln was unabridged.

"The Hell-cat, too?"

"*She* invited these people, so she ought to know who in blue blazes they are. Those were *his* words. Out loud. Not in her presence, of course."

"Eight hundred fifty of her closest friends," Hay said.

"Precisely. So, Johnny, accept the manna when it falls."

"Even at Maillard's prices?" Mrs. Lincoln had hired the celebrated caterer of New York to create masterpieces of the confectioners' art— the model of Fort Sumter, the frigate *Union* with forty cannons, Jackson's Hermitage, a Chinese pagoda, a Roman temple, all of it spun from sugar, every spar and strut and swirl—burdening tables beyond the State Dining Room's locked doors.

A half smile from Nicolay. It annoyed Hay how good that made him feel. Nicolay's expressions of pleasure had to be earned.

Hay said, "Where is Bob?" The Lincolns' eldest son, Robert, had finished his examinations at Harvard and arrived by train in time for the ball.

"Upstairs, I suppose. The covers over his head."

"I envy him."

Hay surveyed the hourglass-shaped women who paraded arm in arm with the men in black. A Noah's ark of two-legged mammals, with hides in the most vibrant of hues—as in nature, Hay reflected, among the menfolk, too. The peacocks of generals with their rainbows of medals, embroidered cuffs, and brass buttons left stylishly unbuttoned. The diplomats, the deadest of deadwood, ennobled in plumes and gold lace. And the fairer sex—the congressmen's consorts trying to out-crinoline the senators' wives. The bejeweled doyennes who were secret secessionists but, for lack of courage or gold, had not fled south. Yet.

"Intolerable bores, all," Hay muttered. "So, Nico, here is a game. Pick out the secret secesh."

"Too easy, Johnny."

"True. So, pick out the radicals." He meant the fire-breathing Republicans in Congress who deemed Lincoln too passive about slavery.

Nicolay chortled. "*Too* easy."

"Right again. Then this. The men of dishonor and their ladies." Nicolay laughed so violently that a splash of colorless punch leapt from his cup and sank into the carpet. "And naturally I mean 'ladies' in the anatomical, not the poetical, sense."

"How old did you say you are, Johnny Hay?"

"Old enough."

Hay happened to glance back toward the president, who was engaged in conversation with a short, pudgy man doing most of the talking. Lincoln towered over him and cocked his head, paying close attention, then flailed his right arm overhead, toward the ceiling. At the floor above.

Abruptly, the shorter man swiveled and bolted toward the double door. The president followed in his awkward heron's gait.

For five or six seconds, the East-room seemed frozen, oddly in suspense. Strains from *La Traviata* wafted in from beyond, unheeded. All eyes were on . . . her. Mrs. Lincoln flicked her ivory fan, its feathers dyed emerald green. Ever so slowly, she spun toward the spot where her husband had stood, and she wobbled like a child's top about to tip. Then, with a visible effort, she straightened herself and suddenly swept toward the door. The ball-goers parted like the Red Sea and let her pass through, then flowed back into one.

"What on earth was that?" Hay said.

"Maybe Willie," Nicolay replied. The boy had fallen ill the previous day, after riding his new pony along the canal. "Or Robert suffocated under his blanket. Or just Tad tearing up the place."

"If it was Tad," Hay pointed out, "the Ancient would never interfere."

⊣►═◄⊢

Day after awful day, eleven-year-old Willie Lincoln's low, muttering delirium alternated with a stupor that occasionally lapsed into a coma. His mother never left his bedside. The president summoned every expert he could find. The swings in the boy's symptoms bewildered the doctors, although with typhoid fever, they said—for such was their diagnosis—often the only pattern was no pattern. His fever came and went, but every time he got worse, he was worse than before. Willie was treated with astringents—acetate of lead, dilute acids—and belladonna. He was given Peruvian bark and beef tea and also doses of brandy and wine. Strong medicines, folk medicines, almost anything that might work. He was bathed in cold water containing chlorate of potash and took laudanum for the pain until it made him too groggy. President Lincoln had forbidden Dr. Stone from applying leeches or blistering to his middle son, although he did permit the calomel. Every four to six hours, Willie swallowed one of the grayish pellets, along with a grain or a grain and a half of Dover's powder—a mixture of ipecac and opium—to curb the fever and diarrhea.

On the afternoon of February 19, a Wednesday, Willie returned from the land of the dying. Hay heard the yowls of laughter from his desk on the second floor of the Executive Mansion. Some of them sounded like the president's. An opportune time, perhaps, to bring the most urgent of the correspondence to his attention.

Bud Taft, Willie's most intimate playmate, was kicking a purplish ball against the scuffed walls of the drafty central hall. Ordinarily the most bashful of boys, he exulted in Willie's revival. His next kick drove the ball directly at Hay's groin. Hay jumped aside and blocked the ball with his knee and sent it skittering through the doorway into Willie's sickroom.

Hay scurried in pursuit. Inside the Prince of Wales Room, the heavy curtains were partly drawn. The sunlight sidled in, lending a cheer to the purple French wallpaper flecked with gold. (That invoice had made Hay gasp.) Steam-heated air gurgled from the registers, to fight the chill. Willie was sitting up in the seven-foot-long rosewood bed, the pillows piled nowhere near high enough to hide the birds and tangled vines carved into the gigantic headboard. On the wall above his head, a cornet of purple silk, crowned in gold, held lacy white curtains that helped relieve the gloom. The president occupied a wicker chair beside the bed; a nurse sat at the foot. The bed was so big, Willie might have gone unseen had he not been babbling with delight.

"Look, Paw, I can *eat*!" Willie cried. He held a misshapen spoon that his father had whittled out of basswood on a rainy Sunday long ago. The boy slurped a whitish, viscous-looking pudding; a globule slid over the edge of the spoon and onto the sheet, settling like a blotch of de-caying cod.

"I can see that, son." Lincoln's high, reedy voice quavered. "You are taking your medicine?"

"Oh yes, Paw. Every bit. I did."

"Good fellow."

"And, Paw, may I see Nanko?" That was one of Tad's goats. "Taddie could bring him upstairs."

"Taddie is also ill, son."

"Then *you* could. Please, Paw. I need to see him, Paw."

"Well, maybe I can, my boy. Maybe I can."

There was a luminescence about Willie. More than intelligence—a liveliness, a life force. Willie was not painfully reserved like his older brother, Robert, nor twisted or odd like Tad, who was eight years old but seemed younger. Tad was a brat, like a boy reared by wolves. He pulled on men's beards, hammered nails into the carpets, sliced the knobs off drawers using the saw in his toolbox, rearranged the books in his father's library, yoked both of his goats to a chair and pulled them sled-like through an East-room reception, all while stammering his baby talk—from a misshapen palate—that no stranger could understand. Hay knew who was at fault—both of them. Neither parent would rep-rimand Tad or Willie or deny them a thing, not after three-year-old Eddy had died. "Let the children have a good time," they would say. So, of course the boys misbehaved. Who could blame them?

Hay could.

But somehow, Willie had learned to discipline himself. He was good-natured and direct, comfortable with both his pals and adults, willing and able to lead (in pranks, best of all) but content to follow. There was a sweetness in the curve of his cheeks and an audacity in his energetic blue eyes. He was a brave and happy boy with a spunk that stopped short of self-indulgence. Willie's round face resembled his mother's—not a surface of it was flat. But in manner, in habits of mind, even in gesture—carrying his head inclined slightly to his right—in his *soul,* Willie was his father's son. They were astonishingly alike. Hay had once watched the president watching Willie puzzle through a problem; ten minutes of concentration produced a clasp of hands and a smile. "There, you have it now, my boy, have you not?" Lincoln had said. Then, to Hay, "I know every step of the process by which that boy arrived at his satisfactory solution of the question before him, as it is by just such slow methods I attain results." Like his father, but no one else in the family, Willie led an inner life.

"But when, Paw, when?" The boy was still stuck on Nanko.

"Soon, son. As soon as you are better."

"Oh, Paw, I know that the medicines ain't gonna be enough."

"Why do you say that, son?"

"Because everybody hushes so when they say my name."

Lincoln opened his mouth and then closed it. Hay pitied Honest Abe, unable to muster a lie when he needed one most.

The president looked up at Hay with unfocused eyes. "And what can I do for you, John?"

Hay glanced to the foot of the bed. "Ma'am," he said.

The nurse seemed not to hear.

"Please, ma'am," Hay said, "if you would . . ."

"As you say, sir," she drawled. The buxom nurse had severe black hair. Shoulders hunched, she crossed to the door and swept it shut.

"Sir," Hay said. Lincoln disliked being addressed as "Mister President"—he preferred "Lincoln," although Hay could not bring himself to presume such familiarity.

The president accepted the goose-feather pen like an obedient child. He signed an act of Congress appropriating $15 million more for gunboats. Hay figured the letters to the feuding governors of New Jersey and New York could wait. But Lincoln needed to learn of the morning's scuffle between Seward and Stanton, the secretaries of state and war, the diplomat versus the brawler, over how splenetic a tone to strike in the president's next epistle to General McClellan.

"Nonsense, *I* will decide," Lincoln said, waving his hand before turning back to Willie, whose spills now resembled a map of Abyssinia.

Hay had turned toward the door when Robert rushed in, a bowl of pudding in his hands. "Here, Willie, for you—brown charlotte."

It was heartening to see Robert so nice to his younger brother—to Tad, too. Robert was eighteen years old and always seemed sad, an intruder in his own family. Hay had known him at preparatory school back in Springfield, the Illinois capital, and they palled around whenever Robert visited Washington City. The semester had started at Harvard, but Robert showed no signs of hurrying back. He seemed to like it here; the boys idolized him and would do anything he asked.

"I already have some," Willie said.

"Oh, but this is so good!"

Hay took his leave. He grieved for this family enduring the saddest of times. In the hallway, neither the nurse nor Bud Taft was in sight.

⊶⊷

Hay tensed for the punch that never came, so he threw one instead. The best defense was a good offense, or so Hay had decided after suffering a blackened eye—it kept the other fellow too busy to punch back. Hay's hard right cross found the Irishman's broad chin, but the man shook it off like a horse's tail shoos away a horsefly. Hay's knuckles cracked—he needed to remember to pull his punches, finger bones being more fragile than jaws. Hay never remembered anything while he was in the ring, not even to breathe, much less to relax. How could he? Someone was trying to hit him.

To-night, it was a large-ish someone. Maybe Hay should feel flattered that his boxing instructor considered him worthy to fight the chesty, ruddy-faced redhead. True, the Irishman had never properly sparred before, hewing to the London prize ring rules. So, Hay determined to teach him a lesson or two. He snapped a jab, which the Irishman parried, then a second jab and a third, each time stepping forward as the man backed away. A fourth jab and a fifth pressed the Irishman into the ropes, and then Hay's right cross got his attention. He followed with a left into the fellow's jellylike belly and a left hook to the ear. Hay marveled at his own capacity for . . . what, exactly? Manliness? Savagery? Courage, mock or genuine? Freedom from—or indulgence in—fear?

Hay was always jittery, his stomach knotted, before climbing into the ring. He liked having sparred better than he liked the sparring. Did that make him a coward? No, he had decided: Without fear, courage had no meaning.

This lesson had been unexpected. He had taken up pugilism in Providence in pursuit of acceptance, to fit in among the Easterners who disdained his rough Western dress and his long hair coiled around his ears, like a Roundhead's. The university had deemed boxing too un-civilized, too déclassé, to taint the campus, so Hay and fistic-minded schoolmates had hired a "professor of pugilism" in the city's seedier sec-tion, who taught them how a gentleman could thwack blackguards and stand up for himself. Knowing he had the guts to face a bigger man in the ring had made Hay less afraid of the world.

Hay had learned other things, too—for one thing, that he could take a punch, which in this capital of ruffians was useful to know. That, and how to respond when the Irishman, recovering, started jabbing back at him, driving Hay back across the ring. His fellow students of the manly art were cheering him on—damn if he would embarrass himself in front of his mates. As the Irishman kept coming at him, Hay pivoted to his right and punched him in the temple, then drove a left fist up into the unde-fended chin. The big redhead toppled onto his back, ending the round.

Hay's second delivered a bottle of water to his corner and sponged off his face and chest. Josiah was Hay's only true pal at the boxing gym-nasium. The street urchin with straw-colored hair had no notion of where Hay lived and worked, and Hay reveled in his not knowing. This shabby place, on the wrong side of Pennsylvania avenue, was as distant as the moon from the Executive Mansion. Its denizens lived in a sep-arate world, quite to Hay's delight. He could come here without be-ing noticed, and when life grew too unyielding, nothing satisfied him more than to pound away on something hard, whether inanimate or human. The Ancient as well as the Hell-cat would be aghast to know his whereabouts, especially as Willie lay ill. Even Nicolay might look at him sidewise. No matter. Hay *needed* this. Not only as an escape from the cauldron of the Executive Mansion but also from his own lin-gering sense of duty shirked. Rare in Hay's acquaintance was the young man of unasthmatic constitution who had not yet volunteered to take up arms for the Union. Yes, it was true, he was probably more useful to winning the war by passing paper to the commander in chief than by ducking minié balls on a muddy field. But still: A red-blooded young man ought to show his mettle in the time-honored way. Here, in the ring, Hay could punch away any feelings of shame.

The thirty seconds of rest expired, and the referee called the fighters back from their corners. Hay felt wobbly, but his opponent looked worse—until they were told to resume, and the Irishman advanced suddenly and plowed his right fist into Hay's solar plexus. The pain radiated through his torso and doubled him over. Then came the punch to his mouth, and it was Hay's turn to tumble back onto the canvas. The second round, all of ten seconds, was over.

Hay sat up quickly and shook his head, and the pain faded—rarely did it take more than a few seconds to pass—enough that he could climb to his feet. He staggered to his corner, and as he arrived, his left leg sagged. Just barely did he land on the stool.

Josiah handed him water and whispered, "Do what you know how to do."

That was the nicest thing he could have said to Hay. Useful, besides.

When the thirty seconds ended, Hay was first to reach the scratch line and also the first to throw a punch. But this time he switched to a southpaw stance, and his jab, jab, jab left the discombobulated Irishman open to a cross from Hay's left. Then came a hard right hook to the Irishman's head. The chess-like quality to boxing—each punch set up the next—kept Hay's mind engaged along with his instincts, before and after the sparring if not in the midst of it.

"Good hook, Mistuh J.," Terrance called from beyond the ropes. The proprietor, a freedman, was Hay's new professor of pugilism.

At Hay's hard right uppercut, the Irishman's mouth opened in a perfect O—a look of surprise, as if the Virgin Mary herself had descended into the ring—and then it closed to a point, just as his torso pitched sideways onto the canvas.

"Oh, I'm sorry," Hay blurted.

"There is no 'I'm sorry' in boxing!" Terrance exclaimed.

Actually, Hay was not sorry in the slightest.

That night, Willie took a turn for the worse. His pulse grew rapid and weak, and he sank into a coma. A pall settled over the Executive Mansion. Hay occasionally ventured into the central hall and saw the president or Mrs. Lincoln or Dr. Stone rush in or out of the Prince of Wales Room. Dr. Stone said Willie was unlikely to last until morning.

Hay was surprised to be awakened by the sunlight—he and Nicolay had forgotten to draw the frayed curtains closed. But now, he dreaded leaving his bed. He persuaded himself to peek from under the quilt: Nicolay had gone. That Teutonic sense of duty put Hay to shame.

He must have fallen back to sleep, because when he opened his eyes, Nicolay was hovering over the bed, reporting that Willie was fine—in any event, better. The boy was sitting up and eating a little, "in thrall to yet another winter's day." It was unlike Nicolay to wax poetic.

Late in the afternoon, Hay was working at his upright mahogany desk, his eyelids drifting shut. For hours the rain had pelted his windows; the fireplace threw off too little heat. Hay huddled over the untidy piles of correspondence. Pleas for office, applications for pardons, diatribes from lawmakers, religious exhortations, unsolicited counsel, slander against public men—such an omnium-gatherum was the president's mail, of which three or four out of a hundred he would show to the president. Into the willow basket at his feet Hay tossed a Rhode Island senator's arrogantly worded appeal to reconsider his brother-in-law's bid (twice rejected by the War Department) to supply the army with used bandages. Then he remembered the senator's artful equivocation on the legal tender bill and retrieved the letter and placed it on the pile requiring a reply. Hay was reaching for the next envelope when a guttural wail erupted outside, in the waiting room that separated Hay's office from the president's.

Hay leapt for the door. He knew whose wail it was, although he had never heard it before.

Lincoln was stumbling the length of the waiting room, past his own office door and in through Nicolay's, at the end on the right. As Hay rushed across the waiting room, a woman screamed beyond the folding double doors. Someone—no, two someones—held a torso by the shoulders and guided it into Mrs. Lincoln's bedroom.

Nicolay's office was narrow and dark, like a passage to purgatory. Nicolay lay on the sofa, propped up on his elbows, half-awake. Lincoln stood by the window, swaying, his body bent.

"My boy is gone," he wailed into his big, bony hands. "He is actually gone!"

Then he burst into sobs and rushed past Hay and out the door.

The burning behind the eyes before the tears arrive—Hay's entire body felt that way. On the verge of . . . something unfathomable. He loved the boy—that, he knew—and the father, too. Hay simply could not believe what he had heard. Yet he knew in his bones it was so.

+>══<+

It occurred to Hay, and not for the first time, that the extent of clutter on a man's desktop was directly proportional to the orderliness of his mind. He liked to think so, anyway, given the jumble of papers that covered both of his desks. But still, he had done what needed doing, whatever Nicolay had no time for—dispatching messengers to the cabinet secretaries and congressional leaders, wiring the president's political friends in Springfield, notifying the diplomats. He was in a fog; he felt nothing at all. Yet phrases leapt into his mind. Hay reached for a pen and tore off a scrap of foolscap.

> *Tearless & calm in the grave he shall sleep,*
> *Weary & worn on the earth we shall weep . . .*

Too plain, he judged—boring. Maybe:

> *Death's thick trailing veils of miasma will rise . . .*

No—too . . . too . . . something, but definitely *too.* It was hell being a better critic than a writer. Still, writing it down relieved him of the need to think about it. Dealing with death must get easier with practice—everything else did. Hay had known little enough of death in his score and three years—two grandparents, an ancient aunt, an elderly neighbor, all in the natural order of things. And the sister he had been too young to remember. Even his grandfather was still alive, who had been patted on the head as a nine-year-old by George Washington himself because *his* father had served under the general's command.

Hay stuffed the foolscap into the satchel that hung from a peg on the wall. It was a gift from his father for passing the Illinois bar exam just days before Hay accompanied the president-elect and his entourage to Washington City. An envelope jutted from the outside pocket—he had not seen it there before. Occasionally, Nicolay used the outside pocket for a message too private to consign to Hay's chair, but he would have positioned the envelope precisely perpendicular to the lip. This envelope was furled—crumpled, almost—and shoved in at a provocative angle. By someone in a hurry.

Hay reached for the envelope and grasped the corner. He laid it along the front edge of his desk and pressed down the corner that begged to curl up. The oyster-white envelope had a crinkly grain that suggested age or wear. It had no postmark or return address. Across the back, in thin black ink, written in a shaky hand, was the name of the addressee:

MR. TRAITOR LINCOLN

Hay had seen countless letters of hatred and threats to Lincoln's life. And to Mrs. Lincoln's—he remembered one that showed a noose around her neck. The president would brush them aside, explaining that his fate was out of his hands, instructing his secretaries to dispose of the letters without bothering him. Hay was about to discard this one, unopened, when a question popped into his mind: If Nicolay had not jammed the envelope into the satchel, who had?

Using his bone handled knife, Hay slit open the envelope and removed a single page of blue foolscap. The roughly textured paper had been folded over twice. Hay flattened it, best he could, across the uneven topography of his desktop. Four lines of a crude cursive slashed across the page, but the boldness of the strokes did not prepare him for the words they spelt.

> *Poor Willie Lincoln*
> *There was one named Barabbas,*
> *who had committed murder*
> *in the insurrection.*

He read the note four or five times. Hay's relationship with the Scriptures was incurious at best. But no one could live for long in any hamlet in the West without acquiring at least a passing acquaintance. Hay knew Barabbas as the bandit whom the crowd of Jews had chosen to

free from crucifixion, in Jesus' stead. Hay remembered nothing, however, about any insurrection, much less a . . .

The noun caught in his throat. What could the note possibly mean
about a . . . a . . . *murder*? Much less a murder in an . . . ? *Now,* there was
an insurrection; there was news of it night and day. What insurrection
had Jesus known?

Hay's ignorance about such things was profound, but he knew who
would know.

Thomas Stackpole sat slack-jawed by the president's office door.

"You still here, Mister Stackpole?" said Hay. Stupid question.

Three hundred pounds of corpulence draped over the doorkeeper's
chair, but the heavy folds of his cheeks betrayed nary a quiver. His linen
suit was laughably out of season; he reminded Hay of the white whale
in that implausible yarn by the author of *Typee* and *Omoo.* Stackpole
was usually sedentary, but he was agile when required. Now was not
such a time.

The door to Lincoln's office was shut. Hay stepped toward it and
raised his fist.

"Not here," Stackpole said in his sweet tenor.

"Where, then?"

Stackpole's neck swiveled toward an indeterminate spot along the
central hallway.

Hay said, "*Where?*"

"Where he passed."

It took Hay a moment to understand. Then he crossed through the
double glass doors and down the hallway. A candle was lit at the far
end. The silence seemed like midnight; his pocket watch said half past
nine. The door to the Prince of Wales Room was open. Hay heard
voices inside.

A single lantern turned the purple wallpaper into the walls of a cavern.
Mrs. Keckly stood by the foot of the bed. More than Mary Lincoln's
seamstress, the stately mulatto had become her aide-de-camp, even
her friend. A blue-and-white bowl was in the crook of her arm, a soft
cloth in her hand, tenderness on her face. She was bathing the elfin

form outlined by the white linen sheet on the oversized bed. Hay remembered that Mrs. Keckly's only child, George, had been killed just last August at the Battle of Wilson's Creek, in Missouri.

Lincoln was leaning over the bed, his back bowed at a painful angle. He lifted the covering and exposed his son's face. The round cheeks were still wet; the lips looked lush. Lincoln's gaze was earnest and long.

"Oh, Madam Elizabeth," Lincoln moaned. "My poor boy, he was too good for this earth. God has called him home. I know that he is much better off in heaven, but then we loved him so." The president's thin voice cracked. "It is hard, hard to have him die!"

Lincoln buried his head in his hands, and his tall frame shook. Hay felt embarrassed at the nakedness, but Mrs. Keckly seemed serene.

After the president regained his composure, Hay said quietly, "There is something I should show you, sir."

⊢══⊣

Stackpole was gone from the president's door. Lincoln lit a candle and took the low seat by the window. Hay unfolded the note, and the president gazed at it without a flicker of recognition, as if it were written in Mandarin. Hay took it back and read the message aloud.

At the first three words—*Poor Willie Lincoln*—a shudder passed through the president, and with trepidation Hay recited the rest. He hardly needed the paper; he knew it by heart. *There was one named Barabbas, who had committed murder in the insurrection.* Lincoln stared through the window into the night.

A minute passed, then a second, and Hay was wondering if he should leave when Lincoln, dry-eyed, said, "Mark fifteen-seven."

"Sorry, sir?"

"The Gospel according to Mark, chapter fifteen, verse seven. The passage about Barabbas. Your father was remiss, I can see."

"In many ways, sir."

" 'And there was one named Barabbas, which lay bound with them that had made insurrection with him, who had committed murder in the insurrection.' "

It always startled Hay how much of the Bible Lincoln had committed to memory. A benefit, he supposed, of a life devoid of burlesque.

"What insurrection?" said Hay.

"The rebellion of the Jews against the Romans. Barabbas was no common thief, nor an evil man. Not if you believe the Jews had a right to live free from Roman rule. Barabbas rebelled openly against Caesar— a brave man, he was—while Jesus preached his own path to the Almighty, peaceful but definitely traitorous. Subversives, both of them, and for their crimes they were sentenced to be crucified, side by side."

So, Barabbas was a rebel—a secesh, from the Roman empire. Hay said, "So why was Barabbas set free, and not Jesus?"

"It was Passover, when the Jews celebrate their liberation as slaves in Egypt. As *slaves*! The custom was for one prisoner to be released. Pontius Pilate left it for the crowd to decide. Jesus was a man of peace, who posed no threat to Roman military might. But Barabbas was a Zealot, accused of murder, and thus beloved by the rebels in the crowd. So it was Barabbas they spared, the man of violence. The prince of peace they left to die on the cross."

"Who did he kill, Barabbas?"

"Scripture says nothing. Not a Roman, or his fate would have been sealed. Another Jew, then. Probably a turncoat for Rome—a traitor to the Jews."

"Or a traitor's son."

Lincoln winced. He pointed to the note in Hay's hand and said, "Who sent this?"

"No one."

Lincoln looked puzzled.

"Nobody *sent* it. It was not sent. It was delivered—by hand." Hay explained how he had found it shoved into his satchel. "No postage stamp. No postmark. Someone put it there."

A long pause. Then, in a voice soft yet firm, Lincoln said, "Find . . . out."

"Find out what?" said Hay, although he already knew.

"Who put this"—Lincoln slapped at the foolscap—"into your satchel. And therefore who . . . might have . . ." His voice broke, and he turned his head away. "Tell me, John"—Hay was one of a handful of people whom Lincoln addressed by Christian name—"do you believe this is possible? That Willie was . . . was . . . ?"

"I wish I knew."

Lincoln's prominent brow hid his eyes. "But it is possible, yes?"

That Lincoln was seeking reassurance from *him*—Hay could not decide whether to feel flattered or frightened. Both. "Anything is," Hay said.

Then, in a lawyerly cadence, Lincoln asked him to keep the investigation secret from everyone but Nicolay or Allan Pinkerton. The Chicago detective had smuggled the president-elect into Washington City in the dead of night, past Baltimore's murderous plug-uglies. "I know you dislike him," Lincoln said—Hay did, though he could not recall saying so—"but he can help you. Pinkerton, Nicolay, others if you think it strictly necessary. Otherwise you would be wise to remember what people would think . . . in the South . . . yes, and in the North . . . if they thought that . . . that the president's son had been . . ." Lincoln stopped, then continued in a raggedy voice. "The hatreds would grow even uglier, John. And where on this bloodstained earth would they ever end?"

Silence again, and then Lincoln spoke in a different voice, flat in tone yet filled with suppressed emotion. "'And so Pilate, willing to content the people, released Barabbas unto them, and delivered Jesus to be crucified.' Mark, chapter fifteen, verse fifteen. Surely *that* one you know, John."

Hay recognized the jab as a jest and was relieved to hear it.

"So, who is our Barabbas?" Lincoln said, more to himself than to Hay. "And who, pray tell, is our Jesus?"

To that last question, Hay feared he knew the answer. He was staring up into his face.

Chapter Two

A tendril of nausea twisted through John Hay as he watched Nicolay slurp down a raw oyster. Hay had acquired a certain tolerance in Providence for unsightly seafood—but at breakfast? With steak and onions and pâté de fois gras? Too early in the season, thankfully, for robins on toast. The chefs at Willard's Hotel ought to be ashamed. By all rights, Nicolay should be as fat as Winfield Scott, the old and gouty general who needed three strong soldiers to boost him onto his horse. But Nicolay remained thin almost to the point of emaciation—from his nervous disposition, no doubt. Even so, Hay knew whom to blame for Nicolay's indulgence in Willard's gustatory temptations: the Hell-cat. The rupture in their affection for Mary Lincoln—and hers for them—had driven the young aides from the table at the Executive Mansion. They took their meals at Willard's instead, requiring a seven-minute stroll.

Which suited Hay, unless the weather was rotten. Willard's was the center of the known universe—the political universe, at least. Crossing the lush and pillared lobby, you might run into (or try to avoid) senators and visiting mayors and magnates and gamblers and wire-pullers for the railroads. Or even that pacifist, Julia Ward Howe, whose overwrought poem, "Battle Hymn of the Republic," published in the latest *Atlantic Monthly,* had been scrawled in a room upstairs. The business of government, honest and otherwise, was transacted upon the rotunda's mosaic floor. And military business as well, judging by the clumps of generals and fancifully attired men of the cavalry hobnobbing with the army's suppliers and would-be suppliers over whiskey at the opulent bar; the fact that liquor was short in the capital (the best was distilled in the South) was forgotten until the tab came due. A crossroads of the capital and of the Union, Willard's was jammed at most hours of the day or night.

But not, blessedly, at a quarter past seven in the morning. The kitchen in the gentlemen's dining room would not open until eight o'clock—except for Hay and Nicolay. They were expected. It was their custom to eat early, a Westerner's advantage over the capital's denizens who slept through the dawn. Ephraim had yawned, two buttons of his tunic still undone, and ushered them to the farthest corner of the cavernous room. Looking out across Fourteenth street at the ramshackle façades of Newspaper Row, they could converse without being overheard.

"You should have fun with this, Johnny—it ought to appeal to all of your worst instincts," Nicolay said. "But instead of going for the jugular, my suggestion is to start at the edges and work your way in. An old journalistic tactic."

Nicolay had begun as a printer's devil at *Pike County Free Press* in western Illinois and wound up as the editor and owner, taking printing jobs for a perennial candidate named Lincoln.

"Meaning?"

"First, ask Old Edward if anyone unusual came in."

"Isn't there always? The cabinet, are they not un . . . ? Oh, I thought you said 'unspeakable.' "

Nicolay ignored the sophomoric humor. "Between the hours of five o'clock—you were in your office, yes, when Willie died? It was not in your satchel before five—you are certain?"

"I never saw it there. Not that I looked. I have to assume so."

A look of triumph played across Nicolay's face. "Johnny, how many times have I told you the *first* rule of . . ."

"Of journalism is," Hay joined in, and together they finished, "never assume."

"I cannot say for an absolute certainty," Hay said, "but I"—to the extent that he could in a chair, he bowed—"*think* it is the case that the envelope was not in my satchel before five o'clock. Clear enough?"

Ephraim brought a pot of coffee—the real stuff, nothing like the chicory or the swill of acorns or okra seeds the rebels drank, owing to the Union blockade.

"And you noticed it when?" said Nicolay, once Ephraim was gone.

"Around nine, I guess."

"You guess?"

"Around nine." Hay hated to feel stupid or, worse, imprecise in Nicolay's presence. No doubt, Nicolay took note of Hay's inaccuracies and mistakes. He kept track of everything; his mind was a machine. That was his value to Lincoln, beyond his judgment, unclouded by sentiment. Even so, Hay knew that Nicolay never judged him by the score. So Hay felt free to say whatever he liked, assured that any idiocy would be forgiven, if not forgotten. "From five o'clock 'til nine—four hours. Anyone could have entered the mansion and ventured up the stairs."

"Then ask Stackpole if he saw anyone enter your office from five until nine. To leave that note. Stackpole would be sitting right across from your door."

"*Assuming* . . . he was at his post," Hay said. "And aware of his surroundings."

Hay nibbled at a hotcake.

"And beyond the question of who," Nicolay said, "is the question of why. Related, obviously. But still, why would anyone *want* to kill an eleven-year-old boy?"

Hay was surprised he knew the answer, but he did. "He was a military target. The son of the commander in chief. If you harm the commander in chief, you harm the Union."

They waited until Ephraim removed their plates. Hay was relieved to see the oysters whisked away.

"Or," Nicolay said, "maybe it was not someone unusual. Maybe it was someone *us*ual."

"Yes, maybe. Who was already inside. Who could enter my office without being noticed. Maybe because he entered it all the time, or from time to time. So that no one would think anything of it."

"Can we make a list of everyone who was in the mansion last night from five o'clock until nine?"

"Can *we*?" said Hay.

"Can you?"

The sun slanted across the patched roofs of Newspaper Row and in through Willard's high windows. Hay noticed a few straggles of gray in Nicolay's sullen brown hair. Twenty-nine was awfully young for that, Hay thought. And there was his delicate health, and Therena's absence, and the unrelenting work.

"By piecing it together," Hay said, "I suppose *we* could."

"Start with Old Edward. He knows everything. Sitting on the secrets of six presidents, he is."

"If Buchanan had any."

<hr>

They emerged from Willard's onto Pennsylvania avenue just as the city was coming to life. The chilly sun struggled through the clouds for the first time in days. Hay squinted to his left. Fourteen blocks southeast, along the broad Avenue, the blurry outline of the decapitated Capitol shimmered in the winter's air, hovering above the lines of leafless elms. Its old, piddling dome was gone, and war had caught the new, grander one when only a rim of it was built.

The City of Magnificent Distances, it was called. Its clusters of grand public buildings were scattered along grand—usually muddy, often impassable—boulevards. The city, barely sixty years old, had never grown into itself, and Hay wondered if it ever would. Here and there a public building aspired to grandeur, surrounded by shanties and swamp and vacant land. Hay was mindful of another magnificent distance, between the city's reality and its self-regard. He preferred Dickens's witticism, during the English novelist's American tour, about the City of Magnificent Intentions. There was something pathetic in the city's allusions (and illusions) to the glory of ancient Rome, to the point of naming its Capitol and its Senate and, more ridiculously, the Tiber Creek, which had trickled from the Capitol westward along the national Mall, before it was made into a canal and open sewer. Indeed, the capital's talent for not seeing the squalor on every side probably counted, Hay figured, as a national strength.

Granted, Springfield was uncivilized, with its unpainted buildings and rustic ways, but it never (well, rarely) claimed to be more than it was. Here, pretense reigned. Not only the work masquerading as play, demeaning both. Aesthetics must be considered: The city was ugly as sin. Washington imagined itself a city, Hay had concluded, only because it was wicked. Well-endowed in the usual vices, especially while Congress was in town, plus the evils peculiar to a capital—political backstabbing, depravities of power, military contracts and kickbacks. But it was less a city than a miserable, sprawling village—in truth, villages, each a huddle of row houses and slums, stinking alleys and backyard privies whose pleasures were carted nightly to a depository ten blocks north of the Executive Mansion.

On the Avenue, an hour and a half past daybreak, an air of disorder had already taken hold. It was too early for the organ-grinders—the monkeys must still be asleep. But the vendors were brewing their coffee, roasting their chestnuts, spreading their selections of socks and scarves. Men in flashy silks—contractors, speculators, office seekers, peddlers of goods and persuasion—scooted into Willard's to start their day of conversation and commerce. Top hats and bowlers vied for position with fedoras of beaver fur felt. On the wide sidewalk, a soldier nearly knocked over an amputee in a ragged blue coat hobbling past on a crutch. In every direction, soldiers ambled along in blue overcoats and trousers, aware that the military patrols never checked anyone's papers early in the day. You could hardly fling a stone across the Avenue—this was the president's quip—without striking a brigadier general or two.

"You see the Ancient to-day?" said Hay.

Nicolay nodded. Hay felt a pang of envy.

"He is in fine whack, I suppose," Hay said.

"Actually, he seems to be. That man is an enigma. Melancholic when he ought to be joyful. Hopeful when he has every good reason to give up the ghost."

"Hopeful?" Hay exclaimed.

Crossing Fifteenth street, a two-wheeled sulky and an ambulance nearly collided, splattering mud on Hay's pantaloons. Damn! He would need to change clothes before to-night. At the opposite curb, the side of the Treasury building lined with gargantuan Ionic columns blocked their way. A lady unashamed of her gaiter boots picked through the slush, scattering two geese and a hog.

A half block to the right, by the State Department's dingy brick building, a left turn brought them back onto Pennsylvania avenue. Here, the sidewalks were broad, but business or pleasure was scarce. Black mud a foot high fouled the gutters. Hay's long, loose overcoat swung open as he barreled along, his felt hat at a jaunty angle, his hands thrust into his pockets.

"One other word of advice, Johnny," Nicolay said, "about how to think through this . . . puzzle. Begin at the beginning."

"What in the devil does that mean?"

"That is the other way to figure things out. The journalist's tactic is to work your way in from the edges, so you know as much as you can when you get to the center of things. The historian's way is to begin at the beginning and work your way through to the end. To understand why things unfolded as they did. Either way can work. Best is to do both. As usual."

"The edges? The center of things? Speak in English, Nico."

"Who *did* this? To Willie, I mean. That is the center of things. Assuming . . . that somebody did. And who left the message in your satchel? That is almost at the center of things, assuming—again—that the same person or persons did both."

"Assume, assume."

"If necessary. And if you are aware of it, and can take that into account, as a *dis*count."

"All right. And the edges?"

"Any situation presents a universe of possibilities. In this case, everyone who was in the building when the note was placed into your satchel. Everyone who had access to poor Willie. And to Tad. The opportunity. Yes, and a motive. You might well be right about why—to injure the commander in chief. Where opportunity and motive intersect, there you will find the center."

"You should have been a detective, Nico." Hay grinned and slapped Nicolay's shoulder. "Or a lawyer."

"Spare me. When we got here to Washington City, Johnny, my first rule was never to be in a room with more than one lawyer at a time.

Because suddenly the conversation becomes unintelligible, in a foreign tongue. The rule was impossible, of course—you and the Ancient, for starters—and within a day or two I gave it up."

"Don't blame me—I wasn't cut out for anything else. Nothing that paid." Hay winked. "Nobody would want to be a doctor after watching my father scrape to get by. getting paid in bushels of carrots— when he was lucky—or half-bales of hay." John Hay considered his father, Charles, the latest in a line of distinguished near failures, a warmhearted romantic who believed in the world as he wished it to be, not as it was. "Nor a teacher, nor a preacher, although I do like to talk. I would not suit the Baptists, for I dislike water. I would fail as an Episcopalian, for I am no ladies' man. So, by a process of elimination, as the least of the evils, I became an attorney at law. And now I get to be a Vidocq."

"A what?"

"Oh, Nico, you need some civilizing. Eugène"—he pronounced it in the French manner—"Vidocq. He was the French forger and thief, who as a thirteen-year-old stole his parents' silver plates, and grew from there. Into a bad arse, the master criminal of his day. Then he had a conversion, an epiphany of sorts, and became the world's first true detective. He started the Sûreté Nationale, and then he ran it. A story odder than fiction. Poe used him as the model for the detective Dupin—you know, in *The Murders in the Rue Morgue* and whatnot. You *have* heard of Poe, have you not?" Hay loved instructing Nicolay, when he could. He described the novel by Victor Hugo to be published in Paris this spring—a college friend had written to Hay—in which the criminal being pursued . . . "And the policeman who pursues him obsessively— Vidocq was the model for both."

"I do not waste my time on make-believe," Nicolay said with the slightest of smiles.

"Yes, you waste it in other ways. All right, then, let us begin at the beginning—what in the blue blazes does that mean? Start with the moment Willie got sick. He was riding his pony, he and Tad. Right after that, he fell ill. Both boys did. But why on earth should I care about that?"

Nicolay shrugged. "It is better to know than not to know."

Hay rolled his eyes at the casual profundity, although he knew that Nicolay, as usual, was correct. "You are full of pearls to-day."

"Every day, Johnny, every day. If only you would listen." That smile, again.

Hay regarded most of his friends as smarter or braver or more talented than he was, which he secretly considered a tribute of sorts to himself.

They reached the iron fence along the north grounds of the Executive Mansion. The gate was open, as it always was. The security around the Executive Mansion was notoriously lax, at the behest of a fatalistic president who insisted on keeping the building unbarred to the people it served. They turned onto the grounds. How starkly white the building was, even under the overcast sky, after the two fresh coats of paint in December. (Hay had seen those invoices, too.) Its unpretentious, democratic nickname—the White House—was catching on. Despite the Greek pillars at the portico, the building was simple and understated, a show of serenity and self-assurance. Except for the tragedy, the turmoil—and the treachery—within.

Hay was surprised to see Old Edward at the crêpe-covered door. Usually he arrived no earlier than ten o'clock, depending on how many friends he met on the street.

"Edward, a word, please," Hay said.

"Certainly, sir."

The crimson parlor was ordinarily reserved for Mrs. Lincoln's use, to receive visitors and to pour the afternoon tea. Not to-day, of course. Hay had heard nothing of her condition, other than she had not left her bed. He had seen the president slip in and out of her bedroom, along with Dr. Stone. And Mrs. Keckly, who carried a chamber pot covered by a red-and-white checkered towel. As for the Hell-cat, Hay was content to assume the worst. It was not only her extravagance and her meddling with the mansion's staff. Something was wrong with her, inside her, in her explosions in temper and her caroms in mood; it seemed her jealousies had settled on her husband's two young aides, for their intimacy with the man she mocked and needed.

Hay had suggested the room and figured to lead Old Edward in, but the doorkeeper put himself in front. This was his bailiwick, after all. Edward McManus was a small, trim man with arctic-white hair curled close to his head. He called himself "the most ancient institution in Washington," having served as the mansion's doorkeeper since Zachary Taylor's tenure, or possibly Polk's. "Goatie," Tad called him, for his white beard. But he moved as gracefully as a gazelle, with an impenetrable politeness and a gliding efficiency, taking the fewest steps necessary to reach his destination. His lively eyes promised an unaffected honesty, such as a president deserved. But anyone who shielded the mansion from unwanted visitors and only occasionally incurred their wrath was bound to be wilier and less deferential than he let on. (After Millard Fillmore succeeded to the Executive Mansion in 'fifty, upon President Taylor's death, the new chief magistrate asked about the propriety of buying a secondhand carriage, and Edward replied that he was a secondhand president.) A man who could detect in an instant a caller's purpose and worth was sure to be perceptive about the nature of men.

The doorkeeper held the door open for Hay. The crimson room was almost garish, with a satiny sheen—the French wall hangings, the grand piano, the upholstered sofas and chairs, the Persian rug, the golden chandelier with its globes of light. The sole object Mrs. Lincoln had spared in her makeover was Gilbert Stuart's painting of the only president who had never lived within these walls, the one for whom the city was named.

Old Edward chose a straight-backed chair for himself and motioned Hay into a crimson love seat. At the obtuse angle, confrontation was impossible.

"What may I do for ye, sir?" the doorkeeper said.

"I need some help, please." Pleading for assistance was often successful, Hay had learned, especially with older men.

"At yer service, sir."

"Last evening, when"—Hay took a deep breath—"when Willie left us, were you on duty at the front entrance, do you recall?"

"How could I ever forget, sir?" Old Edward tilted his head. "Fer the grand bulk of the time, I was, sir. Though not ev'ry moment. Once, I ushered Senator Browning and his missus upstairs." Hay had sent a messenger for the Brownings, knowing the president would want his old friends from Illinois nearby. "And another time or two I departed me post for a few minutes each. Once to fetch Doctor Stone. And once to . . ." He hesitated and looked embarrassed.

"Understood," Hay said. No man could stand at his post for hours on end without attending to the necessary. "Edward, I need to compile a list of everyone who entered the mansion last evening, from the time that . . . from, say, five o'clock 'til—how late were you on duty?"

"Until eight, sir, as me usual. Then dinner in the kitchen."

That left an hour unaccounted for, from eight o'clock until nine, besides Old Edward's occasional forays from his post. Assuming, of course, that the perpetrator, if there was one, came from outside.

"Did anyone relieve you at eight?" An unfortunate choice of verb.

"No, sir."

"Anyone on duty at all?"

"Only the Pinkerton men, a few of them outside, in the bushes mainly. On Mister Pinkerton's orders. The president is not to know."

"While you were at the door, did anyone unusual come in?"

"Unusual, sir?"

"Anyone who was a stranger to you?"

Old Edward coiled his face and half shut his eyes. He took a pride in the keenness of his memory that Hay attributed to advanced age. His evenness of tone, when he resumed speaking, reminded Hay of a trance.

"Three that I recall, sir. Paying their condolences. A young man with a full black beard and a soiled frock coat, a few minutes past six. Then an old colored man, a freedman, I would judge by his posture, with a ridge of silvery hair and a face like driftwood." Hay admired the poetry—ah, the Irish. "He came around seven. And then an old woman, an *odd* woman, white whiskers on her chin, wearing a heavy gray shawl. Just before eight. I was heading down to the kitchen for my dinner."

"Did they come inside?"

"No, sir. Not a step. At the door I turned them away. Two of them left their cards, all but the colored gent. He had none. I can find them if you like. The cards, I mean."

"No need. The news got out quickly. About Willie."

"I suppose it did, sir."

"Any notion of how?"

"Could not say, sir."

"I thought you knew everything, Edward," Hay said with a smile.

Old Edward's eyes crinkled with pleasure. "Nobody knows everything, sir. Not since Erasmus."

Hay shook his head—a doorkeeper schooled in the classics. "And during that time, did anyone leave?"

"Of course, sir. 'Twas the end of the day."

"And who was that, do you recall?"

"The usuals, sir. Ye and Mister Nicolay, of course."

Hay had gone to the War Department to wire the tragic news to Uncle Milt—Charles's younger brother, a lawyer in Springfield, had cornered the family's ambition and taken his nephew under his wing—and then met Nicolay for a somber dinner at Willard's.

"Who else?"

"From five o'clock on?"

Hay tried to remember when he had last noticed his satchel and seen nothing amiss. He could not say for sure and saw no point in guessing. He would rather know too much than not enough. (Oh Lord, he was turning into Nicolay.) "Yes, from the time that Willie"—this time he could manage a euphemism—"passed."

"Oh, I see," Old Edward muttered, although Hay doubted that he did. He hoped not, anyway. "Let me think."

The doorkeeper's eyes fluttered shut. He took his time before he reopened them and turned toward Hay.

"The Brownings, the senator and his wife," he said. "And Judge Taft and the missus. Neither of the boys, nor Julia. Too painful for the Madam, as I understand it, to see those boys here." Old Edward had dropped his voice to signal that the information about Mrs. Lincoln was privileged. "Doctor Stone left shortly before eight and said he would return. Missus Welles and Aunt Mary and another nurse or two." Mary Jane Welles, the wife of the navy secretary, had ministered to Willie and, now, to Tad. "And Tom Cross and another messenger, and Mister Stackpole and . . ."

"Was he on duty at the president's office—Mister Stackpole?"

"Could hardly say, sir. Downstairs, I was. You were there, across the way, were you not?" Not really a question. "And, now that I think of it, there was Mister—excuse me, Major—Watt." That was John Watt, the Executive Mansion's longtime gardener.

"Coming in or out?"

"In. Just after seven."

Why would a gardener arrive after dark? "Not out?"

A moment of focus, then a shake of his head. "Though the conservatory has its own exit." The greenhouse was attached to the western wall of the mansion.

Old Edward reported that Messrs. Seward, Stanton, and Blair—nearly half of the cabinet—had stopped by, each staying for varying lengths of time. The doorkeeper was exact about the comings and goings. Hay asked Old Edward to prepare a list of people who had arrived or left the building plus everyone who had remained on the premises—the cooks, the chambermaids, the messengers. Any of them might have slipped an envelope into Hay's satchel. And one of them had.

"Something else, if I might trouble you further," Hay said.

"Anything, sir." The doorkeeper put on a patient look. "Almost anything."

"The morning that Willie and Tad fell ill, they went out riding. Early, before you arrived. Would you happen to know who took them out?"

A pensive look, staring at the chandelier. Hay had the impression that rather than trying to retrieve a fact, Old Edward was deciding whether to reveal one.

"Tom Cross, I woul' suppose, sir. 'Tis usually he who accompanies the lads outside the grounds." Hay thought of the messenger as an irascible Negro, although the Lincoln boys had always seemed content in his presence. "On tha' morning in particular, sir, I cannot say fer certain."

"And where might I find Mister Cross?"

"Now, sir?"

The president's messengers had their hideaway in the basement of the mansion. Tom Cross would be in around noon.

+>━━<+

It was the right thing to do, and Hay knew it. He had pledged to be mature about this—he *liked* to do the right thing. When he could.

This did not obligate Hay, however, to seek him out. Surely, if Allan Pinkerton was half as sharp a detective as he believed himself to be, he would already know what Hay was up to. The logotype of his detective agency was an eyeball, was it not? So, when Hay saw the Scotsman shuffling out of the president's office, a snarl on his face, silence seemed the better part of valor.

No such luck.

"Mistah Hay!" Not a greeting but a command. Followed by an invitation into Hay's own office, which Hay accepted with forbearance. It was the right thing to do.

Hay was quick to offer Pinkerton a seat, to prevent Pinkerton from offering first. With a barrel chest and a thick black beard that swallowed his face, the famous detective had a glowering presence. Hay had never seen him smile. Pinkerton fixed Hay's gaze—in a contest, it seemed to Hay, who was determined not to lose. One thing boxing had taught him was to look levelly into another man's eyes with a comfort that did not expire. After a half minute or more, Pinkerton eyed a piece of lint on the cuff of his frock coat and picked it off.

"I understand I can be o' service," Pinkerton said.

"As what?"

"As a truth-finde', o' course. The president told me o' yer . . . efforts. Perhaps some . . . professional guidance woul' be welcome."

"Always ready to learn from a master," Hay said.

Pinkerton missed the meanness. "What do ye know so fa'?"

Hay showed him the note and succinctly described the biblical message—*murder in the insurrection*—and his plan to begin at the beginning, attributing the tactic to Nicolay, to slip any jabs.

Pinkerton said, "Wha' the bloody hell does tha' mean?"

"I will start with Tom Cross, who took the boys out riding the morning they fell ill."

"A bloody waste o' time, if ye ask me."

"I do not recall that I did." *Damn it,* Hay thought—*he* would *be mature.* "What do you think I should do, then?"

"Ever'thing ye can think o'."

"My plan, exactly," Hay said. "Such as?"

"Question ever'one who might've entered yer office when ye were gone. When, exactly, was tha'?"

"I'm going to do that. About to start." Hay gestured toward the door as if Pinkerton was holding him up, which he was not.

"Very well, then." Pinkerton seemed less than pleased. "And ever'one who ha' any contact with . . . the boy. Or took care o' him."

"Yes, that is next."

"And if he *was* killed," Pinkerton went on before Hay had finished, "what do ye propose was the mechanism? Was he shot? Of course not. Stabbed? No. Strangled? Hardly. Poison, perhaps. Most likely, he was not murdered a'tall. And this is the note o' a lunatic, which belongs in the trash."

Hay took back the note, but he hoped the detective was right. Pinkerton left without offering to help, to Hay's relief.

Hay had no recollection of having been trapped in a cave as a lad, yet venturing into the basement of the Executive Mansion put him on edge. He descended the staircase and followed the mildewed corridor, with its low, arched ceiling and the green paint that peeled from the walls. Hay crinkled his nose at the smell—a dead varmint, with luck a runt. An incongruous aroma, sweet and warm, wafted from the kitchen at the distant end. Freshly baked bread.

Whenever they were idle, which seemed to be most of the time, the president's three messengers occupied a closet that was halfway to the kitchen, across from a storeroom. The unpainted door was ajar. Hay's knock brought a barked order to enter.

The windowless room held a pockmarked desk, two hard-backed chairs, and a sagging cabinet that must have dated to John Quincy Adams's day. Behind the desk sat a muscular young Negro who lacked eyebrows or any hair on his head. His intimidating physique made him a suitable bodyguard for the boys. Ordinarily, Hay tried to stay clear of Tom Cross; last evening, Hay had practically begged the man before he would walk a half block to tell the secretary of state about Willie. Hay wondered if his own pugilistic training would prevail over Tom Cross in the ring and decided: not a chance.

"Yes, sir, Mister Hay, here you be." Tom Cross's dark eyes locked onto Hay's. This was his lair; he was in charge.

Hay nodded toward a chair. "May I?"

His host nodded.

Hay seated himself and explained the reason for his visit. "This was seventeen days ago. No reason, I suppose, for you to remember. You often took them riding in the morning, did you not?"

"Ever since he got dat pony." It had been a birthday gift to Willie, four days before Christmas, from Senator Browning and his wife. "Willie love dat little gray. Ride 'im ever' chance he get. And wherever Willie went, Tad went too." The scowl in Tom Cross's forehead had softened, and his hard eyes had taken on—there was no mistaking it—a sparkle. "But dat morning, I do remember. 'Twarn't me dat went wit' the boys."

"Oh? You know this?"

"'Course I do."

"How, if I may ask?"

"I says so, di'n't I? You ask me a question, and then you go doubtin' my word?" His eyes had turned stony; he sat picking his nose.

"I am not doubting your word, Mister Cross. Merely trying to understand why I shouldn't."

Tom Cross broke into a toothy grin. "A good one, sir—yes, sir. Tuesday the fourt' is what you're askin'. The fourt' o' Feb'ry—my boy's birt'day. My youngest boy, name o' John, like you. Turned six. And so I makes him his favorites for breakfast. Dat would be cinnamon porridge and flapjacks. He especially likes it when his daddy flips 'em. Says dey taste better dat way."

Hay could not help but smile. "Who took the boys out, then?"

"That would be Mistah Williamson."

"Alexander Williamson—the tutor?"

"Him's the one."

Hay pictured the frail, redheaded man who could not stand up to a downdraft.

"Does he usually take your place?"

"Never had."

"Why this time?"

"Was the Madam's suggestion." Tom Cross shrugged. "Why not?"

⊱—⊰

Alexander Williamson worked mornings as a clerk at the post office, so Hay waited until early afternoon to find him at home. The Lincolns had engaged him as a tutor for the boys, recommended by the commandant at the Soldiers' Home. The Hell-cat's insistence that he work without a salary (to free up money for her dresses and drapes) explained his second—actually, his primary—job.

Hay kept to the muddy sidewalk as he strode east along G street. The day was damp and disagreeable. Beyond Fourteenth street, he passed Foundry Methodist Church and then the Epiphany Church—rivals for God's favor, Hay imagined. Vacant lots separated the buildings like the gaps in an old man's teeth. On a moonless night the previous fall, near the livery stable at G and Thirteenth, Nicolay had been jumped and robbed; beneath his goatee, the nick of the knife left a scar. A soldier gone from his post—Nicolay had noticed the uniform. Not only cutthroats and pickpockets threatened the public safety in Washington City. So did the men who were bound by honor and duty to protect it.

329 G street was just past an overgrown lot, almost to Twelfth street. A hare scuttled under the branches that crossed the sidewalk. The three-story brick row house looked solid enough, though unkempt; on the top floor, the shutters hung askew. Hay mounted the three low steps to the postage stamp of a porch and knocked on the faded red-orange door.

No response.

He knocked again. A child shouted inside, and light footsteps approached. The door swung open, and after a long moment, blond ringlets peeked past the edge. Then a vertical pair of saucy blue eyes and, next, a wrinkled nose and, finally, a quarter moon of a grin. A girl of four or five, sideways.

When Hay asked if Mr. Williamson was at home, she grinned. He wondered if the girl spoke English. Or maybe she was deaf, although

she would not have heard his knocking. When he asked again, she giggled and swung the door shut. Footsteps retreated; a minute went by,
then another. He raised his fist to knock again when heavier footsteps
drew near. The door opened.

In the dark rectangle of the doorway stood a cipher of a man. Alexander Williamson was all pastels. Of medium height, he slouched and
looked shorter than he was. Hay had seen him a hundred times but
had never looked closely, for the simple reason there was little to see.
The tutor was slight and had a pale, bland, expressionless face, like a
daguerreotype plucked from the chemicals before its time. Thin russet
hair flopped over his forehead. His frock coat was rumpled and unbuttoned, and his cravat hung untied. Was sterner stuff beneath? Probably
not. The thought of Alexander Williamson as a bodyguard made Hay
laugh—no, cringe.

"Please forgive me for disturbing you at home," Hay said. He waited
for an invitation that was not offered. "May I come in?"

No reply. Was everyone in this household a mute?

"It is about Willie."

Alexander Williamson stepped aside and, without a word, ushered
Hay into the front parlor. The shades were drawn, and newspapers
covered the center table. There was a faint smell of ammonia. Hay seated
himself by the front window, in the least uncomfortable armchair. A
rag doll with orange hair leaned on the crack of the cushion.

"R-room enough for two," Williamson said with a Scottish burr.

A pleasantry—Hay began to recalibrate his ankle-high opinion. "I
hope I am not interrupting your dinner."

The tutor seated himself facing Hay. "'Tis finished, Mister Hay. And
what is it you want?"

Impatience, with a tint of belligerence. In Hay's experience, timid
males were at war with their timidity. Or did the man have a reason
to fear this intrusion?

"You went riding with Willie and Tad along the riverfront," Hay said.
"The morning of February fourth. A Tuesday."

"Not the r-river. The canal."

"Oh." Hay wondered if someone had mentioned the river or if he had assumed it. *Never assume,* Hay could hear Nicolay intone inside his head.

"A teeny bit of the r-river as well," Williamson said. " 'Til we turned back."

"I see. Had you ridden with the boys before?"

"Nae."

"So why *that* day?"

"I was asked."

"Who asked you?"

"Mister-r Cr-ross."

Hay wanted to say: "Of all people, why *you?*" Instead: "When did he ask you?"

"Th' afternoon just before. Was passing him in the cor-rridor, I was, when he called me name. Hardly had a notion he knew it. Would I r-ride with th' boys th' next morning? Odd, it seemed t' me, but I could no' think of a r-reason why nauw."

"Did he say why?"

"Did it matter?"

"I suppose not. And you said yes."

"I live near-r enough." The tutor hesitated, appraised Hay's face, and seemed to make up his mind. "I am not due at the post office 'til half past eight. And I am very fond of those . . . boys. A young man, almost, Willie is . . ." Hay noted the tense. "Ne'er have I known such a lad. *Nauw* a sinful word from the boy, even in fun. And such a hor-rror of acting r-rude. Like his father-r, he is, yes? And what a mind in that boy! *McGuffey's Eclectic R-readers,* the first *and* the fifth—he r-raced through 'em both. He would r-read a page of his speller once, maybe twice, and he could spell ev'ry wor-rd, with nauw a blunder. Many a time he com-plain I assigned him too *lit'le* work. And ne'er tire of asking a question, 'til he tired out a tutor like meself. The last time"—Williamson's voice caught—"it was the Latin word *calculus* he was wanting to know the meaning of. Means a 'pebble,' as surely ye know, Mister-r Hay." Which Hay, in fact, did. "And wanting to know which words in English 'tis it the source for. So I tell him—'to calculate.' He's a-nodding at this, like *he* is the tutor and I, his blue-r-ribbon pupil. Nae, but *why,* he's wanting to know. And so I tell him, because in these ancient times, schoolboys a-carried a small box of pebbles to *calculate* with, when their teacher posed a problem of sums." A pause. "The last question he e'er-r asked me, it was."

The tutor gasped for breath, exhausted at the outpouring of words, perhaps more than he had spoken at a stretch in a month. His eyes were wet.

Hay said gently, "Did anything unusual happen? On the ride by the . . . canal."

"Such as?"

"Anything unusual."

"Ne'er did this before, Mister-r Hay. How shoul' I know wha' is usual and wha' is nauw?"

Hay suppressed his exasperation—this would be easier if he knew what he wanted to know. "That morning you arrived at the mansion. At what time, do you recall?"

"A quar-rter before seven, I woul' say. In the dark."

"The boys were awake?"

"Boys are."

Alexander Williamson described an uneventful outing. They had trotted across the mansion's back lawn in a smattering of snow and out through the gate onto Fifteenth street, then south to the canal. Willie rode his new pony, and Tad took the younger Taft boy's pony, his short legs sticking out to the sides. They rode west along the canal until it joined the Potomac at Seventeenth street, by the seawall. A little beyond, the flurries turned into a squall, and Willie complained of a chill. "This is a lad who ne'er complains, and so we came back." By twenty past eight.

And by early afternoon, Hay thought, Willie was sniffling and sick in his bed. That was fast—probably too fast.

"No run-ins with strangers?"

"Ne'er laid eyes on a blessed soul. Well . . . there *was* something a mite . . . un*usual*"—a Scotsman's tubular pronunciation—"I suppose you migh' call it."

"Oh?"

"Along the path by the canal, just shor' o' Seventeenth street. The boys ha' gone ahead a lit'le. I saw it before they did. I shouted at them to duck, and they did. It missed them, nauw by a lot. A rock, or somethin' like it. From on high."

"Out of the sky?"

"Such things happen, so Scripture say. I am a God-fearing man, I am, Mister-r Hay. Though I am s'pposing tha', in this particular instance, the arm of mortal man migh' ha' played a role."

"This rock, or whatever it was, it was thrown from where?"

"Hard to say. From the Island, migh' be. Except nary a soul was across the canal, none I could see. Nor ahead of us on the path, or behind us. So over the fence, must ha' come. The fence of President's Park." Union troops were camping on the square of land between the canal and the Executive Mansion. "Unless it *was* from God, and what woul' be the sense in that?"

"But it missed them, this . . . it *was* a rock?"

"Thanks be to God, it did. A projectile of some sort. Enough to make Willie fall off o' his pony, face first in the mud. Nauw injury, to speak of. Thanks be to . . ."

"No injury—you are sure of this?"

"None I coul' see. For three years I studied medicine in Edinburgh, Mister Hay, and someday soon I hope to resume my studies here—been jabbering to Doctor Stone about it. Anyway, I helped Willie up, and he pushed me away and climbed right back on his pony. He was like that, you know—knock him down, and up he pops again. A br-rave lad. 'Twas uninjured, best I could see. When we r-returned I asked Doctor Stone to look at the boy. Said he would."

"Doc Stone was there? At twenty past eight?"

"All nigh', I understood."

"Why on earth?"

"With Missus Lincoln, so someone said."

"And he found nothing the matter with Willie?"

"Was late for my post at the post office, I was. Can hardly feed these mouths"—he flung his arm toward the rear of the house—"on what I earn from teaching those boys."

Hay was starting to like this man.

Still, something bothered him about the tutor's recounting, but he could not think of what. He had no reason to doubt its veracity. That Willie took a spill was plausible, even without a rock from the sky. Hay knew that rutted path. Branches and boulders grabbed at the ankles of man and beast; in places, there was hardly a path at all. Why anyone would *choose* to follow such a path was beyond . . .

That was it: Why had they followed that path at all? As Hay understood, the boys usually rode along the Potomac, not the canal. From Fifteenth street to Seventeenth street, the waterway stank, even ignoring the brambly path. A nonsensical route, slippery in the snow.

"Had you ridden there before?"

"Walked, once or twice. Not r-ridden."

"Then you knew what kind of path it is. Why on earth did you go *that* way?"

"Because . . ." Williamson stared up at the chandelier and its coating of soot. "There is a r-reason, Mister-r Hay, and not a br-rave one." Hay was charmed by the tutor's self-deprecation. "I *meant* to leave the grounds by the Seventeenth street gate, and I started out that way. From the stables down to the car-rriage path, intending to head off to the r-right, but . . ." The tutor squinted at an image that Hay was unable to see.

"Yes?"

"But . . . *he* was there. Behind the spruce tree, down to the r-right."

"Who was?"

"Major-r Watt."

This was the second reference to-day to the gardener's inflated rank. Hay had handled the paperwork himself last September that commissioned John Watt as a lieutenant in the Union army—the Hell-cat's doing—and a lieutenant is what he still was. Not that he actually did anything for the army—not the Union's, anyway. "What was he doing there?" said Hay.

"Standing behind the spruce, staring at us."

"Staring? Was he doing anything?"

"Snipping at branches, best I could tell."

"He is the gardener."

"But at seven o'clock in the morning, with snow in the air-r?"

"Why did you go at all, given the weather?"

"It wasn't r-really snowing when we left, and Willie insisted. His new pony. When it threatened to ge' ugly, we turned back."

"So, why did you change your direction when you saw . . . Lieu*ten*ant Watt?"

A long sigh. "It was like he was trying to hide from us, behind the spruce. Now, it sounds stupid, I know, when you say it out loud. But there was something about . . . he seemed to be *spy*ing on us—that's what I thought at the time. Through the branches of the spruce, he was staring at the boys, staring hard."

"Did he say anything?"

"Nae."

"And because of this, you changed direction."

The tutor's freckled face tightened. "They were my r-responsibility, the boys were. So yes, I changed direction. Better to be too careful than not careful enough."

The apologia, Hay thought, of cowards through the ages. Though to be fair, Williamson was right: The boys *were* his responsibility.

"Why would he want to spy on the boys, do you suppose?" Hay meant to sound incredulous.

" 'Tisn't so doo-lally as it sounds, Mister Hay. The man hated those boys, tha' he did. Tad, anyway. Ever since tha' time with the strawberries."

"With the *what*?"

The tutor recounted the morning, not many weeks before, when the boys were learning their lessons in the oval study upstairs and Watt barged in. He tore at Tad for eating the strawberries set aside for a state dinner. "And for digging in his gardens and trampling on his plants. There was fury in his eyes. He held a grudge against those boys . . ."

Hay found it hard not to laugh. Unauthorized ingestion of strawberries was a novel motive for murder, even for Poe.

" 'A wildcat,' Major Watt called 'im. And in truth, he was not far wrong. No force on earth can keep that boy away from something he wants, 'ceptin' maybe Willie. But the laddie don't take kindly to being yelled at. That gardener made Tad cry, which to me tipped the boy's guilt. But it made Willie mad as a rabid raccoon, that a grown man attacked his brother and made him cry. Willie's voice got low and . . . I would have to say, a little mean. He said something to Major Watt, about having to learn to add, that two plus two do not equal five or six. Made no sense to me. But it did to Major Watt. Without a word, he turned on his heel and he left. And Willie went right on with his lesson, about ancient Greece, as I recall, as if nothing had happened. Nothin' at all."

"Nothing sinful or rude from his mouth, so you say."

" 'T'ain't sinful if it's the truth in pursuit of justice. And it must ha' been, because the man up and left."

Hay was well aware that the gardener padded his invoices for seed and shrubs. The president knew, and apparently Willie did, too. Maybe Willie knew something more, or thought he did, or Watt thought he did, which might have been worse.

Even dangerous.

⊱──────⊰

Hay grimaced at his desk, pawing through the piles of correspondence in search of something cheery. He tried to immerse himself in the text of Jefferson Davis's inaugural address, to be delivered in Richmond the following day at noon. (A Confederate senator's daughter had smuggled it in her crinolines out through rebel lines.) *The tyranny of an unbridled majority, the most odious and least responsible form of despotism* . . . Hay stared at the words so grandly misused and took none of them in. He preferred to peer through the window across the North Lawn. Beyond the iron fence, along the wide Avenue sidewalk, citizens stared back at the mansion in mourning.

He was almost relieved to hear Thomas Stackpole's voice out in the waiting room. Hay's legs ached; it felt good to move.

"Nobody," the doorkeeper replied to Hay's opening question.

"Between five and nine o'clock—nobody at all entered my office?"

"Not that I saw. Except for Mister Nicolay."

"Oh? When was that?"

"Around six, I would say. Looking for you, I gathered. In his usual hunched-over way." Stackpole's neck sagged into his shoulders. "He went in and came right out. And I did, once."

"Whatever for?"

"The president asked me to find you, but you were gone."

"Why, do you know?"

"No."

"Anyone else?"

"No."

"You sure?"

A scornful silence—deserved, Hay conceded.

"Were you there the entire four hours?" said Hay.

"Most of it. I left for dinner. And errands."

"In the building?"

"Yes."

"How long were you gone, would you say?"

"An hour, a little bit more. Then I left around a quarter past eight."

"Left for good?"

"For home."

Another forty-five minutes during which someone might have placed an envelope in Hay's satchel, unseen.

"Strawberries? Be serious." Nicolay flung a copy of the latest House Appropriations idiocy, its red tape unloosed, onto Hay's desk. "Johnny, how do we know he was murdered at all? Beyond that message, which looks meaningless to me."

"Except that somebody left it here, in my satchel. *My* satchel."

"And *how* was he murdered, assuming—*assuming*—he was? Have you thought about that, Mister Vidocq?"

"All right, you made your point."

"Well, then?"

"All sorts of ways," Hay said. "Smothered. Typhoid fever from an infected blanket. Poisoned. An autopsy should help."

"The Ancient says no. An embalming instead—evidently it is one or the other. He wants to take Willie home, to Springfield. In seven years, or three."

"When did he decide this? I thought I was . . . Oh, never mind."

"While you were out at the tutor's. He had been talking to the

Hell-cat, coming from her bedroom, looking . . . nothing if not distraught. What else did the tutor say, beyond strawberries?"

Hay told of John Watt leering at the boys on the South Lawn and of the projectile that fell from the sky. "And now the felonious gardener has everyone calling him Major," Hay said. "Which makes him a liar *and* a thief. He took the Hell-cat to Philadelphia and New York—picture this in your mind, Nico, the two of them trooping from store to store—teaching her how to pad invoices."

"How much, I wonder," Nicolay said.

"Quite a lot, I would think—most of what he knows."

"No, how much he stole. Suppose he feared exposure—from his star pupil in thievery. This would be a way to stop her."

"What would be?"

"Harming her son," Nicolay said.

"Or threatening to."

This suggested to Hay another reason for John Watt to murder Willie. If the Hell-cat was foolish or gluttonous enough to invite a scoundrel to tutor her in the intricacies of illegal accounting, she had left herself open to blackmail—or worse. By killing her son, the gardener could assure her silence, beyond hurting the commander in chief and simply getting rid of a boy who knew too much.

A few minutes past eleven o'clock that night, the president stuck his head into Hay's office and invited him along to the War Department's telegraphic office to examine the latest dispatches from the field. For Lincoln, it was a way to relax. To-night, the sleet was so sharp that the Smithsonian Institution had canceled Louis Agassiz's lecture on the leaps of induction in Darwin's fanciful new theory of evolution. Lincoln wore overshoes and wrapped himself in a thin overcoat that left his wrists exposed. A safety pin the size of a derringer fastened his favorite gray shawl. But no derringer, no qualms about safety. Lincoln believed that whatever to be was to be. Idiocy, to Hay.

Hay debated telling him of his suspicions about John Watt. But what did Hay actually know, and how could he say anything without mentioning the missus? Hay felt protective toward this man who towered alongside him, almost as if he, Hay, were the adult and Lincoln, the awkward naïf. Part of why Hay loved him—and he did—was the man's endearing air of incapacity. Lincoln was puppylike in his enthusiasms, often unmindful of the practicalities—rather like Hay's father in that regard. In his goodness, too, which for both men was unremarkable and absolute. Hay found it inspiring, albeit unnerving, when a man always— *always*—tried to do the right thing. Not exactly Hay's mug of beer. Which inclined him to regard Lincoln with a sneering disbelief: How could anyone be that good? For Lincoln, social ambition meant nothing at all. His too-short sleeves and mismatched stockings were merely the symptoms. It was his carelessness—his not caring—about worldly things that flustered Hay. How could a man rise so far in the world and not care a greenback for its opinion? He claimed never to have finished a novel. He read a lot, but the same things again and again—Scripture, of course, and Shakespeare and Robert Burns. As a boy, he read *Robinson Crusoe* and Pastor Weems's paean to George Washington—little else. About poetry, he knew next to nothing, if you considered Burns and Byron something (and he had memorized Poe's "The Raven"). About European history and anatomy and ancient languages, nothing. About cities and natural philosophy and even slavery, nearly nothing. About the habits of the high and mighty, and of women, Lincoln was blissfully unaware—and incurious. Little beyond the boundaries of Illinois or the banks of the Mississippi River or the Ohio had lain within his ken. Hay excused himself for feeling a little more— he searched for the fairest word—refined.

To-night, Lincoln seemed preoccupied—understandably so. Although with what, Hay had no way of knowing. Hay was skilled at reading people, but never had he known a man so hard to understand. They were striding in silence, but for the crunching of frozen mud underfoot, when Lincoln said, "I have never met this Grant, but I reckon I like him." The untried brigadier general had captured Fort Henry, on the Tennessee River, and now his troops and Union gunboats were besieging Fort Donelson, the rebel stronghold just to the east, on the

Cumberland River bluffs. "He is my first real general. He is a *general*! He *does* things. Nobody need tell him twice—or once. The rest of them ask my permission to piss in the mud. So they can leave the burden of failure on *my* shoulders, like this here shawl. *If* they can be moved to do anything at all."

Hay was thrilled at the allusion to General McClellan, whose Army of the Potomac sat in the mud just north of Manassas, in northern Virginia, instead of marching toward Richmond. "Did you hear from him, sir?"

"From Grant?"

"From McClellan. To your five questions. And the war order." In January, Lincoln had issued General War Order No. 1, commanding all land and naval forces to advance on the enemy by February 22— one day away. Nothing further had crossed Hay's desk, but not everything did.

"Not in writing, mind you. More eloquent than his words is his silence. And his actions—his *in*action."

"All is quiet along the Potomac, as they say, sir."

"Yes, John, too quiet." The president skidded a step ahead of Hay. "I am only the commander in chief. I command, but do my generals obey? This Grant, however, he does not swagger like a general—he only fights like one."

"And drinks like a private," Hay said. "A four-finger imbiber, I am told. By a friend . . ." Hay nodded at the sturdy brick building ahead that housed the War Department. He had learned this tidbit over a lager at the Willard's smoky bar.

"Whatever brand of whiskey that man is drinking, please deliver a barrel to each of my generals in the east. Have someone else deliver it, John." A teetotaler's sly glance. "I would want it to arrive."

They passed between the orderly rows of boxed spruce and fended off the swirls of sleet. Suddenly, something lurched across the bend in the path. Hay froze. Half the size of a man, four legs—a fawn. Surely more frightened than they were. Lincoln had noticed nothing and stumbled along.

They crossed the lawn without further adventure and passed through the wrought iron gate. The path descended into a hollow and ended at the War Department's side door.

The telegraphic office was on the second floor, next to Secretary Stanton's. Even at this late hour, it rattled with the *clackety-clack* of metal on metal—the swift tongue of lightning, thought Hay. (He made a mental note to use that in a poem.) The room had incongruously high ceilings and smelled of perspiration from the labors of the blue-clad young men seated in rows at telegraph keys, scribbling with steel-nibbed pens. Or possibly the scent of discomfort was Hay's own, imagining a *D. B.* branded on his forehead—*deadbeat.*

The soldiers at the telegraphic office were safe from cannonballs *and* moral quandaries. At the door, the towheaded clerk with scarcely a whisker on his chin greeted the president like a tent mate.

"Yes, *sir,*" he said with a loose salute, "to-night you shall enjoy what you read."

The boyish soldier handed Lincoln two or three yellow flimsies, and the fifty-three-year-old president pored over them, line by line. Then he stood straighter and read them again. Hay studied his face—so ugly it was beautiful, he had heard someone say. A fissure ran at an angle from each nostril to the edge of the bristly beard. Now, the face wore a mask of concentration. A mask. Always a mask, separating what was inside from everything—and everyone—else.

A full minute passed before the president whispered, "John, Fort Donelson is ours."

Hay gasped. Ten months after Fort Sumter fell, the Union had won its first important victory in the war. It assured the capture of Nashville, with its factories for cannons and percussion caps and its storehouses of bacon, and opened a corridor for invading the South.

"Twelve thousand rebel prisoners!" the president burbled. "And, John, listen to this. When the Confederate general applied for an armistice, Grant wired back"—Lincoln's voice caught—"wired back, 'No terms except unconditional and immediate surrender.' Magnificent! The man is a poet, John."

As they strolled back toward the Executive Mansion, the odor of coal oil lingered. " 'Unconditional surrender.' " Lincoln rolled the phrase around on his tongue. "Worthy of *Richard III*, it is." That was Lincoln's favorite Shakespeare, next to *Macbeth*, cautionary tales about the temptations of power. "Ulysses *S.* Grant. *U. S.* Grant. Unconditional surr—"

Lincoln's small smile was the first Hay had seen in days.

Chapter Three

SATURDAY, FEBRUARY 22, 1862

John Hay awakened to the tolling of church bells. They pealed like a dream from his boyhood, of a future with nothing but Sundays and sunshine. He squeezed his eyes shut, holding on to the yellow blooms of spring in the village of Warsaw, at the western edge of Illinois, the curled smoke of steamboats on the Mississippi, sleighs sliding past fields of winter wheat.

But now, the bells grew sporadic, the rhythm fractured. These were not church bells; it was not Sunday. The noise was cannon fire, from the Union forts surrounding the city, answered by batteries across the Potomac, which sounded close, *too* close.

Hay sprang to a sitting position. Had the battle for the capital begun?

"Nico!" he cried out.

He was glad nobody heard him, because he remembered. It was Washington's Birthday. This was celebratory fire from the Union's cannons. The Union's alone.

Now he was awake, like it or not. His head still longed for the feather-filled pillow. Torn as usual between comfort and duty, he chose the usual. "All shit and no sugar," he muttered to himself as he slid out of bed.

He performed his morning ablutions with dispatch. He donned two pairs of woolen socks and stopped by the kitchen for a mug of weak coffee and a slice of aerated bread and left the mansion through the rear basement door. He headed east along the gravel path, toward the stables. Hay had no intention of riding, however. He would see more, notice more, if he walked.

It was cold and drizzly; the icy air felt thick under the pewter sky. Hay pulled his greatcoat tighter around him and tugged his slouch hat over his ears. This was less brutal than in Illinois or Rhode Island—those were honest, manly winters, with skin-slicing cold and quilts of snow. Here, the winter was a devious affair, dustings of white that soon melted away, a moist chilliness that wheedled its way through every line of protection.

The gravel path led from the stables down onto the cobblestoned carriageway. Eight or ten feet to his right stood a majestic spruce. *That* spruce, without doubt. Its branches curved like slats across the bottom of a king's canoe. Hay went behind the spruce and saw what he expected: nothing of note.

Hay reversed course and followed the carriageway toward Fifteenth street. Outside the Treasury building, blocks of stone were piled high, for an extension to the already-mammoth building to be built where the State Department stood. *Money runs the world,* Hay thought. *Such a mundane truth—try to fashion a poem out of that!*

Hay exited the grounds and turned south along Fifteenth street. His footsteps echoed off the high, whitewashed fence to his right, the eastern boundary of President's Park. The absence of noise was eerie. No pedestrians except for a pair of scrawny Negro boys kicking a yarn-wrapped ball down the center of the rutted road. At the next side street, off to Hay's left, the tents of Hooker's soldiers stirred with morning life. A block farther south was the vacant lot where Hay had once watched the soldiers indulge in a rowdy game they had learned in the camps, called base ball. Hay reckoned people would prefer their sporting competitions kept simple and direct, man against man, as in the ring.

Now, his task was anything but simple and direct. Hay needed a course of action, requiring intuition *and* cold logic, such as a poet and a lawyer—and yes, a fighter—might conceive.

Begin at the beginning. To see whatever Willie and Tad had seen on their last day of health, to experience what they had experienced. As if he could. And *if* he could, what on earth would that tell him? Hay could not say what he was looking for. He could only hope he would recognize it if he crossed its path, or it crossed his.

Hay smelled the canal before he could see it. Not as rank as in summertime, when the odor through the south windows of the Executive Mansion was as foul as the ghosts of ten thousand drowned cats. But even in winter, the smell was, to be kind, complicated. *The National Intelligencer* had quoted an olfactory savant who recognized "seventy separate and distinct stinks." Hay could do no better than three or four, which was enough. Human excrement, for certain, and the inedible animal parts from the slaughterhouse across the canal. And ammonia and possibly the fish heads discarded at Centre Market, which had flowed—that is, oozed—downstream. All of this, incubated and permeated by rain and sleet and mud and the occasional sunlight and the piercing cold. By the time Hay reached the canal, he was breathing through his mouth.

What once was the glory of Rome
By the new Tiber's malodorous banks . . .

Hmm, possibilities. He fished out a pencil and his calfskin notebook—he always carried those—and scrawled.

Where the soldiers thought only of home
And of their . . . sweethearts' . . .

What rhymes with *banks*? *Ranks . . . pranks . . . blanks . . . spanks . . . manx?* No, no, no. The problem went beyond rhyme. It was his usual one: He had nothing to say.

The stone-sided canal was low and calm, too calm. The isles of ice in the water stymied any movement and concealed the noxiousness beneath. An unclean place, a cesspool—literally. Across the lifeless canal, behind the slaughterhouse and its stockyards, stood the stump of an obelisk, a monument to the man whose 130th birthday was to-day. It had reached only a third of its intended height before the money ran out. Truncated, like the country he had fathered.

Hay watched a crow fly low across the horizon. He reached for his pencil and notebook:

> *Over the Capitol's white dome,*
> *Across the obelisk soaring bare*

Not bad.

> *To prick the clouds, crows travel home,*
> *And find somebody waiting there.*

Singsongy, true. And did crows have a home? Where somebody (was a "crow" a "somebody"?) waited? He shoved the pencil and notebook back in his pocket and set off westward along the canal.

He regretted it immediately. The brambles on the path tore at his trousers and scratched at his side-buttoned boots—Nature, in control. Why not write an ode to the indoors, where Hay stood a fighting chance? He thought of the boys' ponies. A misstep would crack a fetlock or send the rider hurtling to the ground or into the canal. Hay weaved his way around the rocks—*rocks!* Someone might have followed them along the path, except there was no place for a pursuer to hide. To his right, a hillock of boulders ascended to the base of the high board fence that marked the southern edge of President's Park. A rock might have rolled down onto the path or been thrown over the fence.

Hay knew he was kidding himself: He was no Vidocq. He had read the stories as a boy of how the Frenchman had known which clues to pursue and which to ignore, how to frame the wily question that unmasked the wrongdoer. What had Hay learned so far? That nobody suspicious had entered the Executive Mansion to leave him a vicious letter, other than the person or persons who had done just that. That the boys' usual chaperone had absented himself, supposedly to cook flapjacks for his son, and was replaced by a novice incapable of fighting off a hummingbird. That the gardener had trimmed a spruce's branches in a suspicious manner, according to a witness who was no arborist. That a rock had dropped from the sky, barely missing the boys, an act of God or a misflung projectile or an attempt on their lives or merely a pale tutor's flight of fancy. That Willie had died of typhoid fever or possibly of some other unknown cause, or of typhoid fever *and* an unknown cause. Too many questions, sloppy questions, and not enough answers—*no* answers. Willie died—that was a fact. Someone had left a note in Hay's satchel—*that* was a fact. Everything else seemed irrelevant or conjecture. To find meaning in this chaos—*that* was the job for a Vidocq. Sad to say, it was Hay's.

Hay was thinking about his multiple shortcomings when he tripped over a branch and fell heavily onto the path. His right shoulder struck something hard, and the surge of pain made him sick to the stomach. Only when it ebbed did he realize his forehead had slapped into the ground, penetrating the crust of ice and coming to rest half-submerged in the mud. Hay lay stock-still, not certain he could move. A veil began to descend, and Hay prepared himself for nothingness, but fought it. He had no choice but to move his head if he wanted to breathe, which he decidedly did. He lifted his head and, to his surprise and relief, spat out a liquid that was darker than mud. The salty taste confirmed it as blood. The sour taste, grainy on his tongue—that must be the mud.

Blood. Mud. Blood. Mud. An incantation to thwart the pain. A clog at the back of his throat made him gag, and he hacked loose a chunk of . . . Hay preferred not to look. An odor rushed in, meaning his nostrils had cleared—a misfortune. Sharper than sewage. Something rotten, something dead—freshly dead.

This is how you catch typhoid fever, it occurred to Hay, *by burying your face in the malevolent mire.* Maybe this was how Willie had—*if* he had.

Desperate to escape, Hay pushed both hands against the ground, until the mud gave way. A sinkhole! Hay suppressed an urge to panic, squeezing his eyes shut, slowing his breathing to regain control. Hay had learned this in the ring, whenever he felt overwhelmed, to calm himself despite getting punched, preserving enough wind to counterpunch (except when he forgot, which was most of the time). Despite the throb in his forehead and the creak in his back, Hay pushed himself to all fours. He caught his breath and, groaning, raised himself to his knees. He reached out to steady himself but remembered the brambles and pulled his arms back. He focused his gaze across the canal, at a rock promontory that, in the glaze of his vision, loomed like a cross.

As he moved, the mud sucked at his boots; each footstep was freed with a slurp. On the ground, just ahead, a carcass, the size of a child. He gasped: *No!* Hay made himself look again. In actual fact, no. Four legs. On its side—a hog? No, a dog. *Was* a dog, stripped of its skin, the flesh a mottled green. In motion, all of it—maggots, writhing. A cold sweat swept over Hay. He restrained the impulse to run, but not an instant longer would he stay. He plotted a route through the mud, between a shrub and a bog, bypassing the mass of tissue that was no longer alive.

The dangers in Washington City lay in every direction. The city itself was sandwiched between Confederate Virginia and slave-holding Maryland. For a week in April of 'sixty-one, the capital had been cut off from the nation it led—the mails blocked, the railroad bridges burned, the telegraph wires severed. Reports last May that a rebel regiment planned to capture the Executive Mansion and kidnap the Lincolns had prompted troops to camp in the East-room. When the threat eased, the troops left, and now bivouacked in President's Park. This hardly justified the want of protection at the mansion itself, but every time Hay or Nicolay raised the matter with the Ancient, the response was a groan. As late as September, Hay had seen Confederate campfires just across the Potomac and heard the musket shots—*after* the Union army had seized the northern rim of Virginia and built a ring of forts to keep the enemy at bay. Rebel troops were still camped in Manassas, a long day's march away, having secured it the previous summer in the rout at Bull Run. Once Hay reached the Potomac, one of the eleven states in rebellion would come into sight.

The path narrowed. The elbows of his coat caught on prickles, and his boots slid in the frosty mud. His shoulder ached, but he ignored it. It was somewhere near here, by the tutor's telling, that the rock had landed from on high. Rubbish littered the canal bank—a wagon wheel, a mashed-down hat, soaked sleeve of a sweater. Rocks of every size and description, scabrous and crusted with moss, slick and gray, streaked with gold and a purplish beige, the dullest of browns. How could he identify a rock that had dropped from the sky eighteen days earlier? And if he did, what then? A rock was a rock. How could it be traced to its thrower? Even Vidocq would be stumped.

But whence, in fact, had this projectile come? Not from the sky, certainly. From across the canal? Alexander Williamson had looked and seen nobody there. Hay wondered about the tutor's eyesight; he wore no spectacles, although he seemed like a man who should. Across the canal, a few cows foraged on the barren bank. No humans in sight.

Hay turned away from the canal to examine the knoll of jagged rocks that climbed to the base of the fence.

The fence.

It was a high wooden wall that, in some forgotten time, had been coated in whitewash. A rock might have been thrown over the top, or *from* the top, or from the hillside. A rock *or something,* the tutor had said. He had seen *something* drop, possibly a brick or a shard of iron. It hardly mattered what. What mattered was the intent of the person who threw it. Assuming, of course, the projectile could be traced to the thrower. And assuming Hay could find it.

At the least, he should look. Disgusting, to muck around in this mud. He poked at the brambles with the toe of his boot. Long yellowish stalks looked like hay—hay! Hay sank to his knees, knowing his favorite trousers, of kelly-green corduroy, would never get clean. (What he sacrificed for duty.) He pulled his leather gloves tight around each finger and, with both hands, dug into the earth.

Here, the mud was hard. Hay felt a twisting of root that seemed unconnected to bushes or trees. A digging tool would help. On a shrub, he saw a branch as thick as a jailer's forearm; one end was beveled, as if ripped from a tree, although the only tree nearby was a sickly willow. Hay retrieved the branch and used it to jab at the earth by his feet. Willie's pony, he figured, would have stayed on the path. But why should he dig here instead of five feet ahead or behind? Ridiculous! Vidocq would not be caught dead poking randomly into the ground. *Think!*

Hay came up dry.

He squatted and considered his options. He could prostrate himself before Lincoln, confess his ineptness for the job, suggest he assign it to somebody else—Pinkerton, no doubt—and accept the humiliation. Or he could think of some other way to . . .

A few feet ahead on the path, Hay noticed an oval of metal protruding from the path. He sprang to his feet and unearthed what looked like a belt buckle—what *was* a belt buckle, made of brass. He scraped away enough of the crusted mud to trace the raised letters across the front:

MVM

A man's initials, or . . . or . . . Hay had no idea what the letters meant. He slipped the buckle into his overcoat pocket. Maybe the commander of the troops encamped in President's Park would know if anyone had heaved an object over the fence. It probably meant nothing, just one of those things, mere happenstance.

Happenstance—there was nothing *mere* about it. Often, nothing mattered more. On a battlefield, Hay reflected, it made the difference between death and life.

†——————†

The morning passed too speedily for Hay, given all that he needed to do. He pored over the paperwork for the pile of pardons—Lincoln was sure to grant every one. He drafted letters to the governors of Maryland and Delaware about the president's proposal for "compensated emancipation"—the phrase was Hay's, and he rather liked it. To free the slaves in the Union's slave states by paying their masters to do the right thing. Either ingenious or a smidgen too clever, Hay could not decide which. If it worked, maybe it would work in the South, although the slaveholders there had sneered when Lincoln endorsed the idea as they rushed to rebellion. Hay tore up his first rough as too whiny and the second as naïve, before he achieved a tone of conviction in peddling principle without pain. Then he started on similar letters to the newspaper editors in Maryland. These, he would sign with his own name.

Hay was drafting a letter of condolence to the governor of Indiana, whose son had met his end at Fort Henry (Hay had learned to simulate Lincoln's signature) when he was relieved to hear a melodic tenor in the doorway. "Joh-n-ny!"

"You want something, Nico," Hay said without looking around.

"And you are the man for the job."

"If you think so, probably not."

"To fill in for the Ancient at the reading of the Farewell Address. At the Capitol, a quarter 'til one."

Hay swiveled to meet his tormentor and made a face.

"I promised Stanton I would see him then," Nicolay said.

"He can barge in on the president like he usually does."

"That is precisely what I am trying to avoid."

"Why can't ol' Hannibal go?" Hannibal Hamlin was the vice president.

"Nobody knows where he is. Or cares."

To stretch his legs, Hay followed Nicolay out into the waiting room. As he turned back to his office, the specter of letter upon letter from simpletons propelled him through the double doors into the central hallway. It was quiet; doors were closed. Hay descended the office stairs to the first floor. As he emerged from the staircase, Dr. Stone was standing outside the green parlor. Hay called to him, and the handsome head snapped back.

"Do you have a minute, sir?" said Hay.

"No."

"The president's business, sir."

"So is this." Doc Stone nodded at the door to the green parlor. Hay remembered with a shudder that the embalming was under way. Then Dr. Stone said, "Very well. A minute."

Robert King Stone was a tall, brisk man with muscular shoulders. He looked forty, if that, hardly old enough (in Hay's opinion) to justify either his arrogance or the position that justified his arrogance as the acknowledged dean of the city's medical community. The unblemished face was of classic Greek proportions, with a sculpted nose, almost feminine cheeks, a jutting chin, and a mane of black hair that swept back from the formidable forehead. The well-starched frock coat took no pains to conceal the gold-and-silver brocaded waistcoat, an instrument for a physician known most for his skill at the bedside. Dr. Stone carried himself as if nothing could harm him, which tempted Hay to try.

The doctor planted his feet, drew a watch from his vest pocket, flipped it open, examined it, then put it back in its place and said, "Well?"

"The morning that Willie got sick, the fourth of February, a Tuesday, he fell off his pony along the canal. You examined him when he returned to the mansion, did you not?"

"I would need to check my records as to the date. But yes, I did."

"And he was uninjured?"

"And what is your interest in this, Mister Hay?"

Hay had been girding for this question and had not yet devised a satisfying answer. "The president asked me . . . he asked me . . . to examine all the possibilities. Of what happened. To Willie."

"We know what happened to Willie."

"What, then?"

"Typhoid fever. Which has killed more Union soldiers than the Confederates have. Or possibly another form of bilious fever. A classic case, to the degree there is one."

"The morning of February fourth?"

"That morning, he was fine. Nothing but a scrape on his cheek."

"That afternoon, as I understand it, he developed a chill and a fever. Might he have caught it that morning by the canal? Falling off his pony, into the mud. And let me tell you, that mud is—"

"Of course not. It takes a week or more after exposure to typhoid fever for the symptoms to manifest. Eight days, typically."

"So he could not have caught the fever by the canal."

"Of course he could have. You understand, Mister Hay, that the Executive Mansion is located in the single unhealthiest spot in the entire sixty-eight square miles of the District of Columbia. The air that drifts in from the canal, from the river, is nothing short of poison. Or he might have caught it from the water piped into the mansion. No telling how many soldiers upriver, on both sides of what passes for a border, use the Potomac as a latrine."

One of President Buchanan's parting gifts, besides the unstanched slide into civil war, was the system of pipes to deliver the Potomac's water to every bedroom in the president's house, including Hay's. The boys had been told not to drink the water from their washstands, but who could say how punctiliously they obeyed?

"So any of us might have caught it, you mean."

"And still could."

To Hay's ear, Dr. Stone sounded pleased. "But it *was* typhoid fever?"

"That is my best professional judgment." Doc Stone's eyes narrowed. "You have reason to doubt it, *Mister* Hay?"

Hay suppressed his annoyance—he could topple this tall and broad-shouldered notable with a single punch. "Which of his symptoms suggested it was typhoid fever, if I might ask?"

"At the beginning, the fever and chills. The delirium. The rose-colored spots. The intestinal, shall we say, distress." Dr. Stone spoke in a rush. "And the high fever, which came and went."

"Is that usual? For the fever to come and go?"

"Not *un*usual. You said a minute, Mister Hay. It has been more than that already. So, if you will excuse me, I am needed inside."

Without waiting for a reply, Dr. Stone reached for the doorknob and entered the green parlor. Peeved at being dismissed, Hay followed him in.

The first thing Hay noticed was the smell of chemicals, sharp and clean—acidic. His eyes watered, and he pressed them shut. He waited for the sting to pass before easing them open.

Through a blurry gaze, everything in the room was either drab green or stark white. The divans and armchairs had been pushed to the walls, flush against the jungle-green striped wallpaper and the gold-fringed tapestries purchased with appropriations meant for gas lamps on Capitol Hill and a culvert under the Avenue—yea, another triumph for the Hell-cat.

At the center of the room, a table was draped in a white sheet, except for the two bare feet that pointed toward Hay.

Hay stumbled backward and reached behind him for the door. A hand at his left shoulder stopped him. Hay spun around.

"You can stay, suh," whispered a short, pudgy man, and Hay knew that he must. Although not why.

The man escorted Hay along the wall to the right, past the side door to the blue parlor. Not quite to the end of the wall, the man halted. So did Hay, to his sorrow.

On the table, the sheet stopped at the shoulders. The head was propped on a headrest that bulged at the neck. The face looked vaguely like Willie's, but it was puffier, round and full—*too* full. A rubber tube jutted out of the nose and snaked to the far side of the table, into a contraption Hay recognized as a pump. A man standing behind it kept pushing on a plunger.

Hay was trying not to see—or failing that, to believe—what he plainly saw and could not help but believe. Bile rose in his throat, and he swallowed hard, then swallowed again, hoping not to vomit. He noticed Dr. Stone leaning against the opposite wall, glaring at Hay, and swore to deprive him of the pleasure of an urgent departure. He shut his eyes and tensed his shoulders and strained to exert his will—over himself, which was the hardest of all. He looked again at the face that protruded from the sheet, of Willie-but-not-Willie—its waxy pallor, its bloating—and forced himself to feel nothing at all. Hay was good at this when he had to be; he always had been.

He observed the embalming surgeon at work, as a diorama with parts that moved. Dr. Charles Brown—Hay remembered his name—had licensed a French method of embalming for use in America and had recently moved here from New York to profit from the war. Embalmers had overrun Washington City, as the closest center of civilization to the battlefields of Virginia; their wagons followed the troops, contracting with soldiers or with their loved ones to deliver the fallen back home, chemically preserved.

Dr. Brown worked with a vacant absorption. He was a slender man, taller even than Lincoln, with side-whiskers as bushy as General Burnside's. Strong forearms brought the most delicate touch; not a muscle moved without purpose. He pulled the tube out from a nostril at a smooth and steady pace, until the end of it broke free. Then he tilted the head farther back, so that Willie's mouth fell open, and inserted the tube and threaded it into the throat. At Dr. Brown's nod, the man at the pump began again to press the plunger. *Whoosh-whoosh-whoosh*—liquid being forced through a constriction—was the only sound Hay could hear, besides his own heartbeat. The pump did its work for a minute or more, and when it stopped, the silence deafened. Hay realized his breathing needed to resume.

Hay could not help but stare, trying not to take in what he saw. Dr. Brown pressed his fingertips into Willie's neck and, with the flick of a knife, made a slice. Using a prong, he pulled an artery out of the morass of muscle and nerves, then threaded two pieces of silk underneath. Another deft cut, and Dr. Brown slipped a rubber tube into the artery and wrapped it in a silk ribbon that he drew tight and tied twice in double knots. As he repeated the procedure on the other side of the neck, a trickle of something splashed into a porcelain pan by Willie-but-not-Willie's head. Dr. Brown pressed his massive hands across the barely recognizable cheeks, which quickened the flow for a few seconds, until it suddenly ceased. This was a boy's blood, his *life*blood. Willie had no need for it now.

Then the pump started pumping again, slowly at first, then faster, until it reached a pitiless pace. Audibly, the liquid forced its way in, pushing the blood ahead of it. Soon the trickle into the porcelain pan resumed and then became a torrent. Dr. Brown poured in an acrid-smelling liquid—a disinfectant, Hay thought.

Suddenly, Hay felt light-headed and desperate to sit. There was an armless upholstered chair at his right, and he gratefully sank into it, then was sorry he had. A burning behind his eyes—from the chemicals, surely—needed release. *Oh,* he pleaded, *anyplace but here.* He forced himself to his feet and was relieved to feel a strong arm holding him up. The short, pudgy man—Hay had seen him in the East-room the night that Willie took ill—guided him to the door that led into the blue parlor. There, the air smelled mercifully pure, and the man found him a seat and then left him alone, just as Hay wished.

Hay hoped he had not embarrassed himself but was surprised at how little he cared. Already, he was regaining control. Slowly he tried to take in what he had observed. It had been shocking, but also soothing some-how, to see the body as an emptied vessel, nothing more—bloodless, in its way. The soul had already fled, yet the wan figure of Willie-but-not-Willie would remain with him, Hay felt certain, for the rest of his days.

Hay had never seen Pennsylvania avenue so dressed up, even on the Fourth of July. And no wonder: There was no grander public holiday than Washington's Birthday. From every apothecary and clothier, every restaurant and hotel, from almost every building along the Avenue, hung the Stars and Stripes. Just east of Eleventh street, something else was hanging from a leafless tree: an effigy of Jefferson Davis. Hay admired the workmanship, superior to a bedsheet—the wavy hair, the tacked-on goatee. At this very hour, a hundred miles to the south, the Confederate president was delivering his inaugural address, claiming the Virginia slaveholder who fathered this country as the Confederacy's own. *Oh yes,* Hay thought, *Father of His Countries.*

The president's carriage slowed to a crawl. "We will get dere, Mistah John."

"The later the better, by my lights, William."

"I do aim to please."

Lincoln had lent Hay his two-horse barouche and his valet, William Slade, as a driver. The khaki-skinned Negro, of a distinguished Virginian ancestry, was known for jests that could make a Bedouin laugh. His face resembled a pecan with a fringe of white hair.

Vehicles of all descriptions jammed the Avenue—barouches and hackneys, army wagons and omnibuses. It was the widest roadway in Washington City and the only one other than Seventh street that was paved. Nor would traveling on foot have quickened the pace. The northern sidewalk was the city's promenade—the Avenu-orama, as Hay thought of it, crowded with ladies in fur caplets, Quakers primly dressed, soldiers in blue, families with balky children, the bootblacks and newsboys, the vendors hawking cutlery, candy, peanuts, patent medicines, and toys. The southern sidewalk was brazen with unrefined commerce— saloons and seedy shops and gambling joints and brothels. Even at midday, the ladies of the evening were taking a stroll. The carriage edged past the Centre Market, which stretched from Ninth street to Seventh, crammed with hominy dealers and sausage makers, all the hucksters with their goods. Not one in a hundred of these people prancing toward the Capitol in their holiday attire would actually gain entry to the House of Representatives chamber to hear a political hack recite George Washington's Farewell Address. This did nothing to discourage their excitement at celebrating the Union.

Past Fifth street, a clattering of cavalry rushed up from behind. Hay's carriage swerved to the curb and allowed the convoy to pass five abreast, their coats a sparkling blue, sabers clacking at their sides. Followed by a general on his white steed, scarf a-flying, a broad smile—George Brinton McClellan himself.

The man is shameless, Hay thought. According to the particulars of General War Order No. 1, *this* was the day the general-in-chief of the

Union armies was to be marching on Richmond. He was advancing on his own capital instead.

On the far side of the Capitol, Hay alighted and joined the throngs of pilgrims. He let them rush past; his seat was reserved. He stopped at the seated statue of the man he had come to honor, which commanded the Capitol's east entrance. The Founding Father was clad in a toga, bare-chested, a muscled arm outstretched. Not even his mother—this was Nathaniel Hawthorne's gibe—had ever seen George Washington naked.

Inside, the airy Rotunda was mobbed. Above, a tarpaulin took the place of a ceiling, while the new dome was being built; a web of scaffolding covered the high walls. Below, the men wore their Sunday best; the women stepped sideways so that their dresses might survive uncrushed. Jabs of perfume made the unwashed bodies only more malodorous. Ah, the common people. So many of them, yes, but so common.

Hay shuffled across the Rotunda and exited through the southern doorway. A luridly painted corridor took him to his destination. Hay flashed his pass at the unshaven soldier and got a wink in return.

As soon as he entered the new chamber of the House of Representatives, he started wondering how soon he might escape.

⊬⊷⊶⊣

It was nearly four o'clock before Hay returned to the Gray House—a more accurate description, although the rain had stopped. Mingling with the people's representatives lent the piles of mute correspondence on his desk a fresh appeal.

"Oh, William," Hay said as the carriage turned from Fifteenth street back onto the Avenue, "would you happen to know of a bird that goes *north* for the winter?"

"Let me think, Mistuh John. I imagine it might be the magpie, which surely flocks to the talk-talk-talkers of the North."

Hay chuckled. "Could be, William, could be. Though I was thinking it might be the crow, which can go due north faster and freer by riding the Underground Railroad."

A roar from the front seat. "I needs a good laugh, Mistuh John, in these sad, sad days."

A streak of blue in the sky was compressing the gray—Hay thought of jotting a line or two, but the metaphor was too gaggingly obvious even for him.

The carriage was turning onto the north grounds of the Executive Mansion when the door to the carriage slapped open. A man leapt inside and lunged at Hay.

He had a knife. Hay noticed the details of the blade—its bevel, the graceful taper to the point, the serrations near the hilt—as it came toward his throat. Hay raised his forearm to knock his assailant's wrist while he edged his head to the side like he was slipping a punch.

Then he counterpunched. Hay's right fist smashed into the devilish goatee of the triangular face, which belonged to a blond young man with an aquiline nose. He looked vaguely surprised—annoyed, rather—at Hay's subsequent left hook to the jaw. The knife flew out of the young man's hand. His head rocked back, and he tipped backward out of the carriage and onto the street.

William Slade stared in horror and brought the carriage to a halt.

"No!" Hay shouted. "Not here!" He was hoping to seem nonchalant but found he was trembling. It was one thing to step voluntarily into a ring, quite another to be attacked without warning. (*As in war,* Hay thought.) "Keep going," he commanded.

William acceded.

Hay pulled the door shut. His right hand stung. Out of the carriage's window, the Avenue looked deserted, peaceful. Hay might have believed the assault had never happened but for his sudden exhaustion and William Slade's protective glances.

"Takes a brave man to venture out dese days," William said. "Robbers 'round de Smithsonian—everywhere. And not just in the night—in the daylight, too, Mistuh John. Whatever is this world a-comin' to?"

"Keep going, William."

Hay's voice was steel, but his mind was a cloud, with only one recurring thought: *This is the president's carriage, the president's carriage, the president's carriage. Surely this attack was meant for* him. *Or for no one in particular.*

So, should Hay tell Lincoln and add to his mountain of troubles? Or take a punch for the president? He did not know how to decide.

The front door was unguarded, and as Hay entered, a man called his name. He glanced around the vestibule but saw only dust motes.

"Mistuh Hay!" It was the pudgy man Hay had seen at the ball, who had rescued him at the embalming. The man bounced across the vestibule, his hand outstretched. "Ah am afraid Ah have you at a disadvantage, suh. The name is Hall, suh, Doctuh James C. Hall. Mistuh Nicolay expected you back before now."

"I will be sure to thank him."

Despite the flabby jowls and the tea saucer of a chin, the man's handshake was firm. He had a genial face, guileless and kind. The prematurely receding hairline showed half a scalp as pink as a baby's, dramatizing the dark curls at his neck. He moved slowly, as if through water, with an expression of unshakable calm.

Then the man took a longer look at Hay, and his mouth puckered in alarm. "Are you all right, Mistuh Hay?"

"Oh my, yes," Hay replied quickly. "A moment's shock. But no, not at you."

Hay reached and touched the man's elbow, all the while wondering, *Who is he? Hall. Hall . . .* Lincoln's stepsister Matilda had married a Hall—his name was Squire Hall—and they had a son. Who was a doctor, Hay dimly recalled. Yes, who had moved here from Kentucky (or was it Indiana?) just after Christmas. Hay could not remember why, if he knew.

"Glad to meet you, Doctor Hall. We *have* met. Glad to meet you, then, with my wits about me." The embalming seemed ages ago. "And thank you for your kindness, when I was . . . in some need of it. I owe you my . . . well, a great deal."

"Ah am most grateful, Mistuh Hay, to have had the oppuhtunity. In that case, might Ah bother you to accompany me, so that we might converse?"

Hay wanted nothing more than to return to his office or his bedroom for a few moments' peace, but he saw no way to demur. They passed through the vestibule into the corridor and, to Hay's relief, headed away from the green parlor and into the crimson room instead.

"No one will look for us he-ah," Dr. Hall said.

Hay wondered who might be looking at all.

Dr. Hall put Hay in the gaudiest armchair and said, "The only place in this room where you do not need to see it."

Hay asked if he was Squire Hall's son; a toothy smile was the reply. "Do you know him, suh?"

"Wish I did. I have heard the president's stories." Though for the moment, Hay could not remember whether Lincoln's stepbrother-in-law was the disbarred lawyer in Frankfort or the saloonkeeper with a heart of coal. "What can I do for you, Doctor Hall?"

"Call me Jamie, please."

"John, then."

"Cousin Abraham told me of your . . . suspicions, suh, and he asked if Ah might help."

"My suspicions about what?"

"Forgive me, suh." Months had passed since anyone in Washington had asked Hay's forgiveness. "He shared with me the possibility that Willie's passing was perhaps not entirely the Lord's work. Ah had mentioned to him what Ah learned at the, uh, procedure this fine day. It was why Ah bid you to stay, so you might witness it yourself, in case it was so."

"So instead, I almost fainted. In case *what* was so, Doc . . . Jamie?"

"Again, forgive me, suh. Let me speak directly. The embalming"— Dr. Hall gestured back toward the green room—"was a success."

"Well . . . good . . . I guess."

"No, suh, not good. It went *too* well. If you will allow me, please, to explain. Typhoid fevuh causes intestinal lesions, so that when . . . please forgive me, suh, for the canduh of my explanation . . . that when the embalming fluid is injected into the esophagus and passes through to the intestines, the intestines cannot keep the fluid in. It will leak, precisely be*cause* of those lesions. And therefore the embalming will not, in such a case, succeed. You understand what Ah am sayin', suh?"

Hay thought he did.

"But this time, suh, it did succeed. Suh, it *did*. The intestines held the embalming fluid in. And therefore, suh, it was *not* . . ."

Hay mouthed the next two words along with Dr. Hall: "—typhoid fever . . ."

"—that proved fatal for Willie," the doctor went on. "No, suh, it seems not. He might have contracted the disease, but not seriously enough to cause the lesions. Suggesting he . . . succumbed, suh, to something else."

"To what?"

"That Ah could not say, suh. Anothuh disease, could be. Th' bilious fevuh that Doctuh Stone thought at fuhst. Or an infection of Lawd knows what variety. Enough diseases thrive within a mile of this here house for th' devil's delight."

"But you are not convinced, are you, that it was some other disease? You would not be telling me this."

"No, suh, Ah am not. Merely a surmise, let me say, but the wild oscillations in his fever and in his symptoms of other sorts suggest that actions by a mortal were involved."

"That sounds ominous."

"An embalming, suh, is not an autopsy. But Ah *am* aware that the embalming surgeon noticed nothing untoward. No marks of a criminal kind. No sign of a weapon, no strangulation—forgive me again, suh, for my canduh."

"Leaving what, then?"

"Ah would have to suppose"—Dr. Hall's dark eyes narrowed—"a poison of some sort."

A punch to the gut. The matter-of-fact utterance gave it reality. *Murder in the insurrection.*

And by the most cowardly of means.

"Of which sort?" said Hay.

◦━◦━◦

Hay found himself retracing his steps toward the canal. His feet knew their destination, although his brain did not catch on until he crossed Fifteenth street and turned east on Ohio. Whoops and shouts erupted from behind the tent flaps in Hooker's encampment. A Saturday night for men who had nothing to do.

Like Hay. Except he needed to get rid of the jitters he felt. He knew of two ways to do that. One was to hit a boxing bag, or a boxer, again and again, as hard as he could. The other was horizontal refreshment. That, he could find a block or two away.

Hay stepped around a hog sprawled on the sidewalk that was browsing in the gutter, as he ambled toward the cluster of saloons and brothels—"Hooker's division." He would have more choices near the Avenue, but here he was less likely to be seen.

Madam Wilton's Private Residence for Ladies was past Thirteenth street. The red lantern contorted the reflection from the frosted front windows. A tug at the bell brought a glance through the white gauzy curtain and the sound of the tumblers in the lock.

"Good evening, sir." The woman's blond wig was askew on her head. Her cheeks looked unnaturally red.

"And the same to you," Hay said.

"You have visited us before, sir." A statement, not a question, requiring no response. She led him into a plush crimson parlor. After some banter about the weather, she said, "Would you have a favorite girl?"

Hay could not remember her name, but he described her—slender, dimpled, blond, the tattoo of a rose on her breast.

"Oh, Rose," she said.

Not yet a Vidocq, Hay thought.

The front parlor had overstuffed divans and marble-topped tables with mermaid-shaped lamps. The horsehair under Hay shifted, and he tried not to think of the countless arses that had preceded his. Failure at the attempt did not last a half minute before a woman in a scarlet gown and cherry wig sashayed in. Madam Wilton herself—no mistaking her.

"To-night, dear sir," she said, "you are a lucky gent indeed. Rose is here, and also Henrietta. If you would like, sir."

"You mean both?"

"For the price of one and a half." Madam Wilton's smile was more of a grimace; this Saturday night must be slow. "If the gentleman should have a mind to."

It was not his mind Hay needed to consult. That was lower down—his wallet, which was thin. And Rose, if memory served, which assuredly it did, would quite suffice for one healthy young man.

She was as lovely as he remembered, her coy smile beyond her smooth yet intricate curves. She stretched out beside him, then beneath him. The tattoo was where he remembered, and she giggled as he rested his cheek against it and she embraced his head. He felt so comforted there, so soothed, as if he would never wish to leave.

Then, from somewhere deep inside, Hay felt a force began to rise. A familiar one, of course, but it was more than that. It was fused with desperation, with danger—with fear—and would not be denied. He was on her, then in her, pounding his way through her, pinning her wrists to the bed.

And when the paroxysm came, and lasted, and lasted, he collapsed in her arms, calmed and drained beyond repair.

Chapter Four

SUNDAY, FEBRUARY 23, 1862

T hey *are* poison!" Hay exclaimed. "Drugs *and* poison—the very same stuff. That is what Jamie said, and it makes sense. You take the right amount, they will cure you." Hay poked into his omelet soufflé. "Take too much, and they kill. That is what all medicines are—poisons, administered in a less-than-poisonous dose."

When Nicolay stabbed at a slice of pork with a knife and a fork, juice squirted out. "So," he replied, "these practitioners of heroic medicine, these Doc Stones of the world, are murderers, more or less. This is what you are saying. Including your dear father, I suppose."

"My father never killed anyone—on purpose, at least. Whether he saved anyone, who can say? But no, they are not necessarily . . . murderers, as you delicately put it. If they can add and multiply, they can give the right amount of a drug and not too much. In theory, anyway. Whether the numbers they add and multiply are correct, that is something else. This is art, Nico, not science."

Hay was well aware of the civil war in medicine. The established physicians in the civilized places (including this one) believed in fighting disease heroically, using any available tool—leeches, lancets, scalding, blistering, opium, rhubarb, remedies of exotic description. Try anything and everything, in case something worked—what was more American than that? Yet the ubiquity of heroic medicine, and its grim aggressiveness, had induced a revolt—a secession of sorts. In Eastern cities, in the most sophisticated circles, homeopathy and its creed—*less is more*—had gained a foothold. Medicines are poison; to cure an illness, administer the slightest dilution of whatever had caused it. *Like cures like.* Each side had its dogma and viewed the other side as quacks. For Hay's money, both sides' assessments were correct.

"Which remedies—excuse me, poisons—does he think Willie might have . . . ?" As unemotional a man as Nicolay could not finish the sentence.

Hay came to his aid. "Three possibilities, says Doctor Hall—Jamie. Arsenic, mercury, or antimony. They all work as remedies or, in higher doses, as poisons. Either—both."

"So, which of the three might be mistaken for typhoid fever?"

"Any of them, to a greater or lesser extent. And all of them are common enough, easy to buy."

"Arsenic?"

"My father kept some out by the privy, on the top shelf of the shed. To kill the rats coming up from the river." And one of the family mutts. "Any gardener would have some on hand."

"Gardener?" said Nicolay.

"How about that."

"Arsenic is a medicine? What for?"

"Syphilis, says Jamie."

"For Willie? He was precocious, but . . ."

"And to whiten women's skin."

"Again . . ."

"For us, the advantage of arsenic is that you can test for it. The Marsh test, it's called. Something with sulfuric acid that turns the arsenic into a gas—Jamie explained it, and I . . . I skipped my chemistry class whenever I could."

"Boasting again, Johnny—what a waste of an education." Nicolay had known next to none. "A test only for arsenic—not the others?"

"As far as he knows. He will check."

"Can he arrange for this . . . Marsh test?"

Hay said, "He already has."

As they left the New York Avenue Presbyterian Church, Hay found himself praying for a merciful God, less as a matter of faith or of hope than out of a habit of hedging his bets. Lincoln hurried ahead, east across Thirteenth street, dodging the hacks and carriages that carried the worshipers home, tugging at Hay's sleeve like a heedless child. Robert trailed a step or two behind. Father and son wore the black armbands Mrs. Keckly had sewn.

There was no mystery about Lincoln's destination. The miniature shop, almost to Twelfth street, resembled a dollhouse, with its two dwarf windows upstairs and a balcony with a wrought iron rail. *A. Stuntz*— written across the awning. Lincoln stood in front of the picture window, inches from the display of bright and beckoning toys—doll babies and pop guns, tin watches and dominoes, railroad engines wound with a key, wooden soldiers clad in red and blue. All, on a Sunday, unreachable, imprisoned behind glass. Hay wondered how many times Lincoln had stood here, clasping Willie with one hand and Tad with the other, before venturing inside and trading the cares of a wartime president for a father's joys.

As they headed back to the Executive Mansion, Robert kept several steps behind. Hay wondered if this show of laggardliness was directed at the president or at Hay, for . . . what? For having accompanied them to church, no doubt. Hay understood the part he played in Robert's emotional predicament, the threat he posed for the president's affections. Robert could well misunderstand—or, understand. With his mother's round face and soft features, the eighteen-year-old was nice looking enough, in a bland sort of way. He was awkward in anyone's presence—his father's, most of all—and jittery at receiving too much attention. Maybe because his father had given him so little of it, was Hay's guess. During Robert's boyhood, Lincoln was mostly away from home, politicking or traveling the judicial circuit. That, and their vastly different natures, Robert being a Todd through and through, probably explained the distance between father and firstborn. This distance made it all the harder for Robert to watch his father treat Hay like a son. Robert had no way of knowing—and it would hurt him to know—that it was the president who had asked Hay to church and that Hay had suggested inviting Robert. And Robert had come, keeping his distance.

Hay knew he was making things worse—but surely, duty to Lincoln trumped Robert's sensitivities—as he sidled alongside the president, crossing Fourteenth street, whispering about . . . Willie. Hay had decided on the blunt approach. It was kinder, he decided, and simpler. Hay had settled on an opening sentence—*Jamie learned something at the embalming*—when Lincoln spoke up.

"I had a visit last evening from 'Bowie Knife' Potter." The chairman of the House Select Committee on the Loyalty of Government Clerks was a radical Republican from Wisconsin who was prone to see treason where others saw a free man's right to speech. His posse of investigators, Hay knew, was tracking down secret secessionists who allegedly honeycombed the government, including the Executive Mansion. "Mister Watt and Mister Stackpole, he has evidence against both of 'em."

"Evidence of what? From whom?"

"Of their secessionist sentiments. Perhaps you oughta ask him. The man is a fool, but if he says he has evidence, I am never averse to evidence."

They resumed the journey in silence, Robert trailing behind. As they entered the grounds of the Executive Mansion, Hay's courage—and swelling sense of duty—revived.

"Jamie learned something, sir"—to his own ear, he sounded squeaky—"at the . . . embalming,"

"Oh?" the president said mildly. He seemed not to be listening.

"It was not typhoid fever. More precisely, not only typhoid fever."

To Hay's synopsis of Dr. Hall's logic and his description of possible poisons, Lincoln showed almost no reaction, as if Hay were reading the minutes of a cabinet meeting. But Hay's mention of the Marsh test for arsenic brought Lincoln to a halt. Robert nearly walked into his father's back, then circled around and hurried into the mansion.

"And so they need *some*thing," Hay said with trepidation, "on which to perform the test."

The statue of Thomas Jefferson, in an oval of grass on the North Lawn, looked vaguely Negroid in the late-morning gloom. Holding the Declaration of Independence in one hand and a quill pen in the other, the Founding Father saucily thrust out a hip.

Lincoln's face looked carved from stone. "The embalming," he said at last, "didn't that ruin a test?"

"Jamie says no. If the . . . material is tested, the arsenic will still be there."

"As long as Mother and I can take our precious boy home, exactly as he is—as he was. As God made him and then, for His own unfathomable reasons, snatched him away."

＊＊＊

Written in a small, meticulous hand, the names filled the left side of a piece of foolscap. Old Edward had listed everyone who was in the Executive Mansion on Thursday evening from five o'clock until nine.

Cooks—six names.
Chambermaids—four.
Messengers—three.
Doorkeepers—Thomas Stackpole and Old Edward himself.

Hay's name was listed, and Nicolay's, and the president's and Mrs. Lincoln's. And Robert's and Tad's. And John Watt's. But not, he noticed, Mrs. Keckly's. An oversight, perhaps. He thought he remembered seeing her—possibly, that was some other day.

He should question all of them, but not to-day. Most of them were at home on a Sunday. He could speak with the few on the premises, but what would he ask them? Had they seen anything suspicious?—whatever he meant by that. Yes, and by any chance, had they left a message in his satchel after murdering the president's son?

Oh yes, Mister Hay, I murdered the boy, since you bothered to ask.

Who was Hay kidding? He had next to no idea about how to proceed. He needed help, but from whom? Nicolay? Nico asked sharp questions, but he was a tad too rational—to Nicolay, two points made a line—and, in his way, too guileless to outthink a devious mind. Hay knew the right person to ask, even if he preferred not to. Lincoln was right: Allan Pinkerton could lend a hand. In framing questions for the mansion's staff. Possibly, in learning more about the in-house secessionists. Hay recognized it was not embarrassment that explained his reluctance, but rivalry.

So, where might Hay find the detective on a Sunday afternoon? At his agency's office, on I street? More likely, at his home, on Sixteenth. Or at the Willard's bar, nursing a ginger ale, soaking up the gossip. Pinkerton might be arrogant and belligerent, but he was not lazy.

Hay was hurrying down the office staircase when he nearly collided with Pinkerton, who was climbing up.

"I was just coming to—" Hay said.

"You leave him alone," Pinkerton growled. The detective's blue-gray eyes were ablaze.

Hay said, "Leave who alone?"

"Ye know who I mean."

Pinkerton's fists balled up, and Hay's did the same. Hay stood one step higher on the staircase, putting him in position for a mean left hook. He edged not quite sideways, his left foot forward—a boxer's orthodox stance—precariously on the step, and barely resisted raising his fists. Pinkerton, with his heft, might best him in a bare-knuckled bout, but he would know he had been in a fight.

"Let me guess," Hay said. "Horace Greeley? Jeff. Davis? I am sorry, my dear Pinkerton, I haven't a notion."

"We need to talk." Pinkerton brushed past Hay on the staircase. "Now."

Hay had seen the detective once before in a state of high dudgeon—hunched forward, his brows dour, the eyes penetrating, his mouth pursed behind the intimidating beard. That was in Harrisburg, once the plot against Lincoln's life had come to light (assuming, of course, it existed). Pinkerton brooked no disagreement whenever he was sure of himself, which was all of the time.

Once they had settled themselves in their rightful places, Pinkerton visibly relaxed and declared, "John Watt. He was arrested this mornin'. *I* arrested him."

"Congratulations. For what? Padding invoices?"

If so, Hay wondered, *was Mrs. Lincoln next?*

"Nothin' so paltry. Fer extortion—blackmail."

Pinkerton waited to see the effect of his words. Hay hated to give him the pleasure, but he *was* shocked. Pinkerton said nothing, forcing Hay to ask.

"*Who*?" said Hay, after a pause he hoped made its point. "Who did he blackmail?"

"The Madam."

Hay felt his jaw drop. At the audacity. The gardener had helped *her* pad *her* invoices. He taught her, tutored her. An apt pupil, a woman as conniving as he was. Indeed, it was the epiphany that John Watt could not be disciplined without implicating the Madam that had ruptured Hay's and Nicolay's relations with the Hell-cat. And so Watt, in turn, had rewarded her studiousness by . . . How on earth *could* he . . . ?

"Blackmailed her how?"

"With three o' her own letters. In which she admits to . . ." Pinkerton stopped.

"To?"

"She asked him in those letters to commit forgery and perjury for the purpose o' defraudin' the government." Pinkerton recited with almost a tangible distaste. "The woman is an imbecile."

"Thank you—I was unaware of this until just now. How much does he ask for?"

Pinkerton paused for dramatic effect. "Twenty thousand dollars. In gold."

Hay whistled as he exhaled. He was certain the Lincolns had no such wealth. "And if they refuse?"

"Then he will deliver them to our enemies in the press."

Them being the letters, Hay understood. But also the Lincolns. Re-introducing Madam President to the electorate as not only ostentatious but also conniving and corrupt. Hay could imagine the thrill these letters would occasion in *The New York Herald*'s appeasing heart. But $20,000 in gold? The initial bid, perhaps.

"He was arrested, you say?"

"This mornin'. In the conservatory. I snapped on the shackles meself."

Hay was impressed. The arrest must have taken place while the president was at church. Probably as planned.

"Where is he now?"

"And why do ye ask?"

"His name comes up when I make inquiries about Willie." Hay recounted the tutor's suspicions about John Watt's behavior on the South Lawn.

"And wha' woul' ye say was his purpose in standin' behind this tree o' yers?"

"Of *mine*? Who can say for sure that he had a purpose?"

"A man does no' stand ou' in the cold at seven o'clock in the mornin' withou' a purpose," Pinkerton said.

"Other than . . ." Hay explained that John Watt's presence had prompted the tutor to reverse his course. Before a projectile nearly struck Willie along the canal.

"From which direction?"

"The projectile?" Hay shrugged. "From the sky, best the tutor could say. Maybe over the fence, from President's Park."

"'Tis applesauce, this theory o' yours."

"What theory? I wish I had one."

"Tha' the presence o' Mistah Watt was intended to cause a change o' direction tha' brought the boys into danger. From the sky, as ye say."

"*I* did not say—the tutor did. And what makes you so sure?"

"A plot needs to work, Mistah Hay. It needs to be counted upon. A man hidin' behind a tree does not assure a change o' direction. It migh' work, it migh' no'. Probably no'. Fer *yer* plot to work, the boys must change direction *and* a rock flung from somewhere must land just so. This is madness. What kind o' plot is tha'?"

Hay had nothing to say.

"This man is a dunce, your tutor. He is—"

"*My* tutor?"

"—just the man I *woul'* want in charge o' a boy I was meanin' to harm. Now who bore the responsibility for tha'?"

Hay told how Tom Cross, the messenger so beloved by the boys, had stayed home to fix a birthday breakfast for his son. "*If*," Hay said, "he was telling the truth about that."

Which gave Hay an idea. "Is that something you could check?" he said, almost adding "for me."

"Ye are askin' Allan Pinkerton if he is capable o' verifyin' a boy's birthday? And his preference at breakfast?"

Hay smiled in spite of himself. "I suppose I am," he said. "Would you?"

"And is there any other blessed thing ye wish me to do fer you—is there, Mistah Hay?"

"As a matter of fact, there is." Hay told him of the belt buckle stamped with *MVM* that he had found on the path by the canal. Might Pinkerton make inquiries among the troops in President's Park?

"Mistah Hay, you have a simple mind."

"Pardon?"

"Ye heard me well and square. Ye are believin', are ye, that the belt buckle ye just happened to discover when ye fell on yer face in the mud, that this was the very belt buckle that just happened to drop from the sky, waitin' to be found by the simpleton who happened to be looking for such . . . a projectile? And this, flung by a source yet unknown? Is this what ye be believin'?"

Hay felt himself turning red. "When you put it that way," he said, "of course."

⊷━━⊶

The door to the study was shut. Hay knocked. A pause, then an invitation from inside.

Lincoln was seated in his upholstered rocking chair at the center of the oval sitting room. This was where he would read a chapter from his mother's worn Bible after dressing in the morning, or a scene from Shakespeare with his lunch of an apple and milk. His volumes of Shakespeare and Burns shared the old bookcases with Mrs. Lincoln's modern English novels. It was a homey room, with no corners and a blazing fire; its informality, verging on messiness, had managed to resist the Madam's redecorative command.

Lincoln gestured Hay into the Madam's matching chair, opposite his own. "It is about Tad, sir," Hay said. "And Bob. I am scared that something could happen to them."

"Robert can take care of himself," Lincoln said, iron in his voice. "What is it about Tad?"

"About both of them, sir. This is not evidence, exactly. We won't know about any arsenic until . . . But I can't shake the thought that . . . if someone wanted to . . . harm Willie, why would he stop there?"

Hay waited for Lincoln to react, but his face was rigid. Hay wondered if he had grasped the implications.

"Then what would you have me do, John?" the president said.

<hr />

"Taddie, Taddie—wake up, my boy."

A father's cry roused no movement in the bed. Hay was terrified until he saw the thin lips twitch. Then the sleeping lad sighed. The president tunneled a hand under Tad's head and lifted it. Tad's eyes drifted open. Seeing his father, he smiled.

"Papa-day," Tad said. "Papa-day."

"How do you feel, my boy?"

"Me hurt, Papa day."

"What hurts, Taddie?"

The boy started to cry.

"Shhhh, shhhh." Lincoln sank onto one knee and held his son's head to his shoulder. Tad's striped nightshirt nearly vanished under his father's huge hand. Only in his oversized ears did the boy resemble his pa.

Once the boy calmed, Lincoln said, "John here has some questions to ask you, Taddie. Is that all right?"

Tad looked up blankly, tears on his face, and nodded.

Hay stood awkwardly behind the kneeling president. The boy's forehead glistened with perspiration.

"Tad, my boy," Hay began.

"I am not your boy. I am *my* boy."

"Of course you are," Hay said.

"No," Lincoln said, "you are *my* boy."

Tad's face glowed.

"What I want to ask you, Tad," Hay said, "is whether anyone gave you something that was bitter to eat. That did not taste good."

Tad shook his head decisively, almost violently, from side to side.

"Mister Watt, maybe?" said Hay.

The boy's face crumpled. "Mean man. Mean to Taddie."

"But did he give you anything to eat, Taddie?" said Hay.

"Not call me Taddie. Not your Taddie. Papa-day's Taddie. My faver's"—the boy's lisp, aggravated by his second teeth growing in crooked, frustrated the *th*—"Taddie. Not call *me*—"

Hay tried to stifle his irritation. "Did *any*one give you something bitter to eat? Mister Stackpole, perhaps?"

"No, no," Tad whined. "Taddie good boy." He hugged his father's neck like it was a life buoy. "Papa-day, Papa-day, Papa-day . . ."

Lincoln rocked his son from side to side and murmured sounds that Hay could not decipher. Tad's eyes drifted shut, and his head rested on his father's bristly beard. Tenderly, Lincoln lowered the boy onto the bed, where he could rest.

*　　＊＝＝＋＝＝＊*

"I never asked him straight out," Hay said.

Nicolay replied, "And why not?"

"Because he would have said no. Pinkerton would never let me get close to his star prisoner. 'I shackled him meself.'" Hay's falsetto made Nicolay laugh.

They were walking back from supper at Willard's. Hay had passed up coffee and plum pudding—and brandy—to keep the roast lamb and mint on his tongue. "How would Pinkerton know," he said, "if Stackpole and Watt were—are—in cahoots? Or if they are both secesh. I want to question John Watt myself. Because I know why I am asking—at least vaguely—and Pinkerton can only guess."

"You don't want Pinkerton to take this over from you."

"Would you?"

"*Now*"—Nicolay's expression turned angelic—"I understand. You want to question Watt because Pinkerton told you not to."

Hay grinned. "Not *only* that."

"Johnny, you are as transparent as glass."

*　　＊＝＝＋＝＝＊*

Jamie Hall was seated in the waiting room, outside Hay's office door. Hay glanced over the doctor's shoulder at the latest edition of *Frank Leslie's Illustrated*. The popular weekly lay open to the center spread, a drawing of the swirling eminences in the high-ceilinged East-room during the Hell-cat's late, unlamented ball. Hay scanned the faces. When *Harper's Weekly* had pictured the president's New Year's reception, Hay's delicate face and Nicolay's Bavarian severity watched from the side. This time, they were thankfully absent. But when Dr. Hall closed the newspaper, Hay saw the headline on the front page and groaned:

THE PRESIDENTIAL PARTY

Amid all the hazards of waging a war, this was the last thing they needed. Damn the Hell-cat!

"We need to talk, suh."

In Hay's office, Dr. Hall said, "The Marsh test, suh. My friend the chemist conducted it this morning. And yes, arsenic. He found it."

"A lot?"

"Enough."

Hay felt the news in the pit of his belly. It was one thing for poison to loom as a possibility and another as a proven fact.

"Would Willie not have tasted it?" Hay said. "It is bitter, yes?"

"It is, suh, but it can be mixed with something else to soothe the taste."

"He was not eating very much, and whatever he was eating was bland."

"It also depends on how much was administered, suh. Here, it must have been a little at a time. It took seventeen days to succeed."

＋━━╌┼

"He is right, you know—Pinkerton is." Nicolay had a wicked grin.

Hay stopped brushing his teeth and blew a bubble as he replied, "About what?"

"That you are an idiot."

Hay rinsed his mouth as noisily as he could and spat into the basin. "Any particular reason?" he said. "This time, I mean?"

"That a plot to hurt the boys would feature as a central element John Watt, our good gardener, hiding behind a shrub."

"A spruce."

"All right, a spruce."

"Let me lay that, if I might, on the frail shoulders of Alexander Williamson. He is the idiot who told me."

"And you are the Vidocq who believed him."

"I believe in checking out all the possibilities. But yes, I will concede that relying on John Watt standing behind the spruce as the key to a murder plot is the act of a simpleton. Which may or may not make me an—"

Nicolay broke in, "Which leaves us where?"

"With John Watt, still. Now we know that he is not simply a blackguard and a padder of invoices and possibly a secessionist but a genuine criminal besides—an extortionist. Who extorted—*allegedly* extorted—the woman he had tutored in how to steal. He has shown the upstanding character of someone who would murder an innocent boy."

"And the opportunity?"

"Absolutely," Hay said. "As a gardener, he has easy access to arsenic. And he goes upstairs at least daily, delivering his blasted flowers every morning to Madam President. Wherever there is greenery, John Watt has an excuse to be. Nobody would question it."

"And the motive, you say, or at least the desire."

"So the tutor says. And on that I do believe him—this grown man Watt screaming at Tad over strawberries."

"Oh, the strawberries. Though there are times that I would like to scream at Tad."

"And whatever Willie knew about Watt that made him back off," Hay said. " 'Two plus two is five.' That could be reason enough to want the boy gone."

"But if Willie knew something that terrible about him, the Ancient would have known it, too. And have done something about it."

"Not necessarily. He hates doing that sort of thing."

"So, whatever Willie knew about Watt's . . . doings, you are saying this was a motive for murder?"

"I am not saying anything. It depends on how much Willie knew. And there is something else about John Watt—his loyalties. Kentucky—that could mean anything. For the Ancient, 'tis one thing; for the Hellcat, quite another."

Hay went on, "And then there's what ol' Bowie Knife himself told the Ancient." He recounted Congressman Potter's supposed evidence of John Watt's and Thomas Stackpole's secessionist leanings. "This, I will inquire about tomorrow. *That* is a plausible motive, I would say. Besides the fact that he is a despicable man."

"John Watt is, or Bowie Knife Potter?"

"Yes."

Chapter Five

The funeral was to start at two o'clock sharp. Nicolay was off at the cemetery in Georgetown, to make sure the borrowed mausoleum was ready for its temporary tenant.

This gave Hay time to find John Fox Potter. No self-respecting congressman, much less a committee chairman, would be caught sober at the Capitol at nine o'clock on a Monday morning. The *Congressional Directory* said he lived at Chipman's boardinghouse, across Seventh street from the Patent Office, between F and G.

Hay swiveled in his chair and was rising to his feet—he would have to hail a hack—when a shadow fell over the room. A body blocked the door.

"The president wishes you to join him, Mister Hay." Thomas Stackpole's jowls drooped over his neck.

"Where?"

"In the green parlor."

Dread. Was Willie-but-not-Willie still there? Could Hay find a way to ask the president if Willie's knowledge of the gardener's wrongdoing might have caused . . . ? Hay found it hard to pose the question even to himself.

He descended the office stairs and crossed to the green parlor door. He remembered feeling wobbly and worse. He turned the knob and pushed the door open. No chemical smell—a relief. The embalming table was gone from the center of the room. In its place was a catafalque.

The coffin rested on top; its metal looked like rosewood. The lid was open.

Inside, white silk billowed up, and Hay had no choice but to look. How untroubled Willie looked. In everyday attire of jacket and trousers, white stockings and low shoes, he looked ready to play. His calm, round face was restful—merely napping, soon to pull his next prank. His brown hair, brushed and parted, gave him away: In life, he was never so neat. That, and the hands crossed on his breast, clutching a bouquet—a camellia, white azaleas, and sprigs of mignonette.

Hay looked along the length of the short coffin, at the survivor beyond. Lincoln sat slumped in an armless chair, his long, bony fingers clinging to the rim of the casket. Hay took the slat-backed chair to Lincoln's left and uncharacteristically waited for his elder to speak.

At last, Lincoln said, "John, do you believe?"

"Believe . . . in . . . ?" Hay glanced upward.

A slight nod.

Hay said truthfully, "I wish I did."

Another nod. In sympathy or in agreement—Hay could not tell.

"This morning I had a talk with Missus Pomroy, Tad's new nurse. She will stay with him 'round the clock, up at the cottage."

Hay was thrilled; for once, Lincoln had taken his advice, moving Tad away from the potential for danger to the presidential cottage at the Soldiers' Home. "When?" he said.

"After." After the funeral, he meant. "Though I shall hate having him so far away. Nearly an hour's ride. If he should cry at night. And with Mother so . . ." Lincoln's hands flew to his face.

Hay wanted to stroke the president's sinewy forearm but did not dare.

Again, silence. Hay felt his eyes drifting shut when a bang burst from beyond Willie's feet.

The door had slammed into the wall. In the entryway stood a quivering figure in black. Mary Lincoln's face was contorted with rage. Her hair was wild, and her blue eyes were ablaze. The Hell-cat in full hell-cattishness, beyond self-control—*any* control. Someone hovered at her shoulder. It was Robert, glowering at his father and at Hay.

"Mother, you must stay in bed." Lincoln had leapt to his feet. "Robert, take your mother . . ."

Mrs. Lincoln planted herself inside the doorway. "Mister Lincoln, you must not send Tad away. You *must* not." Her voice shook; so did her shoulders. "I could not bear . . ."

Until now, her gaze had been fixed on her husband. But something caused her to lower her eyes, onto the coffin. She staggered to her side, and Robert grabbed beneath her arm as she sank. Robert was toppling under her weight when two strong arms jutted out—Lincoln had arrived at impossible speed—and lifted his wife to her feet, letting Robert fall to the floor.

"It was my fault," she sobbed. "My fault. *My* fault."

"Puss, Puss, Puss," Lincoln cooed, swallowing her up in his arms.

"It was the ball. I never should have . . ."

"No, no, no, no."

Robert, on his feet again, stood by the side door. The airless room, the anguish and intimacy—Hay's breath grew short. He had fled from this parlor before. This time, he gave the casket a wide berth and had nearly reached the door when there was a shriek at his back: "It was *you*, John Hay! It was you."

Hay turned.

"Mother!" Lincoln shouted. "Control yourself. This instant."

"It *was* you. It was, it was, it *was*." Her cry had turned into a wail. "You will not take Tad from me, too."

Hay thought: *Too?*

"If you take my Tad from me"—her keening kept on—"I will have nothing, *nothing*, left."

At the corner of Hay's eye, Robert turned and slunk from the room.

❦

John Fox Potter was not at his boardinghouse. The pinch-faced Mrs. Chipman allowed as to how the congressman had left already—for the Capitol, she presumed. Hay went on to the seat of government, to the House of Representatives side. He climbed the grand staircase and passed through the high wooden doors.

Inside, everything was marble, remote from the world outside. The vestibule was eerily empty. The House was not scheduled to start its work—*work* was a leg-pull, Hay thought—until noon. Lawmakers slept late, then started their evenings early.

Potter was unlikely to be sitting in the empty House chamber. In his office, then—in the attic, the sentry said.

Hay hurried through a round hall and found a circular stone staircase that belonged in a castle, barely wide enough for two people to pass. The attic was two flights up. He followed the marble passages into a warren of narrow hallways and low ceilings. By the door to a WC, Hay sighted his man.

"Mister Chairman," Hay called to the hulking frame.

The congressman turned and looked down on his interlocutor. A wilderness of whiskers concealed most of his face, other than his furrowed forehead and cavern-deep eyes. "Bowie Knife" Potter was taller and stouter than Hay, but surely a hard right to the ample belly would double him over. Such a silly nickname, in Hay's mind, and one the congressman bore with too much pride. He had earned it back in 'sixty, when a House debate over slavery provoked a Virginia congressman to challenge him to a duel. Instead of pistols, Potter chose the wide-bladed Bowie knives, which the Virginian deemed uncivilized and backed out. The Wisconsin lawmaker became a hero across the North.

Hay said, "A mere moment, if you could, sir." On Capitol Hill, unctuousness was de rigueur.

"If I can," Potter replied.

Not exactly a yes.

Potter's hideaway was no larger than a pantry, higher than it was wide. Rickety shelves lined with gray boxes covered the walls. The congressman towered over a desk piled high with yellow flimsies, tamed by a toy cannon on top.

"What may I do for you, Mister Hay?" said Potter in a tone that implied: *or may not.*

"And for the president."

"He is taking our investigation seriously, I am pleased to see."

"You could say that, I suppose."

"I just did."

Another reason to dislike the man.

"I am interested in particular, Mister Chairman"—Hay made sure to use the honorific every sentence or two—"in two of the . . . your . . . allegedly . . . disloyal clerks."

"Yours, you mean."

Hay nodded rather than admit it. "John Watt—you are aware of his arrest yesterday?"

Potter looked startled. "I am not surprised in the least," the congressman recovered. "I warned the president about his traitorous views. In person, man-to-man. And still he refused to—"

"I am here, am I not? On his behalf. Please, Mister Potter—Mister *Chair*man—can you tell me what your investigators learned about John Watt?"

"That he is a venomous, traitorous—"

"Specifically, Mister Chairman, if you would. If you *could*."

"That he has had intimate relationships with secessionists—a Capitol policeman said so. Plant, I think his name is. We took evidence against more than five hundred government employees, and we have reason to believe that at least three hundred fifty of them are disloyal. You cannot expect me to remember the details on each and every one, Mister Hay. But another witness told us—I believe it was the postmaster of Washington City, Mister Clephane—that the gardener has the reputation of being in league with secessionists."

" 'Has the reputation'? 'In league with'? This isn't evidence."

"Every accusation we make, Mister Hay, carries the accuser's name. Nothing is concealed or taken on faith. You may value the testimony as you see fit."

Hay happened to know that Potter's investigators had not bothered to verify any of the accusations from men who might have designs on the jobs of the accused. "May I see the affidavits?"

"A complicated question, as you are doubtless aware. You are asking if the executive branch of government might examine the investigative files compiled by the legislative branch." Potter had served as a county judge in Wisconsin before running for Congress. "I understand that this president takes an expansive—and quite possibly unconstitutional—view of his constitutional powers. I, however, do not."

Constitutional powers. Potter's price, Hay judged, would be steep. His initial price.

"The purpose of your investigation, as I understand it, is to compel the government to take action against its disloyal clerks." Hay spoke with as little expression as he could muster. "Here I am, to take action. The president will do whatever he must to defend the Union. That is the oath he took upon becoming president, and he will fulfill his oath. This, you cannot doubt, sir."

"Of course I can," Potter replied.

"On what grounds, Mister . . . ?" The honorific would not come.

"An assessment of character, shall we say?"

Hay could punch the man or just stalk out—or shift the conversation. He suppressed what he wanted to do. "Did any of your . . . witnesses"—a nicer word than *informers*—"suggest that John Watt is intent on harming anyone?"

"Harming who?"

Potter was sharper than Hay had assumed. "Anyone."

"I would believe anything of the man. Either you are loyal to the Union or you are not. We have evidence that he is not, in the men he keeps around him."

"Who were already working with him in the Executive Mansion."

"And have remained in their posts. And in Mister Watt's case, with a military post as well. A traitor is a traitor, Mister Hay. You may not be aware that my ancestors were Puritans." Hay was unaware but not surprised. "One of them served on the commission that condemned Charles I to the block. There is right, sir, and there is wrong. My ancestor did not compromise with evil, Mister Hay, and neither shall I." Potter's words rang with conviction, but he sounded bored, as if he had recited them a thousand times before. "And your second man?"

"Thomas Stackpole."

"I warned the president about him as well. He is worse."

Again, Hay heard a mishmash of half accusations. The president's doorkeeper had been heard spouting treason and been seen with known (that is, suspected) secessionists. A secesh beyond doubt, he was, in the congressman's eyes. A dangerous man.

"How dangerous?" said Hay.

"Any secesh is dangerous," Potter said.

This was not an answer. Hay could not picture either John Watt or Thomas Stackpole slipping arsenic to a boy—well, maybe he could. "I need to see the evidence," he said.

They settled on a postmastership in Kenosha, pending the president's okay.

⊁━⊰

Black crêpe masked the mirrors; the crêpe on the windows was white. The only sounds in the East-room were footsteps and the occasional cough. Hay sat behind Robert's right shoulder, hoping to catch his eye. He did not know what he would say, other than his condolences, heartfelt. On both sides of Robert, chairs stood empty, reserved for his parents and surviving brother.

William Seward leaned across the aisle, fatigue on his clean-shaven face, and mouthed, "How is he?"

"Persevering," Hay whispered back.

A hundred mourners encircled the part of the floor that Willie-but-not-Willie was supposed to—but did not—occupy. The coffin had remained in the green parlor, at the family's—that is, the father's—behest. Two and a half minutes before two o'clock, by Hay's pocket watch, Lincoln shambled in. First Seward, then everyone else, rose from their seats and remained standing until the president seated himself on the aisle, next to Robert. No missus, no Tad. No Willie.

At two o'clock sharp, the Reverend Gurley strode into the East-room and down the aisle like a bride who fears a jilting. It was not Phineas Gurley's fault that his parents had given him a name suited to Dickens. Nor could he be blamed for his sloping forehead or bulging eyes. But the curl of his lips, his sprawl of side-whiskers, his archly pious demeanor—on those, Hay felt it fair to hold him to account. That most preachers positioned themselves between God and man—and not necessarily below the midpoint—was a given. Still, it offended Hay how the pastor regarded himself as the president's intimate, refusing to understand that Lincoln *had* no intimates.

The silence in the hall was formidable. The Reverend Gurley, at the lectern, peered down at the president for five long seconds, then five more. Hay started to squirm, but Lincoln was gazing at the ceiling and paid no mind.

"Sad and solemn is the occasion that brings us here to-day," the pastor began at last in a sonorous voice. His vast forehead glistened, in faith or in fever. "A dark shadow of affliction has suddenly fallen upon this habitation and upon the hearts of its inmates. The news thereof has already gone forth to the extremities of the country . . ."

Why use a single syllable, Hay thought, *when three or four would do?*

"The beloved youth, whose death we now and here lament, was a child of bright intelligence and of peculiar promise. His mind was active, inquisitive, and conscientious; his impulses were kind and generous; and his words and manners were . . ."

How tiresome to listen to an oily old fool extol the virtues of a whole-souled boy, but every word of it, Hay reflected, was true. Hay's own vexation at Willie had been directed at the prankster in the boy, at the mischief maker, the mutineer against the world of adults, which any self-respecting American lad aspired to be. As John Hay had been. And Tad, who went too far because no one would stop him.

"—and on Thursday last, the silver cord was loosed, the golden bowl was broken . . ."

Outside, beyond the drawn drapes, thunder made the mansion shake.

⊹⊱━⊰⊹

Only upon setting out for the cemetery did Hay learn of the damage from the storm. The carriage he shared with Nicolay and—to his chagrin—with Allan Pinkerton was tenth or twelfth in an uncoiling line of dozens more. In front of Postmaster General Blair's house, across the Avenue from the Executive Mansion, branches lay scattered in the roadway. The gale had peeled back the copper roofing at the central post office and at the Georgetown College infirmary—this was the driver's report. At the Baptist church on Thirteenth street, the leaden bell had plunged through the roof.

The rain had stopped for now, but the gusts of wind packed malice. Pinkerton sat facing the rear, in his flat bowler hat, his gaze fixed past Hay's shoulder. He smelled of tobacco.

Hay pointed to the downed elm and said, "*That* is the hand of God, Nico. And the dead sparrow I saw back there in the gutter."

"You were wise, Johnny, not to pursue the ministry," Nicolay said.

The carriage swerved side to side to avoid the branches in the road. At Twenty-third street, it skirted the equestrian statue of George Washington, which faced his native and now-rebel state to the south.

"The Cross boy's birthday," Pinkerton said. "'Twas the fourth of February. And yes, Tom Cross cooked the breakfast. Though whether it was hotcakes or scotch pie or merely a pitiful porridge, this I was unable to learn."

Pinkerton *was* capable of sarcasm, Hay was pleased to find out.

"And the commander at President's Park?"

"General Elias. A marvelous fellow. Never notices a thing. It is possible for someone to climb to the ramparts in President's Park, which has a direct view o' the path by the canal. Although it woul' take a strong and accurate arm to hit someone."

So, the idea had made at least a modicum of sense. Hay felt less foolish than before. Except it was wrong—why not take his lumps?

"You were right"—Hay volunteered to take his lumps—"about the . . . unlikelihood of that sort of attack." Hay told Pinkerton about the arsenic in Willie's remains and the evidence—or gossip—of secessionists in the Executive Mansion. "The *alleged* secesh. Do you think you could help me with those?"

No reply.

The carriage crossed the bridge into Georgetown, over the mouth of Rock Creek. Georgetown was a sleepy southern village, older than Washington City (and named not for *that* George but for King George II of England, whose successor lost the colonies to the colonists). Shabby shops lined Bridge street.

The funeral cortege continued west. It took a roundabout route, north up High street, for a bone-rattling ride, then turned east at the reservoir, along Road street, past the row houses huddled in clusters. Four blocks along the heights of Georgetown, the sad procession arrived at Oak Hill Cemetery.

A pair of white horses tugged the hearse up the hillside, until the road tapered into brown stalks and mud. Once the rig halted, six pall-

bearers slid the casket from the carriage and lifted it—achingly light—
to their shoulders. The bareheaded president ambled behind, a
loose-limbed Westerner on uneven ground, climbing through a wilderness of bare branches.

Hay followed on foot. Last year's leaves, dead and wet, banked against
the tombstones. He tried to picture Willie gamboling across the South
Lawn but could not escape the thought of a cloaked figure hovering over
a supine body, feeding him . . . what? He shook his head, and his right
foot stepped off the path and sank into a gulch. Immediately, the cold
soaked up through his boot and past his ankle. Scrambling to catch up,
Hay limped up the hill, just as the coffin reached the ridge. Just beyond, the slope dropped away, and Hay could hear the loud, rushing
Rock Creek far below.

The pallbearers waited with their burden outside the mausoleum's
iron gate. Over the arched doorway, carved in the limestone: WILLIAM
THOS. CARROLL. The Supreme Court clerk was very much alive, although three of his children rested inside. Lincoln had boarded with
Mrs. Carroll's kinfolk a decade and a half before, during his single term
in Congress.

Lincoln stood behind the coffin, resting a gloved hand on the edge,
raising his other, moving his lips. Then the pallbearers carried the casket
inside, and Lincoln followed. Hay heard metal scrape against stone,
and the pallbearers emerged, empty-handed. Lincoln stayed inside.

Hay was of no use here, and the ache in his foot had risen past his
calf. He nodded to Nicolay and weaved through the straggle of mourners. On the path, he balanced one foot in the mud and the other on the
mashed-down thatch, hoping to avoid the brambles along the edge.
Lines of poetry bounced around in his head.

> He groveled on the grainy floor,
> And kissed the dead child o'er and o'er.

Hay had no idea what it meant, nor did he want to know. Or maybe:

> And at my door the Pale Horse stands,
> To carry me to unknown lands . . .

More melodic, at least. Too obvious, perhaps. (*Perhaps?*)

"Mistuh Hay!"

Hay recognized Jamie Hall's Kentucky drawl and let the president's stepnephew catch up. His overcoat looked two sizes too large.

"We need to talk, suh."

"My carriage," Hay said. His companions would find another ride back.

Dr. Hall kept hold of Hay's wrist as the carriage twisted down the hill and remained silent until they reached the street. *As if the graves had ears,* Hay thought. Then he spoke so softly that Hay strained to hear, "About the arsenic."

"Yes?"

Dr. Hall said he had visited the embalmer at home to inquire about his procedures—"just to be certain."

A sinking feeling. "Certain of what?"

"That nothing Doctuh Brown did in the . . . procedure, suh, might have spoiled the Marsh test."

"And did it?"

"Strictly speaking, no suh, it did not. Except that the blood used in the test was tainted with the embalming fluid. The fluid itself is mainly acetate of alumina and the chloride of alumina—if you would forgive the detail, suh. For funerals in which the coffin will be open, however, the good doctor adds two other ingredients. Carmine, for a pinkish coloration. And . . . arsenic."

The carriage, taking a corner too quickly, tilted on two wheels.

"Damn! What on earth for?" said Hay, redirecting the pique he felt for the driver.

"If you would forgive me again, suh, for my canduh, it is used to fend off . . . insects, as Ah understand it. Not in Europe any longer, suh, only he-ah. In Europe, the embalming fluid uses no arsenic at all. It was outlawed years ago. Seems that a lord of some renown in Paris died a trifle too unexpectedly for the authorities to ignore it, and after he was embalmed without due delay, doubts were raised about the, uh, circumstances of his demise. Arsenic was found in his tissues, and suspicion turned to his mistress, who was charged with the murder."

"By Vidocq?" exclaimed Hay.

"By who?"

"Please, go on."

"At the trial, the embalmer testified that the fluid he had used contained arsenic, and the mistress went free. The embalmer's name was Jean Gannal." Dr. Hall tortured the French pronunciation. "The same Doctuh Gannal whose method of embalming the esteemed Doctuh Brown has licensed over he-ah. The one he used in preserving Cousin Abraham's son."

"Which contained arsenic, you are saying."

"Yes, suh, it did. Perhaps arsenic *was* the culprit in Willie's . . . passing. But because of the arsenic in the embalming fluid, it is impossible to know."

Hay sighed. "We are back at the beginning, then."

"Ah would not say that, suh. No, suh, Ah *would* not."

"And why is that?"

"From the success of the embalming, we know—well, we suspect—that it was something, suh, *some*thing besides typhoid fever. Even if we do not know what."

"What else could it have been?"

"If it was a poison, or a medicine serving as a poison, this leaves us now, suh, with two choices. Antimony or mercury. Possibly something more exotic, but Ah would doubt it."

"Because?"

" 'Twould be that much harder, suh, for a, uh, puhpetrator to find some. Why use something exotic when something common will do?"

"All right. Then which of those two do you suppose . . . ?"

"Both are remedies; both are poisons. Either, in excess, can be fatal. But there is no fever associated with antimony. *No* fever. So it would not be mistaken for typhoid . . . well, *fever*. And Willie, so Ah am told, had a fever from the fuhst."

"Unless it was antimony *and* typhoid fever."

"Possible, Ah suppose, but unlikely. Mercury is far easier to acquire and to administuh than antimony. Blue mass pills or calomel—all too common, suh. *All* too common. In every apothecary. In half the households, Ah would guess—more than half."

Hay's father always had both of them on hand. "And the symptoms?"

"Of a toxic amount of mercury? For the most part, they match ty-phoid fever. Starting with a fever and chills. Then the intestinal trou-bles—at both ends. And red patches 'round the mouth. And a dullness in spirit that could pass for a stupah."

"Delirium?"

"Close enough, suh. An agitation, confusion. Easily mistaken, Ah would think."

"Any symptoms that do not match?"

"Cannot say, suh. *That* you might ask Doctuh Stone. He bein' more familiar with . . . poisons, if you will, than Ah am. With the effects of mercury *and* with Willie's symptoms."

As the carriage crossed over Rock Creek, back into Washington City, the sky had started to lighten. An ambulance clattered toward them, its nag looking near to collapse.

"But there is no way to test for it, you said."

"Ah did say that, suh, and it is good of you to remember, but it seems Ah was mistaken. Doctuh Brown tells me there *is* a test for mercury, published in a journal in London back in 'twenty-two, by one James Smithson—yes, *that* Smithson." The British chemist and mineralogist had never set foot in America but bequeathed his fortune to build the red sandstone castle devoted to science on the young capital's national Mall. "A complicated procedure, it uses gold and nitric acid to detect the minutest amount of mercury *and* to measure its concentration. Meanin' it could distinguish between a therapeutic, even a heroic, amount of mercury and a toxic amount that was meant to . . . to cause harm."

"Is the line that clear between . . . heroic medicine and . . . and . . . ?" Hay could not bring himself to say *murder*.

"We can hope, suh. We can hope."

The carriage stopped at Seventeenth street to allow a line of geese to cross the Avenue then turned into the grounds of the Executive Mansion.

"Nobody in this country has conducted this test before," Dr. Hall said. "Doctuh Brown has consented to conduct it himself. But . . . he will need . . . material to test."

Hay waited for Dr. Hall to continue. Then the wording sank in. *Material.* Not blood. Hay thought of the boy who had just been . . . no, not buried. More like stored on a shelf. What had been done could be undone, with a grisly ease.

Hay said, "Would you rather I ask him?"

"Ah will, if you prefer."

"No, I will."

"Nico, you are useless."

"You are looking for a painless way to ask a father to let someone slice off a piece of his son. There is none. I say, and for the third or fourth time, just ask him. He wants this solved, and he will do what he has to. He always does."

This was true.

They crossed Fifteenth street on the way back from Willard's. "And," Nicolay went on, "why do you ask my opinion if you mean to ignore it?"

"Nico, how can I know what to think until I know what you think, then think the opposite?" On the far sidewalk, Hay crouched like a boxer. Nicolay poked him in the sternum.

Upstairs in the mansion, Lincoln's office was empty, but the door to the oval study was open. Hay walked in and saw the president slumped in his rocking chair, eyes shut, a *National Intelligencer* in his lap. Hay turned to leave—this could wait. Hay would prefer it.

"John, stay. What I can do for you, my boy?"

The fire in the hearth had dwindled to smoke and embers; a candle glimmered on the table next to the president. Hay lowered himself into the opposite chair. "There is something I need to ask."

"Then ask."

Hay explained how the Marsh test had found arsenic in Willie's blood, but that the embalming fluid also had arsenic, so . . .

"There is no way a court could judge, I can see that," Lincoln said.

"And so the next step is to test for mercury, which Jamie thinks is likelier than anything else."

"Sensible. Doc Stone gave him calomel, which I said he could do, so long as it warn't too much."

"Too much of it, Jamie says, can"—Hay caught himself before saying *kill*—"cause harm."

"Too much of anything, John, can cause harm." Lincoln's face looked stricken; the left side was in shadow. "The sins of the father killed the son, I swear to you, John. *My* son."

"That is nonsense, sir. You know that."

"I know nothing of the kind."

Suddenly, Hay understood what he meant. Hay was one of the few people who knew of Lincoln's past addiction to blue-mass pills. The blue pills—actually, gray pellets the size of rabbit turds—only intensified the bouts of melancholy and the rages that Lincoln had swallowed them to cure. Or so Lincoln had come to believe. Because the previous August, one sweltering day, he had stopped taking the pills altogether, and the rages ended.

"You sent it to him through your blood, you think? Or by contact, skin to skin? Or possibly by an ether in the air? Six months after you *stopped*? This has nothing to do with the other, sir. Nothing. Yours was a medicine, and his was . . ." Here Hay was, soothing Lincoln. Terrifying.

"Medicine, to a point. But that is not why I am responsible, John. He is my son—*was* my son, more than my son. *That* is why. More than anyone on earth, he is—was—who I am. What I gave to him was the essence of my self. He is part of me, and whatever happened to me was bound to happen to him—and for the same reason, whatever that reason was. And whatever happened to him must, therefore . . ."

"This is"—Hay took the risk—"gibberish, sir. This was not your doing. You *know* this."

"It was not intentional, John, but it was my doing. And the answer to your question is yes."

"Yes, what?" Hay had not asked his question yet.

"You may collect whatever part of him you need. Or Jamie may. As long as I can come along. So I can see my boy again."

Chapter Six

The brick stables lay ahead, on the South Lawn, behind the boxwood hedge. A plaintive whinnying greeted him inside—Willie's pony, unridden for twenty-one days now, ever since the boy had fallen ill. This morning, the pony would have to wait. The other horses stood alert, on edge, quiet but for an occasional snort. Hay passed through the aromatic mixture of hay and manure, heading for the farthest stall.

"Shhh, Hasheesh," Hay cooed as he stroked his mare's charcoal-gray mane. The animal poked him for the cube of sugar he slipped her from the pocket of his greatcoat. Hay had named her in loving memory of that long night in Providence when he and his friends had partaken to excess. He had not ridden the mare in more than a week, and she hated to be ignored; it would take a few minutes, at least, to earn her forgiveness. He lifted the saddle, slipped on a bridle, and led her outside. He fed her another sugar cube and mounted. The mare gave a shake, to show which of them was in charge, then settled down.

The Avenue, too, had calmed from its usual morning rush. Hasheesh ambled along, and Hay was content to let her. Low buildings and low commerce lined both sides of the street.

Hay thought, This *is the central boulevard of the national capital? Is there a meaner capital in architectural adornment?* Other nations' capitals had physical grandeur and cultural weight. Surely, Washington City would never be a London or a Paris or a Rome.

Hay had left Hasheesh at a livery stable behind the headless Capitol

and now was hunched over a table in a tiny windowless room, leafing
through the thin gray file marked *Watt, John*. So far, nothing Hay did
not know already. The original invoices from the nursery in Philadelphia, before the numbers had been altered. A train ticket between Washington and Wilmington on the twenty-first of October, one day after
(best Hay could recall) the Hell-cat had traveled the identical route.
Testimonials—more accurately, antitestimonials—from the witnesses
Potter had mentioned. *"The associations of John Watt, gardener at the
President's House, are with known secessionists, and very intimately so . . . ,"*
*"heard him say that the Southern Confederacy must be acknowledged. That
the United States never could conquer the south," "that Jeff. Davis was the
best and bravest man in America . . . ," "much elated at the result of the
battle of Bull Run," "that the federal army was composed of rubbish, and
that the soldiers were cowards . . . ," "has the reputation of being in the
league with the secessionists . . ."*

Hay tossed the pile down. He picked up a letter from Julia Taft, the
Taft boys' older sister, about how the gardener had been so kind in showing her the strange plants with the long Latin names. Most curious was
a letter in a painfully slanted hand:

Sept. 13th, 1861
Executive Mansion

My dear Mr. Potter:
   *I am very much surprised to hear that a letter has been received in
the Commissioner's office—charging Major Watts as a Secessionist. I
know him to be a Union man, & have many opportunities of hearing &
judging him. The date after the battle of Manassas, I never saw a more
troubled man. . . . There is no better Union man than Watts, & no one
who has a greater contempt for Jeff. Davis.*

                                        Yours sincerely,
                                        Mrs. President Lincoln

Her case might have been stronger, Hay thought, had she not mis-
spelled Watt's name. And if her brother, three half brothers, and three
brothers-in-law hadn't enlisted in the Confederate army.

Hay felt like washing his hands but wiped his palms on his pants and reached for the file labeled:

THOMAS STACKPOLE, DOORKEEPER

On top was a biographical sketch: Born in Sandwich, New Hampshire, in 1822. A wife and seven children, ages six to seventeen. At the Executive Mansion since 'fifty-three, first as a night watchman, then as a messenger, then as the keeper of the president's door. Originally hired because his cousin had married President Pierce's sister's son—a random connection, but no more than Hay's to Lincoln. Still, how had a native of New Hampshire become a secessionist—if, in fact, he had?

Hay examined what looked like an investigator's notes. Occasional words were decipherable—*cotton, permits, Hammack.* No surprise: John Hammack was a restaurateur on the Avenue, near Fifteenth street, known for his oysters, terrapin, and secessionist fire. Seems that Stackpole had dined at Hammack's on three successive evenings in December, twice with none other than John Watt. Hay was aware of the maneuvering for the government's coveted permits to trade for Confederate cotton—a license to print money, or greenbacks. Yet, was it suspicious to dine with one's colleague more than once?

The next set of notes was more legible. Written at the top: *R. May*—evidently, the interviewee. Apparently the account of a meeting the previous June or July (the last two letters were smudged).

R. May has a sister living at Bailey's Crossroads, Fairfax County, Virginia, who is a secessionist. She frequently comes to Washington, and told witness that she would carry any information to Manassas she could get. While in Washington, witness's sister stops at the house of one William Brown, a master plasterer. Bill Spaulding and his partner, S. Parker, who are secessionists, congregate together at Brown's house, and Stackpole is frequently with them. On one occasion, R. May saw Parker and Stackpole in conversation and heard Stackpole say, "When we go down there, and tell them what we know, they will be all right."

The committee, Hay was confident, had never bothered to ask Stack-pole about this or anything else. Who was this R. May, betraying his own sister? A war of brother against sister. Potter must have told Lincoln of this accusation that Stackpole was a Confederate informant, if not a spy—nothing so juicy would he keep to himself. Did Lincoln not believe it, or did he not care? Hay wanted to trust the president's trusting judgment. But suppose it *was* true—that Stackpole had passed information to the rebels, directly or indirectly, military or political. This man who sat outside the president's door. Down the hallway from the president's sons.

Hay leafed through the file and started on the notes of an interview with John W. Haynes, one of the district volunteers who guarded the Executive Mansion.

On Saturday night, in April, when there was a general apprehension of an attack by the rebels on the city, witness was on guard at the President's House. Witness noticed many times during that night that Stackpole came out and passed through the little gate on the side into the street, and appeared to be in conversation with some person. The first time he came out was immediately after one of our intelligence men had gone in, and witness then saw that the person Stackpole was conversing with was Bill Spaulding, a noted secessionist, residing in this city. Witness further testifies that Stackpole came out from the President's House nearly every time that any one passed in, to make report of the situation. Witness thinks Stackpole passed out and in at least eight times during that night. In one instance, witness said to Stackpole, "if Jeff. Davis comes here tonight I will put a pill through you." Stackpole replied, "you would not do that, would you?"

Hay sat stunned. What innocent explanation could there be? Again, this Spaulding, a wall painter. Hay half remembered a broad-faced, muscular Irishman with a perpetual smirk, balancing on a ladder in the second-floor hall. Was he also a secessionist—an *accused* secesh? Why should Stackpole be telling him anything, much less eight anythings?

The next dirt-streaked document was a military-looking report from the sentries at Long Bridge. On the night of February 6—that was two days after Willie fell ill—Stackpole and William Spaulding had crossed over the Potomac into Virginia, claiming to be on government business, which Hay was reasonably sure they were not.

The rest of the Stackpole file looked useless. Scrawled notes of two or three interviews with witnesses whose names Hay did not recognize. A limp layer of foolscap, covered with architectural plans—of what, Hay could not tell.

As he raised the pages from the table, a card slipped out. It was cream-colored with a claret border, of heavy stock, embossed across the top in an elegant script: *Elizabeth Keckly*. Below, in an overcurlicued hand, the message expressed the undersigned's regret that she would be unable to testify to the honorable committee as to the character of Thomas Stackpole.

This was curious. Hay wondered why she would refuse. Because the dressmaker knew too little about him—or too much? And why had she even been asked?

━━━✦━━━

No time like the present. None of Pinkerton's men were in sight. And damn it, what if they were? Pursuing the president's business trumped Pinkerton's decree. Hay descended from the attic of the Capitol.

Edward Ball was a burly man in his fifties with a bloated face and a sweep of white hair. A former congressman himself, from Ohio, the sergeant at arms for the House of Representatives led Hay down a narrow staircase, then another, into the Capitol subbasement. They had climbed down into the earth; the air was moist and smelled like an ancient tomb. Hay recalled that George Washington was to have been buried here, until Jefferson objected to a monarch's resting place and Martha wanted her husband at home. Hallowed ground, this remained, with a waft of decay.

Hay followed the sergeant at arms along a sloped walkway between the unpainted brick walls. Their lanterns flickered, and Hay's blew out; he reached ahead to the sergeant at arms and relit it. The low arches of the ceiling supported the unimaginable weight above. Everything was solid, enclosed—entrapped. Yet with a layer of muck underneath.

From muck thou art, and unto muck shalt thou return.

"So, why is he here?" said Hay. Edward Ball had known where to look. "So no one can find him?"

"Precisely," the sergeant at arms said.

They took two or three turns, and halfway along the corridor, a boy-ish guard slouched in front of double wooden doors, a musket at his side. He offered a halfhearted salute and opened the unlocked door. Hay stepped through and motioned his companions to stay behind.

Inside, the swirl of air currents indicated a room of some size. A store-room for lumber, judging by the scent of pine. In the farthest corner, the flame of a candle shriveled to the wick and, with a sizzling sound, burst higher. Hay's eyes took a half minute or more to see much of anything. There were no bars; this was not a cell. It was a large room with almost no furniture and the mustiness of a cave. Surely, vermin swarmed the walls and invaded the straw mats that covered the floor. Seated in a hard-backed chair, staring at Hay, was John Watt.

His face looked even sparer than before. His sunken cheeks, covered in whiskers, reminded Hay of Lincoln's, even to the mole. His ears were too big—like Lincoln's, too. His hair was tousled, as if he had just wo-ken from a broken sleep, which possibly he had. He was lean but had a farmer's wrists, hairy and thick, protruding from torn-off sleeves. His eyes, closely spaced, were as hard as a snake's.

Hay considered what he knew about John Watt. Not enough. A fix-ture in the Executive Mansion since the flower-loving Fillmores. A talented gardener, by all accounts, proficient with orchids and crêpe myr-tle and, yes, with spruce. Skilled also in finding the trapdoors in proce-dures. How long he had been padding his invoices was unknown, maybe unknowable. Mrs. Lincoln, inadvertently, had given him—and herself—away when she ordered Nicolay to sack the Executive Mansion's stew-ard, who happened to be John Watt's wife, so that the salary might be diverted to more decorative pursuits. *That,* Hay realized, was the garden-er's motive in blackmailing the Hell-cat. It wasn't only the opportunity for profit from extortion but also something sweeter—vengeance. How perfect, for it had been something in Mrs. Lincoln's tone, and her in-sistence that John Watt had no cause to kick, that prompted Nicolay to examine the gardener's invoices. In the organic fertilizer account, Nicolay noticed a *2* redrawn as a *5;* the difference equaled the excess cost of the state dinner for Prince Napoleon. Then the four hundred-plus dollars added to the invoice for seeds, bushes, and fruit trees from a nursery in Philadelphia—this covered twelve extra place settings of the new maroon-edged china. She and the gardener deserved each other (this was Hay's opinion) in whatever their deathly embrace.

Hay took the hard-backed chair across from Watt.

Watt said, "Why in th' devil's name you here?"

"Why are *you* here?" Instead of in an ordinary jail, Hay meant.

"Cooked up. Out of hate."

"Why should they, whoever they are, hate you?"

"You tell me."

"I do need to ask you a question or two."

"Has I a choice? Or is this an eastern polite?"

"You are speaking to an Illinois man, Mister Watt."

"So yer sayin'."

Hay suspected Watt knew more about Hay's background than Hay knew about Watt's. "And where in Kentucky are your people from?"

"Lexington. Yes, the same." That was where Mrs. Lincoln was born and raised. "I am honored you are a-messin' 'bout my birth and breedin', Mister Hay. A pleasant way to spend an afternoon."

"I am not here to ask about the . . . charges against you . . . the extortion . . . the letters."

No change in expression.

"Nor about the invoices that were, shall we say, inaccurate."

Silence.

"This is about Willie."

Watt stirred in his chair, betraying a curiosity in spite of himself.

"Very early on the morning of February fourth," Hay said, "you were standing by the carriageway on the mansion's south grounds, while the president's sons were riding down to the river—well, the canal. You remember this, yes? Tell me, Mister Watt, what were you doing there?"

A half smile emerged on the gardener's face—an ugly sight. "You may call me Lieutenant Watt, if you like," he said.

"Not Major?"

"Some do call me that, out of respect."

"And have you enjoyed your military service, Lieutenant Watt?"

"Unlike yerself, you mean? I am proud to be serving my country, *Mister* Hay."

"We are all in your debt. Now, to ask you again, what were you doing on the South Lawn so early that morning?"

"You say *v'ry* early on that morning. Mebbe for an educated man such as yerself." Watt exaggerated his drawl. "Not for a gardener."

So, it *was* Watt on the South Lawn. "You recall the morning I am asking about, then."

"Cain't say that I do. 'Twas more than one."

"On this morning in particular, you were standing by a spruce tree just below the carriageway. Does that narrow it down sufficiently?"

"I s'pose it do. And may I ask *you,* Mister Hay, why you find my mornin' routine all so allurin'?"

"So, why were you there? Was it to"—Lincoln had once told him that, in a courtroom, surprises work—"spy on the boys?"

"*Spy* on them?" Watt laughed. "Why would I ever do that? They are not military tar—"

Watt stopped and looked surprised. Which, unless he was a consummate actor, suggested that the thought of the boys as targets was a new one. Implying Watt's innocence—of this, at least.

"A pity, yes," Watt went on, "what happened to the boy. But God has His ways, has He not? Boys die ever' day. A body cannot feel sad 'bout each and ever' one of 'em."

Hay wanted to punch the man and felt himself rise from his chair. Halfway up, he stopped—Watt was goading him, and he must not give in. With an effort, he resumed his seat and said, "Your sadness, Mister Watt, is your business. *My* business is to ask what you were doing on the south grounds early on the morning of February fourth. A Tuesday."

"*Yer* business, Mister Hay?"

"It is, yes, Lieutenant Watt. Representing the president."

"We are mighty, are we not?"

Hay refused to play. "You were standing by a spruce tree very early on a winter's morning."

"Trimmin' its branches."

"But so early—barely past dawn?"

"Now, the trees on the grounds are *also* yer business, Mister Hay? And how and when to tend them?"

"In this case, they are. Please answer my question, Mister Watt."

"Gladly. A cold morning gives a clean cut."

Hay sat back. Was that true? He had no idea. It sounded plausible enough. More than plausible—poetry. *A cold morning gives a clean cut.*

Hay felt like a dunce. Worse, Pinkerton was right.

Another tack, then. "Jefferson Davis, would you still describe him as the best and bravest man in America?"

"In Confederate America," Watt replied nonchalantly. "Ain't that America, too?"

"That seems to be the question at stake. Then tell me, were you elated at the results at Bull Run? Or should I call it Manassas?" Beauregard, the Confederate general, had referred to the Southerners' triumph by invoking the city, not the creek, and the nomenclature became a shibboleth dividing North from South.

"You may call it what you like. My sister's boy was shot in the shoulder there."

A new fact. "On which side?"

No reply.

"Has he recovered?"

A glare.

"And tell me, is the Union army composed of rubbish?" Hay was enjoying this. "Are the Union soldiers cowards, Lieu*ten*ant Watt?"

"*Our* soldiers ran from Manassas, Mister Hay."

"I know this—I saw it myself."

"All the way to Washington City. The Great Skedaddle was not a pretty sight. Or am I no longer permitted to speak the truth in your America? Are factual statements now regarded as treason?"

"You admit these statements, then?"

" 'Twas my understanding, Mister Hay, that this is a free country, still."

"A free country at war against itself, Mister Watt."

"An unfortunate fact of life."

"But a fact nonetheless."

What a blackguard, Hay reflected as Hasheesh ambled home. A thief—for what else was padding invoices but thievery?—a liar, a blackmailer, an instigator, a secessionist sympathizer, a mean-tempered man. But was he a murderer? Watt had sounded surprised at the thought of Willie as a target. And Pinkerton *was* right, about a stupid way to run a plot. Watt would be impulsive; poisoning, if done slowly, took patience. Ordinarily, gardeners had patience; this one did not.

Unless the gardener was a master at hiding who he was, or if he was working with somebody else.

Or somebodies else.

⊢━━⊣

Inside the entrance to the Executive Mansion, Old Edward hovered like a falcon, his eyes alarmingly bright. He smelled faintly of varnish. From drinking, was Hay's guess.

"You have heard, sir," Old Edward said, "abo't Nashville?"

"No. Good news?"

"'Tis ours, Mister Hay. Requirin' nary a drop of our boys' blood. Like a stroll on a Sunday afternoon. Yesterday, it was the capital of Tennessee of the Confederate States of America—if you will pardon the phrase, sir. Now it is the capital of Tennessee, U.S.A."

Hay had never heard Old Edward so effusive. Pro-Union sentiment, even fueled by whiskey, should not surprise him in the Executive Mansion. To-day, it did.

"Wonderful news, Edward."

"And thank the good Lord, sir, fer General Grant."

"True, true. Have you seen Mister Stackpole of late?"

"Aye, I have, Mister Hay. Heading"—Old Edward pointed to Hay's left—"to the conservatory, I should think, sir."

Hay marveled at the doorkeeper's talent, even while squiffed, for keeping track of everyone's whereabouts without leaving his post. But why on earth was Stackpole in the greenhouse?

At the western end of the mansion, Hay passed through the double glass doors. Heavy, damp heat slapped his face. Flowerpots and clay planters hung on hooks from the sloped ceiling of the greenhouse;

countless others lined the shelves from ankle to shoulder height. Hay felt light-headed from the cloying smell of flowers of every hue—roses, gardenias, jasmine, camellias, orchids. He pressed a clammy palm over the lip of a waist-level pot and became aware of being watched.

"It *is* strong, is it not, Mister Hay? In the gardenia family—*Gardenia jasminoides,* I believe, although Major Watt could tell you for certain. Quite pleasing, once you get used to it."

Hay thought that might take a while.

Stackpole's musical voice belied the bulk that covered the edges of the stool. Seated by the counter at the conservatory's northern wall, Stackpole shifted but did not rise at Hay's approach. His muscle tone looked so slack that if Hay punched him, the skin would only languidly re-emerge. His lips stretched into an insincere grin, which Hay supposed was better than no grin at all.

"I was not aware this was your domain," Hay said.

"Major Watt is otherwise engaged. He asked me to attend to certain matters in his absence."

"I thought he had assistant gardeners for that."

"No one he trusts quite like myself, may I say."

Hay thought, *If this were a conspiracy, would Stackpole acknowledge it so readily?* "To do what?" he said.

No reply.

Hay said, "And how did he convey his wishes?"

"He left me a note."

"May I see it?" Hay was not sure why he had asked.

"No," Stackpole replied. That chilling grin, again.

"All right. Then let me ask about this. To-day, I was examining the investigative files at the House committee on the loyalty of . . . Potter's committee."

"That committee of cowards and charlatans."

"The very one. Nevertheless . . ." Hay described the testimony that Stackpole had met with a secessionist from Fairfax County and had spoken to the painter Spaulding eight times—"in the middle of Seventeenth street, at the Avenue"—the night Washington City feared an attack. "Named witnesses."

"Name them."

Hay remembered both names, and he knew that the Sixth Amendment to the Constitution assured the right of the accused to confront his accusers. But this was no legal proceeding, and Potter had insisted on secrecy. "I don't think the names matter. People in a position to know." Hay wondered if that was true. "The report, with witnesses' names, will be published soon enough."

"If you are asking me to explain, Reginald May is a liar and hypocrite." So, Stackpole knew one of the names already. "An abolitionist of the most intolerant sort who has been fighting his sister over inheriting their father's nineteen slaves. I do know the lady in question, and she *is* from Fairfax County, out in Virginia, and if you saw her, Mister Hay, you, too, would have been present in that parlor if you could. In fact, I am glad that you weren't."

A leer, his face a full moon. Hay could only imagine how a comely young lady would view the attentions of a bloated, married man.

"And the information she carried back to Manassas?"

"Nothing *I* told her. Beyond that, I cannot say."

Hay thought, *Cannot or will not?* "And your conversations with Mister Spaulding on Seventeenth street. A contact of some sort?"

"To this, I plead guilty. He is my sister's husband. You remember that night, do you not, Mister Hay? Minute by minute, we waited for the enemy to attack. Inside the president's house, we heard the cannons. I was worried for my family, and for my sister's family. My duty was to remain at my post, and so I counted on Mister Spaulding to protect my family as well. I confess to keeping him informed so that he might know whether and when to flee the city."

"Even if nobody else knew?"

"To the charge of protecting my family, I plead guilty, Mister Hay. Perhaps someday you shall understand."

Stackpole swiveled on the stool. His profile resembled Nero's, with bulges.

"You are a New Hampshire man, are you not?" said Hay.

"That I am, and proud to say so. Rugged country, rugged people." Hay could guess why Stackpole had left. " 'Live free or die,' as we say.' "

"Does that apply also to slaves?"

"New Hampshire has no slaves. So, yes."

Hay thought, *How can you ask a man if he is a secessionist? And get a candid response? Maybe with a direct question.* No, Hay decided. In the president's home, only a fool would say yes, and Stackpole was nobody's fool.

"Does it trouble you," Hay said, "that there are slave pens just a few blocks from here?"

"I cannot say, Mister Hay. Does it trouble you?"

The truthful answer (although Hay was not about to say so) was no. Hay did not like to meddle with moral ills, preferring the company of comfortable men, the men who could read, who understood the world as it was, in its glorious grays. He was wary of principle, on principle. Then why did it offend him that Stackpole might feel the same? An amoral doorkeeper, protecting Buchanan and Lincoln alike—what could be the trouble with that? Answer: if he sat a few doors distant from the president's beloved sons. His explanations for Potter's charges were plausible, even persuasive. Why, then, did Hay not believe him? A phlegmatic man, slow to act and yet—this was Hay's impression—merciless whenever he moved.

+=+=+

The exhumation was scheduled for four o'clock, and Hay went to alert the president. Hay found him in Tad's bedroom, dozing in a chair, a Bible open on his lap. Tad was asleep, a cherub's face, his hair in chaos.

The creak of Hay's step on the floorboards awakened Lincoln. "What time is it?"

"Past two."

"In the afternoon?"

The day was dark but not that dark.

Hay mentioned the exhumation, hoping Lincoln would decide not to come.

"Is Jamie going?" the president said.

"Yes. And Doc . . . Doctor Stone."

"When do we leave?"

+=+=+

The carriages arrived at the cemetery at half past six. The president had pushed the excursion past dark—public knowledge, he said, would help no one. Hay suspected the president was trying to hide this most intimate of undertakings from himself. Who could blame him?

The lanterns twisted up the path like drunken soldiers. Hay slipped on the trampled mat of leaves. As he neared the ridge, the rush of Rock Creek grew louder.

By the quarter moon, Hay distinguished the stovepipe hat from the surrounding silhouettes. Lincoln stood in front of the mausoleum, as still as a tree trunk.

The wind picked up. Lincoln pulled his gray shawl tight around him and waited. Minutes later, Dr. Stone emerged from the vault, carrying a small wooden box. He nodded to Lincoln, and brushed past him, and started down the hill. Lincoln removed his hat and stepped into the crypt. By the light of a single candle, a father fell to his knees before the best in himself.

⊢═══⊣

Hay's pocket watch showed twenty minutes before midnight. The front entrance to the Executive Mansion was unguarded and unlocked. Hay was reaching for the door when a man snarled from behind him, "Who goes there?"

Hay swiveled, his fists cocked. A small, wiry man jumped from the shrubs, and a lanky figure appeared at the corner of Hay's right eye. Both of them had pistols, aimed at Hay's chest.

"Ah, Pinkerton's men!" Hay exclaimed.

Papers were furnished; explanations were proffered and accepted.

Inside the mansion, the gaslights were low; the silence was profound. Hay's footsteps creaked on the staircase. He was desperate for a bath.

Hay slowed as he approached the bathroom beyond Tad's closed door. A cold bath promised pain, but he had no patience to heat the water. He would check on Tad instead.

That Tad was still here was the Hell-cat's doing—that, and the Ancient's willingness to let her have her way. Hay's uncle Milt thought of Lincoln as a henpecked "poke easy" he had only haltingly come to admire. Hay stood nervously outside the boy's door, his sense of duty struggling with the memory of twisted bedclothes. The strength of his reluctance to open the door persuaded him that he must. A rule his older brother (and boyhood hero), Leonard, had beaten into his head—literally—after John backed down from a fistfight: Giving in to your fears hurts more than the bruises from facing them.

The hinges squealed as he leaned on the door. Inside Tad's room, the air felt dense. A medicinal smell competed with the sting of kerosene. Tad lay on his back, motionless, his hair matted on his forehead. The boy's lips curled, as if he were pulling off a prank in his sleep. A rasp, then long breaths of contentment. Light flickered across his face; Tad's color had improved.

A cough, not from Tad but from the foot of the bed.

"Missus Pomroy!" he exclaimed to the silhouette. A woman bent forward, her hands in her lap. It was not Mrs. Pomroy, who was generous in girth, but the thin, buxom nurse with the severely cut hair. To-night, she had a weary smile.

"He looks better," Hay said.

"He is," she replied. Her drawl straddled the line between silken and abrasive.

"Out of danger?"

"If the Lord wills it. A good boy, underneath." She was aware, then, of Tad's surface. "I've handled tougher."

"Only an optimist can work as a nurse," Hay said with a smile.

"Eugenia," she said, extending her hand.

"John Milton Hay." Her hand was strong but clammy. He asked if Tad had slept soundly, hoping insomnia was a symptom of mercury poisoning; catatonia, he knew, signified typhoid fever.

"Off and on," she said.

"And his fever?"

"Up and down."

Hay checked his watch and decided to stop off in his office before heading to bed. The draft of a letter to Andrew Johnson lay half-written on his desk, informing the dimwitted, hard-drinking (from Hay's War Department friend, again) Tennessean of his appointment as the military governor of his newly conquered state. Hay crossed toward his corner desk in the dark. His left hip bumped something hard—he yelped.

The felt-topped table had been moved. He felt his way around the edge of it and waved his arms like the antennae of a praying mantis and tiptoed to his desk. The lantern was where he had left it; its concave waist was a comfort in his hand. He struck a match, and the flame burst to life.

He tried to read the letter to Senator Johnson: *martial law . . . established authorities . . . brigadier general of volunteers . . .* Words formed into phrases, but sentences seemed beyond reach.

This was asinine. He needed sleep.

Lantern in hand, he twirled from his seat. Something caught his eye. Jutting from the outside pocket of his satchel that hung on the wall was a triangle of white.

Not again!

He knew what it was before he plucked it out. The envelope was crumpled and smudged. His hand shook.

Hay sank back into his seat. He returned the lantern to the dust-defined circle on his desk, shoved the letter to Andy Johnson aside, and positioned the envelope in the emptied space. It was oyster white, linen-like, faintly lined, rough to the touch—all, as before. Thick black ink. A raggedy cursive.

A different addressee, but the same recipient.

FATHER ABRAHAM

No postmark. Delivered by hand. Somebody's hand. Into his satchel.

Hay's hands hovered, fingertips poised, as if over a harpsichord. He turned the envelope over. It was unsealed—meant to be read. He lifted the flap and removed a folded sheet of foolscap. He unfolded the paper and smoothed it out on the desk. Written in a rough but legible hand, it read:

And ye are risen up against my father's house this day, and have slain his sons.

Sons.

Plural.

Chapter Seven

Grogginess dampened Hay's jitters. The president was in the oval study, finishing his breakfast, rocking harder than the coffee would explain. Hay consoled himself with the thought that regarding the war or anything else, the worse the news, the more Lincoln wanted to hear it.

Lincoln fingered the envelope with an almost feminine care and extracted the message inside. As he read it, his back stiffened like the barrel of a shotgun. At last, he said, "Judges."

"Pardon?"

"Judges. The book of Judges, nine eighteen. The murderous reign of Abimelech."

A name that was new to Hay. The things Lincoln knew, he *knew*. "Which testament?" Hay said.

"The old." Without condescension. "He was the son of Gideon, the Israelite commander, by a Canaanite concubine. When Gideon died, Abimelech wanted the kingship for himself, except that his seventy half brothers had a contrary notion. So, for seventy pieces of silver, Abimelech hired local cutthroats and murdered all but one of his half brothers. The youngest one escaped. *He* prophesied Abimelech's demise—accurately. The prophecies we remember are the ones that went wrong."

" 'Have slain his sons,' " Hay said. "His *sons*! Not just one."

"I know, I know, I know." Like a chastened child. "This time I shall prevail, no matter what Mother thinks."

⊬⊷⊶⊣

Old Edward's black suit was, as always, fastidious, and his high collar was starched.

A master plowman might have parted his snow-white hair. His dignity was intact and, by extension, so was the mansion's and that of everyone under its roof. Yet something about the doorkeeper looked unkempt. The way he stood—yes, his shoulders slumped. From fatigue, no doubt, or from illness or drink or from the weight of the world on his back.

Hay asked Old Edward for a moment of his time and was led into the cloakroom. It was like stepping into a remote and primitive place, suffused with the smell of wet fur from parties past. At the back wall, Old Edward pushed aside a row of forgotten overcoats, revealing a pair of slat-backed chairs. The two men sat across from each other, their knees inches apart. Old Edward's watery blue eyes were alert.

"I need the same thing as last time, if you could, please," Hay said.

"The same what, sir?"

"Sorry. A list of who was here, on the premises. For last evening between, say, six o'clock and midnight. You were not here past . . . When did you leave?"

"Me usual. Around eight."

That left four hours after Old Edward's departure. Maybe Pinkerton's men had kept track of everyone who came in or left.

"A list, then, please, of everyone who was in the building between six and eight. Best you can."

"How soon do you need this, sir? By yesterday?"

"If you could, please."

⊬⊷⊶⊣

"Just the man I wanted to see," Hay said, and for once, he was telling the truth.

"To be o' service," Pinkerton replied, with a deference Hay assumed was a pretense.

The detective was loitering near the door to the president's office, as if Jenny Lind was about to emerge, and resisted the invitation into

Hay's office. The compromise was a whispered conversation in Hay's doorway.

"Last night, after eight, did your men see anyone leave the mansion?"

"Me men, why woul' they—"

"No games, please. They stopped me outside here, so I know they were here. I found another message last night in my satchel, like the first one. Someone left it there sometime between six o'clock and just before midnight. Maybe one of your men saw—"

"They were watchin' for intruders, no' fer anyone on their way out."

"Someone might have come in and then left. Or just left."

"I will ask."

"No, nobody." Thomas Stackpole showed a wisp of a smile. Hay wondered what amused him. "Not before half past eight, when I returned to the bosom of my family."

Parody—that was his source of amusement. Hay brushed it aside. Half past eight. For three and a half hours, anyone might have entered his office unseen.

"Not even Nicolay?"

"I am aware of the meaning of words, Mister Hay. When I say *nobody,* that is what I mean."

Hay spent half the afternoon questioning two cooks, three of the chambermaids, a messenger, and a stable boy, each of them on duty the night Willie died; all but the stable boy had also been working last night. Nobody knew anything. No one had seen anyone enter Hay's office. An Irish chambermaid had entered the Madam's bedroom just past eight o'clock. "Too many flowers," she said, holding her nose. Her blond tresses and saucy stance aroused him. "Like a funeral."

Hay still knew nothing worth knowing. That whoever had left these messages was well-versed in Scripture, which eliminated precious few people other than himself and probably Nicolay. So, should Hay quiz his interviewees on the Bible and grow suspicious if they passed? All right, then, what else did he know? That no one had been seen entering his office, although somebody had. Not John Watt—he was confined beneath the Capitol. Unless someone had delivered the message on his

behalf. Thomas Stackpole, perhaps. The doorkeeper was certainly familiar enough with Watt's conservatory, and both men stood accused—
rightly or wrongly—of hobnobbing or worse with secesh. Both of them
had served in the Executive Mansion since . . . well, since Hay was a boy.
Hay was fairly certain that the two were working in cahoots. But in
murder? Tad had said specifically that neither John Watt nor Thomas
Stackpole had fed him anything, so it was unlikely (assuming Tad told
the truth) they would have poisoned Willie. Unless somebody else had,
on *their* behalf—a conspiracy, indeed.

━┿━━┿━

Hay knew full well his destination, although his motivation stumped
him. At half past five, Kate Chase would probably be clinking a champagne glass with one or another of her beaux. The last place Hay could
expect to find her was at home.

But he needed to clear his head, and the mere act of visiting, whether
she was there to receive him or not, would count as evidence (to himself if not to her) of his affections. So, here he was riding Hasheesh east
along E street, ambivalent enough to let the mare nose toward a dog
in the roadway. At least her father would be at his desk at the Treasury.
Hay loathed Salmon Chase—so did Lincoln, who liked almost everyone—and he was confident the feeling was mutual.

The rutted street and muddy sidewalks bustled with the expiring
workday. A drunken soldier staggered off the sidewalk and into the
street. Hasheesh knew enough to steer clear.

The Chases' three-story brick mansion stood at the corner of E and
Sixth. Hay tied the mare to a post in front, stripped the calfskin glove
from his right hand, mounted the porch, and rapped on the cherrywood
door. Almost immediately, the door swung open. Hay's heart sank.

A butler was at the door, but the secretary of the Treasury was
leaving. He was an imposing man, tall and portly, with a hairline
that retreated like Napoleon in a Russian winter. His manner was
imperious—and humorless. "Salmon the Solemn," wags called him.

"What do *you* want?" Salmon Chase barked.

"Your daughter," Hay replied. That came out wrong. Accurate, but unlikely to persuade, which at the moment was the only measure that mattered. "Is she at home?"

"I do not see what business it is of yours."

"None at all, Mister Secretary, I assure you. I was under the impression that she was expecting me."

A lie.

Which worked.

"Reginald, see if she is receiving." And the secretary slipped past Hay out the door.

So, she *was* there. And within reach. His stomach tightened.

Inside of ten or fifteen seconds, a petulant voice cried out, "Mister Hay, shall you never leave me undisturbed?"

"Do you wish me to?"

A gamble.

"I would be devastated."

She stepped off the sweeping staircase and grabbed Hay's hand and led him into the library. The room was luscious but unpretentious, its walls lined from floor to ten-foot ceiling with shelves of books. (Purchased at estate sales, was Hay's guess.) A fire blazed, and Kate Chase guided Hay into one of the matching upholstered chairs. She continued to stand. Hay, swearing to himself, returned to his feet.

And kissed her. Hard.

Hay was starting to lie in apology—"I have no idea what came over . . ."—when she kissed him back. He grasped her shoulders and felt the strength in her back as she nestled her torso into his. Their kiss deepened and lingered. He was pondering the depths beyond the deepest kiss when suddenly she pushed him away.

He opened his eyes. A look of mockery on her face, Kate Chase bowed slightly and said, "You see, Mister Hay, you needest not fear mine."

She remembered!

Which meant—surely it did—that she cared. Either that, or she wanted him to think that she cared. Because she wanted something from him, in exchange for . . .

Her violet eyes met his.

Whatever the price, he would pay it. And Hay kissed her again.

⊁━━━⊰

Hay fell asleep at last, despite the roiling down in his nightshirt.

A shriek woke him up. From down the hall. By the time Hay reached Tad's bedroom, Robert and the president were there.

"I heard him screaming," Robert explained unnecessarily. He was half lying on the bed—the rest of him cantilevered—cradling Tad's head in his hands. The boy was whimpering, eyes wide open. His father stood at the foot of the bed, looking numb.

Lincoln said, "What happened, son?"

"A knife, a knife, a knife," Tad sputtered. "At me, at me."

"You said a rope," Robert said.

"No, no, a rope, a rope, a rope. *And* knife, a knife." Tad started to shake, and Robert held him closer.

"Who was coming at you?"

"Ve man was."

Hay said, "You were dreaming, Tad."

"No, no. It was a man. A real man. Wiv a knife."

"You said a rope," Robert said.

"No, a rope."

Hay said, "What did he look like, this man?"

"He was big, like my bruvver. A pillowcase on his head. All I saw o' him was ve knife."

"The rope," Robert said.

"No, ve rope. *And* ve knife."

The president drew Tad away from his eldest son and curled the boy into his chest, kissing his forehead, chirping at him like a mother robin to her young.

"Whatever you say, I believe, Taddie boy," the father said to his son. "Because I know it is true in your heart."

Chapter Eight

Hay slept with an old man's bladder, grateful for the chamber pot beneath his bed. As dawn broke, he was using it again when there was a hectoring outside his closed door. Nicolay's bed was empty, but it was not his voice or demeanor. Recognition floated just beyond reach. Eventually, the shouting and the knocking fused, and Hay shouted back, "Come in, Bob!"

The door flung open, and Robert Lincoln burst through. "I will not leave!" he cried. His smooth, round face was contorted and wet; his tangle of hair looked unwashed. "He wants me to go. And I refuse. I will not."

"Who is *he*?" said Hay, although he knew.

"And so do you."

"I do what?"

"Want me to leave."

Hay sat up. His nightshirt felt damp. "Did he tell you that?"

"In so many words."

"All I said is that both of you are in danger here. You and Tad."

"From what?"

"Bob, it was not typhoid fever that killed your brother."

Robert looked frightened. "What was it, then?"

"We might know more later to-day." Hay debated telling Robert about the messages received and decided he had a right to know, at least about the second one; it was his life at stake. Hay knew it by heart: *And ye are risen up against my father's house this day, and have slain his sons.*

"Plural," Hay said. "Which is why both of you need to leave. In my half-baked opinion."

"But Tad is here."

"Not for long."

"Threats are not uncommon, correct? They come in every post."

"This did not come in the post. Somebody put them in my satchel—in *my* office. Without a postmark. And it was not the first one."

"How many others?"

"Just one."

"So, who put them there?"

"Ha, if I knew that . . ."

"Someone *here,* you are saying."

Robert's fear was understandable. Having your life endangered, and by someone on the premises, maybe someone you *knew,* must have been scary as hell. Robert should have been told already. By his father, not by Hay.

⊬⊸⊸⊩

All morning long, the interruptions never ceased. Lord Lyons in search of the president, who was determined not to be found. A messenger delivering a copy of General Halleck's order in Arkansas to hang any rebel soldier involved in poisoning Union troops, which Hay judged too painful for the president to see just now. The *New-York Times* man desperate for information about the rumors of battle on the Upper Potomac—Hay knew nothing because there was nothing to know. An office seeker who collapsed on the stairwell under the strain—served him right, was Hay's reaction. Hay was busy drafting a demurral to Thaddeus Stevens's demand for a postmastership in Pennsylvania for a deserving mulatto when there was a knock at his doorframe. Rather tentative, Hay was pleased to note. And for once, the intruder was someone he was happy to see.

"It *is,* suh." Jamie Hall's pudgy figure fairly loped into the room. "Mercury. Too much of it. Much too much. A toxic amount, without doubt."

"Without doubt? No chance it was an accident, or a miscalculation? Or medicine that was *too* heroic—*over*heroic." Hay realized how acutely he hoped this was so.

Dr. Hall made a show of considering these possibilities, then exhaled noisily and shook his head.

"There was nothing heroic about this, suh. Nor overheroic. No, suh, there was not. In my opinion, this was intended to be."

+=≻━≺=+

"Either one, Jamie said—calomel *or* blue-mass pills," Hay said.

Lincoln's reaction was confined to a twitch of the mole on his cheek. He stood by his office window, fingering the spyglass. "Enough to . . . ?"

"Yes."

"According to . . . ?"

"The laboratory man who conducted the Smithson test."

"Smithson test?"

Hay wondered if Lincoln hounded for details to avoid thinking about what they meant.

+=≻━≺=+

The list of names on the seat of Hay's chair bore Old Edward's precise hand. Hay glanced down the first page, then the second, which listed everyone on the premises when the second message was left. The usuals. The four living Lincolns. Nicolay and himself. Mrs. Keckly. Nurses. Dr. Stone. Cooks and chambermaids, messengers and guards. Two assistant gardeners—Hay tried but failed to recall their countenances, curious why *two* assistant gardeners should be necessary on a cold winter's night. And William Spaulding—but why would a housepainter work after dark?

Silly Billy. Hay had heard the man's nickname from Willie. Hay had understood why it made Willie giggle—because it portrayed the man as the opposite of what he was, which was a bully. This was obvious to Willie and surely to Tad. And to Hay. He pictured Spaulding high on a ladder, in the State Dining Room or the second-floor corridor, looking down at whoever was looking up. A painter could go anywhere without explanation. Hay could not visualize the painter actually applying paint.

Hay posed the question to himself: What would Vidocq do?
A blank.

Hay had too many suspects and not enough facts. And a conjecture: that a conspiracy of secessionists inside the Executive Mansion had administered poison to Willie and possibly to Tad, while leaving two messages in Hay's satchel. By solving one imponderable, Hay would solve the other. So, why not tackle the easier one first? The messages.

For those, he had some facts—namely, the lists that Old Edward had prepared of everyone in the mansion when the messages were left. The previous list had twenty-seven names, and this one—Hay counted the entries on all three pages—had thirty-one. At least twenty names looked in common, although if more than one person was involved, the same name need not be on both lists.

He put the two lists side by side. The president and Robert were on both, and Hay and Nicolay, Mrs. Keckly, Thomas Cross and Thomas Stackpole and William Spaulding . . . *Silly Billy*. Both times a message was left, he was in the mansion. Stackpole's brother-in-law. The two had been seen together consorting out in Virginia with a Confederate . . . an *alleged* Confederate informant—that is, a spy.

The sunlight was a delight. Hay passed in front of the War Department and crossed Seventeenth street. He imagined Stackpole and Spaulding conferring in the intersection, eight times in the course of a night. Hay crossed the Avenue, dodging the erratic procession of wagons and hacks.

The address was 190 Pennsylvania avenue, three doors west of Seventeenth. An apothecary was on the corner, then a milliner next door. Then a shabby brick building with a door handsomely painted in yellow and midnight blue:

PARKER & SPAULDING
House and Sign Painting
and Glazing
2nd floor

Hay passed through a smoky vestibule and climbed the stairs. The banister was gone; its supports protruded from the wall.

At the top, he passed from day to dusk. The plain brown door straight ahead bore no indication of what lay beyond. On the door to the right, Hay examined the letters still nailed in place:

PA KER &   PAUL ING

Quite an advertisement for a housepainter, Hay thought.

Hay's knock drew no response. He twisted the knob, and the door swung open. The front room was empty but for a low-hanging chandelier and a Corinthian column embedded in the wall. Otherwise, no furniture, no occupants.

"Halloo!" Hay called out.

"Thomas?" came a shout from the back room.

Hay grunted noncommittally.

A strapping man with a broad, stupid face stepped into the room. He had a swagger and a smile that suggested brutality, not mirth. Silly Billy, indeed. His woolen jersey had a splotch of purple paint on the forearm.

"*You.* What's ya want here?" Spaulding's drawl was belligerent. "Or is it Mister Parker yer after?"

"No, it's you I came to see. To ask you some questions"—Hay hesitated, then decided that courtesy worked even on oafs—"if I might."

"About?"

"Thomas Stackpole."

"Be quick with 'em, then, Mister Hay. I am a man of affairs."

"Then let me start with this—what were you doing at the mansion last evening?"

"Which mansion would ya mean?"

"The Executive Mansion. You were in more than one?"

"I got clients in many a mansion."

"It looks like you are giving them up." Hay swept his arm around the barren room.

"And in cities other than this'n." Which was not an answer. "In Baltimore, in Phil'delphia. Wilmington, time to time."

"And Richmond."

"Not during the past year, sorry to say."

"How about the year coming up?"

"Ya never know what will happen when ya wake up in the mornin', Mister Hay. Surely ya'are old enough to know that."

"You are *from* Virginia, are you not? Born there."

"Story of me life, I see. Very well. A Virginian I am, and proud to be so. Seven years here in Washington City. Seven years of fat, as the Scriptures say. This one, the fattest of all."

"Despite the war."

"Because of it. Ain't just the sutlers and the embalmers making out like horse thieves. Painting a house t'ain't so reliable as squirtin' a dead soldier or hawking tripe to the troops. But the more war, the more buildin', which must be painted at least once to keep the termites away. Old buildings, too, them's worth it now to keep 'em in shape. This means work, which means gold. Well, it used to mean gold. Now, greenbacks."

"And your hope as to which side wins the war?"

"That nobody win. That the war keep on for the rest of my workin' life, and my chillun's too. Sadly, 'tis out of my hands."

Spaulding was a few inches taller than Hay and thirty or forty pounds heavier—all muscle, Hay could see in the slant of his shirtfront. Hay backed up a step, beyond a jab's reach.

"So, are you closing up here?"

"Cutting me costs. But yer not here fer the state of my business."

"No." Although that was not without prurient interest. "What I want to know is what you were doing at the Executive Mansion last evening."

"Cannot s'pose why ya care such a lot. But v'ry well. Examining the places I touched up in the State Dining Room. In the corner, where the rain leaked through. To make sure it's all lookin' right."

"And it was?"

"Oh yes, we do good work here, Mistuh Hay. If you should have any doubts."

"No, none." Hay could check this with Old Edward. "Were you in my office at any point?"

"Why would I want to do that?"

Again, not an answer.

"I assume you saw Mister Stackpole there. Your brother-in-law, as I understand it." Hay waited for wonderment and was disappointed. "You were expecting him just now, I gather."

No reply.

Nor did Hay learn anything about Spaulding's unauthorized trip across the Long Bridge, or the Confederate trading permits, or the spy in crinoline at Bailey's Crossroads. Spaulding was not as stupid as he seemed. He might well have stolen into Hay's office, under Stackpole's protective eye, and left a crudely written message. But in that case, Stackpole could have left it himself. Why bring an extra person into a conspiracy? Unless, of course, the conspiracy was Spaulding's.

As Hay descended the narrow stairs, he felt more confused than when he had mounted them. He was crossing the Avenue, returning to the Executive Mansion, when he saw Thomas Stackpole waddling toward him.

"Billy is waiting for you," Hay said, savoring the look of surprise.

The man Hay needed to see—but preferred not to—was leaving Tad's bedroom.

"Doctor Stone," Hay called out.

"What is it this time?" The physician's handsome, craggy jaw jutted more than usual.

"Questions the president wanted me—no, instructed me—to ask you."

"Then he can—"

"Come with me," Hay said sharply, then added, "Please. In here."

Hay strode into the oval study. To his surprise, Dr. Stone followed. The room was empty. They seated themselves in the upholstered rocking chairs across the center table. Dr. Stone's expression had shifted from annoyance to curiosity.

"As I imagine you are aware," Hay began, "there were some . . . irregularities in Willie's death."

Hay doubted that Dr. Stone was aware, unless he had caused them.

"I was in charge of the case." The doctor was matter-of-fact, confident in his authority over lesser beings. "There is nothing of which I was unaware. How does a layman such as yourself define 'irregularities'?"

Subtlety, Hay reflected, was not the good doctor's strong point. Hay would oblige. "A toxic amount of mercury in his tissue."

"Impossible!" Dr. Stone lunged forward in his seat. "Who says this?"

Hay described the Smithson test that the embalmer, Dr. Brown, had conducted.

Dr. Stone's eyes narrowed. "Either the test is nonsensical or the man is an amateur. I administered only as much calomel as a boy his size could take—and no more. I took his size into account—I swear it. Those were my instructions, from his father, and I fulfilled them. You can tell him that. Or I will."

"Nobody is accusing you of anything, Doctor Stone." Although the verve of the doctor's denials struck Hay as curious. "I am merely stating facts, trying to understand them. Let me ask you this: Did any of Willie's symptoms . . . diverge from the typical symptoms of typhoid fever?"

"No case is precisely the same as any other, Mister Hay. So any patient's symptoms will diverge, as you put it, from what might be regarded—incorrectly, I assure you—as typical. Nor can we say for certain that this *was* typhoid fever. A bilious fever of some sort. Or possibly typhus, which as you know"—a steely look—"is a distinct disease, despite the similarity in name. But I have neither the time nor the inclination to educate you, which I assure you is a cause for regret."

Dr. Stone's prominent chin invited an uppercut; his chiseled cheek was ripe for Hay's right fist. The doctor started to stand, but Hay would not be deflected.

"You have seen many cases of typhoid fever, or bilious fever, or whatever you think to-day that it was. Please, did you see any symptoms that did not accord with . . . ?"

"I understand your question, Mister Hay. And I am trying my damnedest not to answer it."

"Successfully, so far."

"You do understand the confidences that exist, that *must* exist, between doctor and patient. Your father is a doctor, is he not?"

"He is, and I do. But your patient is . . . no longer with us. And your patient's father has asked me—instructed me, *ordered* me—to make these inquiries. If you like, we can both go to the grieving father so that you can hear his order in his own words. Or you can believe me."

Dr. Stone considered his choices and made up his mind. "There was one symptom Willie exhibited that did not fit with typhoid fever. A green stool, rather like spinach." The doctor watched Hay to gauge his discomfort. "This *is* a symptom of mercury poisoning."

"Why did you not mention this before? Or wonder about it, at least?"

"To repeat myself, Mister Hay"—this time, the honorific was without mockery—"there is no typical case of typhoid fever, or of bilious fever. A single symptom, or the lack of it, signifies nothing."

Hay could not shake the feeling that Dr. Stone was hiding something. He had certainly had the opportunity to administer a toxic amount of mercury. But he had, in fact, promised to "do no harm." Had he done any? Probably. Doctors do. But if it was inadvertent—heroes often fall on their faces—he was not really to blame, unless he had purposely violated the president's, the father's, orders. And if it was purposeful, because of . . . what? . . . a sympathy with the South? Speculating was pointless. Hay's gut told him . . . *maybe*. That it was conceivable Dr. Stone was involved, that he had been heroic and then some. Probably for some untreasonous reason. But, in any event, it was worth learning more.

"Then why did you keep administering it—the calomel—if he showed signs of taking too much?"

Dr. Stone leaned toward Hay and said with conviction, "So he would live."

Yes, Hay wanted to ask, how well had that worked? But he kept his silence.

⊢⟩━⟨⊣

Hay was toiling at his desk, waiting for Nicolay so they could stroll to Willard's to dine—to *drink* and dine—when he felt a shadow at his back.

Pinkerton.

"What do you want?" said Hay, bracing for a tirade about his meeting with John Watt.

"Information. To give ye."

"I am all ears," Hay said, knowing that nothing was free.

"About the secesh. In this buildin'."

"Please." Hay gestured Pinkerton into a chair.

It was not a pretty tale. The detective recounted some of the incriminating stories in Potter's affidavits, and in the exact language, but adding some of his own. Of Thomas Stackpole and John Watt seen carousing in a tavern with a trader known to have sold muskets to the rebels. (Hay could not picture Stackpole "carousing" at all.) Of Stackpole tending to Watt's orchids in the gardener's absence. Of Watt conferring with Dr. Stone in the conservatory late one night.

"So?" said Hay.

That Stackpole had spent part of his boyhood near Washington City—where or why, Pinkerton's men had not learned yet. Did Hay know that William Spaulding had married Stackpole's sister? (Pinkerton frowned at Hay's reply.) Or that Spaulding had been seen in Watt's presence, in the greenhouse, just before the gardener's arrest?

"What?"

"Oh yes," Pinkerton said. "Conferrin' head-to-head."

The makings of a conspiracy, indeed.

Chapter Nine

FRIDAY, FEBRUARY 28, 1862

J ohn, I want you there as a witness." Lincoln had popped his head into Hay's bedroom at first light. "I daresay you will enjoy it. But not a word to anyone, please."

Hay glanced across his bedroom—Nicolay was gone, probably already at his desk.

"Besides him," Lincoln said.

Stanton, the emotional war secretary, had burst from the president's office the previous evening, muttering, "A damned fizzle, a damned fizzle," and Hay had been delighted to learn why. General McClellan had sent pontoon boats up the C&O Canal, alongside the Potomac, to help secure the railroad at Harpers Ferry. However, the boats were four to six inches too wide to pass through the locks. Stupidity. Or arrogance— an assumption the material world would yield to the general's will. In either case, in Hay's mind, a stroke of luck.

Hay's hurried breakfast, at his desk, was watery coffee and a misshapen apple of the sort Lincoln favored for lunch. He was examining a wormhole that lacked a worm when a booming baritone sounded too hearty for so early an hour. The general in chief had arrived.

Hay crossed the waiting room and entered Lincoln's sanctum. George B. McClellan was barreling toward the far window, his hand outstretched, grabbing at the president's. Hay figured a jab, then two or three punches to a belly thickened from the capital's larders, followed by a hard right cross to the overconfident chin—this would flatten the general with a satisfying thud. Lincoln beckoned the Young Napoleon to a seat, but the general stayed on his feet, and so did the president. (And so did Hay, who longed to sit.) The difference in their heights was laughable, and Hay understood McClellan's pleasure in being perverse—he often felt the same.

The general scowled in Hay's direction. "And why is this young whippersnapper here?"

Hay would have been hard-pressed to explain.

"I appreciate youth, General, as you can attest. The capable Mister Hay is my secretary. But this is a conversation between you and me. About the pontoon boats in Harpers Ferry."

There were to be no pleasantries. McClellan's handsome face froze.

Without a pause, Lincoln said, "Why in tarnation could you not have known whether a boat would pass through that lock before you spent a million dollars—gold, not greenbacks—taking them thar? I am no engineer, but it seems to me that if I wished to know whether a boat would pass through a lock, common sense would teach me to go and measure it first."

McClellan's cheeks turned as red as his lips. Hay wondered if the wellborn general had ever been scolded before.

"Have you never heard of a measuring stick, General? Please explain yourself." This was Lincoln as a courtroom counselor, cross-examining a hostile witness, a man he had known since the 'fifties, when McClellan was the chief engineer of the Illinois Central Railroad and Lincoln often represented or fought the company in court.

McClellan's mouth moved but nothing came out. Lincoln would have waited until noon, Hay felt sure, but the general said at last, "Your Excellency, I am only as good as my military intelligence."

Hay's mouth fell open in surprise: McClellan was blaming the blunder on Pinkerton.

"How else can I learn the facts on the ground, Your Excellency?" Cockiness had returned to McClellan's cadence. "I cannot be expected personally to visit the locks with a measuring stick, or does Your Excellency consider that the most strategic use of my time?"

"How you spend your time is your own business, General. But the results of your performance are my business, the nation's business, and

I must hold you accountable. According to War Order No. 1, you were to be marching on Richmond by the twenty-second of this month. To-day is the twenty-eighth, and here you are before me, no closer to Richmond than you were. If you are not using your army, General, perhaps I could."

"I also rely on Mister Pinkerton for his estimates of enemy strength." A pugnacity swelled McClellan's chest. "And let me assure you, Your Excellency, that if I am furnished a suitable number of troops, I shall execute your war order without delay."

"The commander in chief's order, you mean."

"Of course, sir—nothing less." McClellan glanced around for a seat. "I have never run from my responsibilities, Your Excellency, and while there is breath in this body, I never shall."

The man's unctuous audacity left Hay in a boil of rage, and he marveled at Lincoln's capacity to keep his calm while dismissing the general as if he were a butler who had delivered cold tea.

+≡≡≡+

Columbian College was located out Fourteenth street, past the boundary of Washington City, but its National Medical College was housed downtown. The drab brick building was on E street, between Eleventh and Twelfth.

The front door, unattended and unlocked, squeaked as Hay pushed it open. Inside, the moldy smell belied the presence of anything medical. He tried the staircase and found fresher air on the second floor. He knocked at the door to his right and, hearing no answer, entered an anteroom of sorts. A podium faced three rows of four seats apiece, all empty.

"Can I help you, young man?" A deep and melodious voice caught Hay from behind.

Hay turned and saw a stocky man with an unruly white beard that did not entirely conceal a smile. Hay considered briefly if the man meant *may* instead of *can* and decided no, he was asking if he might be capable of aid while reserving judgment on whether he would offer any. Hay needed both—the *can* and the *may*—or he was wasting his time here.

"I hope so," Hay replied.

On the brisk walk from the Executive Mansion, Hay had considered how to solicit damaging information from the colleagues of a man he had to assume they revered. His stratagem required only a single untruth.

The man invited Hay into a shabby office barely big enough for one person. Dr. George M. Dove was an affable man with stooped shoulders and a pliable, if half-hidden, face. He introduced himself as a professor of the theory and practice of medicine—"and an admirer of Mister Lincoln's, if I may say so. What sort of appointment does Mister Lincoln have in mind, if I might ask?"

"I am not permitted to say, I am afraid." A doctor, Hay knew, would respect a confidence. "But you would trust Doctor Stone, I imagine, with your own children's lives?"

"Of course, of course, of course," Dr. Dove said, a trifle too quickly to suit Hay.

"*Has* he treated your children?"

"No, Mister Hay. Both of my children passed on without his assistance."

Hay felt his cheeks burn. "Oh, I am sorry. How long have you known Doctor Stone?"

"He arrived here in . . .'forty-eight, as I recall. I was already on the faculty here. Or 'forty-nine, he came. As a professor of anatomy. Not long out of medical school himself. Quite the genius, we were told."

"And was he?"

"In his way. We all are," Dr. Dove said gravely. "Then he left for a few years and returned in, let me say, 'fifty-eight. As a professor of ophthalmological anatomy. 'Fifty-nine, perhaps—please forgive my imprecision." His eyes twinkled.

"Where did he go for those years?"

"Taught and practiced in Richmond, as I understand it. His wife is from Richmond, or nearby. He met her there. From a fine old family. Good stock."

"Still there, I take it."

"I would imagine."

"And sympathetic to the rebels."

Dr. Dove squirmed at his desk. "That, I cannot say."

"And Doctor Stone?"

"Doctor Stone what?"

"His sympathies."

A piercing look. "This is something we never discuss."

"Because?"

"We are colleagues here, sir. Whatever our private beliefs."

"Do you know Missus Stone?"

"Oh yes. A lovely woman. She is here now, of course."

"What brought them back to Washington City, do you know?"

"An offer from the school. And an invitation from President Buchanan himself."

"To do what?"

"To serve as his personal physician."

"Which he did, as I understand."

"And capably. Until the end of his term. And then for Mister Lincoln. Perhaps on Mister Buchanan's advice. Making him, I suppose, the only living soul who has seen both presidents as God made them." A rumble started in Dr. Dove's abdomen and burst forth as a horselaugh. "And another man on our faculty, who *was* on our faculty, Doctor Garnett, left to serve as the personal physician for Mister Davis—Jefferson Davis. Who I gather is rather cold to the touch." Another laugh. "Tell me, Mister Hay, is President Lincoln a warm man?"

"In his way," Hay replied. "Though remote."

"As all great men are."

"Were Doctor Stone and Doctor Garnett particular friends, would you say?"

"Not that I noticed. None of us have much time for friendship."

"Or inclination?"

An easy, affectionate laugh, one that would console at a bedside. Hay was prone to trust anyone who shared his sense of humor.

Hay said, "Is he liked by his colleagues, would you say?"

"Liked? Admired, certainly."

"Oh?"

"He is a young man who has come very far. Not everyone likes that. And to be fair, he is not overly concerned if they do. He has stepped on toes. But he has never stepped on mine. Nor would he." A tight smile. "I think highly of the man—in every way."

"As does he."

"No doubt he does. As do I. And, I might assume, as do you. That is why we are here, is it not? In the capital, at the center of things. For the most part, we selected ourselves. I did. Maybe you did, too."

"Not a sin, I hope."

"Not exactly a virtue," Dr. Dove said. "But Doctor Stone, for what it is worth, was born here."

⊬═══⊣

The wisps of clouds did nothing to impede the stream of sunlight. Worse were the clouds of dust the cold wind stirred up. The National Theatre was dark to-day, its poster boards empty, and Hay shielded his eyes as he stepped past.

Hay was trying to make sense of Doctor Stone. Yes, his wife's family was probably—no, surely—loyal to Virginia and the South. But that was *her* family, not his. And yes, he had lived for a while in Richmond, but he was a native of Washington City—itself a swamp of secessionists, of course. Who could tell, Hay thought, what was in anyone's heart? Maybe the heroic doctor had simply given the boy more calomel than he had intended—such a Narcissus would never admit it. But that was arrogance, not murder. Surely, the line was distinct between heroism and harm. Any other conclusion was absurd.

Hay assailed himself for getting sidetracked, for veering from suspect to suspect. He needed to focus on the *un*heroic, on the names that appeared on both of Old Edward's lists, on the possibility of a conspiracy among the mansion's secessionists. Hay had questioned most of the overlaps already, to no avail. In search of a conspiracy, he had questioned John Watt, Thomas Stackpole, and Silly Billy Spaulding. *Start at the edges and work your way in*—Nicolay's advice. Hay had started at the edges, and he was still there. So, what should he try next? *Think! Think!* Where was Vidocq now that Hay needed him?

The northeast gate of the Executive Mansion was open to everyone, even to Hay (as Nicolay was wont to jest whenever they passed through). Just as Hay approached the front door, it opened. Did Old Edward use a secret peephole, or did he just know?

"You saw my list, sir?" the doorkeeper said.

"Yes, thank you."

"Useful, I hope."

"Not very, I'm afraid."

Old Edward looked hurt.

"Only because your day ended at eight," Hay rushed to add, "which left four hours unattended. And because so many people were here, it is difficult to know where to start."

"It would depend, I imagine, on what you are looking for."

"You are a wise man, Edward."

"I try to be, sir." A warm Irish smile. "But if I might offer a piece of information?"

"Please do."

"Was just wanting to say, sir, that Tom Cross was on the premises Tuesday night until ten or eleven o'clock, mostly here or under the portico."

"What was he doing all that time?"

"I was not here, sir. You would have to ask him."

"How do you know he was here, then?"

"I know."

Hay did not doubt it.

Hay took four or five steps into the vestibule before he turned back. "One other thing. Billy Spaulding, the painter, says he was here Tuesday night to check the repairs in the State Dining Room. Do you remember this, by any chance?"

Old Edward tried hardest when you challenged his capacity to keep track of things.

"I *was* here, and he did come in. But not for the dining room, sir. The touching up there was finished six weeks ago. The other night, he was heading upstairs."

"What on earth for?"

"You would have to ask him, sir."

⊹⊱⋆⊰⊹

The sunlight had not filtered down into the basement of the Executive Mansion. The door to the messengers' cloister was closed. Hay knocked and did not wait for an answer.

Tom Cross was hunkered over the desk, his bald black scalp work-ing angrily. One eye tilted up toward Hay.

"Whachoo want?" The husky voice sounded self-restrained, for which Hay was grateful.

"A question or two."

"Go."

Hay suppressed a spasm of anger. "Is another time better?"

"I mean, go on. Ask."

"Oh. Thank you." Politeness to a Negro—Hay supposed he could get used to it. "Old Edward says you were here late the other night, Tues-day night, near the front entrance."

Hay waited for a confirmation but got a one-eyed stare. He said, "Do you recall what time you left?"

"I do."

Hay waited and said at last, with only mild derision, "And what time *was* it?"

"Near ta eleben o'clock."

"And starting when, would you say? Please."

"Nine."

"Did you see anyone enter or leave in that time?"

"Yes." Again, he stopped.

"All right—who, then?"

"Miz Cornelia."

"The cook, you mean—Cornelia Mitchell."

"Yes."

A long pause.

"And?"

"Mistuh Robert come home, by carriage."

"About what time?" Hay felt like a parent inquiring after a wayward child.

"When de wind come up. Not long befo' I go."

"All right. And?"

"Mistuh Stackpole."

"I thought he had already left."

"Mebbe he left ag'in."

"When was this?"

"Soon after I got t' he-ah."

"Good. Anyone else?"

"Only Missus Keckly."

"When was this?"

"When I left. I was waitin' fer her. To drive her home, at de Madam's request. 'Cause so dangerous after dark."

"Rather late for her to be leaving."

"She gwine leave befo' dat, so I'se a-waitin' all that time, 'til she ready."

"What held her up, do you know?"

A long, low sweep of his massive head. "She lookin' mighty troubled 'bout sumpin. All she sayin' was, 'A woman's work ain't never done.' 'Cept she don't say *ain't*. And I says, 'Neider is a man's.' And she laughs, and so do I. And den I takes her home."

⊹══⊹══⊹

A broad-backed man was seated in Hay's swivel chair, inspecting the papers on his desk. Hay clapped his hands and snapped, "What the hell?"

Allan Pinkerton turned and, showing no sign of remorse, said, "I ha' been waitin'."

"You are finished waiting. Now get out of that chair and leave my things alone. I could have you arrested for this."

"Nonsense," Pinkerton said, yielding the seat to its owner. "Ye expect me to arrest meself? Snooping, ye do understand, that's me business. Yours, too, now."

"Well, don't do it to me."

Pinkerton took the hard-backed chair. "News to tell. Tha' William Spauldin' is gone. Across the Long Bridge, yesterday."

Why was Hay not surprised? He imagined the painter on his gray—no, white—horse, swaggering over the planks that spanned the Potomac. Fading into the darkness, both arms in the air.

"What time was that?"

Pinkerton cocked his head. "Why do ye ask?"

Hay told of his visit to Spaulding's office the previous afternoon, apparently just hours before he went south. "His office was empty of furniture, abandoned, except for him. And something he told me about the night before was a lie. For no good reason I can see. Well, let me restate that—no good reason except an incriminating one. He said he was here to inspect the State Dining Room. Instead, he went upstairs, where the boys are. According to Old Edward, and why would *he* lie?"

"Ye talkin' the nigh' the second message was left."

"No, the night after."

"Was he also here the nigh' before?"

Hay retrieved Old Edward's lists from his desk drawer, sorry that Pinkerton saw where it was, knowing he would need a new hiding place.

Hay riffled through the list. "Yes, he was."

"And the nigh' o' the first message?"

A check. "No."

"Ye sure?"

"What kind of . . . ? Never mind." Hay did not want to know what Pinkerton thought of him. He could guess. "Yes, I am sure."

"What time was tha'—yer visit?"

"One o'clock. No, closer to two."

"Six or seven hours, then, before he went south. What did ye talk about?"

"That he is a Virginian and makes no secret of his loyalties. He is a secesh through and through—that seems clear enough. He offered the most innocent explanation for why he consorts with rebel spies. And for his previous excursion across the Long Bridge, also unauthorized. With Stackpole, that time."

"Did ye say ye suspected him of . . . anythin' a'tall? Even hint at it? Though I suppose yer very presence was a hint."

"Maybe it was, but I could think of no other way to question him except by being present. You seem to assume he is not coming back. He did the last time."

"No' sayin' tha' for sure. But 'twould seem so to me. Leavin' at night, in such a hurry and all, leavin' nothin' behind."

"His family?"

"I will check," Pinkerton said. "He showed a pass signed by the president. Tha' is wha' the sergeant on duty at the bridge remembers. Woul' ye know anythin' about tha'?"

At last, the explanation for Pinkerton's presence. "Nothing," Hay said. "Nicolay might know. Or the president."

"Or Stackpole?"

"No reason he should," Hay said. "Unless he wrote it himself. Which, now that I think about it . . ." Hay swallowed hard and plunged ahead. "I could use some help here."

Pinkerton's eyes seemed to soften. "With Stackpole?"

"I will talk to him."

"Because ye ha' been so successful in questionin' him so far?"

Hay thought fondly of punching Pinkerton's rounded gut. "I will take care of that, thank you very much. But I want to know more about his background. And if I am missing anything. That you happen to know of."

A snarl.

"And," Hay continued, "if anyone else might be . . . involved." With some trepidation, Hay offered his theory about a conspiracy of secessionists. Out loud, it sounded farther-fetched than it had in his mind. Still, Spaulding was gone, John Watt was in custody, and Stackpole was . . . well, seated outside the president's door. "Are there others?"

"I will pu' me best man on it, Hay. Meaning, me."

⊬━━━⊣

"We know where he went," Hay said. "I just want to know why."

Thomas Stackpole remained absorbed in a copy of *The Congressional Globe*. Hay doubted the doorkeeper's interest in the proceedings of Congress.

"Over the Long Bridge last night. Without his family, or yours."

No reaction.

Hay said, "Do you know where he went?"

Stackpole kept his eyes on *The Globe*.

"Is he coming back, do you know?"

Stackpole looked up but stared impassively as if Hay were speaking Urdu.

"Where is your family?" said Hay.

"Safe." The high pitch of Stackpole's voice startled Hay—again.

"At home, then."

"I cannot see what business this is of yours, Mister Hay. What do you suspect me of? And my brother-in-law? Of being a secesh, I take it." Stackpole's fat cheeks quivered—in anger, Hay supposed.

"Are you?"

"You have asked me this. I am a Union man, and I have been since President Pierce lived here. Longer. Ask me again and I will tell you the same."

⊹⸺⸺⊹

Lincoln dozed in the upholstered rocker, cradling *Richard III* in his lap. Hay was backing out of the oval study when he heard, "What can I do for you, John?"

"In this winter of our discontent?"

A wry smile. "If the Almighty has a purpose here in this house, He is keeping it well-hidden from me. What is on your mind, John?"

"I am confused, sir."

"The beginning of wisdom, I should say."

Hay sank into the opposite chair and poured forth the fragments of evidence and suspicions. "Too many suspects, and any of them might have . . . There is really nobody in this building I trust entirely other than you and Nico. I am not always sure about myself."

"I am. Tell me what you know."

"What I *know*? I *know* almost nothing. I feel stuck—stupid, even. I know that Willie . . . passed away. That two messages, without postage, were left in my satchel. That a toxic amount of mercury was found in his . . . tissue. Apparently too much for it to have been an accident. If *apparently* is the same as *knowing*."

"Which it is not."

"Agreed. What else do I *know*? I have the names of everyone who was here in the mansion around the time those notes were left in my satchel—that is, to the best of Old Edward's recollection, which is pretty good but probably not perfect."

"He would disagree."

"In any event, the list is not necessarily exhaustive."

"You have spoken to everyone who is on both lists."

"Just about. Nothing out of the ordinary."

"So, who do you suspect?"

"Besides everyone? The secesh, most of all. The ones that Potter's investigators named. Do *they* know anything? None of the accusations against them would stand up in court."

"Which does not mean they are false."

"Granted. But you asked me what I *know*."

"I am also interested in what you think you know." Lincoln's face had relaxed. Hay was pleased to have helped.

"I think I know that secessionists were behind this. And I think I know that there *are* secesh, or secesh sympathizers, which I know is not necessarily the same, but there are some here in this building. They work here. Two are gone. John Watt is sharing quarters with the roaches and rats under the Capitol—he disliked the boys and maybe was trying to spy on them, but probably not. And this painter Spaulding—do you know him?" Lincoln's attention had returned to his lap. "He crossed the Long Bridge last night. Did you sign a pass for him to go?"

A slow shake of the bowed head.

"And Stackpole. He seems to be pals with John Watt—they have both worked here for a very long time—and this painter Spaulding is married to his sister."

Hay was describing Stackpole's behavior the night the Confederates were expected to attack when Lincoln waved his hand and said, "Yes, yes, Potter told me. And I think it is hogwash."

"And his visit with the lady from Manassas."

"A man knows who he knows. I have known many a man—and lady, too—of Confederate sympathies."

"You are content to have him sit outside your door."

"Yes, of course. I even lent him money—three hundred eighty dollars, and without collateral."

"Really! For what?"

Lincoln gave Hay a stern look and said, "A family emergency, I would imagine. I never asked. So yes, I have taken the measure of this man and, yes, I trust him."

Hay wondered, and not for the first time, if Lincoln trusted too much.

"And Doc . . . Doctor Stone," Hay said. "Might he have administered too much calomel, inadvertently or . . . . not?"

"You think not?"

"This is far from anything I know, or from anything I *think* I know, but . . ." Hay recounted Dr. Stone's connections to Richmond, through his wife and his own sojourn there.

"Hardly evidence of a willingness to betray his medical oath."

"True."

"But you are right," Lincoln said, "we must reach beyond the evidence and look for the truth."

Hay could not remember having said something so wise but hoped that he had.

"And we do have the one witness," Lincoln went on, "who we *think* was a witness. We can ask him again."

Chapter Ten

We need to go." A rough hand shook Hay's shoulder. "Now."
His grandfather was waking him up for school. Hay tried to push the hand away.

"John, I need you to come with us."

Hay's eyes snapped open and stared up into Lincoln's.

"Where to?"

The president explained the morning's destination and the need for dispatch. Although the Hell-cat was unlikely to awaken for hours.

Hay said, "Should Bob come, too?"

Lincoln left without responding.

Hay dressed swiftly and prattled with Nicolay (how nice to rise earlier for once!) and drank the dregs of last night's huckleberry tea. Dirty and hungry, he wended his way down to the north portico, where a barouche was parked. The matched pair of shiny black horses pawed the gravel. Tad was already inside, asleep, his head resting in Mrs. Pomroy's ample lap.

Hay climbed in and sat facing the rear. Mrs. Pomroy sang out, "And how are you this very fine morning, Mister Hay?"

Too much cheer at too early an hour. "I got out of bed, didn't I?" Maybe he *was* becoming an Easterner.

Mrs. Pomroy's smile broadened. Her iron-gray hair and gentle blue eyes suggested a woman of competence and kindness. Neither her countenance nor (Hay guessed) her character showed any sharp edges.

"And how is *he*?" said Hay, nodding at Tad, who looked angelic at repose.

"Recovering, thank the Lord. A tough little fellow, he is. 'Twill take more than the devil to defeat him. Or a nightmare."

"You will be staying out there with him?"

"Oh yes."

"And your own family?"

"My husband and children are . . ." She pointed at the ribbon of mourning that hung from her bonnet.

Hay started to say, "Child*ren*?" when the president climbed into the carriage.

"His other valise," Lincoln said. "The oxblood—you have that, too, Missus Pomroy?"

"Oh yes," she said.

"You sure?" Lincoln seemed nervous.

"Oh yes."

The carriage rolled away from the mansion, past Lafayette square, and headed northeast along Vermont avenue. The morning was crisp and clear; the streets were deserted. Tom Cross drove slowly, easing the ruts, skirting the bumps. Tad stirred but did not waken. Hay saluted Lincoln's restraint in not pulling his son onto his lap and disturbing his sleep. The president gazed out the window, his hand engulfing his young son's ankles.

Lincoln said lazily, "And did you always feel you could say, 'His will be done'?"

Hay thought Lincoln was speaking to him, and he was stumped for a reply.

"No, not at the first blow," Mrs. Pomroy replied. Hay realized they were resuming a conversation begun earlier. "Nor at the second. My dear husband and then my young son. Then my oldest, on the battlefield."

Lincoln turned to Hay and said, "At Bull Run." Hay had ridden out, with much of Washington City, to watch the battle's devastation and returned, shaken, to the capital the following dawn.

"It was months after my . . . my affliction that God met me at a camp meeting." Mrs. Pomroy told of the church gathering in the fields of Maryland and of the certainty and comfort she had felt ever since.

"Simply by trusting in God," she said, her cheeks shining, "and feeling that He does all things well."

Her voice was thick, but her tone was matter-of-fact. Hay glanced over at Lincoln and saw his hands clasped to his face.

They rode in silence northeastward along Rhode Island avenue and turned north onto Seventh street. Signs of civilization became sparse— scattered houses, a low stone wall, a field cleared of trees, the howl of a dog or a fox. The clip-clop of the horses merged with the rasp of Tad's breathing. Hay felt himself dozing off.

They crossed Boundary street, leaving Washington City behind, and pressed steadily uphill. The landscape in Washington County was a tangle of bushes and trees. Tad gave a snort and jolted awake. His body arched, and Lincoln reached for the elfin boy and lifted him to his shoulder like a colicky infant.

"Where, where?" said Tad, gesturing ahead with the arm that swung free, clinging to his father with the other.

"A quieter place," Lincoln said, "so you can get all the way better, my Taddie, like you used to be. And maybe the Taft boys will come to play." Mrs. Lincoln had banned the playmates from the Executive Mansion as too painful a reminder of the son she had lost.

"Oh, Papa-day, weally? I miss, miss Holly. I do, I do. And Bud, too." Then he burst into tears.

His father wrapped his long arms around him, and the swaddled boy fell back to sleep. Lincoln, too, fell asleep, or so Hay thought, until the president said, "There's a divinity that shapes our ends, rough-hew them how we will." It was a statement, not a question, and was directed to Hay.

"Pardon?"

Lincoln repeated it. "From *Hamlet*, John. What did they teach at that school of yours?"

"Nothing so callow as Shakespeare."

" 'There's a divinity that shapes our ends.' We can control the little things in life, John, but the big things are out of our hands. Which is the only thing that makes any of this bearable. That the ways of the Almighty are larger than we can know."

Larger than I can know, anyway, Hay thought.

Forty-five minutes passed before they crossed into the manicured grounds of the Soldiers' Home. This was where veterans of the young nation's three past wars came to molder and die. The carriage rolled to a stop in front of a many-gabled stucco cottage with a weathered look. The superintendent had nagged Lincoln to stay here in the summertime, to escape Washington City's viciously humid heat, like Buchanan had done (as if that were a recommendation). A ploy, Hay guessed, to put the president in the superintendent's debt at budget-writing time.

Tom Cross opened the carriage door, and the cold pressed in, along with a whiff of the woods. For a minute or more, father and son sat without moving. Then Lincoln sighed and stepped down from the barouche. Refusing all offers of aid, he cradled Tad in his arms and mounted the ramshackle steps, crossed the wide porch, and entered the house. Tom Cross and Hay followed with the valises and a small trunk of Tad's toys—including (or so Hay judged by the weight) his collection of tin soldiers, minus the ones he had mangled out of frustration. Mrs. Pomroy carried a portmanteau of her own.

By the time Hay found his way upstairs, Tad was sitting cross-legged in bed, talking without cease and (to Hay's ear) without sense. He was hard enough to translate at normal speed, but with the excitement of a new place and the sunlight spattered across the bare walls, his words blurred into babble.

"Yes, Taddie. Yes, Taddie," Lincoln sang in his nasally twang. "Yes, Taddie. Yes, Taddie."

Some way to rear a hellion, Hay thought. *The child is always right.*

"Now, you may try him again, if you like"—Lincoln had turned to Hay—"with your question."

Hay thought, *Just one?*

"Now, *my* boy"—Lincoln's face softened, talking to Tad—"John here wants to ask you something, and I want you to listen. All right?"

Hay wished he had prepared. Some lawyer he would make.

"Papa-day, you stay wiv me."

"Of course, Taddie, as long as you like. But first, I want you to listen to John here."

Hay took a chair by the bedside, and Tad looked at him with dark, watery eyes. The boy's curiosity was strong, but no equal to illness or sleep.

"Taddie, my—" Hay stopped himself. "Tad, I need to ask you a question about some medicines you took. Do you remember Doctor Stone giving you medicine?"

A wary nod.

"Gray pills—did he give you some to swallow?" Hay felt a stirring at his back. "Or blue pills?"

Tad stared back at Hay like a porcelain cat.

"Tad!" Hay said. "Doctor Stone *did* give you gray pills, every day, did he not? And watch you swallow them down." He wondered if the eight-year-old was a little too young to take pills.

Tad nodded once. His wide eyes never left Hay's.

Lincoln said, "But did you eat 'em down, Taddie, like a good boy?"

"Yes, Papa-day, yes. Me and Willie, too. Oh, I miss Willie, Papa-day. I miss Willie, miss, miss, miss Wil . . ."

Tad was trembling and caved in to tears. Lincoln wrapped his oversized hands around the boy's oversized head and tucked him into his chest. Primitive noises burbled out from . . . Hay found it hard to tell from which of them. Together, they rocked in a chair that had four straight legs.

Lincoln looked up and mouthed to Hay, "Any more questions?"

Hay raised an index finger.

With a seesawing of his hands, Lincoln roused Tad from his dozing. "Taddie, Taddie, are you awake?"

The boy raised his head and offered a beatific smile, which Hay hated to squelch.

As gently as he could, Hay said, "Tad, did anyone else besides Doctor Stone give you pills, gray *or* blue?"

Tad seemed not to have heard him, and Hay was about to repeat the question when the boy's eyes filled with tears and he nodded, then stopped, then nodded again. His head began to bob at an accelerating pace, until he seemed to be losing control. Lincoln's pressed his palms against Tad's cheeks, and the boy calmed.

"Who was he, Tad?" the president whispered.

"A lady," Tad said, more clearly than before.

In unison, Lincoln and Hay said, "A lady?"

"A lady, Papa-day, a dark lady."

"Yib?" said Lincoln. That was Tad's nickname for Mrs. Keckly.

Tad shook his head fiercely.

"Young or old?" said Lincoln, cross-examining the witness.

"A dark lady," Tad said stubbornly, then he started to cry, and this time he would not be consoled.

Hay borrowed a brown stallion from the Soldiers' Home superintendent, with a promise to return it as soon as he could (although he was careful not to specify when). Lacking a carriage roof, nothing to shield him but his greatcoat, his felt hat, and the cable-stitch scarf Kate Chase claimed to have knitted, he was grateful for the sunshine. The trip back seemed shorter, as it usually did and, this time, it actually was: The stallion loped downhill more swiftly than a barouche could carry four adults and a boy to higher ground.

A dark lady, Hay thought. A dark lady who was not Mrs. Keckly. Assuming, of course, that Tad was telling the truth. The boy lived in a world of his own. Quite possibly he was telling the truth, or what he thought was the truth, but the truthfulness was confined to *that* world and no one else's. The only person who knew the difference for certain was Willie. Nobody else, not even the father, whose love for Tad showed a desperation that frightened Hay. When Willie died, no one's loss was greater than Tad's.

Who, then, was the dark lady who had—Hay would assume, yes, that Tad was telling the truth—given Tad, and presumably Willie, the gray pills? The dark lady was not John Watt or Thomas Stackpole or Silly Billy Spaulding, that much was evident. He might also assume it was not Mrs. Keckly. Tad had said so. But that meant taking it as fact that Tad was a credible witness.

One of the nurses, perhaps. Hay wondered how many of them, besides Mrs. Keckly, had dark skin. He had seen none of their names (none he recognized, anyway) on both of Old Edward's lists. Or even on one of them, best he could recall. Suddenly he realized why. They worked for eight or twelve hours at a stretch; they had neither arrived nor departed in the time spans Hay had specified, and Old Edward might have been unaware of their presence upstairs. By now, too many days had lapsed to count on asking him again.

Still, Hay's first step was clear: to question Mrs. Keckly. He had seen her gliding in and out of Tad's bedroom and Mrs. Lincoln's. She was everywhere, hardly noticed, like the wainscoting. She had made herself invaluable to the running of the place, scheduling the boys' round-the-clock nurses, making herself indispensable to the Hell-cat (and therefore to the president) in matters far beyond gowns. She also seemed to be a heroine of sorts to the Negro servants, or so Hay had gathered, owing to the impressive distance she had traveled in her life. Born a slave somewhere down in Virginia, she had used the artistry in her fingertips to amass the $1,200 to purchase her freedom.

As Hay continued south along the extension of Seventh street, the distance between the houses decreased. As he crossed Boundary street, back into the city, he felt his stomach constrict.

Mrs. Keckly lived and worked on Twelfth street, just north of K, in the Negro section of town. Here, the trees were sparse and the sidewalks nonexistent. He was looking for *388* and found it painted in crimson above the door of a four-story row house with elaborate brickwork and cornices carved over the windows. Hay pulled on the frog-shaped doorknocker and let it fall. Inside, an echo died away. A dressmaker probably saw clients only by appointment; for the grandes dames, she went to them.

Hay rapped again on the door and, this time, the eye-level ovals of opaque glass filled with a swirl of shadow. Light footsteps approached, and the door opened.

Elizabeth Keckly stood in the doorway. Her charcoal lace gown had an unapologetic bodice. Even on the stone slab of the doorstep, she stood a few inches shorter than Hay—but statuesque, her back erect, her hair tightly braided. Her skin, the color of prewar coffee with cream, gave off a glow. On her unlined face, the polite but inscrutable expression suggested that nothing could trouble her, nothing in the universe, on either side of death. Certainly not a bantam such as John Hay.

"May I come in?" said Hay, more tentatively than he would have liked.

Her moment of hesitation showed who was in charge. Then, without a word, she stepped aside. Willing to relent, but out of choice, not obligation. Here, she was the mistress of the premises, and wished it known.

"Thank you," he said, to show his breeding—actually, to mask his lack of it.

As Hay followed her into the front parlor, Hay realized with a shock that not since boyhood had he entered a Negro's home. Twice, he had accompanied his father to a deathbed and waited in the doorway of a shack. And once, in Springfield, he had taken Uncle Milt's cook to her home, toting a sling of apples and pears, but declined her invitation for supper. Slaves were unknown in Illinois, except for the fugitives rushing through, and the few frightened freedmen had kept to themselves (as the white folks did). In Providence, the freedmen were too fancy for most of the college men; some of them had Negro butlers of their own.

Mrs. Keckly's home was neither fancy nor poor. If not for the photographs of colored men and women in the hallway, Hay might have mistaken it for a white person's home. Her parlor was as overfurnished and damask draped as any attorney's. Mrs. Keckly guided Hay into a wine-colored armchair with prickly upholstery. She remained standing.

"I am terribly busy, Mister Hay. I have a gown that must be ready this afternoon—it is for a senator's wife—and another one by morning. These are clients who would not countenance a delay. If you would permit me a moment or two to instruct my assistants, I would be grateful." With a swish of her crinolines, and without waiting for a response, she swept out of the room.

On the round table at the center of the parlor, the morning's *National Republican* was folded to page 3. An item was circled in blunt pencil:

Slave-Catching in Washington

The following is the reply of Mr. Keese in relation to one of his supposed slave-catching operations. Mr. Keese declares our statement that his victim was a defenceless woman to be "an unmitigated falsehood," and challenges our Reporter to prove his assertions. We have always relied with confidence upon the statements of our City Reporter, and have no reason to doubt his veracity in this case. We understand him to accept the challenge and he will doubtless on Monday prove more than Mr. Keese will desire to see.

Then came the slave-catcher Keese's letter of vituperation, reminding the *Republican*'s readers that the Fugitive Slave Act was still the law of the land. Hay wondered if Mrs. Keckly had a personal interest.

Hay pulled out his pocket watch—when would she return? He was examining the top shelf in the bookcase—*The Last of the Mohicans, Uncle Tom's Cabin,* a volume of Keats, two of Hawthorne—when he felt, rather than heard, a presence at his back. He spun around guiltily and found Mrs. Keckly in the doorway, delivering a level stare, as if he had violated a confidence, which possibly he had.

"How, then, may I help you?" she said.

"I have a few questions I need to ask, if I could, please. At the president's request."

"The president asked that you . . . question *me*?" Mrs. Keckly looked down her almost-aquiline nose at Hay as she lowered herself into the overstuffed divan. "The subject, Mister Hay?"

"He asked that I look into . . ." Hay started with the least threatening, though least promising, piece of the puzzle. "I had occasion to look through the investigatory files for the House Select Committee on the Loyalty of Government Clerks—you know the committee I mean?"

"Everyone in this city does."

"And in particular, the file for Thomas Stackpole. In which I found a note from you, declining to testify to his character." Mrs. Keckly's head jerked up, but Hay could read nothing in her expression. "May I ask why?" he said.

"Why what?"

"Why you . . . declined. And why they asked you in the first place."

"And may I ask why you are asking?"

"Because I am trying to . . . understand Mister Stackpole and his . . . loyalties, shall we say?"

"I know nothing about that. Which is why I declined to say anything at all."

"Why did they ask you?"

"That, you would need to ask them. I can hardly enlighten you as to the committee's reasons."

Plural.

"But they thought that you could," he said. *And probably would.*

"They are not infallible, Mister Hay. None of us is."

"I am relieved to hear that," Hay said with a smile he hoped was charming.

He studied her strong, sad face, the determined eyes; the corners of her mouth drooped low. Her beauty was in force of character, in her surprisingly delicate features that told of resolution and an inner calm.

"Let me ask you something else, then," Hay said. "I understand you arranged for the nurses for Willie and Tad."

"Until to-day." She seemed resentful at Tad's departure.

"At Missus Lincoln's direction, I imagine?"

"And the president's."

Lincoln had not mentioned that—no reason to. "Let me ask you this, then. Willie and Tad were in separate bedrooms most of the time they were ill. Did you arrange for a nurse for each of them or a single nurse for both?"

"For each of them, when I could. But it is hard to find experienced nurses. The war hospitals need them just as much. More."

"So there were times when one of the boys was left alone."

"I did the best I could, Mister Hay, and if you believe it was not good enough, then I beg you to—"

"Oh no, Missus Keckly, nothing like that. I do not blame you in the slightest. It is the facts of the situation I am trying to ascertain. I hold no one at fault."

Except for murder, Hay thought.

"Then why do you ask?" she said. The set of her jaw suggested a patience that could outwait Hay until Jefferson Davis became a Yankee.

"I wish I could explain further, but I cannot. I assure you, however, that I do need to ask."

She sat stony-faced.

"I have another question, please," he said—"a request, really. I would like to have a list of the nurses you engaged. Could you draw one up for me? *Would* you, please?"

Mrs. Keckly seemed tongue-tied for a moment and said, with a tremor in her voice, "Did one of them do something wrong?"

"I should hope not. But I *would* like a list."

"Now?"

"Not all of them. But the ones you can remember. Starting with yourself, yes?" Hay withdrew the calfskin notebook from his pocket.

"Yes, of course. And Missus Lincoln, at times. And the president, when he could. Mary Jane Welles." That was the navy secretary's wife. "And Old Aunt Mary. And one or two others, perhaps—I would have to think."

"Which of them"—Hay did not know how to say this—"which of the boys' nurses are . . ." He rejected *darkies*. "Negroes?"

Mrs. Keckly stiffened. "Besides myself, you mean?" she said.

"Yes, besides yourself."

"Old Aunt Mary. Mary Dines."

Hay pictured the gray-haired, squared-jawed woman—*old* was accurate—shambling in and out of the mansion's bedchambers, dragging a pail.

"Any others?"

A hesitation. "No."

"No one?"

A steely gaze was her reply.

<hr/>

Other than his mustachioed landlady in Providence, Old Aunt Mary was probably the gentlest old woman Hay had ever met. *The furthest thing from a murderer,* Hay thought as he spurred the stallion back to the Executive Mansion. Murder*ess*. Hay knew her only in passing, but he prided himself on his ability to penetrate façades. The notion was ludicrous. And if Mrs. Keckly was as pure as Lincoln believed, and if—*if*—no other nurse had a darker hue, then Hay was chasing a dark lady in some other guise. Who either worked in the Executive Mansion or had visited it.

Old Edward might know.

Hay instructed the stable boy to arrange for the stallion's return to the Soldiers' Home (Hasheesh would bridle at smelling a rival nearby) and found Old Edward at his post. His white shirt showed a smudge just below the cravat. Hay weighed the embarrassment the doorkeeper would feel against the greater embarrassment he would feel later, and told him. Old Edward was grateful in excess.

"And what may I do for you, Mister Hay?"

Hay described the list he wanted, of every Negress employed in the mansion, plus any who were on the premises on Tuesday evening past—"To the extent you can remember."

"I can remember," Old Edward said. "It will be very like the list I gave you already, Mister Hay."

"Shorter, I would guess."

⊱━━━⊰

Hay heard the sobs while he was climbing the staircase. He hoped the Hell-cat's door was open—frightful decibels, should it be shut. It *was* open; thank goodness for that. Hay was surprised at the sympathy he felt for her. Maybe he *was* good at heart.

He crept across the hallway and stood outside the doorway to her bedroom. Her back was to Hay, facing the president, and suddenly she raised her right arm and, without an utterance, slapped him across the cheek. Hay startled, but Lincoln did not react at all, as if he she had swatted a fly on the bedpost. As if it had happened before.

"We *had* to move him, Puss." The president's reedy voice was whiny and hoarse. "There was no choice. He was not getting well here. And getting nightmares. He will get better up there."

"But why . . ." Sobs punctuated her effort to speak. "Mister . . . Lincoln, but why . . . could I"—then in a gush—"not see him first?"

"Mother, you know why. You were sleeping when we left. And your tears would have upset him. You know that."

"It was b-better for hi-i-im not to . . . s-see his . . . mother, you mean." She was trembling, the sobs slipping out.

"Mother, Mother, Mother." The president coaxed her toward the far window, his arm girdling her waist. He pulled the curtains aside, and with a solemn gesture, he pointed toward the capital's southernmost reach.

"Mother, there is a large white building on the hill yonder," Lincoln said. He meant the Government Hospital for the Insane. "Try and control your grief, or it will drive you mad, and we may have to send you there."

Her sobbing revived.

Hay felt soiled—this was something he ought never have seen. What *had* he seen? Were all marriages, he wondered, cauldrons of violence and fear? Had the president grown impervious to anyone else's pain? (No, that could not be.) Or was the Hell-cat simply beyond salvation?

⊢⟩═⟨⊣

William Seward was all in gray, and despite that—or because of it—he glittered at the head of the table. His disorderly gray hair, his gray-and-maroon waistcoat, the pallor that seemed wise rather than irresolute—Hay marveled at how lively the Confederate color could look. The grays blended suavely with the mahogany furnishings and the wine-colored walls. The secretary of state's mansion, along the eastern edge of Lafayette square, stood within a rifle shot of the president's house. Its elegance suggested a woman's touch, although owing to her neurasthenia, Frances had shunned the swamp of Washington and stayed in upstate New York. Hay could conclude only that the taste was Seward's.

Sophistication was merely one of the qualities Hay admired in the secretary of state. His profanity was another, and his ease with a Havana and a scotch. Also, his unpredictable insights and his fearlessness about ugly truths and his shrewdness in grasping a situation without revealing any thoughts of his own. And his cutting humor, even when it was directed at Hay.

How else to interpret the *placement* at this evening's table except as an instrument for the host's private amusement at Hay's expense? Hay was seated between two dowagers and directly across the table—but separated from ease of conversation by an arrangement of tulips and a pair of crystal candlesticks braided with orchids—from Kate Chase. She was a vision in a black frock that revealed more than it concealed. A male admirer sat at each elbow. On her right, Mr. Sprague, the boy governor of Rhode Island, counterpoised by a handsome but stupid congressman from New York whose support Kate's father would need if (when?) he ran for president again in 'sixty-four. Another of Seward's pranks, no doubt. So, Hay found himself exchanging labyrinthine sentences with the woman to his left, a tiny woman with a silo of thin white hair, who claimed as her son the loudmouthed senator from Massachusetts currently haranguing Seward about the president's "folly of constipated emancipation." *Serves Seward right,* Hay thought. The secretary of state was making pitifully little effort to suppress a smile.

Through the turtle soup, the shad, the lamb, the asparagus, the terrapin, the french kisses—Hay lost count of the courses—a constant, vexing presence was Kate Chase's merriment. Hay took it personally, for he was morally certain that was how it was meant. Why did he let himself be tortured so?

"And yes, my dear Mister Hay, the quality of the Madeira has been frightful of late"—Hay politely allowed the jowl-drooping dowager to his right to prattle on—"and we can only pray that this terrible war will be finished by spring, however it might . . ."

It was over the dessert of charlotte russe that Kate Chase trilled his name, with her patented admixture of deference and mockery. "Oh, Mister Hay, you can imagine my dear father's joy when he learned of your opposition to his reasonable request."

"Regarding?" said Hay, although he could guess. A newspaperman in Ohio who was a political ally of the treasury secretary's had decided he had the talents to serve as the minister plenipotentiary to Czar Alexander II. Hay was surprised that Miss Chase was so unmindful of the capital's customs as to bring up a matter of business—of office seeking, no less—over dinner. Too much Madeira, perhaps. Or the latest evidence that the Chases, father and daughter, operated in the absence of shame.

"Oh, Mister Hay, I do believe that you are aware already. Unless the thwarting of qualified applicants has become a matter of daily routine."

"Oh, that is my hope for the day when I awake each and every morning. For every position, we have a luxuriance of qualified applicants. This is a fertile country in that regard."

"You do have a way with words, Mister Hay. If perhaps you would indulge me, then—I understand you are a poet. In your soul, I mean." She moved one of the vases aside.

"My soul is a complicated place, Miss Chase. Someday, perhaps, you will be so good as to explain it to me."

"If I had the time, I might enjoy that. But more immediately, I was hoping you would write a poem for us here."

"Now?"

"You say you are unable?"

"Never. Any subject in particular?"

"Oh yes," she said. "Me."

Hay saw this could come to no good. Every escape looked like cowardice, and any attempt to . . . well, every line, every *word,* was a peril. He would need to navigate between the Scylla and Charybdis of flattery and malice. Hay was prone to say he liked a challenge more frequently than he actually did.

"Easy subject," Hay said, dismayed at the silence around the table. "Allow me the honor of trying. *A young woman known well for her chestnut hair.* No, *A young woman* renowned *for her chestnut hair.*"

Kate Chase leaned toward him, her long lashes fluttering; her crinkled smile sent spasms through Hay.

"*Spent her days . . . mooning over her papa's fate.*"

That brought a scowl from Kate Chase, but the rest of the table perked up.

"*Only at night . . . nighttime . . .* No, *night . . . Only at night when the stars looked oh so fair.*"

Cliché had reared its ugly head, and the rhythm was a-kilter, but Hay saw no choice but to soldier on. He considered the rhymes for *fate,* then took on a performer's voice, to project to Seward's end of the table. (At Brown he had auditioned for the part of Iago but lost out to an Episcopal minister's son.) "And . . . if I may . . ."

Hay glanced at Seward, who smiled like a proud father.

> *A young woman renowned for her chestnut hair*
> *Spent her days . . . contriving her papa's fate.*

At the end of the table, a thump of delight.

> *Only if blocked by vases—yes, yes—moved here or there,*
> *Could—no, would. Would she resist letting a man kiss . . .*
>   *fair Kate.*

The deep blush on Kate Chase's cheeks was Hay's prize—her embarrassment at the flattery she could hardly renounce, tied to a poke at her deserving, Iago-ish father.

"A second verse!" the Prussian ambassador cried out. Silverware clattered.

Hay said, "I shall retire after one round, my dear sir, and declare myself grateful I am still on my feet." He half stood and bowed.

"Hear, hear!" Seward shouted before inviting the women to take their coffee in the front parlor. The men adjourned to the drawing room, where they sipped brandy, puffed on segars, admired the crackling fire, and talked of the war. Of General Pope's sweep down the Mississippi River toward the Confederate heartland, of the two Union gunboats that silenced a Confederate field battery in Tennessee, of Jefferson Davis's proclamation of martial law, of interpretations of General McClellan's behavior—here, voices were raised—as that of a prudent man or a coward. On the last, Seward was silent, as was Hay. Not a word about the Harpers Ferry pontoons, Hay was relieved to note. In Washington City, some secrets stayed secret (although if this one escaped, Hay reckoned, no harm done).

After a second brandy and before a second Havana—Seward's taste in both vices was impeccable—Hay rose from the cracked leather armchair to take his leave. Four or five guests lingered, but Seward signaled him to stay. Eleven o'clock had passed before only Hay remained.

Seward put down his glass and picked up his segar, which had gone out. He pushed his Cyrano nose into a handkerchief and showed no inhibition, which Hay took as a compliment. "Hay, what is the use of growing old?" he said, staring into the fire. "You learn something of men and things, but never until too late to use it."

"Well, teach it to me, Governor, and I shall be glad to put it to use."

"I would be glad to, my boy—I bet you would. And let me say, I have also learned something of women, Hay, and one thing I have learned is that *that* young woman is not the right young woman for you."

"Miss Chase?" Hay was surprised at his relief to hear this. "Why do you say that?"

"I do understand the attraction—I am not too old for that." A twinkle in Seward's eyes. "But she is not a kind person. Kindness is something that every man needs from a wife. You especially, my dear boy. And patience. Our Miss Chase is cruel when it is necessary—even women can be forgiven for that—but also when it is unnecessary. The only man she will ever make happy is her shit-ass of a father. Indeed, she *is* her father, in a . . . comelier package. Let the good governor of Rhode Island achieve his fondest wish."

"It seems he will whether I let him or not."

"Then be grateful, my boy."

Seward was probably right, but surely the secretary of state had not taken him aside to offer romantic counsel. "What else have you learned, Governor, that might be put to good use?"

"I am curious at the moment about what *you* have learned. How is your investigation coming?"

"What investiga—"

"There are two?"

Now, Hay understood the summons. Seward's relationship with Lincoln was more than professional or political; it was personal. The rivals for the Republican presidential nomination in 'sixty had truly become friends—Seward's doing, mostly. He had courted Willie and Tad with a gift of kittens and prevailed on the president to come along for carriage rides in the late afternoon and conversed with him for hours in comfortable chairs about war and politics and life. Whenever Lincoln wrestled with a decision of state, Seward saw dangers and opportunities that others overlooked, and he was unafraid to say so. Maybe he *could* help Hay.

Hay said, "What did he tell you?"

"The basics." Seward poured Hay a fresh snifter of brandy and seated himself near the fire, oblique to his guest. "Now, *you* tell me."

Relieved to have Seward to confide in, Hay unburdened himself—the pair of messages in his satchel, the implication of the successful embalming, the arsenic in the embalming fluid, the toxic presence of mercury, Dr. Stone's heroic intentions, the accusations of disloyalty in Potter's files, John Watt's attempt at extortion, Tad's dark lady—"*If* there was one, and with Tad, you never know. Someone did poison Willie—that seems clear—and maybe tried to poison Tad. Only because Tad is a . . . blackguard in miniature did he survive. That is my working theory, anyway. Until this morning, I was thinking it was a secesh conspiracy at work. John Watt, Stackpole, the painter Spaulding, who has gone south, by coincidence or not—*those* blackguards. But now I am not so sure. This dark lady—if it was not Missus Keckly, who could it be?"

Seward stared into the fire, nursing his snifter in his delicately formed hand. Light flickered over the hand-tooled bindings of books that stretched from floor to ceiling. A room of dark wood and leather, in which confidences seemed easy and right.

"You have ruled out Missus Keckly?" said Seward.

"Tad has."

"But as you say, Tad's word is . . . not the Gospel according to . . . Mark, was it?"

"Do you have some reason to think that *she* . . . ?" Hay stopped; the words hung there. "Why would a mulatto, any Negress, conspire with secessionists? They should hate one another."

"You are assuming there was a conspiracy. And that secessionists were involved."

"Yes, Nicolay always says, 'Never assume.' I keep assuming."

"We wouldn't need rules to live by if we did not break them from time to time."

"Or always."

"Even more so, then," Seward said. "About Missus Keckly, I would be careful about making assumptions. She is a complicated person. A lot is going on underneath."

"How on earth do you know this?"

"I pride myself on an ability to read men—and women, too. You might say that is how I earn my keep. This is what I *do*."

Hay said, "So, what is going on underneath?"

Seward shifted in his chair. "That, I do not know. But something."

Chapter Eleven

SUNDAY, MARCH 2, 1862

There was nothing so annoying, in Hay's mind, as an unselfish act that goes unnoticed. Hay had declined the president's invitation to church so that Robert might spend time with his father undisturbed; since the inauguration, by Robert's account, father and son had spent no more than ten minutes alone. Robert had responded to Hay's generosity by refusing to go. Nor would he tell Hay why. Probably it was the pain he had felt at the toy store after church, plus all the years of pain before that. Hay was exasperated both at Robert and at his own exasperation. It was not his job, he told himself, to fix the rift between father and firstborn. What a sad, sad house!

Hay wished only to escape into the cold air. He could not bother to descend into the mansion's basement for bread and currant tea, and so he hastened out the front entrance. The sky was charcoal, heavy with the threat of snow. He pulled his greatcoat tighter around him and felt—heard—a rumble in his belly. He ignored it.

He crossed the Avenue to Lafayette square. The iron gate, adorned by eagles, was unlocked. The bare branches of the sycamores and tulip trees offered skeletal protection. Straight ahead, Andrew Jackson sat astride his horse rearing high—the "tippy-toe" statue, as Tad called it. Cavalry horses were kept in temporary stables at the rear of the square, and Hay stepped over the evidences and exited through the back gate. Across H street, worshipers surged into the daisy-yellow confines of Saint John's Church—the church of presidents, it was called, although not of this one. Hay steered clear, turning west. Only then did he remember whose house lay ahead.

The three-story gray manse with the Corinthian-columned entrance was stately to the point of inertness. This could not be said for the man who answered Hay's knock. Not a butler but the navy secretary himself. Gideon Welles's bushy snow-white whiskers looked glued on, like one of Pinkerton's men in tawdry disguise. The curls that reached his shoulders, along with his ethereal ways, had inspired the newspapermen to dub him "Marie Antoinette." His unwillingness to venture an opinion no matter what the cabinet was discussing peeved Lincoln. Hay's opinion was that Welles was a fool.

"And what do *you* want?" said Welles. He scrutinized Hay like a beetle under a microscope.

"Good morning, sir," Hay replied, wielding courtesy as a shot to the gut. "Is your wife, by any chance, available for a conversation?"

"We are leaving for church, young man, and I suggest you do the same."

"I need only a few minutes," Hay said, uncertain this was so.

"What for?"

Welles's face was stern, and Hay thought of refusing to say. But that way, he would not get past the door, and he must. A white nurse might tell him of a dark lady, which a colored nurse might not.

"About the nurses who tended to Willie and Tad—the other nurses," Hay quickly added.

A hesitation, then with a Connecticut archness: "I shall see if Missus Welles is indisposed." Hay expected to be left on the doorstep, but the navy secretary ushered Hay into the parlor.

Hay had learned you could never judge a man's true nature from examining his parlor, but you could always tell what he wanted others to think of him. The nut brown and maroon of the upholstery and the drapes reminded Hay of a New England patrician's sanctum. A vase of orchids and a Bible sat on the center table's octagonal marble top; crossed cutlasses were mounted over the doorway. Volumes of Emerson, Thoreau, and Hawthorne lined the walnut bookcase, their bindings uncracked. Only *Uncle Tom's Cabin* showed signs of intrusion. On a higher shelf sat the carving of a skull from some primitive land.

"Mister Hay." The cultured voice came from the doorway. Hay turned and saw the plain but poised countenance of Mary Jane Welles. "May I be of service?"

"Thank you, yes."

"And please, if you would have a seat. There is no need for you to stand."

"Oh, I like to look at books."

"Then perhaps you shall write one someday. I understand you have a talent."

"Who on earth told you that?"

"One can spend hours by a boy's bedside and learn many things. Could I offer you some tea, Mister Hay? I would offer coffee but you might think I was showing off."

Hay understood why the Hell-cat had taken to Mary Jane Welles. She wore her empathy on her sleeve, and her friendship with Mrs. Lincoln offered the imprimatur of eastern breeding upon this outlander from the West. And yet she was homely enough—her nose was blunt and bony, and gray curls hung to her neck—to pose no threat.

"Your husband tells me you are leaving for church. I do not wish to delay you."

"God can spare me for a few minutes."

"In that case, yes, please, tea would be lovely," Hay said, slipping into his manners for the Providence salon. He hoped something solid would come with the tea.

A shake of the bone-china bell summoned a servant. Once the servant was gone, Mrs. Welles waited for Hay to speak. Either from politeness or a defensive crouch.

"You are a nurse by training?" he said.

"In Hartford, I was. Not since coming here, until Missus Keckly asked. Anything I could do for Missus Lincoln, I would do gladly."

"And for the president, too?"

"Of course."

"I am pleased to hear that, because I need to ask you some questions at his behest."

Hay established that she had been a nurse to Willie as well as to Tad. Had Dr. Stone ever asked her to administer medicines?

"Laudanum, when the pain was strong—that was for Willie. And when he was agitated, a little brandy, on his mother's lace handkerchief. He would take it no other way."

"Nothing more than that?"

"No, nothing more."

"Calomel? Blue-mass pills?"

"No." She looked desperate to inquire but, as a cabinet wife, knew not to.

"What can you tell me, then, about Mary Dines?"

"Old Aunt Mary? What would you like to know?"

"Is she trustworthy?"

"Entirely. Whatever she says she will do, she does. That is my experience. I would trust her with my life."

"With your child's life?"

"I already have. Last fall, with our Hubert, when he had typhoid fever. I recommended her to Missus Keckly, when she asked me."

"Your son recovered?"

"Yes, thank the Lord. He was horribly ill, but Old Aunt Mary has a knack for soothing a child. As settled as the earth, she is, and as reliable. A child senses that—Hubert did. Tad did, too."

"How was she freed, do you know?"

"That, you would have to ask her. I do know who owned her. You might have heard of him. A former senator and war secretary by the name of Jefferson Davis."

Hay gasped. The Confederate president's former slave was caring for the Union president's sons.

The servant returned with a silver tray, relieving Hay of the need to reply. An ornate teapot and two fluted cups—sacredamn, no food! Mrs. Welles poured, and Hay sipped a beverage that looked and tasted rather like water. New England austereness. Homeopathic tea.

"Does Missus Keckly know this?" Hay managed. "Or the Lincolns?"

"Missus Keckly does. That is how she knows Old Aunt Mary. From the Davises."

"What do you mean?"

"Missus Keckly made gowns for Varina Davis until the day she and her husband left for Montgomery to take the rebel presidency. Varina begged Missus Keckly to go with them, but it was out of the question. If you had purchased *your* freedom, would you move to Alabama of your own volition, even with a guarantee you would remain free?"

"So, *that* is their connection, through . . . ?"

"Oh yes, Varina Davis. A hostess of some repute, while they were here. Warm, vivacious—nothing like her husband. When he served in President Pierce's cabinet, they often hosted at the Executive Mansion, substituting for Franklin and Jane on the occasions the president had overimbibed. Mister Davis was a senator from Mississippi when Missus Keckly came to Washington City and Varina learned of her talents."

"How on earth does a woman of . . . color make herself known?"

"As in any business—word of mouth. Recommendations from her clients in Saint Louis. That was where her owner's daughter took her, as I understand it. Her first gown here she made for Missus Lee."

"*That* Missus Lee? The general's . . . ?"

"The same. A lavender silk, a remarkable creation. It was still the subject of conversation when we arrived a year ago. Such a silly city this is."

This was the most remarkable woman Hay had met here. As down-to-earth as a man. More than her husband was, for certain. Hay decided he would believe anything Mary Jane Welles said.

"One thing led to another, or should I say, one *dress* led to another. Eventually, to Missus Lincoln."

"From Robert E. Lee's wife to Jefferson Davis's wife to Abraham Lincoln's wife—for a mulatto seamstress, this is fancy footwork."

"Not in this small town. It was Missus Keckly's mention of Varina that persuaded Missus Lincoln to hire her. After some haggling, of course, as to price."

"Then I should like to talk to whoever recommended her to Missus Lincoln."

Ever so genially, Mrs. Welles said, "You already are."

"She is never *not* there," Hay said, "so nobody notices her anymore." He picked at his stringy capon. This was not a day that Willard's deserved its culinary reputation, due to (Hay judged magnanimously) the press of the after-church crowd. "She could easily have left a message in my satchel."

"Or two," Nicolay said.

"Yes, or two. And she had access both to my satchel and to Willie. And to Tad."

"Except Tad ruled her out specifically. Unless there is more than one Yib."

"Assuming"—an arch nod at Nicolay—"he was telling the truth."

"True," Nicolay said. "But we are forgetting something, Johnny. Her son. He was killed last summer. Could she kill another woman's?" Nicolay sipped distractedly at his tea; his sweetbread with peas was growing cold. "Unless . . ."

"Unless?"

"No telling, Johnny, what a death can do to someone. Different people handle it differently. In awful ways, sometimes."

"Not *that* awful, surely."

"You have not seen enough of life, my dear Johnny, to know what is possible and what is not."

"And you have?"

"I have." A look of pain crossed Nicolay's thin face, and Hay realized with a jolt how little he knew about his friend's orphaned boyhood.

"Please forgive me, Nico." Hay meant it. "So, something like this is possible?"

"With a human being, anything is possible. Anything wicked, I mean."

The Island, located south of the canal, was a place Hay ordinarily tried to avoid. The landscape, almost treeless, grew spongy and bleak, like the moors in *Wuthering Heights*. Colored gangs roamed even in daytime; dead dogs and cats littered the street.

Hay was riding Hasheesh, to facilitate an escape should one be necessary. To the south of Maryland avenue, signs of civilization resumed, if you counted (which Hay did not) the ramshackle buildings of unpainted boards that a gale could blow away. The occasional passersby had tattered clothes and ebony faces. Hay turned right at C street, coaxing

Hasheesh to brave the mud and slush. The houses leaned against one another like drunkards; any that collapsed would drag the rest of them down.

The house at 263 C street stood third from the corner, on the left. Its exterior was painted carmine, almost crimson. Old Aunt Mary was not in hiding.

Hay tied Hasheesh loosely to the porch railing and stepped to the door. The coats of paint did not conceal the cracks that radiated through the wood. How many strange doors had Hay knocked on of late? This one sounded thinner, and it swung open right away, as if someone had been watching from the window.

That someone was a woman Hay had seen many times before but had never addressed. Old Aunt Mary was . . . sixty, seventy, eighty? An elderly Negress's age was, to Hay, unfathomable. She was a short, cylindrical woman with sparse white hair and tawny skin marred by yellow splotches across the cheeks. Her features were surprisingly delicate; her gaze, steady.

"Missus Dines," Hay said.

"Oh yessuh, Mistuh Hay, been expectin' you."

"You have?"

"Please be welcome in my humble home."

The crinolines beneath Old Aunt Mary's long black skirt rustled as she led Hay into the parlor. He expected a dingy interior, the walls speckled with patches of plaster. Instead, the furniture was worn but solid as ballast. The yellow wallpaper and the rag-woven rugs felt relaxing. Hay chose a smoky-brown chair stuffed with horsehair. Old Aunt Mary tottered on her feet, as if taking a seat would show disrespect.

"Please, sit," Hay said, uncomfortable with offering hospitality to his hostess, more so when she obeyed. "By what magic were you expecting me?"

"No magic, Mistuh Hay." Old Aunt Mary's face lit up; her smile revealed her two top teeth gone. "Missus Keckly say she gib you my name."

"But you knew I was coming *now*?"

"Ah s'pose Ah did, yes, suh."

"May I inquire how?"

Her smile was suffused with a grandmotherly understanding. "Yes-suh, you may inquire, but dat don't mean Ah kin explain it."

Hay laughed. "Well, then, you must also know why I am here."

"Canno' say dat I do, suh."

Hay wished *he* knew. Where to begin? He complimented the warmth of her home, hoping he did not sound surprised, but she seemed not to hear him at all.

"Were you on duty that night," he said, "the night Willie took a turn for the worse?"

"What night was dat, pray?"

"February the fifth. The night of Missus Lincoln's ball."

Old Aunt Mary's brow furrowed. Hay noticed a clutter of freckles across the bridge of her nose. "Oh no, suh," she said. "Dat was the night of my dear nephew Absalom's burying time. We was sittin' with poor Absalom, over on Elebenth street, near to L."

"Ah. How often *did* you work as Willie's nurse? And Tad's?"

"Tad, almost neber." If that was the case, she was unlikely to be Tad's dark lady. "Willie, near t' ebery day. What a fine boy, he be. A fine boy."

"Willie, then," Hay said. "He was taking certain medicines for his . . . illness. Including gray pills—calomel. Did you happen to give him any of those?"

Old Aunt Mary shook her head.

"Or see anyone who did?"

"Of course," she said. "Doctuh Stone."

"You saw him administering pills to Willie."

"Yes, suh. Dat what doctors do."

"Gray or blue, did you see? And how many did he give . . . at a time?"

"Gray chalky pills. About so . . ." Her forefinger and thumb moved an olive pit's width apart. "Three of 'em. No, four."

"And Willie swallowed them down without any problem."

"A good boy, dat boy was."

The attribute that everyone agreed on—the one that got him killed.

"Did Doctor Stone ever ask you to give any pills to Willie?"

"No, suh."

"Did anyone else?"

"No, suh."

"Did you see anyone else give him those pills?"

"No, suh."

"Missus Keckly?"

"None Ah seen, suh."

"The nurses, were they all white women, besides Missus Keckly and yourself?"

"Yes, suh. All o' dem but Eva."

"Eva? Who is that?"

"All Ah knows is Eva. A fidgety girl. Miz Keckly knows her, from out in Maryland somewhe'e."

Why had Mrs. Keckly said nothing about an Eva?

"You also know Missus Keckly, yes? Or knew her before?"

"Good Lor', eber'body know Miz Keckly."

"In your case, through Missus Davis, Varina Davis, yes? When she was a seamstress and you were a . . ."

Hay was unversed in the etiquette of asking someone about her previous condition of servitude.

"A slave, Mastuh"—there was no mistaking it—"Hay. The Davises were kind t' me, dey were. Got nuthin' bad t' say 'bout 'em. Not a thing. Mastuh Davis is a chilly man, but to white folks, too, and de missus is a kind lady to eberyone."

"Your emancipation, Missus Dines, how did that come about?"

"The kind of people dey are, Mistuh Hay. When dey a-leaving for the South, they gib us a choice, t' come wid 'em or t' be free. And Ah choose t' be free."

"As easy as that?"

"Nothin' in dis life is easy, Mistuh Hay. Surely youse is old enough t' know dat."

"I am getting there," Hay said.

+ ⚡ +

Hasheesh sagged back into the stable, relieved to be home. So was Hay. Snow had started, in wet, fluffy flakes. Hay had read recently that every snowflake was unique, which struck him as outlandish enough to be true. He bypassed the Executive Mansion basement, with its confusion of odors, and hurried around to the front.

Old Edward was just inside. Hay brushed the snow off his shoulders and said, "On a Sunday?"

"I thought I might be needed."

"Always."

"Thank you, sir."

"Edward, do you know of an Eva, one of Willie's nurses? A Negress."

"Yes, sir."

"Do you know her surname, by any chance?"

"Socrates, I believe, sir."

"You believe?"

"Socrates. Could hardly forget."

"But she was not on your lists, that I recall."

"She must not have been here at the times you asked about."

"Is it possible she *was* here and you didn't see her or remember?"

Old Edward stiffened.

"I meant," Hay hastened to add, "she might have been upstairs all that time."

"Of course it is possible," the doorkeeper said. "She *was* here the night before last, that I can say for certain."

"Oh? As a nurse, do you know?"

"Talking with Missus Keckly." He pointed over Hay's shoulder. "By the conservatory door."

"About what, any notion?"

"I cannot help you with that, sir. But possibly Mister Pinkerton can. He is waiting for you upstairs, in your office."

Hay groaned. Old Edward tittered.

"One last thing," Hay said. "Do you know where she lives, this Eva Socrates?"

"It depends what you mean by 'know,' sir. In Georgetown, as I understand it. As for a street address, you might look in Mister Nicolay's personnel files. Or ask Missus Keckly."

Upstairs, Pinkerton had seated himself in Hay's chair, his broad back hiding his hands. Hay cleared his throat, but the detective did not turn.

"Pinkerton! What in hell are you doing?" Hay took a boxer's stance, left foot forward, fists raised.

"Workin', as usual." Pinkerton swiveled and showed Hay a smile that bared stained teeth.

"At *my* desk?"

"More interestin' than most. Ye ough' to be feelin' flattered."

"I told you last time—"

"Then ye should put yer correspondence where—"

"I shall have to." Hay wondered if a safe would fall through the floor of this worn mansion; maybe a locked drawer would suffice. "And to what do I owe this unsolicited pleasure?"

Pinkerton moved to the uncomfortable chair. "I have heard from me man in Richmond tha' William Spauldin' has arrived. Fer the purpose o' treason, I can only assume."

"Or commerce."

"No' judgin' from his characte' and the facts."

"What facts?"

"His known secessionist leanin's. His earlier meetings with rebel spies. The sudden nature o' his departure. His use of fraudulent, and apparently forged, papers to pass through the sentry at Long Bridge. By deduction, Mister Hay."

More like lazy reasoning, Hay thought. "And what is he doing in Richmond?"

"No word on tha' yet."

"Very well, then. Please let me know." Hay half rose to prompt Pinkerton's departure.

"Somethin' else," Pinkerton said.

Hay sat.

"Ye asked me to perform a job, and tha' I did, and to the customer's specifications." This last, obviously meant in jest, told Hay more than Pinkerton had probably intended, in explaining why he exaggerated the enemy's strength, telling McClellan what he had wanted to hear. (The greater the enemy, the nobler the victory.) "About Mistah Thomas Stackpole. Who the man is."

"I am in your debt," Hay said. "So, who *is* he?"

"He is a large"—a smirk—"and rathah accomplished gentleman, and one with a complicated past. He *was* born in New Hampshire. And his cousin did marry Franklin Pierce's nephew, which is how he came to the Executive Mansion in the first place. And William Spauldin' is indeed married to his youngah sister, Abigail. All as you say, Mistah Hay." Another smirk. "And fer several years, as a boy, for four years and nine months, to be exact"—now, Pinkerton was showing off—"he lived in Maryland. Not fa' from here, to the east."

"Doing what?"

"His fathah worked on a farm but left abruptly, for reasons a lit'le unclear. They all went back to New Hampshire, where his wife's family—Thomas's mother's family—hails from."

"How old was he then—Thomas?"

"Ten or twelve."

"And this was when?"

"Back in 'twenty-three, give or take."

"A while ago, then," Hay said.

"To ye more than me."

"And Stackpole, *our* Stackpole, wound up back around here again."

"By the grace of President Pierce. And he ha' been here ever since, as par' o' the furniture. An overstuffed divan."

Pinkerton *did* have a sense of humor.

"What are his . . . sympathics?" said Hay. "Is he secesh, do you know?"

"His associates are, no question. About him, no proof. 'Tis a man's heart ye askin' abou'." Hay was impressed at Pinkerton's capacity for nuance. "But it does seem so. Took as a wife a southern Maryland girl. Nary a Union man or woman lives and breathes in such a place."

These were facts? Maybe not, but Hay could see that they counted. Perhaps this business of detection was less a matter of finding facts and arranging them than of filling the gaps in between. That took imagination.

Hay hoped he had enough.

"There is more," Pinkerton said. "With me men, there always is." Hay bowed his head to show a deference he did not feel; maybe he was learning Washington's ways. "Those trading permits with the South, our Mistah Stackpole sold them to John Hammack, the restaur—"

"Yes, that I know." Actually, Hay was not sure that he did. He understood the pecuniary value, however, of a government license to trade with the enemy.

"But you may no' know *this*. How do ye suppose Mistah Stackpole *got* those trading permits?"

Pinkerton was right, and Hay wanted to know. "Tell me, please."

The detective—*the real detective,* Hay thought—smiled without remorse. "The mistress o' the household," Pinkerton replied. "Who di' ye think?"

"I suppose I might have guessed," Hay said.

"In hindsight, Mistah Hay, everythin' is obvious."

+——⇥+

Nicolay had no record of an Eva Socrates, which meant she was not getting paid, at least under that name. Nor could Hay recall having seen the young Negress around the mansion. He might have seen her and not noticed or remembered, of course. He did this (as he pointed out to Nicolay) with white people, too.

Hay discovered her address by serendipity. It was midafternoon, and Hay was famished; the gnarly biscuit and weak tea he had scrounged for breakfast had burned off. He headed downstairs to the kitchen, angling for a slice of apple pie, until he smelled the oatmeal muffins, freshly baked. The iron black stove sat high, like a throne.

"Is yer nose dat brings you he-ah, my son?" Cornelia Mitchell said.

"It is," Hay replied. "The most dangerous of the sensory organs."

"Besides de hands."

The cook cackled at her own wit. She was the sort of quiet, wiry old Negress who attracted confidences. Her fierce brow and gray braids belied her dimples and the ease of her smile. According to Old Edward's lists, she had been in the Executive Mansion after Willie had died but not when the second message was left. Hay accepted the muffin she offered on a maroon-edged plate. Steam rose from the center, and he took a bite. The flavor was subtle yet sublime.

"Wunnerful," Hay said with his mouth full. "Does the president eat these?" As far as Hay knew, Lincoln's indulgence in sweets began and ended with raw apples and the occasional cherry pie.

Cornelia Mitchell raised her chin, looked levelly at Hay, and said,

"How a man chooses to eat is the business of his own private self. I will go to my grave, Mistah Hay, and never tell a soul."

Hay accepted the comeuppance with a tasty swallow and a grin. "And how the boys eat—ate? Good appetites, yes? Willie and Tad?"

"Oh, always. Healthy growin' boys. Until dey ailin'. And den dey still eat milk porridge or rice boiled in milk or pudding at any hour o' de day or night. Light on a belly dat's leapin' around."

Just the thought of it made Hay queasy. "Let me ask you something else, if I might. A young woman named Eva Socrates—do you know her? She was one of the—"

"I does. And I'se de better for it."

"Because?"

"She a fine young lady what know her own mind. And has the fool courage to tell it, which I admire. And fear. Because Lord, it can bring a bad end."

"Has it, do you know?"

"I know nothin' about nothin'. Neber have, neber will. Nicer dat way."

"Well, your secret is safe with me. Not that I believe you for an instant. Would you happen to know, by the ghost of a chance, where Eva Socrates lives?"

The cook slid the kettle back onto the fire and satisfied herself that it was balanced. She said, "Why do you *need* to know?"

"To ask her some questions. About what happened to the boys." That was more than he had intended to say. "I am working under the president's orders."

She looked at him, not blinking. "In Georgetown," she said.

"Where in Georgetown, do you know?"

"Yes, suh, I do." She described a neighborhood called Herring Hill, up the hill from Bridge street, where the freedmen lived, not far from Willie's resting place. "Montgomery and West streets, the southeast corner."

"What do you *not* know?" said Hay.

"People tell me things. Cain't say why."

⊁——⊰⊱——⊀

The snow stopped as Hay was setting out for Georgetown, but the fluffy white on every branch and roof transformed the ordinary into beauty. Allowing Hasheesh to lounge, Hay flagged down a hack. An easier trip to bear than the last time: A Negress's shack was an easier destination than a graveyard.

Hay considered his approach to Eva. The question he wanted answered—did she murder an eleven-year-old boy?—was unlikely to elicit a useful reply. He might ask if Willie had been frightened about his medical care (or anything else) and he could inquire about Doc Stone of someone unafraid to express an opinion. What reason could he offer for asking? Actually, no need to give one. He could simply ask Eva if she had administered calomel to Willie and then watch her response. He could inquire about Old Aunt Mary and the other nurses. And about Mrs. Keckly, Eva's benefactress—careful, however, not to show more than a casual interest.

There was an art to this Vidocq stuff.

By the time he crossed the bridge from Washington City to Georgetown, Hay had pretty much decided to rely (as usual) on instinct. He directed the hack to take an immediate right, north along Montgomery street. The wind whipped past, and Hay pulled his slouch hat low over his forehead. Shanties pressed against the creeks of mud that served as sidewalks. No lights inside, no signs of life, other than the bark of a dog in the distance. At West street, the carriage turned east, back toward the creek. Here, the narrow houses were spaced like cornstalks in a drought; a scream in one might not be heard in the next.

On the southeastern corner of Montgomery and West, a frame house had visible cracks between the slats of walls that had never seen paint. The ground-floor window lacked shutters or drapes. Hay peered inside. The room was empty of furniture or movement. Hay knocked on the front door. Hay thought he smelled something burning—no, burned—and rapped harder. No response.

When he punched at the door in frustration, a noise wafted from the porch of the neighboring house, beyond a vacant lot of brambles and stones. The dark-skinned woman was as thin as a river birch. Her voice jiggled, "Gwine."

"Pardon?"

"They gwine. Wit' ever'thing, best I see."

She had looked, no doubt. "Where to?" he said.

An expressive shrug.

"When?" said Hay.

"Yest'day. In the night."

"Who left?"

"All of 'em."

"Eva, too?"

"Dunno. Tell me one from de next."

"A young woman, maybe twenty years . . ."

But the neighbor had turned away and was heading inside.

A flicker of light inside Lincoln's office illuminated nothing. Gradually, Hay became aware of a silhouette by the far window, black against iron gray, unmoving.

Then it moved.

"Sir," Hay projected a whisper.

"I am looking at the stars." Hay recognized the slump of the shoulders, cradling the tube of the telescope that was pointed toward the southern sky. "When you look at the stars, John, everything on earth seems so small."

Hay desperately tried to think of a jest. "How powerful *is* that telescope?" he said.

"You are coming with me," Lincoln replied.

As they crossed the South Lawn toward the stables, the stars glittered overhead like shattered crystal, reflecting off the snow on the ground. Lincoln saddled up Old Abe, his easygoing gray steed, while Hay apologized to Hasheesh for the lack of a treat. The mare was nonchalant.

"There is something I need to tell you, sir," Hay said as they passed through the Seventeenth street gate. "About Missus Lincoln, sir."

Lincoln stiffened at the second *sir.* "There is nothing about that woman I do not know."

That woman?

Hay told him of Pinkerton's report about the permits to trade with the South that Stackpole had received by way of Mrs. Lincoln's favor.

Lincoln took the news without a flutter. Hay had the impression he was relieved.

All was silent along the western stretch of New York avenue except the *thwap thwap thwap* of hoofs pulling out of the mud.

"And, John, how does this concern Willie?"

"No reason to think that it does, sir."

"Then why is this within the province of your investigation?"

"I am not saying it is, sir. It is something I learned, sir"—he thought of pinning this on Pinkerton but decided not to—"and I thought you might want to know. Maybe I was . . . mistaken."

"No, John, no. I would rather know than not know. Always."

The response Hay had hoped for. "Let me tell you this, then, or maybe you already know. That Missus Keckly used to make dresses for Varina Davis. And that Old Aunt Mary was ol' Jeff. Davis's slave. Just a point of interest, nothing more."

"Honorable people, the Davises. Ol' Jeff. was born a few counties away from me, you know, in Kentucky. He is not an evil man. He is a man of his circumstances, as most of us are. I might have been him; he might have been me."

They continued west along E street, passing a few dark houses per block, islands of habitation.

"How is Tad?" Hay said.

"Better, to-day."

"You saw him?"

"After church. Robert and I."

"Bob went to church? I thought he . . ."

"He changed his mind. With that boy, who can explain?"

The Naval Observatory stood on a hill beyond Twenty-third street. Slices of its silvery dome shone through the leafless trees.

"They say the day I was elected to this godawful job, a bright star was seen in the daytime sky, about sixty degrees south of the sun. In Illinois, so the newspapers said. And you know *they* are never wrong."

As they entered the observatory grounds, a drizzle was rinsing the snow from the gravel roadway. The dome vanished behind the tree trunks until the night riders rounded a curve. Next to the silver hemisphere was a sliver of moon. Lincoln stared at the sky, transfixed.

The dome vanished from sight as they arrived at the observatory entrance. The two-story brick building was as unprepossessing as a school. Lincoln tried the doorknob. It turned. Inside, gaslights illuminated the arch of a double staircase that spread like a butterfly's wings across the foyer.

"Hallo!" Lincoln shouted.

No reply.

Lincoln called out again. Upstairs, metal scraped against metal. The president loped toward the left staircase. Hay followed.

"Hall!" Lincoln shouted into the space that gaped above them.

Hay wondered if this was another of Lincoln's stepnephews. Not one he had heard of.

The switchback staircase opened into a round room with a hemispherical ceiling gashed by the largest telescope Hay had ever seen.

"The Equatorial, they call it," Lincoln whispered as if in the presence of something sacred. "A fourteen-foot refractor." To Hay, it looked like a python ready to pounce.

Lincoln called again, "Professor Hall!"

From somewhere above, a nasal voice replied, "Whoever you are, I am at your service. Begging your patience."

Footsteps clopped down a metal ladder from the telescope's nether reach. Following the legs, the torso, and the shoulders appeared the head of a meek-looking man. His beard was too lush and his forehead too expansive to suit his shortness. Yet his erect posture announced that the only opinion that mattered to him was his own. He betrayed no surprise in finding at his feet the nation's chief magistrate.

"Mister Lincoln, what may I do for you, sir?" The astronomer spoke with a patrician New Englander's lilt. He was no Kentuckian.

"Just to look into the heavens, if I might, Professor Hall."

"I will be glad to assist you in any way I can."

"And how is little Asaph?" said Lincoln. "How old is he, now?"

The astronomer's smile split his face like an overripe melon. "Two and a half, sir, and into every kind of mischief. He understands everything and ignores what he pleases. A keeper he is, sir."

Hay worried that Lincoln would crumple, in grief for Willie, but instead he smiled, probably thinking of Tad. And Willie.

"And *your* son," Asaph Hall went on, "you know he was here last night."

"Who? Not Wil . . . ?"

"Robert. Almost at midnight."

"Whatever for?" the president exclaimed.

"Same as you, sir. Just to look."

Chapter Twelve

T he very idea is absurd," Nicolay said, sipping his tea. The gentle-man's dining room at Willard's was empty but for a table of scar-faced men giggling by the opposite wall. "Old Aunt Mary is a kind, kind lady."

Hay licked huckleberry jam from his upper lip—his mustache was filling in at last—and continued his assault on the diamond-shaped doughnut. "No argument here."

"As much as you would like to give one, you mean."

"Well, of course. And I agree only to a point, Nico. Remember who Old Aunt Mary was owned by. The Confederacy's stick-up-his-arse."

"Until when, do you know?"

"Until they went south, she said. I was hoping you would know, as the repository of all information, useful and otherwise."

"Let me get this straight," Nicolay said. "Are you suggesting that the president of the . . . you should pardon the expression . . . Confederate States of America is conspiring to murder *our* president's child, or children, using two freed slaves as his conspirators?"

"Both of them, in Tad's words, dark ladies," Hay said. "And do not forget Doctor Stone. A former resident of the unholy capital of that unmentionable geographical entity. Who married a maiden of that un-holy capital. And whose former medical colleague is now the personal physician to the president of the aforesaid entity. And let us not forget that the painter Spaulding was recently seen in that unholy capital of that entity. Is all of this a coincidence? Maybe. Or might they all be working together—conspiring, as it were? Improbable, perhaps. But impossible?"

"And John Watt? And the ever-present Mister Stackpole."

"Them, too. These are not stupid men. Presidents come and presidents go, and in the asylum we now call home, they survive."

"If this is a conspiracy," Nicolay said, "it is the least disciplined, least organized, most ramshackle conspiracy one can imagine. They are incapable of buttoning their shoes. Should the fate of the Confederacy rest in their hands, then . . ."

"Then maybe there is a God after all," Hay said.

On occasion, even Mrs. Lincoln's prim sister was bound to answer the call of nature, and Hay waited so that he could steal into the Hell-cat's bedroom. He had refrained from seeking Lincoln's permission for fear of being refused, figuring that no matter how severely he sinned, Lincoln would forgive him. Eventually.

Mrs. Lincoln's bedroom, adjoining her husband's, was larger than his. And darker, day or night. A thick reddish globe shaded the gaslight; the taffeta drapes reminded Hay of a coffin's lining. The chamber's occupant lay still, on her back, in the four-poster bed. Her cheeks were puffier than Hay remembered, and the hair that sprawled over the pillow was threaded with gray. The questions he had hoped to ask—about her letter in support of John Watt, about her familiarity with calomel, possibly about Stackpole and his trading permits—melted like a penny candle. Hay felt like an intruder. He *was* an intruder.

He was turning to leave when a shrill voice—*her* voice—chilled him. "He was here again."

"Who was?"

"My darling boy. At the end of the bed." Her eyes were shut.

"Just now?" said Hay, exhaling. He had been holding his breath.

"Every night."

And mornings.

Hay wanted to say, "You were imagining this. Willie was not at the end of your bed." But who was Hay to jab at a mother who was grappling with a grief he hoped he would never understand?

⊱━━⊰

Dr. Stone was hastening from Tad's vacant bedroom toward the office staircase when Hay pounced. The good doctor was never not in a rush.

"Sir!" Hay cried out in his most deferential yet insistent tone as his quarry turned and said, "You, again."

"Please, sir. One—"

"One minute, correct? Your customary exaggeration."

"Guilty as charged."

Candor earned a smile. Hay reached inside his coat and withdrew a folded-over paper and waved it at the doctor. "The president's say-so."

Dr. Stone stuck out his hand. "If you would."

Lincoln had taken Hay's dictation . . .

> *My dear Dr. Stone,*
>   *Please answer Mr. Hay's questions about the medical condition of my sons Willie and Tad, as far as you are able.*
>
> > *Obliged,*
> > *A. Lincoln*

. . . with a single change. Before *questions,* Lincoln had inserted *reasonable.*

The oval study was empty but for the ghost of its usual occupant. Seated in the president's upholstered rocking chair, Dr. Stone's feet did not quite reach the floor.

"What, then, are your reasonable questions?" said Dr. Stone.

"The first one is: How much calomel did you administer to Willie? Is that reasonable enough?"

"Not in the least, but I shall answer it. Twelve grains of calomel, twice a day. Now, what else?"

"How many pills is that?"

"That would depend on the size of the pills."

"Of whatever size you administered to Willie."

"The smaller ones. Four of them at a time."

"A heroic dose, yes? How much is a toxic amount, would you say?"

"Three times that. Are you accusing me of something, *Mis*ter Hay?"

"Of course not." Hay refused to squirm. "And Tad? How much calomel did you prescribe for him?"

"Eight grains. Commensurate with *his* size."

And his orneriness, Hay guessed. "And he swallowed the pills you gave him?"

"Tad? Yes."

"All of them?"

"I just said so."

"Is he not a little too young? I would think a child would need to be ten or eleven before—"

"Nonsense. Any child Tad's age can swallow a pill, if he has a mind to."

If, Hay thought. He asked to see Willie's medical chart—"There is one, yes?"

"No."

"No chart?"

"There *is* such a chart, yes. But the president asked me to answer all reasonable *questions,* and I am answering your latest question, which *is* reasonable—may you examine my patient's chart? And my answer to your reasonable question is no. You may not examine the chart, not without the express permission of my late patient's, this minor patient's, parents."

"Parents, plural?" said Hay.

Singular would do.

Hay was wondering how to inquire about Mrs. Stone's family in Richmond when the doctor stood and turned toward the door. Hay let him go. He could think of no query that would elicit useful information or leave the doctor in any mind to help.

⊰═⊱

Hay hoped to find a moment alone with Lincoln, to gain permission to examine Willie's medical chart. But Stackpole was absent from his post,

allowing more than the usual chaos among grovelers and grumblers besieging the president's door. Hay spent the next three hours answering
mail. Soothing a half-witted Republican congressman from Maine who
threatened to bolt on the homestead bill. Replying to diatribes from the
allegedly honorable mayors of Baltimore and Wilmington about the
niggardly rates for compensated emancipation. Offering the president's
endorsement of the constitutional convention in the western counties
of Virginia bent on joining the Union as a separate state—in a word,
Hay thought, *seceding.*

His mind wandered to Dr. Stone, so urbane, so haughty, so handsome, but not a liar. Nor a killer. *First, do no harm*—especially to a
president's son. Beyond considering, was it not? If Dr. Stone had administered only a third of a lethal dose—there was no proof but no
reason to doubt him—somebody else must have administered the
rest. A dark lady, by Tad's unreliable account. Which could mean only
Mrs. Keckly or Old Aunt Mary or . . . Eva.

Where was Eva? *Who* was Eva? And who had seen her last before she
fled? To that, Hay knew the answer, by Old Edward's reliable word:
Mrs. Keckly.

Hay retrieved his greatcoat.

Hasheesh sniffed at the half apple as far beneath her worth, but Hay
held the superior bargaining position—it was all he had with him—
and the mare, in the end, had to accede.

New York avenue was empty in the late afternoon, and Hasheesh
grazed along the gutter in search of edibles, reminding Hay of Nicolay's description of the city as a national pigsty. Hay's patience lasted four
or five minutes, then with light kicks to the haunches he wheedled the
mare along.

As Hay crossed K street, an overloaded wagon rushed past, bearing
sheaves of winter wheat from the port of Georgetown. Whether from
stubbornness or stupidity, Hasheesh refused to yield the right of way,
until Hay kicked her.

"You will get us both killed!" he cried. "Actually, no—*you* will survive." He almost kicked her again.

The upper stories of Mrs. Keckly's house, halfway along the block
on Twelfth street, showed the bright lights a seamstress needed. Hay

was a few houses away when a hooded figure bolted from Mrs. Keckly's doorway. From the rear, a familiar shape leapt into a carriage.

"Follow her," Hay whispered to Hasheesh, caressing her mane. "At a distance."

The mare bobbed her head; she understood.

Even along Vermont avenue, the procession of vehicles carrying men to their homes after work gave Hay and Hasheesh some cover. But as the carriage rolled on, habitation gave way to long blocks of brush and trees. Darkness settled in, and Hay imagined pairs of eyes peering through the leafless limbs. Hay edged to the side of the roadway, hoping to remain out of the carriage driver's notice.

Hay had ridden this way just two days earlier. Suddenly, he realized Mrs. Keckly's destination was the same. The Soldiers' Home.

He thought of breaking into a gallop and heading her off before she could reach Tad. But he forced himself not to hurry. He had no grounds for suspicion—and no evidence. Hay wanted to know her intentions, to catch her in the act—preferably, just before.

Hay kept a loose hold on the reins, staying a hundred feet behind the carriage. The mud in the roadway, now empty of other travelers, muffled the sound of the hoofs. Across Boundary street, into Washington County, the road's gravel gave way to dirt. Thick-trunked trees lined both sides.

As they climbed into wilderness, the temperature dipped, and the air felt heavy, thick. Hay cursed himself for not bringing a scarf. The mare's breathing grew labored, and it was a relief when at last Mrs. Keckly's carriage turned right. The sky had grown lighter—the moon was rising behind the clouds—as Hay followed the carriage beneath a canopy of bare-branched trees and onto the Soldiers' Home grounds.

The carriage halted in front of the cottage; other carriages were parked farther on. As the cloaked figure alighted and climbed onto the porch, Hay waited behind the trunk of a maple. The door opened in the Crusader-arched doorway, and Mrs. Keckly went in. For surely it was she; her posture unmasked her.

Her carriage stayed put, and Hay made up his mind. There was a gathering of some sort in the cottage. He would never manage to reach the front door unnoticed, nor pass through it without being seen from inside. He could not let Mrs. Keckly know he was here. Another route into the house—this was paramount.

Hay dismounted and lashed Hasheesh to the lowest branch, swearing her to silence. Kneading his sore rump, Hay crossed to the stucco wall, then crept along to his right. Thorny leaves pulled at his coat. He darted around the corner and saw a portico that protruded from the house. There was a door underneath it. Four, five, six strides, and Hay arrived.

The door was locked.

For Tad's protection.

Ahead, just above eye level, was a veranda, which (best Hay could reconstruct) ran along the dining room, the drawing room, and the parlor. Instead of doors, it had tall windows that, in wintertime, were sure to be latched. Around to the right side, underneath the veranda, Hay spotted steps that led down to a plain wooden door.

The stairway was short but steep, and Hay felt his way. Prickly vines crisscrossed the sidewalls that rose up around him. At the bottom, Hay stepped on something angular and unforgiving. His heel landed hard. Only by leaning into the fall did he not twist his ankle. But his palm thudded into the doorjamb. He shook off the pain and pulled himself up into a pugilist's crouch and stepped to the door.

The doorknob felt cold, even to Hay's gloved hand. Stiffly it turned—rusted, for certain—and yet it did turn, and kept turning, screeching, until Hay heard the click of a release. He leaned into the door, which gave way; its hinges squealed like a panther's prey. The momentum hurled him into a dark, fetid room.

He caught his breath and tried to gauge his surroundings, without much success. Shuffling ahead, Hay bent his forearms in front of his torso, as if preparing for a flurry of blows, hoping not to bump into a scythe or a plow—or a person. How many double eagles would he pay right now for a penny candle? Slowly, his eyes grew used to the dark. By his mental map, he needed to press ahead and to the right, to reach the staircase that led to the first floor, then to the second. Where Tad slept.

You can work your way through any maze—Hay had read this somewhere—by placing your fingertips on the wall at the entrance and never lifting them, until the twists and turns lead, eventually, to the exit. This was not the time, he decided, to test the truth of this. The room stank of damp animals and rotting wood; there were things he preferred not to touch. A trickle of perspiration rolled down his spine.

An opening in the far wall led into another low-ceilinged room, which smelled even worse. It was empty, as far as Hay could see, which was not very far. To his right, above eye level, a horizontal line of light looked like the crack under a door at the top of a staircase.

Hay rushed toward it and thwacked his right knee against a hard object poking up from the floor. The pain radiating through his leg made him sick to his stomach. Squeezing his eyes shut, Hay reached to steady himself on the blackguard of his misfortune—a wagon wheel, Hay determined by feeling the spokes. He waited for the pain to pass, as in the ring, and it did. Once the nausea ebbed, Hay straightened himself and tottered to the foot of the stairs, glaring up at the door as if the fire of his attention could open it.

Hay climbed the stairs and, at the top, turned the door handle—soundlessly, to his relief—and pushed. No give. Swearing to himself, he leaned his shoulder into the door. Not a hairsbreadth did it move. He pressed on the door at his waist, and it bowed. The door was not locked; it was stuck.

So, could be unstuck.

Hay stooped and shoved his shoulder, and the door popped open. It sounded to Hay like a cannon shot. He froze, listening for footsteps.

Blessed silence.

Slowly he pushed on the door; a third of the way open, it creaked. Hay heard a high, thin voice, and a second, then a third, all cooing at once, at a distance. Meaning, the owners of the voices were listening to no one but themselves, surely not to any intruder at the cellar door.

Intruder? Who was the intruder here? And where had Mrs. Keckly gone? He assumed one of the voices was hers but couldn't be sure. If so, then whose were the others? And what were they doing here?

Inch by inch, Hay pushed open the door. He bent his torso around the doorframe, glancing down a corridor with a diamond-patterned tile floor. Halfway along, near the front entrance, a half dozen cloaked or coated figures huddled. They moved as one, toward the far end of the corridor. Trailing them, and unhooded now, was Mrs. Keckly.

Hay followed.

The mysterious figures disappeared through a door, which closed behind them. Now, the corridor was empty but for Hay. As he crept closer to the door, he heard a man's mellifluous voice from inside. Hay wondered what was going on—and feared that he knew.

He considered his options. He could remain in the corridor, to be seen by anyone who came late or left the room. Or he could retreat to the staircase and assure himself that Tad was safe upstairs. Or he could slip into the room of the mellifluous voice and find out . . . what?

First things first. Hay rushed upstairs and stole into Tad's bedroom. Mrs. Pomroy jerked awake, raising her double chin from her ample bosom. She nodded toward Tad and smiled at Hay, before returning to slumber.

Hay retreated down the stairway, his fingers brushing the banister touched by presidents, and heard a low, guttural wailing beyond the closed door. The crack under the door was dark—this was his chance. Hay twisted the knob ever so slowly and pushed the door open a crack. The wailing continued, and the darkness was absolute, except for the gaslight that flicked on—with regularity, Hay noticed. Seven or eight seconds of black, then a moment's glitter of gaslight, and then the afterglow, fading to darkness. Then, again.

Hay waited until the next flare of light fizzled, then slipped inside. He stepped behind the door and backed into the wall. In the moments of light, Hay saw that every surface in the room—floor, walls, ceiling— was paneled with wood. Must be the library, as comforting as a cocoon.

Abruptly, the wailing ceased. The heavy silence was broken by coughs. A drum began to thump, with a hypnotic beat that slipped into syncopation. Then a banjo twanged, and a bell began to tinkle.

"Music in the air," the manly voice purred. The accent was British, cultured—*too* cultured, Hay thought. "And to-night, we shall hear from the loved ones we have lost. Loved *ones*."

The gaslight flared again, and Hay caught a glimpse of a slope-chinned silhouette standing across a table. Lord Colchester—that was his name. *Lord*—ha! Claiming to be the illegitimate son of an English duke. A charlatan, more like it. Hay had heard of him in many a salon—a suave and dashing fraud who made the city's matrons swoon, and shrewd enough to deliver what people wanted. All over the capital, and in other places, too, mediums were popping up like mushrooms after a rain, offering séances for grieving mothers and anyone in fear of death—that is, everyone.

The round table was empty but for a bowl of roses. Around the perimeter, heads bobbed up and down, resembling Jews at prayer. Once the music ended, Hay heard a sniffling along to his right.

"Is there anyone here with us? From the other side?" The earthbound voice was whining. "Is there someone who wishes to speak to us? We are here to listen. We *are* here, awaiting thy pleasure. In supplication to our Lord, who knoweth of the souls beyond the grave . . ."

Trying not to snicker, Hay scolded himself for a closed mind. Until he heard the feathery voice wafting from the wall to his left, by a white fireplace flanked by floor-to-ceiling cabinets. "Oh, my mama, my mama, my mama . . ." The voice was a young man's, a simpering young man's, with British diction.

There was a gasp at the table and a strangled cry, "George! Oh, my *George!*"

"Oh no, Mama, Mama, no crying, please. I am here with you now. It is I, it is I. I am fine, more than fine. I am *happy,* Mama. Please do not cry!"

"But, George . . . George . . . where are you, George?"

"In good hands, Mama. The best. Rest assured, please to God." The voice was fading. Hay supposed it was hard to sustain a pretense for too long.

"George, George, George, please, *please* do not go. Stay. I beg of you, please . . ."

So painful was this to hear that Hay was almost grateful when Mrs. Keckly burst into sobs.

"Your George shall return, if not to-night, another time—that, I can promise you, my dear." Lord Colchester's unctuousness reminded Hay of the Reverend Gurley's. "For our Lord, who in His eternal kindness is kind to His children and to the mothers we bless. May we be fortunate this night of our Lord to reach another soul whom He has taken to live beneath His eaves. I speak of your son William Wallace Linc—" A shriek muffled the final syllable. "If you would make your presence here known."

Hay could not believe his ears—what was *she* doing here? Was the Hell-cat not confined to her bed?

A scratching on the wainscoting accompanied a tapping behind the wall. The figure in front of Hay rose from the seat and pushed the chair back with such force that it tumbled over, landing at Hay's feet. As Hay pressed harder into the wall, the person to the Hell-cat's left—a man, judging by height and breadth—pulled the chair aright and pressed a hand onto her shoulder, forcing her down into the seat. A rasping: "This is why you are here, Mother."

Mother. Robert clasped his hand over hers.

As if on cue, a childish voice wafted from near the hearth. "Mama, I am here, dear Mama, here I am. I am your Willie, Mama, your dearest boy." An angelic voice, of indeterminate gender.

"Oh yes, Willie, my favorite boy!" Mrs. Lincoln cried. The gasp came from her left. "Are they feeding you all right?"

"Oh yes, Mama, I am eating well indeed. And feeling ever so fine. I am cured, dear Mama, and I can run and play with the other boys whenever I like. But, oh, I do miss Taddie terribly much. Oh, and you, Mama, you! And Paw."

"Willie, my Willie, my Willie, my dearest boy, we miss you ever so much."

"But I am here, Mama. And here I shall stay. And someday, you shall come, and we shall be together again. With Taddie and Paw. I promise you, Mama, I do."

Robert jumped from his seat and hurtled through the door. His Hell-cat of a mother tore herself away from her dead son and careened after the one who still lived.

While the assembled sat stunned, Hay sidestepped out the door. Mother and son were propping each other up by the wall of the corridor. They paid no attention as Hay hastened past.

Chapter Thirteen

TUESDAY, MARCH 4, 1862

H ay was stumbling across the waiting room barely after dawn, making a beeline for the WC, when Allan Pinkerton accosted him.

"He is gone!" the detective shouted.

Was no act sacred?

"*Gone!*" said Pinkerton.

Hay suppressed the desire to punch him—a hard hook would suffice. Instead, he said, "Who is? And what damn time is it, anyway?"

"Late enough. Stackpole."

"He never comes in before eight. Later, often."

"No, he is *gone*. South. We go' word."

Hay felt the press of his bladder and willed himself to ignore it. "From?"

"The sentry at the Long Bridge. Stackpole wen' across last night, supposedly on official business. Flashed a pass."

"No business I know about. Maybe Nicolay does—though he is *asleep*." Hay's eyes bored into Pinkerton's, but the detective was oblivious. "Or ask the president."

Pinkerton's beady black eyes lit up.

Hay snapped, "Not now!"

"The Ancient said nothing to me." Nicolay was awake when Hay returned, spitting into the porcelain basin. "So, how *did* he get across?"

Hay clambered back into bed. "I doubt he waddled. And no horse could hold him. A carriage, then."

"Brilliant deduction, Johnny."

"Oh, just a skill, Nico, like any other."

A snort. "You should say something to the Ancient. Better you than Pinkerton. Maybe he did send Stackpole on some secret mission. He is a man of secrets, you know."

"Who—Stackpole?"

"Him, too."

In pursuing the dark lady, Hay had almost given up on the notion of a secessionist conspiracy. But Thomas Stackpole *was* up to no good—that seemed clear. The only question was: of what sort?

+>==—=<+

"Who *is* this Eva? And where on earth did she go?"

"What does it matter, Mister Hay?" Mrs. Keckly's dismissiveness struck Hay as near to arrogance. Then he realized she meant: Why should *you* care?

"Please allow me to be the judge of that. And why was this Eva missing from your list of nurses?"

"An oversight, nothing more. I am getting old, Mister Hay." Mrs. Keckly tried a sheepish smile. Hay guessed she looked older than she actually was—in her forties, more or less. An erect posture must take its toll. Even seated, as here in her parlor, Mrs. Keckly did not permit her back to touch the divan. A Renaissance sculptor might have found his masterwork.

Hay had planned to surprise Mrs. Keckly in her dressmaking chambers, but she was a hard person to surprise, not after everything she had overcome in her life. Which was literally beyond his imagining—to have been born into slavery, in a hut with dirt floors, and ravished by her master's neighbor (for such was the talk), leaving her no recourse but to worship her son. Gaining her freedom, losing her only child—a visit from an urchin like Hay should cause her nary a quiver.

And yet, she seemed shaken. Something in her demeanor had shifted—the lift of an eyebrow, perhaps, or a twist in her neck.

Hay had resolved to say nothing about the séance. There was nothing he needed to know—he understood why she had gone. Truly, he did. Nor, beyond the Hell-cat's presence, did it seem to touch on Willie's death. But Hay found it curious that a direct question about the missing nurse had met a stone wall.

"We are all getting older, Missus Keckly, even the young," Hay said. Then: "Do you know where she went? I must say, you seem . . . unsurprised she is gone."

"Why should I not be? People like her come and go."

Like her? "How did she happen to come? You hired her, yes?"

"I did. She came highly recommended."

"By . . . whom?" With Mrs. Keckly, Hay wanted his grammar pristine.

"An old friend, whose judgment I trust."

"All right. Then where did she go? You must have some notion."

"I cannot help you, Mister Hay, I am sorry."

"No doubt you are. Still, I implore you. Who is your old friend, then?"

"Her name is Sally."

"Sally what?"

A pause, then a whisper: "Sally Socrates."

"Ah," Hay said. "Eva's . . . mother?"

No response.

Hay said, "How do you know her?"

"From long ago—*long* ago."

So, she had hired her old friend's daughter, someone she felt she could trust. Nothing wrong with that. That was how Hay got here.

"Where is your friend—here in the city?"

"Oh no. Out in Maryland. A place called Riversdale. The Calvert estate."

Hay had heard of the Calvert plantation, spread over ten thousand acres in Maryland, beyond the District of Columbia's northeastern line, and he remembered why: Its owner was Charles Calvert, a sanctimonious congressman (was that redundant?) who was a member of "Bowie Knife" Potter's secesh-hunting committee. Even as Calvert urged the president to create a Department of Agriculture, he had likened him to a tyrant.

"She lives there, your friend?" said Hay.

Mrs. Keckly squirmed. "Yes."

Then it struck Hay: This was a *plantation*. With slaves. Mrs. Keckly's friend was a slave. Meaning that Eva was . . .

"A fugitive!" Hay cried out. "A slave—Eva. An *escaped* slave."

Mrs. Keckly's eyes shone like onyx. Slavery was still legal in the District of Columbia, and the Fugitive Slave Act was in force.

"Where is she, then?" said Hay.

Silence. She *knew*.

───※───

Mrs. Keckly had given Hay the address—541 H street, nearer to Sixth than to Seventh—of the nurse he had met at the Executive Mansion a couple of times before. The door opened before Hay's second knock.

"May I help you, Mister Hay?" A lithesome drawl.

Eugenia Jenkins was a handsome, although not a pretty, woman. Not at all delicate. Stern lips and determined eyes promised no nonsense. Her shiny black hair, parted precisely at the center, plunged down both sides of her face. She had a brisk, efficient manner and a demeanor that Hay had found neither friendly nor unfriendly.

"I hope you can," Hay replied. He applied his most charming smile. "May I come in?"

The parlor was sparse in furniture or any air of permanency. Hay wondered if she was moving in or out. The remnants of a fire simmered on the hearth, and Hay took a wicker chair that felt too close to the heat. His hostess continued to stand. He noticed a few black hairs coiled under her chin.

"Eva Socrates," Hay began. "What can you tell me about her?"

"A wicked one." Eugenia Jenkins scowled, sinking into the mismatched chair.

"Why do you say that?"

"You needed to look at her once and you knew it."

"She is a runaway slave, did you know that?"

"I am not surprised."

Hay took that as a no. "You worked with her, did you not?"

"I did not."

"Both of you were nurses to Willie *and* Tad."

"At different times."

"You never overlapped?"

"Once or twice. We never spoke more than two or three words."

"But that was enough to know she was evil?"

"You could see it in her eyes."

"That is preposterous," Hay said. "Evil isn't in somebody's eyes. It's in what they think and do. What did she *do?*"

"You are a naïve young man, for which I offer my congratulations. For remaining so innocent in this city of sin."

Hay resented the notion he was innocent of anything. Was he not skeptical to the point of cynicism? Was he not devoted to the low life as well as to the literary salons? Did he not crave experience of every description? *Innocent*—how dare she!

"You seem entirely too familiar with our fair city," Hay said. "You were born here, Miss—Missus?—Jenkins?"

"A morning's ride away. My husband is ill, a weak heart, so I come here. Bought this place, for a boardinghouse." Her drawl had thickened.

"And so you wound up as a nurse at the Executive Mansion."

"I heard there was a need, and I offered myself."

"How did you hear this?"

"Was no secret of it. The newspapers saying the boys got sick. I was in need of work."

"You had experience as a nurse?"

"Enough. As a mother."

"And Old Aunt Mary? Is she skilled as a nurse?"

"Only with affection. Which is usually enough."

"But not always?"

"No, not always."

"Did you ever see her give medicine to Willie or Tad?"

"No, not at all. That sweet old lady, she would never hurt a cockroach." Mrs. Jenkins glared at Hay, as if to reproach him for thinking her animus toward Eva was simply the result of dark skin. "They are all God's creatures, she would tell you. Which I suppose they are. But God made higher creatures and lower creatures. Is she skilled? No."

"Please tell me, were there other nurses with dark skin?"

"Missus Keckly."

"Is she a nurse, really?"

"Whoever is willing to nurse is a nurse. You may have noticed, Mister Hay, the considerable need. There is no magic involved. A smattering of knowledge and an ability not to faint at the sight of blood."

"Did you see *any*one administer medicine to Willie, other than Doctor Stone?"

She paused and shook her head.

"Or anyone coming into Willie's room who had no business there? Or into Tad's room? Mister Watt, perhaps? Or Mister Stackpole?"

"I do believe I saw Mister Stackpole in Willie's room once or twice, looking for the president, so he said."

"The president was not there either time?"

"No. He seemed surprised to see me, but both times he turned and left."

+=+=+

Hasheesh poked along H street, and Hay let her, caught in a confusion of images that passed for thought. Maybe Hasheesh felt the same—she ignored a turkey's carcass in the gutter. Whenever Hay tried to follow a strand of conjecture and fact, it seemed to lead back to Mrs. Keckly. Certainly, Eva did. Old Aunt Mary, too. Mrs. Keckly had hired all the nurses. She certainly had the run of the mansion. And the séance, which had nothing to do with anything. Other than death.

Mrs. Keckly could not possibly be a secessionist—could she? A mulatto? Yet, her relationships with the grandest dames of the Confederacy suggested . . . what? A willingness to put money before morals? Possibly. But how could he reproach a woman—a former slave, yet—for earning her way? Or maybe Nicolay was right. (Wasn't he always?) The death of a child—who could tell how a mother might react?

Hay needed to learn more about Mrs. Keckly. And he knew who could probably tell him whatever he wanted to know. The African.

+=+=+

"I was in Warsaw once, ye know," Pinkerton said, "me wife and me, *yer* Warsaw." Hay had caught him browsing again at his desk—again, unflustered. "We was robbed o' ever'thing we had."

The closemouthed Scot was not one to engage in small talk; a gratuitous insult to Hay's hometown must be motivation enough.

"I can guess who did it," Hay said.

"From your skills at detection, Mister Hay, or from insight into yer family and friends?"

"From insight into Warsaw. We have three drunkards, two fancy girls, and one thief. A rather nice old fellow, is Daniel—with a long face and gray, curly hair, correct?"

Pinkerton was nodding.

"He would never have harmed you."

"You migh' tell tha' to me wife."

"It would be a pleasure," Hay said. "In the meantime, do you have something to tell me now?"

"We found Stackpole."

"Excellent. Where?"

"Almost to Richmond. On the road. Me men, in pursuit."

"What was he doing?"

"Travelin' in a carriage, papers in order, his Confederate tradin' permits in hand. We shall learn more, I assure you, after he is brought here."

Hay shuddered to think what that meant.

"There is something else you might do, if you would," Hay said. He stood over the seated detective and rather enjoyed the advantage, except that Pinkerton seemed not to mind.

Pinkerton agreed right away to search for the fugitive slave. Maybe he *was* being helpful. Hay wondered if he might need to perform the distasteful though oddly satisfying task of changing his mind about somebody.

┼══╌══┼

Hay and Nicolay left Willard's, emboldened by an after-dinner brandy—in Hay's case, two. The Avenue was uncommonly boisterous for a workday night. Past Fifteenth street, they joined a stream of people, many or most of them Negroes. Hay checked his pocket watch—just past nine. At ten o'clock, any Negro caught on the street would be subject to a ten-dollar fine and a jail cell until morning. The prospect seemed not to disturb them, as they flounced through the open gate of the Executive Mansion.

Then Hay saw the source of attraction. Above the portico, on the second-floor balcony, a tall and windblown figure leaned over the ledge. They had missed the opening words.

"—day one year ago." Hay had forgotten this was the anniversary of Lincoln's inauguration. "All that we had feared has come to pass. Our beloved Union has broken apart. Many young men have died in their country's service, and many a mother and wife and sweetheart . . . and father . . . grieves." Lincoln's thin voice had grown husky; his listeners stood transfixed. "A year ago, the future looked perilous. And still, it does—about that, let there be no mistake. And yet . . . and yet . . ." A master of timing was at work. "We are so much mightier now than we were a year ago. Our army of six hundred thousand volunteers—*volunteers,* ready to perish to preserve our blessed Union—is as steadfast and noble as any on earth. In the West, the tide of secession has been reversed. Across these united states, we are stronger in our resolve *and* in our knowledge of what the task before us will require. Knowing the worst is the first step toward making things right, and we shall. For there is something else we have learned beyond doubt. Whatever the price required, we shall pay it, and with the help of the Almighty, we shall prevail."

Lincoln turned away. There was a low, muffled sound that Hay thought was gloved applause, until he recognized the yelps of approval in hundreds of throats, black and white. He glanced over at Nicolay and saw tears trickle down the side of his nose and vanish into his beard.

The corridor upstairs was silent but for the creaks in the floor. Hay had the impression the hall had been vacated only moments before. No light was visible under the president's door. Nor the Hell-cat's. Only under Robert's.

Lifted and burdened by additional whiskeys, Hay passed through the double doors and crossed the empty waiting room into his office. He skirted the felt-topped table and veered around the uncomfortable chairs meant for the sort of conclaves Hay sought to avoid. He lit the kerosene lantern and sank into his swivel chair. A sheaf of papers crinkled underneath him.

He found a wad of pages closely covered with scrawl and cleared a place on his desk. Hay leafed through them, deciphering a word or syllable here and there—*temp., tongue, gastric, cal.* Each page had a date at the top, working back from *February 20* to *February 4.*

Willie's medical chart. The president had asked, and Dr. Stone had assented. Now, Hay needed to make sense of it.

Chapter Fourteen

Robert Lincoln used the corner room on the right, beyond the one in which Willie had died. The door was closed, and Hay knocked softly and pushed it open. The room was small and, at first glance, empty of life. Then Hay noticed the lumps in the bed, like a boa constrictor that had swallowed a camel. Nine o'clock had passed, the sun was high, and the Prince of Rails—as Robert hated to be called—had a blanket over his head.

Not for long.

"Bob! Bob!"

The blanket retracted, and a face emerged. How cherubic it looked. Innocent.

"I was dreaming." Robert slurred the words. "A sunny morning, by a river. Mother was smiling."

This felt familiar to Hay. "I can give you everything except the sun"— he drew open the drapes—"and your mother's smile."

Robert's face crumpled.

Hay started to apologize, but there was nothing he could say. "But the river," he rushed on, "I can give you. We need to cross it. We owe the African a visit."

——◆——

Hay had thought of Jamie Hall as a pudgy counselor who was wiser than his years, not as a practicing physician. This morning, however, he was busy with a patient, and Hay waited outside. A child's squeals beyond the door suggested the doctor held the upper hand.

Patience was not among Hay's virtues. (That was a virtue he figured could wait until he got old.) He used the time to examine every detail in the modest waiting room—the unraveling rug, the hard-backed chairs, the grayish molding, the faded painting over the hearth of a darkened woods. He peered through the dirt-streaked window, down upon the Avenue. Across Tenth street, a carriage nearly collided with a meandering hog.

The crack of the door jolted Hay from his reverie of pseudodetection. A hawk-faced woman leaned on a walking stick as she led a boy with a mottled face. Jamie, behind them, saw Hay and beckoned him in.

As Hay took a seat on a gurney propped between two desks, the doctor smiled and said, "And to what do Ah owe this pleasure?"

"I need a favor."

⊱—⊰

Robert was waiting by the stables at a quarter past noon. The fine drizzle had given way to haze. Hay saddled up Hasheesh, while Robert debated riding Willie's pony, who needed the exercise, before choosing his father's easygoing gray. Hay pushed aside the memory of being attacked in Lincoln's carriage. Maybe inviting Robert was a stupid idea. The danger was to *sons*. But Robert also needed the exercise, and not only physically. Hay remembered how the African had taken to Robert the last time. This time, he needed the African to open up.

"Not to scare you," Hay said, proffering a black hooded cloak. "We shall go incognito."

"I spend my life like that," Robert said.

Hay led the way, just in case of . . . of what? Surely, nobody would be looking for men on horseback at the Fifteenth street gate. Hay glanced around and saw nothing nearly as suspicious as two men in black hooded cloaks.

They turned south on Fourteenth street, toward Long Bridge. "Remember, tell the sentries we are visiting the troops," Hay said.

"Which ones?"

"The New York Seventh, up on Arlington ridge."

Their dealings with the constituted authorities would be every ounce as dishonest, Hay reflected, as Thomas Stackpole's had been.

The line at the bridge was a snarled procession of sutlers hauling wagons piled with goods for the troops. Hay considered pushing to the front—this was the president's son, after all—but anticipated the scorn this would draw, and rightfully so. Patience.

Half an hour brought them to the bridge. The lanky, pale-skinned sentry had a cowlick and a haughty manner. He asked for their passes, which Edwin Stanton had personally signed that morning, splenetic at not knowing why. ("Robert, too?") The sentry examined Robert's permit and squinted into his face, then cocked his head and declared, "You is him, him is you. Yer pappy is a monkey stew. Pass through."

Beyond the guardhouse, the shabby wooden bridge had slatted sides and roof. The hoofs on the boards echoed—*plunk, plunk, plunk*—in the misty air. (Every night, the planks were removed across the bottom to prevent Confederate cavalry from crossing in the dark.) The sky was gray, and the far shore was gray. Below, the Potomac was gray.

"John," came the grunt from beside him, "what do you want him to tell us?"

"Whatever he knows. Which I suspect is a lot."

"Does he know *her*—Missus Keckly?"

"She made dresses for Missus Lee. And besides, he seems to know everyone, certainly everyone born in Virginia—everyone with dark skin, I mean. And many with white skin, I would guess, if they dined at the Lees' table. And everything *about* them. A veritable oracle of Delphi, I hear. Or do they admit to such mysteries at Harvard?"

"Nothing so blasphemous. So, why bring me along?"

Hay laughed. "Your handsome face."

The previous spring, Hay and Robert along with Nicolay had ridden up the long hill to the old mansion, after Union troops forced Mrs. Lee to leave (while her husband was off leading the rebel troops) soon after Fort Sumter. The slaves had stayed behind—the Lees' property, in effect, watching their property.

"And why do you want to know more about Missus Keckly?"

"She has been acting strangely of late. And she is in a position to do harm if she wishes."

"Harm to . . . ?"

"To anyone. Your brother." Hay was referring to Tad, but he also meant Willie.

"Why would she . . . ?"

"I don't know." Which was the truth. "I was there, you know, at the Soldiers' Home."

"Actually, I do. I saw you as I was . . ." Robert trailed off.

"Leaving," Hay helped out.

Long Bridge *was* long, nearly a mile to the Virginia shore. A pair of terns circled overhead, uncomfortably far from the ocean. On the river below, puddles of water had collected where the ice had thinned.

"My mother should never have gone. It was her idea—Missus Keckly's, I mean. I figured it could do her no harm. Once Mother has made up her mind, there is no arguing with her. It did get her out of bed."

Ten minutes seemed like an hour, before they returned to solid ground. The muscles under Hasheesh's neck relaxed, while Hay's back constricted. The Union had captured all of the hillside, but Arlington ridge still felt like enemy land.

A long, low marsh lay before them; a squad of waterfowl skidded to a stop by the shore. Swaths of oaks and maples had been felled, to protect Washington City from concealed belligerents, leaving the high ridge more desolate than last spring. White tents covered the hillside. Spirals of smoke rose from encampments, and soldiers ambled every which way, like ants in a daze. At the crest of the ridge stood a pillared mansion—stately Arlington House. Their destination.

Hay led Robert along the shoreline. All was quiet but for the cawing of the crows. To their right was the iced-over river; to the left, a line of fir trees spared from the axe. They turned uphill, past fallow pastures, and reached the iron gate of the Arlington estate.

From behind the brick pillar, a soldier emerged. "Your papers," he growled. He was a fussy little man with darting eyes who raised Hay's Interior Department credentials to within a half foot of his face. Hay marveled at the myopic sentry protecting this army headquarters from attack.

"We are expected," Hay said, although they were not.

"Who by?" the sentry said, squinting at Hay.

"James Parks."

"Mister Parks." This very white sentry offered a look of surprise—and respect.

Hay dismounted and led Hasheesh through the gate. Robert followed with Old Abe. Across a rutted road, the hill rose steeply. Beyond the treeless expanse, the mansion stood isolated—splendid. Hay was struck by how much it resembled the Executive Mansion, in its neoclassical symmetry, the Greek pillars lining the front portico, the wings at each end.

Hay and Robert approached and tied up their mounts, and Hay looked back down the ravaged hill, across the tent tops and the surviving woods, beyond the iced-over river. Off to the left was the Executive Mansion; to the right, the dome-less Capitol. Both of them within a cannonball's range.

In the open stretches of power maligned,

The line popped into Hay's mind—what the hell did it mean? Still, he rather liked it. So, keep going.

Stands a headless temple at a cannonball's range.

He had lost the rhythm—that, he could fix—but now he needed a rhyme for *maligned. Mind? Hind?* (Ha!) *Find? Fined? Blind?* Oh yes . . .

What if the enemy, forsworn—forsworn?—and confined
Should shoot its embers into . . .

Aargh. So, what rhymed with *range? Mange?* Oh, *change.*

What if the enemy, unshorn *and confined*

Should he end the verse with a question? Too late now . . .

Shot his way into the White House, terribly strange?

Awful, awful. His calfskin notebook remained where it was.

A shout at his back reclaimed his attention. A soldier lounging on the porch called on the civilian intruders to present themselves. Hay climbed the worn wooden steps, Robert a half step behind. The pillars, he saw, were made not of marble but of wood (or was it plaster?) that was painted to look like marble, in ochre and off-white.

"And who are you, boy?" Liquor on the soldier's breath was evident three feet away.

"I am John Hay, President Lincoln's assist—"

"And *you*?"—over Hay's shoulder.

Robert drew himself up and said, "I am the president's son."

"Dern't take me fer stupid, boy. His son is bumpin' up daisies."

Robert leapt at the soldier, and Hay bounded between them.

"Bob, Bob." Hay pushed him back. "Be smart."

The sentry drew his revolver and pointed it at Hay's head. Hay ignored it, pleased that he could.

"And strong," Hay told Robert.

"I am," Robert said, leaning forward.

"Strong*er*."

Robert relaxed.

The front door swung open at Hay's touch. The Negro butler in livery looked out of place in the center hallway, as colonels and lieutenants and adjutants scurried past.

"Yessuh, may I help ya?" The butler's close-cropped gray hair brightened his mahogany skin. He belonged to a distant time, before this hillside had ever seen war.

"We are here to see James Parks," Hay said. "Mister James Parks."

"And who may I . . . ?"

"I am John Hay, an assistant to President Lincoln. And this is Robert Lincoln, the president's son."

The butler's lack of reaction was disappointing, although Hay supposed that important personages were as common in the Lees' home as Southern drawls.

The butler ushered them into the parlor on the right. A jumble of furniture and crates filled the high-ceilinged room; the Oriental rug was rutted and worn. The walls, a robin's-egg blue, showed gaping rectangles where paintings had hung. The red velvet divan by the front wall was piled high with papers. The only places to sit were the pair of corner seats, upholstered a ghastly green, which faced the marble fireplace. Robert plunked himself down. Hay remained standing.

Robert said, "Why would he tell us anything?"

"Sometimes, people just like to be asked. I think he has every reason to help us."

"Why would he want to do that? And what do you suspect Missus Keckly *of*?"

"An interesting question." The rich baritone made Hay jump. It came from the back wall, which was not a wall at all but a series of archways into the next room.

The African was a small man without a hair on his taut brown skull. His ears protruded and one eyelid drooped, which lent him a remote and cockeyed look—*fittingly ethereal for an oracle,* Hay thought. Yet he stood with perfect balance, his weight distributed on the corners of his feet, his legs and hips and torso in alignment. No one could knock this man down.

The African's gaze fastened on Robert, whose face was cast toward the floor. "Mastuh Lincoln, 'tis an honor to have you in this house again. Your father, I pray, is well."

"As well as can be expected." Robert did not meet his eyes.

"My sorrow, in my heart." The African's fist swung to his breast. "And for the one who gave you birth. And for yourself."

Robert's head sank into his palms.

"And tell me, then, what brings you here on this beautiful morning that God created?" The African directed this to Hay, recognizing who was in charge. Understanding the distribution of power was part of his duties.

"Elizabeth Keckly," Hay said. "You know her, yes?"

"Of course. She was a favorite of the madam's. And why"—the African nodded toward Robert—"do you ask?"

The African crossed the room and stood with his back to the hearth. The low fire danced behind him. The collar on his black coat was frayed, although his shirt was a starchy white. The amusement in his eyes suggested he knew what Hay would say before Hay said it, which he probably did.

"I wish I were allowed to tell you," Hay replied.

The African nodded. "What can I tell *you* then, sir?"

Can, not *may*—a good sign, Hay thought. "About her character, her friendships, her loyalty—her loyal*ties*. Let us begin at the beginning. Where was she born, do you know?"

"I do. In Dinwiddie Courthouse, sout' of Richmond. On a plantation owned by Armistead Burwell." He pronounced the surname as a single slurred syllable. "A mild-mannered man."

"You knew him?"

"Knew of."

The African stopped—his mind had gone elsewhere. A secret to deft detection, Hay recognized, was to sense when something had gone unsaid. Better still if you could guess what it was.

Try a blunderbuss. "Knew of what?"

"Rumors, not'ing more."

This time, he tried silence, hoping to elicit a longer reply. He cringed when Robert said, "Never believe a rumor."

"And why is that?" the African said.

"Because they are lies." Robert's tone was grim.

"Always?"

Robert flushed. "Almost."

Hay said, "What were those rumors, Mister Parks, if you would?"

A hesitation, then: "What you'd expect. Lizzy's mother—Agnes, was her name—she was a fine-lookin' woman, and Mastuh Burwell got his way wit' her. Lizzy, she several degrees lighter than Agnes. Agnes's slave husband, the ebony Mister Hobbs, he not Lizzy's daddy."

"Hardly uncommon, as I understand it, for a master to . . . take up with his prettiest slave."

"That is so, sir."

Hay suspected the African knew this all too well. "What was he like—Mister Burwell?"

"Not an evil man, really. Less brutal than most o' 'em. It *hurt* him when he had to sell off a husband from a wife. Though he would—business is business, you understand. Is it more o' an evil or lesser of one, to know the pain he cause and to cause it ne'er'less?"

The eloquence of the African's shrug acknowledged the agonies that human greed unleashed so serenely.

"You knew Agnes," Hay said.

The African's posture softened.

"That I did. A fine lady—the finest. Wit' dignity, and a mind of her own. It give her no end of troubles, which she endured with a sufferance to make the Savior proud. All of this she passed on to Lizzy. Everyone hear o' Lizzy Hobbs, fer her beauty and willpower and . . . her airs, you might say. How she held her head, as if she was meant for somet'in' better than the hovel." Hay thought the African gave off similar airs. "Which, as it happened, she was."

"With your help, perhaps?"

"Not hardly. Only bringing to the madam's attention"—the sweep of the African's hand included the mansion and the ghosts of Lees—"what ever'one already knew. That here was a woman of talent, with her fingers and her head."

It *was* astonishing how far Mrs. Keckly had traveled in life. "Her mother passed on not long ago, I understand," Hay said.

"Around the time *your* troubles"—the African nodded at Robert, who sat curled in the chair—"began."

"Losing your mother cannot be easy." Hay exhaled and added, "And a son."

Silence. The African's face was granite. When he spoke again, his voice sounded flat and distant. "One was in the natural order of things—the other was not. Something changed in her, then. In Lizzy. Both times."

Hay waited for him to go on, then exclaimed, "So, you have seen her? Here, I suppose?"

"It happens. The Long Bridge is not as long as you think, Mister Hay. There are many ways to know things, and many levels of knowing."

Hay groaned inwardly; he was stuck at one way, one level, at most. "What changed in her, then?"

"Exactly what one would expect, Mister Hay."

"Which is?" Hay hated to ask dumb questions, but not all of them could be smart.

"Lizzy learned something," the African said. "From her mother. At the end."

Again, silence. This time, even Robert knew to shut up.

Their patience paid off. "About Lizzy's father. That it was *not* Master Burwell, as everyone had believed. Including Lizzy. Nor was his plantation the only place she lived as a girl. That much I know and no more."

"Do you know where this other place was?"

"Not in Virginia. Beyond that, I know nothing at all."

Or he knew, Hay thought, and would not tell.

Hay and Robert returned the sentry's salute and continued down the hill. The sunlight was failing; the sky looked heavy with snow. Below, the Potomac was devoid of life. As they neared the riverbank, the path grew muddy and steep, and Hay worried that Hasheesh might stumble. He thought he noticed a movement in the clump of trees to the left. He looked hard but saw nothing but fir branches shivering in the wind.

Hay waited at the bottom of the hill for Robert to catch up. Hasheesh found a snack in an overgrown bush.

"You all right, Bob?"

"Yes."

Too curt. Robert was brooding—in this way, if in no other, his father's son. The source of Robert's perpetual sadness, Hay surmised, was more than Willie's death or Tad's malady or his mother's forays into madness. It was *because* he was his father's son. Having to watch his younger brothers—and Hay, too—reap the fatherly attentions he had never known.

Hay pulled back on Hasheesh's reins, as she kept bucking her head to the field of food. Only under protest did she point her muzzle forward.

The path swept along the river, which a wall of spruce concealed. Everything seemed still, eerily so. A shout echoed from afar—of a sentry, perhaps, by Long Bridge. Hay thought he saw a white oval flitting through the trees. Not an oval so much as a triangle, pointed toward the earth. A face—yes, it was. Ghostlike. Vaguely familiar.

A noise exploded from the woods, and Hay's left shoulder felt a slash of heat. He flopped to his left and, only by the fiercest hold of his calves, kept Hasheesh beneath him. With his right hand he grabbed at the loosened reins as the mare launched into a gallop, toward the bridge. There was hair in his face—his own?—and both of his shoulders went numb. In a voice of command he had never used, Hay shouted at Hasheesh to halt, and for once in her life, the mare obeyed.

He pressed his fingers of his right glove into his left shoulder. Pain pulsed into his chest. He felt faint and wondered wildly, *Damn, where is Robert?*

Then Hay remembered where he had seen that triangular face before, and he swore to himself not to forget it.

And then he forgot it as the sepia faded to black.

Chapter Fifteen

Opening his eyes seemed so preposterous it was not worth trying. Hay roamed around inside himself. The fog was impenetrable. Nothing he thought made sense; nor did he care. Only gradually did he become aware that he was awake—and alive. His upper left torso throbbed. *Drawn and quartered,* he hummed to himself. *Drawn and quartered . . .* He yielded to self-pity, his lonely pleasure, before willing himself back to sleep.

He must have succeeded, because when he became sentient again, he felt a warmth across his cheeks. Pressure slipped to both sides of his jaw and started to slide toward his neck. Hay opened his eyes. A face hovered above his—rutted, roughly whiskered, with a beatific smile.

"Good as new, soon 'nough." The prairie drawl reverberated with emotion restrained as Lincoln brushed a hair from Hay's forehead. "The doc says."

Hay tried to sit up and say, "Doc Stone?" But it came out as a croak, and he dropped back onto his thin pillow, exhausted. He squirmed, and the undercarriage wobbled—a cot. He was dimly aware of someone thrashing to his left. When he twisted toward the noise, his left shoulder blazed into pain. He squeezed his eyelids shut and longed for oblivion. When he opened them again—seconds later? hours?—the kindly gray eyes were gazing down upon him.

"Did I ever tell you, John," Lincoln said, "about the soldier who was wounded at Dranesville?" Jeb Stuart's rebels had skirmished with McClellan's troops just before Christmas, in northern Virginia. "A young lady accompanied me to the hospital, and she asks the soldier where he had been shot. 'At Dranesville,' says he. 'But *where?*' 'At Dranesville,' says he. 'But *how* were you wounded?' A plucky young woman. 'At Dranesville,' he says again. So the lady asks me to help, for she feels a deep interest in the poor soldier. She steps aside and I ask him, 'My good man, where were you wounded?' 'At Dranesville,' he tells me. 'But where did the minié ball hit you?' 'It passed through my testicles, sir.'

"I call the young lady back, and she asks me, 'Well, Mister President, have you found how the man was wounded?' And I say, 'Yes, at Dranesville.' And she says, 'But where was he struck?' Taking the young lady by both hands, I say, 'My dear girl, the ball that *hit* him would have *missed* you.'"

Lincoln's own guffaw overwhelmed the giggle that rocked Hay's torso and caused extraordinary pain. But for an instant, Hay forgot where he was. Then he thought, *Where* am *I?*

He must have spoken this because Lincoln said, "In the Patent Office, the top floor, the hospital here." After the waves of wounded soldiers filled the churches, schoolhouses, and public halls, the federal government had opened its own buildings next.

"What better place to . . . convalesce," Lincoln said. "With the telescopes and threshers and sewing machines—these things I love so." Lincoln was the only president to hold a patent, for a device to lift a boat over shoals. He pointed to the glass-front cabinet at Hay's feet. "Look at the model of this Gatling gun here. The latest version, with the reloadable steel chambers. Six barrels, two hundred rounds a minute. They use percussion caps, you know. Doctor Gatling personally swore to me—were you in the room?—that his gun would fire so fast, and the carnage would be so dreadful, that this single invention would bring an end to war, all war. I would venture to say he has yet to be proven correct."

Hay understood the reason for Lincoln's prolixity, and he was touched. It was meant as a lullaby, and it worked. The fatherly grasp on his uninjured shoulder was a steadying force.

The next time Hay awakened, something was blocking the sunlight. His shoulder felt a twinge, nothing worse, and he resisted the temptation to test it. Millimeter by millimeter, he opened his eyes. The vaulted ceiling was high above him; through the skylights the sun struggled to break through the clouds. Everything was a blur.

"You all right, John?"

The reedy voice beside his head was familiar. Another way in which Robert resembled his father.

Hay was overwhelmed with embarrassment at his awful—unforgivable—lapse of judgment. Inviting Robert along might have gotten him killed. The saving grace was that he, Hay, had been hit with the bullet surely meant for the president's son.

"Bob, are *you* all right?"

"Me? You are the one who got shot."

"Why would anyone want to shoot me?"

"Who wouldn't?" said Robert. The glint of a smile. "Whoever it was, was not much of a shot."

"Seems to be true, by the weight of the evidence." Hay clasped his left shoulder with care. "A graze, nothing worse."

>—<—<—|

The next time Hay awoke, sunlight was reflecting off the cabinet's glass panes. He was relieved to be alone—well, not alone. He propped himself on his elbows; to his right and to his left, a double row of cots led to the distant walls.

When he sat up, his shoulder hurt like hell. Might a bullet or a minié ball have lodged inside? He had not seen a doctor to ask. He started to sag back but steeled himself. If these soldiers could brave their wounds, so could he.

Except that the moans from nearby cots undercut his premise. "Mama, Mama"—from Hay's left. A carrot-haired boy, scrawny, no more than sixteen or seventeen. The coarse blanket traced the outline of one leg and not the other, and the stump of his right arm rested on top. Hay could think of nothing to say, and he had learned from painful experience that if he had nothing to say, it was wise to keep his mouth shut.

In the high-ceilinged gallery, with its graceful windows and marble columns, the cots were out of place. Each was occupied by a bandaged head, a half limb, a tangle of man and bloodstained cloth. Hay could do nothing for these men—these *boys*. Write a letter home, if his neighbor was—had been—right-handed? He had no business being here, with soldiers who had left parts of themselves on a field of blood. He was taking up a bed from someone who needed it more.

Yes, Hay thought, *that is what he could do.*

This would take planning. He was wearing only his undershirt and ankle-length drawers; his street clothes were probably under the cot. Along with his boots, he hoped. Hay leaned over to look, and everything went gray; he flung his hand to the floor, catching himself just in time. Pugilistic instinct.

No, he was not ready yet.

He waited until after the midday meal, brownish liquid with chunks of something—was it vegetable or meat? He had no appetite but ate all of it, knowing he needed the strength. Most of the men, the lucky ones, dropped off to sleep. No one still awake would care what he did, unless Lincoln's presence had prompted the nurses to keep tabs.

Hay took his time. He sat up and waited for the straight lines of the cabinets to become sharp before he swung his feet to the floor. The carrot-haired youngster was drooling in his sleep. Hay reached under the cot and found his trousers and slipped them on without drawing anyone's attention. And his boots. The right lace snapped when he pulled it; no matter. His frock coat, folded neatly at the end of the cot, was ripped in the shoulder—from the bullet, he assumed. He slid his injured arm into the sleeve without wincing—surely, no bullet was inside—but in arching his back to maneuver the other arm in, he yelped in pain. He glanced around; no one had noticed. Out of politeness or indifference or slumber—no matter.

Hay climbed to his feet and felt the room spin, then sank back onto the edge of his cot. He let a minute pass, then tried again to stand, this time more slowly. His stomach rebelled. The best remedy for nausea, his professor of pugilism had taught, was to walk around. No better time than the present. One foot in front of the other. Concentrate, concentrate. Grit and concentration, Hay crept along the wide corridor, past the glass cases stocked with the nation's cleverest brainwork. Striding toward him was a woman in a brown burlap dress—a nurse.

"Privy," Hay muttered, brushing past. He wondered too late what she thought of his frock coat. He was assuming, of course, that she had bothered to look.

The corridor ended, and the hallway to the right had iron balustrades along both sides. The fresh smell was startling, a measure of the stink in the ward. The brightly colored tiled floor brought him to a grand hall with reddish pillars and marble walls. An alcove sheltered a staircase, and he leaned on the brass railing, hoping no one would see him descend. Two staircases delivered him to the ground floor, where the Patent Office was conducting its affairs, paying no mind to the damaged men upstairs. Hay found the door to F street and escaped through it. The sight of the Treasury Department's fearsome façade, a half dozen blocks to the west, was a comfort.

Midday traffic clogged the street. Hay fished for his pocket watch—it was gone! Any of the orderlies might have filched it. He would think about this later. First, he must get home.

The squeaks of wagon wheels and the neighing of nags ruled the road. Along the sidewalk, unruly soldiers wrestled with vagrants and clerks for space. People stared at Hay. Did he look that terrible? The lack of an overcoat, perhaps—he had left it behind. Suddenly he felt dizzy. He thought of turning back—in the hospital, he could lie down—when he spied a hack at the curb. A woman with packages was hobbling toward it. Hay got there first.

"The president's house," he said. "And hurry."

Hay was running as fast as he could along the river—no, down a road—until his ankles started to burn, then his calves, his thighs. He was trying to outrace . . . something unseen. His pursuer was close behind—Hay heard the hoofs and harsh breaths. No, those breaths were his own. His pursuer overtook him and pressed a snout into Hay's shoulder. Pain hurtled through his chest, just as a sweet, sarcastic voice cried out, "Mister Hay! Mister Hay!"

Hay smelled Kate Chase before he saw her. A scent of lilacs so overpowering—truly, a woman who could make a man ill. He opened his eyes and smiled at her presence. She *was* beautiful. His wound did not extend below the waist.

"The most beautiful thing you ever saw, *n'est-ce pas?*" she purred. "And the biggest." Kate Chase tapped at the landmass between her neckline and her neck, made of amethysts and pearls. Above the necklace was a pair of mercenary eyes, belonging to a woman beyond Hay's means.

"Spriggs, is it not—the generous gentleman? I gather he has asked for your hand."

"How you jest about my Billy Sprague. Jealousy, I would guess. And a mean spirit. How . . . *wise* I was to have spurned your advances."

"Not all of them," Hay pointed out.

"Most."

At her coy smile, he missed her all the more.

She said, "And what are you doing in bed at this time of day?"

"What time is it?" Hay could not remember having arrived. "And what are *you* doing here?"

"I went to your office, and it was empty. So I came looking. To tell you—to *show* you."

To rub it in, he thought.

"And why are you still in bed?" she said.

"I was shot."

"Don't be melodramatic."

"No, I was."

"Who would want to shoot you?"

Hay laughed, which hurt. "My question, exactly."

Hay tried to think about life without Kate Chase. He felt a flutter of disappointment, but an organ that did not ache at her news was his heart. Indeed, he felt pleasure at the prospect of her absence from his life. Seward was right, and he was free of her. Hay took a deep, painless breath. A bullet he had dodged.

Nicolay strode in just as Kate Chase was leaving.

Hay said, "Tell me, Nico, who would want to shoot little ol' me?"

"You are feeling better, I see."

"I mean it—who would?"

Hay told him of the figure of the man he had glimpsed—*thought* he had glimpsed—in the woods. "The same blackguard who attacked me in the Ancient's carriage. I am morally certain it was he."

"Johnny, for you to be *morally* certain about anything is a . . . Besides, you told me this morning that whoever it was, was aiming at Bob."

"I did?"

"Yes, when Stackpole and Old Edward carried you up here."

"They *did*?" So, Stackpole was back at his post. The corpulent keeper of the president's door sharing Hay's deadweight with the diminutive Irishman—Hay wanted to laugh but remembered not to. "When was that?"

"Just before noon," Nicolay said. "You looked like something the cat dragged in."

"Tad's goats, more like."

∗⇥⟞━⟝⇤∗

"We found her!"

Hay was dozing and dreaming of laudanum—half dreaming, half desiring—and someone was shouting. Easy to ignore.

"We found her, I tell you!"

A rap at the doorframe opened Hay's eyes. His left shoulder throbbed, and his right fist cocked at his ear. He was disappointed that the blur of Pinkerton was too distant for his cross to connect.

"Come in," Hay said unnecessarily. "Was she lost?"

"Ye tol' me she was."

"*Who* was?" They were speaking in riddles.

"Eva, your runaway slave."

"Oh." Hay *was* groggy. "You found her—where?"

"The first place we looked. Ou' in Riversdale. The Calvert plantation."

"What on earth was she doing there? That is where she escaped *from*. She went back?"

"And was escapin' again. Me men wen' to make inquiries, and they saw her leavin'. Actually, scalin' a low wall."

"Then let me talk to her—to-day, if I can."

Pinkerton's thick beard jiggled on his face.

Hay pressed, "Did she explain why?"

No reply.

"What did she *say*?" Then it dawned on Hay. "Tell . . . me . . . what . . . happened."

"She was tryin' to escape," Pinkerton said. "From *us*!"

"Is she dead?"

Hay marveled that keeping a blank face must be harder than it looked. "She was a fugitive slave who was tryin' to escape," Pinkerton said. "But I do have somethin' that might help explain why she wen' back." The detective reached inside his coat and pulled out a ledger and handed it to Hay. Its cover was splotched and felt rough to the touch. "She had it on her. Stole it, as sure as a hen on an egg."

"For what earthly purpose?"

"Tha' is yer problem, Hay. And I see, my lad, ye have been up to no good."

The right shoulder of Hay's nightshirt had been ripped, to make room for the bulge of bandages.

"That distinction belongs to someone else, identity unknown." Hay recounted the previous evening's events, leaving out the parts he could not remember, which was most of them.

"Coul' ye see who di' it?"

"I had the briefest look, and from a distance." Hay told of the vague resemblance to the man with the blond goatee who had attacked him before. "In the president's carriage—he might have thought I was Bob. This time, too."

"Ye don't look a thing alike."

"Last time, the blackguard never looked. He opened the door and lunged. This time he was too far away. Or just a bad shot."

"Aye, bu' the first time—it *migh'* ha' been Robert inside. This time, it *was* Robert, nearby. Bu' . . . bu' . . . ye say tha' Robert was riding behind."

"I didn't, but he was," Hay said. "Behind and to my . . ." It all seemed such a haze. "To my right."

"And the rifle sho' came from behind you, and to your left—is tha' correct?"

Hay had to think hard, but yes, that was correct.

"So, shootin' at ye," Pinkerton said, "took a very different angle than to shoot at Robert. Which leads me to believe he was aimin' at . . ."

"First time was outside the mansion—anyone could have waited. But this was in Virginia."

"Meanin', ye were bein' followed, more likely than no'."

"Or Bob was."

"Across the Long Bridge. The man coul' no' have known where ye were goin', correct? Meanin', he migh' ha' left an impression in a sentry's mind."

"*If* it was the same man," Hay said. "But again, why would anyone want to shoot me?"

"Oh, please," Pinkerton said, "let me count the ways."

Hay laughed, then winced at the pain.

The knock at the door was timid—ladylike. Hay was dozing when he thought he heard it and decided to wait until he was sure. Soon, he was sure.

"Come in!" he shouted.

With the possible exception of General McClellan, it was the last person Hay expected—or wanted—to see.

"Some apple charlotte, suh—from Cornelia, downstairs."

"Oh, thank you, Missus Lincoln. It looks wonderful indeed."

Had she forgotten her fury, or forgiven him?

"I could not manage it myself, suh."

Ah, a hand-me-down. But a kindness, nevertheless. The bowl held a smudged spoon and most of a cooled apple crisp. Hay's gratitude was real.

"You are feeling better, Mistuh Hay?"

"Much better, thank you."

"You were shot in the shoulder, as I understand, suh."

"That is my understanding as well." Mostly, he remembered being surprised. "It takes more than a graze, ma'am, to incapacitate me." But, he suspected, not much more.

Hay tried to imagine the Hell-cat in a war hospital, drifting from cot to cot, dispensing kindness, one dose per missing limb. Here, she crossed her arms across her breasts, gazing down with a practiced beneficence, and Hay understood her reason for looking in on him. "Mother" is what Lincoln called her, and that is what she did best—*at* her best. The sicker the child, the better she got.

The calligraphy across the cover was confident—a Gothic script of understated size.

Chas. B. Calvert
of
Riversdale
Prince George's County
Maryland

This was the congressman himself, that farmer turned politician. Inside the ledger, the handwriting was legible, professional. The first page was labeled *Rock Creek Farm*.

Alexander	65	$50
Betty	60	30
Drucilla	51	1
Rachael	48	75

The middle column must be the person's age, the column on the right—Hay felt ill—the price. Of Calvert's slaves.

Joe	45	250
Isaac	40	750
Airy	38	250
Mary	31	250
Caroline	29	300

None of the names was familiar—no Eva. The Mary was surely too young to be Old Mary Dines. No dates, nor whether these were purchases or sales or merely valuations. Or why Isaac was valued so highly, and poor Drucilla at a dollar. Hay imagined himself put on the market, judged by his raw economic worth, and shook his head.

The list went on for three pages. Then the *North-West Farm* filled two pages more. Seventy or eighty slaves, all told. A list of property—of assets. Without the corresponding liabilities, financial or moral.

Hay was sitting up in bed, so engrossed in the casual evils of names and numbers that he did not hear anyone enter.

"Ah do beg your pardon, Mister Hay, at this difficult time."

Hay was delighted to see Jamie Hall in an ankle-length sealskin coat. "A doctor is just what I need right now. A minimalist, a homeopath, best of all."

"On that, as on everything else, suh, Ah straddle the proverbial fence."

"As any man unafraid of castration would do."

A merry laugh from Dr. Hall, which Hay joined. He was feeling better already.

Hay said, "In all honesty, Doctor—Jamie—is there any reason I must remain in this bed?"

"Other than the prospect of collapsing from a loss of blood, Ah can see no particuluh reason a'tall. You are feeling up to snuff, I may infer, suh?"

"You may. I can hardly feel my shoulder at all."

"But if you treat it unkindly, you will. Homeopaths *and* the . . . heroic physicians will tell you that, suh. This is why Ah would counsel more rest. *If* you were asking."

"Which I suppose I was, to my regret."

"Do you have a doctor of your own?"

"Seems I must make do with you, if you will have me."

"Ah implore you not to count on me for a judgment such as that. Ah am a poor country doctor."

"As my father is."

"Ah am pleased to know that you come from worthy stock."

"I am relieved to know it as well. And what brings you here, my friend, other than kindness?"

The pudginess in Dr. Hall's cheeks stiffened, to signify the serious man. From inside his coat, the young doctor extracted a sheaf of papers. Only now did Hay remember bringing him Willie's medical chart. Yesterday morning seemed an eon ago. Hay snapped as close to attention as he could in bed.

"Ah found a pattern of sorts, Ah would say. A spike in the boy's fever, suh, every day or two. Of three degrees Fahrenheit, on average. It went as high as 105.6. That would last for eight hours or thereabouts and then fall back."

"What kind of pattern is that—every day or *two*?"

"Every two days for the first week, suh, every day *or so* after that. A pattern, to my uncertain eye. Not a perfect pattern, suh, but a pattern."

Hay was alone again, fighting off sleep, when the slave ledger returned to mind. He had left it on the table by his bed. He opened it and found his place.

Negroes kept

Basil	27	700
Isaac G. C.	40	750
Caroline	29	300
John Hanson	10	425
Anna Maria G. C.	1	80

The list, covering two pages, ran to three dozen names; the valuations totaled $10,000 or more. *G. C.*—what did that mean? The same initials showed up four more times on the facing page. The *C.* stood for *Calvert,* perhaps. The *G.* for . . . no way to tell.

The next page, labeled *Hired out,* listed a dozen names. When Hay turned to the facing page, a chill climbed his spine.

Negroes Sold to Armistead Burwell

Names	age	val.	sale
James	29	$700	$700
Hanson	23	700	700
Henry	19	700	700
Matilda	28	225	225
Priscilla	5	250	250

Nothing familiar. On the next page, near the bottom, was a list of sales to Armistead Burwell from Calvert's North-West Farm. Halfway down, Hay froze:

Agnes	24	250	250
Elizabeth	7	300	400

This was it. It had to be. Agnes and Elizabeth, listed successively, of ages that plausibly made them mother and child. Then Hay noticed the valuations. Why would Calvert value a seven-year-old girl more highly than a fertile and comely woman in her childbearing years? Hay leafed back and noticed something peculiar: Among all the sold-off slaves, only Elizabeth fetched more than her valuation. Why would Burwell pay so much for the girl, unless . . . unless she *was* his child?

Except she was not his child. The African had said so, and Hay believed him. Maybe, Burwell had never known that. But Agnes had known the truth, and Hay had to assume that, now, Lizzy did, too.

Any other reason to overvalue a seven-year-old slave girl, Hay preferred not to know.

"This is even crazier, Johnny, than your usual notions."

"Most of which turn out to be right."

"Some of them."

The concession thrilled Hay. "You told me yourself, Nico—start at the edges and work your way in. I need to know more before I ask her again."

Nicolay returned his hog-bristle brush to its place. "Are you sure Missus Keckly sent her?"

"Who else?"

"This Eva might have gone on her own. There might be something about *her* in there. You probably stopped reading it, right?"

The price of speed, Hay understood, was a lack of thoroughness, which was one of the reasons he and Nicolay complemented each other so well.

"But Missus Keckly's name *is* in there," Hay said, "Elizabeth. Right under her mother's. Who else could it be? And Eva is from there and worked *here*, nursing Willie and maybe Tad. You are saying this is all a coincidence?"

"No, no. That she worked here is not a coincidence. Missus Keckly hired the nurses. If they knew each other from the Calvert place, it is no coincidence at all. Nor is the fact, the evident fact, that Missus Keckly and her mother are listed in a slave ledger. They were slaves. The African said she lived someplace else. Now we know where. In Maryland, a half day's ride from Washington City."

"*You* should have been a lawyer," Hay said. He did not mean it as a compliment. "But let us *assume*"—a pointed nod—"that it *was* Missus Keckly who sent Eva to steal this ledger, pre*sum*ably because Eva would know where the ledger was. How would Missus Keckly herself know, after so many years? She could hardly sneak in and out unnoticed."

"And put Eva in such danger? By sending her back to the place she had escaped from once before?" For Nicolay, a look of outrage was even rarer than frivolity. "This Eva was a fugitive, for the Lord's sake! Anyone might have seen her and turned her in. And there, they *knew* her. What a risk she took! She must have owed Missus Keckly a lot—a *lot*. And Missus Keckly, she showed a certain . . . heartlessness, would you agree? If, in fact"—Nicolay was returning to form—"she sent her there at all."

"Well, consider the alternative," Hay said. "That Eva stole this ledger on her own accord. For her own reasons, whatever they were. Say, to gain leverage over Missus Keckly somehow. Maybe Missus Keckly had learned something incriminating about *her,* or threatened to turn her in. Because she was a fugitive, perhaps."

"But there is nothing incriminating in the ledger. And besides, Missus Keckly is the last person to—"

"Or Eva was . . . a murderer. A murder*ess.*"

"But then, why would Missus Keckly protect her at all? Which she did by not telling you Eva was a nurse."

"Because she was the daughter of a friend. Or because Missus Keckly would also look guilty for having hired her. Or maybe she was—or is—part of a plot."

"Johnny, this is absurd."

"No. Merely unlikely. But so is every other possibility, except for the one that is true. She *is,* however, a woman of secrets, Missus Keckly. Not even the African knows them all. Making dresses for Varina Davis and Missus Lee and now the Hell-cat, surely she was privy to more than her share. And she knew how to keep them, no doubt about that. There must be something she is trying to hide. Granted, I saw nothing in the ledger that would . . . Well, let me read it through to the end." Hay sank down onto the bed. "Tomorrow, on the train."

"The train? Leaving me with your work?"

⊹⊱━━━⊰⊹

Hay was on the verge of sleep when he thought he heard the president chuckling. He opened his eyes—the gaslight in the bedroom stayed on all night—and saw Lincoln in the doorway, in his stocking feet. The short nightshirt hung over his long bare legs, bunching up in the back; it reminded Hay of an ostrich.

"Look, look at this!" Lincoln cried. A book rested in one hand, a lantern in the other. Thomas Hood's *Whimsicalities* was open to a drawing of a hive and the boy, covered with bees, who had broken it apart. AN UNFORTUNATE BEE-ING—the caption left Lincoln in stitches. Hay and Nicolay—for he, too, had awakened—guffawed out of courtesy, and from the pleasure in hearing Lincoln laugh.

"John, how are you doing?"

"I will live, sir." Hay managed a wry smile, embarrassed at his pride in the glancing wound.

Lincoln sat on the edge of Hay's bed. "Yes, but will you live well?"

"When do I not?"

"This is why we keep you around here, my boy."

"I thought it was for my dashing looks," Hay said.

"No," Lincoln replied, "that is why you keep *me* here."

Hay, fully awake now, was hard-pressed to continue the banter. "Sir," he said, "there is something we need to discuss."

Hay filled in the president on the death of the escaped slave—directly at the hands of Pinkerton's men, indirectly at Mrs. Keckly's.

"Madam Lizzy!" the president exclaimed. "I would trust her with my life. Are you insinuating"—he pronounced it *insiniating*—"that she had something to do with . . . ?" Lincoln's displeasure shook the bed.

"No, no," Hay said, lying. "But she knows more than she is saying."

"Do you know anyone who tells everything they know? If you do, you are friends with a fool."

Or are one, Hay thought. Most of the mistakes he had made in his life, and especially in Washington City, had come from telling the truth. "There is something else," he said.

Lincoln's reaction to the report of a pattern—"of sorts," as Jamie Hall had said—in the spikes in Willie's fever was not what Hay had expected. Relief, tears, fist-shaking anger—any of these would have made sense. Instead, the furrowed brow, the cold and calculating look, caught Lincoln in the pure act of thought.

Hay had nearly dropped back to sleep—Nicolay was lightly snoring—when Lincoln said, "So, you do suspect a nurse."

"A dark lady," Hay said.

"You think the one who is dead?"

Hay shrugged. "Could be."

"We need a schedule," Lincoln said, "a schedule of Willie's nurses. Missus Keckly could prepare one, if she doesn't have one already. Then lay it down on a table, next to the pattern of Willie's spikes in fever. To see who was on duty when the fever spiked, or just before."

Simple, Hay thought. *And brilliant.*

Lincoln was turning to leave, then looped back. "I almost forgot," he said. From the breast pocket of his nightshirt, he pulled out a gold pocket watch with delicate links in the chain. Hay thought for a moment it was his grandfather's, but it was too shiny.

"Yours," Lincoln said. "I was afraid someone might . . ."

He had shined it.

Hay felt tears brimming behind his eyes at this kindness. The man's troubles extended to his stricken family and a sundered nation and every soldier in the field. Here, Lincoln had made time for a stripling whose shoulder was grazed. *The grandest gift any man could give another,* Hay thought, *is a moment of his finite days on earth.*

Chapter Sixteen

Hay was awake, and his shoulder was stiff. He twisted his torso to the right and ever so carefully left. An ache, then a stab of pain. Less than he had known in the ring. Pugilistic pain was transitory, however. This was not.

He could stand it—he *would*. He needed only to adjust expectations. His buoyancy lasted until he tried to sit up.

Nicolay was gone—it was past eight o'clock—and Hay shuffled into the basement in hopes of sustenance. The aroma of gingerbread drew him into the kitchen. Cornelia Mitchell was slicing potatoes.

"Hello, dear," she said. "You on de mend?"

It seemed everyone (other than Kate Chase, of course) knew. This embarrassed him a little—it was just a grazing. "I am, thank you."

"Mebbe dis will help." She shifted her scimitar from the overmatched potato to the steaming loaf of gingerbread and sheared off a thick slice. A jar of butter stood nearby, and she slid it toward him, along with a trowel.

"And tell me, dear, how's your investigatin' goin'? Find your man?"

Cornelia Mitchell obviously knew more than Hay had told her. He broke off a corner of the gingerbread and placed it on his tongue. Warm, it was as luscious as it looked—how often did that happen?

"What makes you think it's a man?" Hay said.

"Ain't it always?"

Hay laughed. "Usually." He considered asking the question that was burning in his mind. Unlike a lawyer in court, a detective had no choice but to ask questions without knowing the answer—how else could he learn anything? "Between you and me, never to be repeated to a living soul"—he waited for an affirmation, which came in a quizzical nod—"what is your opinion of Missus Keckly, may I ask?"

Hay looked the cook in the eye, and she held his gaze. He could sense the calibrations going on inside her. Neither of them moved until Cornelia Mitchell said, "She is a lady."

"That, she is. But she is hard inside, yes?"

The cook straightened herself to full height, shorter than the ears of a doe. "Think of where she started out and think of where she is. Softness dunt git ya along, Mistuh Hay. Dunt raise ya no twelve hunnerd dollars. Don't bring ya into the mansion here. Mind ya, hardness do dose things—dat is de way of de world. And de sooner youse unnerstand dat, the smarter a young fella ya'll be."

Hay rather admired the implicit insult. "Was it hardness that got you here?"

"Naw, dat was my gingerbread. But here's in de cellar, Mistuh Hay. She upstairs."

"Let me ask you this, then." He was confident the cook was a churchgoer. "Is she capable of evil, do you suppose?"

Cornelia Mitchell laughed. It was a merry laugh, which succeeded in mocking the question but not the questioner. "D'ya know anyone who ain't? Anyone who know Scripture"—she gave Hay an appraising look—"know dat each of us is good and evil both. The only question is de proportions."

⊷═══⊷

The House of Representatives was in desultory session. That lawmakers would labor on a Friday was astonishing in itself; that they would keep ordinary business hours was too much to expect. Thaddeus Stevens, the randy Pennsylvanian—his mulatto housekeeper's domestic duties were rumored to include the night shift—was explaining in acerbic tones a technical point about his bill authorizing the government to buy back hoarded coins by selling off bonds. "—asks us to allow him to sell these seven-and-three-tenths notes for the purpose of raising the coin required for immediate use . . ." The few congressmen on hand gathered in clusters or sagged at their desks.

One congressman seemed to be listening, the one Hay was hoping—and yes, expecting—to find in his second-row seat. Earnest and alert, keeping farmers' hours, sat Charles Benedict Calvert. To-day would go more smoothly with his say-so.

Hay took the empty seat across the aisle. The freshman lawmaker was a small man with a confident demeanor. His bulbous forehead, formidable baldness, and the set of his bewhiskered jaw announced a serious man whose service to a nation in peril was the gift of his time. He meant to waste none of it, and thus he listened with diligence to the Ways and Means Committee chairman's elucidation, paying no notice to the man who was a year and a half too young for a seat in this chamber.

In a penetrating whisper, Hay said, "I need your help, sir."

Calvert's head swiveled, but his torso kept facing the front. "What may I do for you, young man?"

Hay introduced himself—Calvert pretended to remember him—and explained what he wanted.

The congressman's face and demeanor changed not at all. "And what is your purpose?" he said.

"You are aware of the escaped slave who was captured leaving your . . . estate"—*plantation*, although factual, seemed contentious—"the other night?"

"Of course."

"She was a nurse for the president's son—sons—and the president has asked me to make inquiries."

"As to what, precisely?" Calvert had the self-possession of a man whose bloodline, not his office, assured his influence. The scion of his state's noblest family—his great-great-great-great-great-grandfather was the first Lord Baltimore—was a farmer by trade, an inventor by avocation, and an overlord by profession and self-assessment. And now a national legislator.

"Her background, her history—her habits, if you will."

"Why not ask her?"

"She is dead. While trying to escape her . . . pursuers."

"Justice, I would call it," the congressman said.

"This was the second time she escaped from your . . . estate. She came back and was leaving again—trying to."

"Delayed justice, then. What do you wish to know?"

"Frankly, whatever I can learn." *Work in from the edges.* "May I ask if you know, or knew, a man named Armistead Burwell?"

"Why you would care, I cannot imagine." Hay held his breath. "But *of* him, certainly," Calvert went on. "He and my father did business together. You might also say they were friends. Went hunting together. Shared their dogs and their duck blinds and other things."

Such as slave girls? "And Elizabeth Keckly—originally, Hobbs," Hay said, "she . . . lived at Riversdale, as a girl. Sold by your father, I believe, to Armistead Burwell. Did you know her?"

"I was a boy then."

"Or her mother, Agnes Hobbs?"

Calvert hesitated, then shook his head. "I was a boy."

"And this Eva, do you know anything about her?"

"I own forty-five or fifty slaves, Mister Hay—I cannot know them all. I do know that she escaped. As I trust you are aware, even if the president is not, the escape of a slave still violates the law."

"I am aware. And Eva's mother, she is still . . . *with* you, I understand. Her name is Sally. Sally Socrates."

"I do know Sally."

"Would you have any objection if I speak with her?"

"Why would I?" Calvert's gaze rested on Hay as Thad Stevens droned on. "Though I remain puzzled, Mister Hay, as to the necessity."

Hay stared up at the stained-glass panels in the ceiling. "There is evidence a crime was committed." He locked his gaze onto Calvert's. "A terrible crime. That is all I can say about it. At the president's request, I am looking into this, and I have reason to believe that Eva might have been involved. And in Eva's . . . absence, I am hoping that her mother might be able to help. Please, sir, I am appealing for your cooperation."

Calvert said nothing. A congressman was lambasting President Lincoln for relieving General Fremont of command—months earlier—for having emancipated the slaves in Missouri. At last, Calvert said, "You do understand the plight of the farmers, do you not, Mister Hay?"

The conversation had moved to a negotiation of terms. "My family was a family of farmers," Hay said. An exaggeration, although not by the capital's standards. "As was the president's. You may rest assured he understands their"—he thought of the wartime surge in prices for flour and cornmeal and pushed it aside—"plight."

"Does that assurance extend to recognizing the importance of farmers in the cabinet? Is that a step the president would endorse?"

"He might well," Hay replied, doubting it. What on earth would come next—a separate department in the cabinet for businessmen, another for workingmen? Ridiculous. Why not a department for spinster teachers?

Evidently, Hay's equivocation sufficed, for Calvert pulled a half folio from the desk drawer, dipped a quill pen into the inkwell, and started to write.

—<del>————</del>—

Hay regarded the railroad station just north of the Capitol as an embodiment of the city it served. From the outside, the Baltimore & Ohio station was a grand affair, with its elegant tower and arched entrance. Inside, it was dingy and damp.

The waiting room was nearly empty in a midmorning lull. Hay purchased a ticket for twenty-five cents in postage stamps and descended the iron stairs to the platform. The air was foul. At the farthest track stood the every-other-hour train to Baltimore, four sleek cars with gold and black lettering. Hay walked to the end and climbed in.

A pair of women wore hats ornamented by vegetables of the cabbage family; businessmen yammered in the middle of the car. Hay took the loneliest seat he could find, at the front. As the train rumbled off, crossing into Maryland, Hay perused the rest of the slave ledger but found nothing of use (further evidence, he figured, for speed over thoroughness). He unfolded the morning's *Intelligencer,* which he preferred to the *National Republican*—what was the fun in reading a rag you agreed with? A report of free Negroes emigrating to Hayti. A letter from Seward disavowing any interest ("drop my name henceforth and forever") in the presidency, written without any prodding. He *was* a friend to Lincoln. Lucky thing—Hay would hate choosing between them.

The railroad car's wood-paneled ceiling and its well-padded seats bespoke luxury. As the woods rolled by outside, the newspaper became a sea of tiny print, out of which emerged the profile of a face with noble cheekbones and an aquiline nose. He tried to picture Elizabeth Keckly, née Hobbs, as a seven-year-old for sale. A high forehead, braids like shinnying poles, a humorless demeanor—Hay doubted she had changed much since the day of her birth. (Did anyone?) Her life showed she was capable of accomplishing anything she put her mind to. Anything.

The second station, twenty minutes along, was a three-sided hut, adjacent to the trunk road between Washington and Baltimore. A sign in Gothic script announced: CALVERT. Hay sighed. The family had prevailed on Maryland's mightiest corporation, the B&O, to provide a station for its private use.

The conductor pointed beyond the grove of firs to a mansion on the hill. After the train chugged away, spewing its black smoke, Hay set off across the treeless pastureland. The lack of concealment made him feel vulnerable. This was unfriendly territory; in the 'sixty election, all of Prince George's County had delivered to Abraham Lincoln, the Republican presidential candidate, a total of one vote.

The mansion at the hilltop resembled a French château—its proliferating gables, its widow's walk, the majestic elms and oaks. The old colored butler greeted Hay by name. Word had arrived faster than a railroad. By telegraph, must be—but Hay had seen no wires. By horseback, then. Charles Calvert was taking no chances. Hay wondered why.

He was ushered past an elegant staircase with a bust of the Greek goddess Hygeia (Hay had been awake that morning at Brown) on the newel post and into the southern wing. The butler suggested he wait in the library for Mr. Webster, the overseer, and Hay allowed as how he might.

Entering the room was like crossing into a virginal country. The French wallpaper covering all four walls told the story of a hunt—the red-clad hunters on their mounts chasing the dogs through woods and across arched bridges and dappled glades. The alcove shelves of well-thumbed books—on history, astronomy, veterinary medicine, and (most of all) agronomy—revealed this as a learned man's refuge. Hay was thumbing through a copy of *On the Origin of Species*—this notion that man descended from the apes struck him as a cosmic joke—when a tall, lanky man in a patched-up coat stalked through the doorway.

"Webster," he snarled. "What d'ya want?"

His robust presence belied his age, which must have been sixty or more. His swept-back white mane sharpened his beardless, falcon-nosed face, and his dark eyes kept Hay in their sights. A man you would want on your side in a fight. Not that Hay meant to start one.

"I know who you are," Webster said, as he sat and left Hay's extended hand unshaken.

"Mister Calvert gave me a letter of—" Hay reached inside his coat.

Webster raised his hand, palm forward. "Yes, I know."

"This is about Eva, the slave who—"

"*Yes,* I know."

Hay swallowed his exasperation and said, "Can you tell me when she first . . . escaped?"

"The twenty-first of December. She ran away that night. My job is to keep track of our staff"—Webster tapped the gray-bound ledger that rested under his forearm—"and our property."

Hay saw no advantage in revealing that the slave ledger was in his possession. "Would you know *why* she escaped?" he said. "And why she came back?"

"Why do any of them leave? Freedom looks so simple from a distance." The overseer's tenor sounded peevish, as if someone were pinching his throat. "They think it will be easy to make it on their own, and they learn to their regret that it is not. And so they give up. This Eva was not the first to come back to Riversdale. Here, they are cared for. They have a home."

Mrs. Keckly was a counterexample, but Hay saw no reason to argue the point. "Do you know—*did* you know—Eva?"

"An empty-headed girl, stupider than most." His lips curled as he spoke. "A troublemaker, like her mama."

"I would like to talk with Sally."

"Impossible."

Hay reached inside his coat and this time unfolded the letter. He insisted that Webster read it and acknowledge its contents. It obliged the overseer of the estate to make available to Hay anyone on the premises and to fulfill any request for nonfinancial and nonproprietary records. Hay had escaped having to add *reasonable*—Charles B. Calvert was a farmer, not a lawyer.

"You recognize the signature, yes?" said Hay.

Webster bristled. "Anything else, then?"

"Yes," Hay replied. "Elizabeth Keckly. You know *her*?"

The overseer's face drained of color—or had Hay imagined it? "She lived here a while," Webster said. "Then she left."

"Was sold, you mean."

A grunt.

"Was she born here?"

"No."

"You are sure of this?"

"I am a liar, now?" Webster's forehead creased, from either concentration or brutality.

Hay said, "You were working here then?"

"And living here."

"As the overseer?"

"Not quite yet."

"How well did you know her?"

"She was a pickaninny. What was there to know?" Webster rose from his seat. "Anything else?"

"Not for the moment, sir."

━━►═◄━━

Albert, for that was the butler's name, arrived as soon as he was summoned. He led Hay into a landau and took the reins.

The gravel road passed an orchard of dwarf pear trees and a field of withered hay. All was silent but for the cawing in the elms.

"Dem crows," Albert said, twisting around to Hay. "Master Calbert say no shootin' 'em. He allow no gun shot nowhere on de estate. Yes, suh, dem crows might eat up some of de corn, but dey also eat all dem varmints dat eat up everything else in the fields. We payin' 'em for der service, ya might say. Ever' livin' thing gotta eat."

"How long have you lived here, Albert?"

"All o' my life, suh. Next is comin' my seventy-second year, God willin'."

"Then perhaps you knew a girl named Elizabeth . . . Lizzy . . . Hobbs, she would have been. Now, her name is Keckly."

"Don't rightly know that I did, suh."

"Her mother was Agnes Hobbs. She was sold to a man down in Virginia, must have been thirty-five years ago, maybe more."

"Yes, suh, that Agnes I do recall. A pretty lady she was, with such an air about her. Of a *la*dy. And, Lordy, she know'd it—she sho' *did*." A cackle. "Proper, she be. Her skin the color of a fawn in spring. Yes, Miss Agnes. Such a smart lady, she was, and determined—tha' fer sure. With enough sense to take what the good Lord gib her and use it to make her way, if you git my meaning, suh."

Hay thought he did.

Their destination was ahead on the left. The odd-looking structure resembled a railroad roundhouse, with a roof that rose to a peak, except that the outer wall was not round.

"Master Calbert's own doin'." Albert's chest swelled. "Wit' eight sides."

"What on earth for?"

"De cows, dey love it. It calms 'em, habbin' dem wide walls and all dat space. So's dey gib mo' milk. Dat's science, so Master Calbert say. And dey do."

So, Charles Calvert was a crank for progress, no matter how silly it looked. Which it did. The roof of the octagonal barn was crowned by a gilt-plated weather vane shaped like a cow. The landau halted at the south gate.

"Through heah, suh," Albert said, helping Hay climb down.

They walked past a tank that exuded an unmistakable odor of . . .

"Yes, suh," Albert said, "de glory of nature. From dose hogs yonder." Pens were set off to the left. "And de sheep dere." Albert pointed right.

"Sally works here?"

"Yes, suh. Upstairs."

In the perimeter yard, dry stalks jutted from the crusty ground. The two-story octagonal barn was painted white—"so's de cows is happy comin' in," Albert chattered. The structure had an unexpected grace,

which Hay attributed to its cupola with sides of glass—"for de
vent'lation," his tour guide pointed out. "For a hunnerd and four cows."

"And for the humans," Hay joked.

"For de cows," Albert said.

They passed through the barn-sized entrance, and Hay sniffed the
scope of the operation—the substances that entered the cows and those
that exited, and the animals themselves. "Not a hunnerd four right
now—more like sebenty," Albert was saying. "But dese are happy cows.
And why not?"

Hay might prefer not being tied to a stanchion, even if the feed room
was nearby. The stalls were arranged in two concentric octagons, and the
entire floor was sloped like a funnel toward the center of the barn—"to
allow dem fluids to flow," Albert explained.

A rickety wooden staircase led to a loft that ringed the open barn.
Here, the air smelled of pinewood and the sharp moistness of hay. By
the outer wall, beyond a stack of bales, a bent-over Negress was sweeping the floor.

"Sally," Albert said.

She was a tiny woman with shoulders as narrow and protuberant as
a grasshopper's. Her hair was streaked in a grimy gray. Most unnerving
was her complexion, which ranged from mahogany in the hollow of her
throat to a mottled, freckled beige on her cheeks. Hay wondered if she
had been scalded as a child or was merely the product of a mixture that
had never mixed. She stared up into Hay's face with weary eyes, waiting to be spoken to.

Hay said, "Albert, would you mind . . . ?"

The butler said nothing; nor did he move. Then Hay understood. The
overseer had instructed him to listen.

Hay gave his name and came to the point. "I work for President
Lincoln," he said and waited for the welcoming smile. When none appeared, he said gently, "I must ask you about Eva."

It occurred to Hay that perhaps she did not know yet that her
daughter was dead. But her face went rigid, and she started to fall.
Albert jumped in, reaching under her arm, and guided her to a seat on
a hay bale. Hay chastised himself for not getting there first. He prided

himself on being quick in the ring, where nothing was at stake but his manhood.

"What about her?" she said in a thin, aggrieved voice.

"She was here, was she not, the night before last?"

An almost imperceptible nod.

Hay said, "Do you know why?"

Sally shook her head.

"Did you see her?"

The Negress's face betrayed a mix of pain and love that was conquered by a motherly instinct to deceive.

"No," she said, her voice strong. She looked Hay in the eye, which he took as a sign she was lying.

"Did you know she was here?"

"No."

Hay glanced over at Albert, whose presence was not conducive to frankness. "I happen to know that she was," he said, "and that Elizabeth Keckly sent her." Which was more than he knew.

No denial—no reaction at all.

"Missus Keckly is a friend of yours, is she not?" said Hay. "Or was, from when she lived here as a girl. She told me so."

"She was," Sally murmured. Her eyes shone with tears.

"When did you see her last?"

A shrug—eloquent, ageless. "I hear tell of her," Sally said.

"Through Eva?"

A pause, then a nod.

"Meaning you saw Eva."

No reply.

Then something struck him. He leaned toward Sally and whispered, out of Albert's hearing. "*You* took the slave ledger. You knew where it was. And you handed it to—"

"No, no, no," she said.

"But how did you know to look for it? Either you saw Eva twice or . . . you got word from Missus Keckly, through . . . Well, what does it matter, I suppose? She is bound to have her ways. No doubt you would do anything she asked."

"She is a good woman. Good to my Eva."

Until she got her killed, Hay thought. "Yes, and a strong woman, too. And smart."

"Smarter than most men—most white men."

"She gets it in part from her papa, I suppose."

Sally shot Hay a shrewd look; his shot in the dark had found its mark. The slave examined the back of her hand, which was the color of the Mississippi mud. In a light and airy voice, she said, "So people say."

"Did they say this at the time?"

"People talk."

"What do they say—*did* they say?"

Sally stared at the floor.

In a low, even tone, Hay said, "Your daughter died for this information, to deliver it to Missus Keckly. I am trying to find out what it was."

"Ask Lizzy."

"I shall. But I am asking you first." Hay debated telling the truth. "So I'll know *what* to ask her."

Sally swallowed and looked across the barn and seemed to make up her mind. "She was . . . lent . . . Miz Agnes was. To Mistuh Calvert . . ."

"*To* Mister Calvert."

A nod. "—and was sent back to Virginnie jest befo' she give birth. Then Mistuh Calvert—the old Mistuh Calvert, Mastuh George—he takes her back. This time, buys her. And den he sells her again, back to Virginnie. Back and forth she go—*they* go—like a sheep between two patches o' clover. 'Cept warn't no clover."

"When you say Virginia, you mean Armistead Burwell's place, in Dinwiddie, yes?"

"*Dat's* the name. He's the one dat lent her and den sold her and den bought her back again."

"Any idea why?"

At her look of incredulity, Hay felt himself blush. "A fine-lookin' woman she was," Sally said. "More than one man might-a thought so. But whichever one had 'er, he must-a been the smartest man in the place—the smartest *white* man. 'Cause Lizzy so smart—and near to white. *Dat* was what people say. And people, what dey say, dey's usually right."

"If she *is* that smart, and I do not doubt it, why did she want that ledger, do you suppose?"

"Why do you ask me? Ask her. All I can say, suh, it warn't the only ledger she ask for."

"Oh?"

"No, suh. But the other warn't there. Gone where it oughta ha' been."

"An earlier one?" The slave ledger Hay had seen showed nothing earlier for Elizabeth Hobbs than at age seven—back in the 'twenties sometime.

"Not'in' like that, no, suh. A ledger of another sort. Listin' the staff what lived here."

The ledger Hay had seen under the overseer's forearm.

Hay caught the day's last train back to Washington City. He had willed it to arrive before the overseer discovered the loss and came in pursuit. Not a theft, exactly. He was not a thief but a borrower—an *authorized* borrower, in fact. Hay had left Webster a note, using Riversdale's own cream-colored stationery. He had promised—in writing!—to return the ledger to Congressman Calvert personally, soon as Hay was done with it. All too cowardly, he had to admit, lifting it from the table in the library and concealing it under his coat. Still, he reasoned, the overseer was nowhere to be found (not that Hay had looked) and the B&O, if running on schedule, was soon to pass through. Which it had, and now his eyes drifted shut. Lines flashed into his mind:

> *Property is theft, he had been told*
> *By a thief who was laden with loot.*

Hay fished his calfskin notebook and a pencil from his greatcoat pocket.

> *He was about to agree when he . . .* hmmm . . . rhyming
> with *told*. Fold. Cold. Hold. Controlled. Or, yes . . .
> *He was about to agree when he found himself sold*
> *For . . . a greenback, an eagle, and . . . a . . . hoot.*

Hmm, that was close to meaning something. Hay slipped the paper back into his pocket and fingered the ledger under his coat and pulled it out. The swaying of the railroad carriage was not the problem, nor the fading wintery light. Most daunting was the ledger's faint writing, a tangle of filaments. Lists of names, best Hay could tell, dating back years, decades, generations. How would he make any sense of it, not knowing what he was looking for? Assuming he had filched—well, borrowed—the right ledger.

The railroad car was empty but for a gray-haired couple who had ex-changed nary a word. Hay rested his head on the side of the railroad car, and it rattled like a drummer boy's jaw. He closed his eyes and pic-tured Sally seated on the hay bale. He chided himself for not asking directly if her daughter might have done ill to Willie. But what good would it have done? She would not have known and, if she had, she would have lied. Or collapsed, just at the thought of it. Why cause point-less pain? There was enough in the world of the other kind.

And what, pray tell, did any of this have to do with Willie's death? So what if Elizabeth Keckly had been fathered by this slaveholder or that one, or if she had lived at this plantation or that one and had known this doorkeeper or . . . ? But it did matter—Hay believed that in his gut. Mrs. Keckly had hired Eva as a nurse, had she not? And Eva—yes, a dark lady—could easily have administered the poison to Willie and Tad, and maybe Mrs. Keckly had known. She had sent Eva back to the plantation, supposedly in search of a ledger that listed the young Eliza-beth's high price, at the cost of Eva's life. Maybe Mrs. Keckly had *wanted* Eva dead, because of . . . Who could say? Her son had been killed, then her mother died, just as Willie fell ill. Nicolay was right; there was no telling the effect. She had something, *somethings,* to hide—that much seemed clear. And she had been too involved in Willie's care, and too involved in the household—still—for Hay to silence his suspicions.

Hay opened his eyes and stared out at a soggy, fallow field. Then he closed them again and pondered who was the smartest man on the Calvert estate. That was easy: the proprietor, Charles B. Calvert. He of the octagonal cow barn and the other innovations. Hay sat up. No, he thought—not possible. He was too young to be Mrs. Keckly's father. Fifteen years older than she was, at most. Well, it was *pos*ible. (Hay, at fifteen, had no slave girl at his disposal.) Charles Calvert's father—that made more sense. Yes, in his elder years. The old man taking an unwilling slave girl for his own—where was the news in that? That would mean that Elizabeth Hobbs Keckly was Charles Calvert's . . . half sister. That would explain why he had gone pale when Hay mentioned her name. The two of them, borne of the same father. What was his name? Oh yes, George Calvert. Ah, *those* were the initials in the slave ledger—*G. C.*

George! The name Mrs. Keckly had bestowed upon her only child.

<hr />

Lincoln stepped out into the waiting room and summoned Hay inside. He looked like hell. Had he slept in days? His cheeks seemed to be slipping from their moorings. No wonder: His son, his *sons,* his wife, the war, his generals—everything was taking a toll. Melancholia seemed a rational response.

Hay had no capacity—or desire, really—to cheer the man up. He had started to recount what he had learned of Mrs. Keckly's background when Lincoln broke in.

"I appreciate all of this, John." Lincoln fumbled around on his desk, absently rolling a rock into a brass-handled bell, causing the lantern to flicker. "But there is no need for you to look into this any further."

"I am not sure what you mean, sir," Hay said.

"I mean, there is no need for you to look into this any further."

"Are you asking me to stop investigating Willie's . . . Willie . . . his . . . ?"

"Exactly that."

Hay opened his mouth, but no words emerged; a trickle of saliva reached his chin. He tried again and said, "May I ask why, sir?"

A long silence. Then: "Nothing will bring him back."

Hardly an answer—that had been true when Lincoln asked him to investigate. Something must have happened. But what?

Hay said, "Surely it matters *who* . . . ?"

"Will that bring him back?"

"Of course not, but it could stop one of his"—Hay saw no choice but to be direct—"brothers from—"

The clap of Lincoln's huge hands resounded like a gunshot. Then, in the mildest of voices, the president said, "I know everything I need to know, John. There is nothing more I *want* to know. My boys will be safe, I assure you."

+=====+

Nicolay's saturnine countenance, dripping with soapy water, drooped. "Did he say why?"

"Only humbug. 'It will not bring Willie back.' 'There is nothing I need to know.' No—no reason. Just, stop."

"He asked you?"

"That was my word. He seemed to accept it."

"He did not order you." Nicolay toweled his face and neck.

"He is not *my* commander in chief," Hay said.

"Of course he is, Johnny. Also, your employer and your landlord. And patron saint."

"Yours, you mean."

"But the way I see it," Nicolay said, "an order is an order, and a request is . . . a request."

"You *should* be a lawyer," Hay said.

Nicolay's balled-up towel was deflected by Hay's flick of a fist.

Chapter Seventeen

Hay forced himself to remain at his desk and turn every page. With so little evidence available, he saw no choice but to make the most of what he had. His shoulder ached, and he longed for laudanum but vowed to wait until nighttime, when drowsiness would serve him well. Hay sat up straight in his swivel chair, planted his feet on the floor, and slapped his cheek, which made his shoulder hurt less.

The ledger was covered in thin gray cotton, of the sort used for cheap coffins. Scrawled across the title page:

Residents of
Riversdale

The earliest pages, starting with 1822, were clumped together. Hay pried them loose—a crushed insect was the glue. The ledger seemed to be a census of sorts, listing the inhabitants, dwelling by dwelling. By each man's name was a dollar figure, which Hay took to be the monthly rent. What would Mrs. Keckly want with this?

Hay found a tactile pleasure in turning the pages, with their rough surfaces and ragged cut. The listings were written in a delicate hand.

Dwelling #708:
Ghagan, Philip, 38, white, b. Ireland, gardener $17
Ghagan, Jane, 39, white, b. Ireland

Ghagan, Dannie, 8, white, b. Md.
Ghagan, Morris, 6, white, b. Md.
Ghagan, Philip, 4, white, b. Md.
Ghagan, Ann, 2, white, b. Md.
Dwelling #709:
Jones, Joseph, 40, white, b. England, farm manager $19
Jones, Elizabeth, 39, white, b. England
Jones, George, 14, white, b. England
Jones, Jenett (f), 11, white, b. Md.

Hay counted four more Jones children—no wonder the rent was higher. Nor did Hay recognize the inhabitants in the other five dwellings.

The 1823 listings looked the same, except for another Ghagan daughter and new inhabitants in Dwelling #704. The Godmans were gone; listed first among the new tenants was:

Webster, James, 45, white, b. Md., asst. overseer $21

That must be the man Hay had just met. He would be in his eighties now—plausible, Hay supposed, if a nasty nature kept a man looking young. The family he had lived with bore a different name:

Jenkins, Archibald, 29, white, b. Md., farm manager
Jenkins, Elizabeth Webster, 20, b. Md.
Jenkins, John Ladoe, 1, white, b. Md.

A married daughter, perhaps, with a husband and son. Jenkins—a familiar name. Hay tried to remember why. From Jenkins Hill, perhaps—the original name of Capitol Hill. He checked the 1824 listings. The family had stayed on, now with a newborn daughter, Mary Elizabeth.

Now, Hay remembered: Jenkins was the name of that nurse. But she was not Mary Elizabeth. Something more euphonious—oh yes, Eugenia. Well, Jenkins was a common enough surname. Oh, and the nurse was *Mrs.* Jenkins—her girlhood surname must have been something else.

Then Hay turned the page and nearly fell out of his chair.

Stackpole, Henry, 35, white, b. Md., asst. overseer $16

This was *not* a common surname. And beneath was further proof:

Stackpole, Anna, 32, white, b. N. H.

New Hampshire—that fit.

Stackpole, Thomas, 11, white, b. N. H.
Stackpole, Peter, 6, white, b. Md.

One and the same. This would make the doorkeeper—Hay closed his eyes to calculate—not quite fifty. The fat, jowly doorkeeper could be almost any age.

And if Thomas Stackpole had known Mrs. Keckly in their youths, then . . . Hay had a sickening thought—that they had not only known one another.

That they were kin.

<hr />

"So?"

Thus, in a word—a syllable—Thomas Stackpole admitted . . . to what, exactly? "Of course I know her. This town is small. Surely you have learned *that,* my dear Hay."

Hay bristled at *dear* and wondered at the loquaciousness. "But *she* is . . ."

"Yes, and I am white. This town is small—and wicked—in that way as well. And out there"—Stackpole's thick finger pointed eastward, toward Riversdale—"is smaller still."

Stackpole's misadventures in Richmond and his involuntary return had not erased his bland yet serene smile. He overflowed his seat outside the president's door, garbed in a drab, dark suit and his customary aplomb. Hay would have preferred inviting him into his office for a private conversation but worried that Stackpole would decline.

"You had a good trip, I take it." Hay meant his smile to be disarming, although Stackpole was never disarmed.

"I did. The trip was profitable, if that is what you ask. And with an escort home, at the government's expense. At the cost to the troops of a few blankets and a cannon."

"Mister Pinkerton's men were not too rough with you, I hope."

"Oh, I can absorb punishment, Mister Hay. You might be surprised." He seemed to wink; Hay hoped it was a twitch. "Even when it is undeserved. They were uglier to Mister Spaulding, I should say."

"I was unaware he returned with you."

"Oh yes, it was a family affair, for which I should be grateful to . . . you, perhaps?"

"You give me too much credit, sir. So you did cross paths with Mister Spaulding in . . . Richmond? Is that where you . . . sojourned?"

"How thoughtful of you to inquire. I went on business, Mister Hay. As did he. We were both of us successful, until Mister Pinkerton's gentlemen interrupted us."

"I was under the impression that your business was working for the president."

"And for *Madam* President, my dear Hay; let us not forget that."

As if Hay could.

He could think of no easy way to ask the question on his mind. Often, the solution was simply to ask it. This time, however, he sidled in.

"How long did you live at the Calvert . . . estate?"

"Why do you ask?"

"Bear with me, if you would."

A pause. "Two years only. When I was eleven years old, we left."

"For New Hampshire."

"You have been making inquiries, I see."

"About everyone. Why did you leave the Calvert . . . place so soon?"

"I was a boy. Nobody told me. And now, there is nobody left who would know. Why does this matter, besides?"

Hay noted that Stackpole had not denied knowing why.

"Missus Keckly, again, if I might," Hay said. Time to be blunt. "Were you more than friends, perhaps?"

"What are you implying, Mister Hay?"

"No, nothing like *that*." Although, Hay was accusing Stackpole's father of exactly that. "I was wondering if she might be . . . related to you . . . by blood." That did not come out quite right.

Stackpole's eyes shrank to a pinpoint. "I will not dignify that with a response," he said, jowls trembling—with rage? with shame? with embarrassment at being unmasked? Hay had no way of knowing. Only one thing was clear: Stackpole would be loquacious no longer.

◄═══►

The correspondence on Hay's felt-covered table had piled up. The Indiana governor's request for a pardon for a cousin (an elastic term, Hay thought) convicted of bribery; that would require an answer, but an easy one. A letter from the Reverend Henry Ward Beecher proposing a Negro for a postmastership in the city of Brooklyn. Hay had started to draft a polite refusal to the famous pastor when relief arrived in a knock on his doorframe.

"You wish to see me, Mister Hay?" It was Elizabeth Keckly, stately and buxom in a plain black gown.

"No. Well, yes. But how on earth did you know?"

She smiled. Stackpole must have told her, and she was inserting herself before Hay knew what he wanted to ask.

"Please, come in."

Mrs. Keckly seated herself in the hard-backed chair without being invited. Hay found this audacious but also refreshingly matter-of-fact.

"How is your shoulder, Mister Hay?" she said.

"Much better, thank you," Hay replied. If this was a bout, he had lost the first round. "As you can see, I am already back at my desk—my own little battlefield."

He immediately regretted the lighthearted allusion to sacred ground, where Mrs. Keckly's only child had given his life. But she seemed not to mind.

"You are a vigorous young man, indeed. The president is lucky to have you."

Although Hay recognized the tactic—he was practiced at being the charmer, not the charmee—he could not help but enjoy it. This was a side of Mrs. Keckly he had not seen before. But why did she feel the need?

Hay thanked her and decided to surprise her with his suspicions in the guise of fact. He said, "Tell me why you sent Eva back to Riversdale. Was it to bring you that ledger of slaves?"

Mrs. Keckly's face tightened, and tears slid down her cheeks.

"You know, then," Hay said.

She lifted an embroidered handkerchief to her face and nodded.

"It is your fault she is dead," Hay said. He meant to be cruel: The greater her shame, the likelier her cooperation.

She lowered the handkerchief and spoke through arched lips. "Not in a world that was just."

"Which world is that?" Hay felt ridiculous playing the realist with a self-emancipated slave. "I think I know why you wanted the ledger," he said. "Your name is in it, and your mother's. But why did you send *her*?"

"You have seen it?"

"Oh yes. I have it."

Mrs. Keckly's eyes grew wide. "May I see it?"

The second round was his. "When you answer my questions," he said.

"Then ask them."

"Why did you want it at all? Everyone is from somewhere. Who cares if you came from the Calvert place?"

"I just wanted to know, is all."

A lie.

"Then let me ask the question I asked before. Why did you send Eva?"

"I could hardly go myself."

"And why is that?"

"In case I was seen."

"By whom?"

"By anyone."

"But why send Eva—a friend's daughter, yes—send her back to . . ."—Hay decided not to say *her death*—"to do this for you? You wanted it that much?"

"No one else knew where it was."

"Sally did."

"You have seen her."

It was unmistakable—there was fear in her eyes.

"I have."

"What did she tell you?" Mrs. Keckly leaned forward in the chair, her face so near to Hay's he could smell the mix of perfume and perspiration.

"That you wanted the staff ledger as well. Why?"

No reply.

The hell with starting from the edges. "Because it listed Thomas Stackpole's family?"

"*What?*" It was almost a shriek.

"Yes, I am also in possession of that one. Well, is that the reason?"

"Oh my, no."

At last, he believed her.

"Isn't that the reason you refused to testify on his behalf? That you knew him—that you are kin to him. That you are—"

"No, no—by everything I hold holy, no."

Mrs. Keckly, her backbone rigid, started to rise from the chair.

Hay asked her for a schedule of nurses but found he was addressing her back. The third and final round was hers.

=+===+=

A Saturday night with nothing to do and no one to do it with, and so much frustration to work off. Nicolay was visiting friends who were too tedious for Hay, with their ever-expanding horde of tots. Lincoln and Robert were taking in a burlesque opera at the Odd Fellows' Hall, on Seventh street—they were together, which was good, and both of them needed a laugh. Hay decided to take a walk, hoping to clear his mind, or even to organize it, although that was aiming high.

The northern sidewalk of the Avenue was crowded with revelers in varying stages of inebriation. A soldier whose tunic was torn brushed shoulders with Hay, who curled his fists in a way he knew was unwise. Hay crossed the Avenue, dodging a carriage and its glazed-looking nag.

On the southern sidewalk, the proportion between the sexes skewed toward women with paint on their faces and a strut in their strides, winking at men without regard to age or girth; Hay felt flattered at their attentions anyway, which he realized was their intent. That he was prey rather than predator did not trouble him; it was arousing.

The first three winks he ignored, from women who were, respectively, too old, too plump, and too rouged. The next girl was none of those—rather shy, in fact, in offering Hay a sidelong glance. As in: *I am embarrassed to be out here, but because of reasons beyond my control, here I am.* As was Hay.

She had passed him when he stopped and turned to look. His shoulder hurt; he would have to make allowances. She, too, was looking back, and Hay found himself smiling—this would increase the price, no doubt—and walking toward her. She waited. She had a sauciness around her mouth and a liveliness in her eyes and pleasing curves in her girlish overcoat.

"Hello," Hay said softly.

"Hello yourself." There was a lilt in her voice.

"A nice evening."

"Not very."

"No, I suppose not," Hay said. "But it can be."

"I am open, sir, to suggestions."

Hay made one.

⊹⪼══⪻⊹

Hay's cravat was crumpled, and half of his collar was detached. Hay tiptoed into his dark office, grateful for the absence of witnesses who might ask where he had been. (His shame at sin was gaining on pride, which Hay hoped was a sign of maturity.) It was too early for bed, but he felt too tired to do anything productive. He meant to collect himself at his desk before facing Nicolay, who might still be awake.

Hay sank into his swivel chair and felt a crinkling beneath him. He reached down and retrieved three or four pages of foolscap, folded and refolded, nestled inside one another like petticoats.

Hay was disbelieving. The schedule of nurses! He shoved the piles aside on the desktop and lit the kerosene lantern. His fatigue had disappeared.

The pages felt brittle as he unfolded and smoothed them out. On the top page, pencil lines crisscrossed, marking off a grid. Each row was marked with a date, from February 6 through February 11; two of the four columns were labeled Willie and two, Tad. Each oblong, Hay gathered, represented a twelve-hour shift. Written inside most, although not all, of them were initials or a name.

The next page continued from February 12 to February 17. On the third page, below the row for February 20, the left-hand columns were blank.

The lettering, slender and crisp, looked nothing like the messages left in Hay's satchel. MJW—that would be Mary Jane Welles. Dines was Old Aunt Mary. EK—Keckly. EJS—Eva Socrates, must be. On the last page, RP—that was Rebecca Pomroy, the nurse now taking care of Tad. Hay figured the boxes devoid of initials or a name must mean no nurse was on duty or one nurse covered both boys. Or Mrs. Keckly could not remember. Or she preferred not to say.

Now, Hay needed to match the schedule of nurses against the spikes in Willie's fever, in search of a pattern. Lincoln's advice remained valid, even after its purveyor had supposedly taken Hay off the case.

Hay lifted a stack of correspondence from his desktop onto the floor and removed Willie's medical chart from the top drawer, then arranged the nurses' schedule and the medical chart side by side. The likeliest way to detect a pattern, he decided, was to note Willie's fever in every twelve-hour block of time. Dr. Hall had estimated a toxic dose of calomel would bring on a surge in fever in two or three hours. So, a nurse bent on evil might want to administer a dose toward the end of her shift, to deflect suspicion. Hay's task, then, was to track which nurse was on duty when the fever was recorded *and* during the previous shift.

Tedious work, Hay's least favorite kind. If this was Vidocq stuff, it was overrated. Hay whittled his pencil to a jagged point and just missed slicing his thumb. Some of the notations of Willie's temperature were daunting to decipher. The 102s resembled the 105s; a couple of the 6s might have been 0s (fortunately, after the decimal point).

The chore took nearly an hour, penciling in Willie's fate in Fahrenheit. His fever was recorded, in various handwriting, at eight o'clock, four in the afternoon, and midnight. On February 6: 102.5, 104.3, 102.9. Steady for a day and a night and then 104.5. Twice, Willie's fever reached 105.3. A spike, then a decline and, twelve or eighteen or twenty-four hours later, another spike. A pattern of sorts, but erratic, the work of a sardonic God or the capricious course of disease or a person who meant to do harm.

Every time Willie's fever reached 104 degrees or higher, Hay circled it. Nine times in sixteen days. Twice, the nurse on duty was MJW, the navy secretary's wife. Mrs. Keckly was on duty twice; and Dines, EJS, and RP, once each. Twice, no nurse was listed on duty—Doc Stone must have measured the boy's fever himself, or Tad's nurse served Willie as well. Once, that would have been Old Aunt Mary and, the other time, EJS. No pattern in particular.

The schedule, clearly, was incomplete. Nor did it mention the Ancient or the Hell-cat, who had sat up with Willie night after night.

Could the Hell-cat have . . . ? The possibility had hovered before at the edge of Hay's consciousness, but he had concluded each time, as he did now: No, impossible. Not even she was that crazy. Still, that would explain why Lincoln wanted the investigation ended.

All of that, he must ignore. Hay returned to the pages before him, to check the spikes in fever against the nurse during the previous shift. The nurse on duty just before Willie's fever broached 104 was EJS. The second time, EK—Mrs. Keckly. The third time, EJS. The fourth, EJS. The fifth . . . again, EJS. Twice, nobody was listed during the previous shift, but two of those times the nurse on duty *while* Willie's fever spiked was . . . EJS.

Eva Socrates. The dark lady.

A murderess.

Who had already paid the price. At the hands of Pinkerton's men.

Chapter Eighteen

SUNDAY, MARCH 9, 1862

Hay started to curse at the blackguard who clutched his shoulder, the wounded one. Then he opened his eyes and saw the fright in Lincoln's face.

"Come join us, please, John, as soon as you can." The president's tenor was a tone higher than usual.

Three minutes later, barely past six o'clock, Hay crossed to the president's office and walked into a maelstrom. Members of the cabinet sat at contradictory angles around the center table. Lincoln, at the head, now wore a mask of unconcern. The portrait of Andrew Jackson over the mantelpiece stared across at the military map of Tennessee on the opposite wall. The office was cluttered with the president's papers, despite the chambermaids' best efforts, but it was free enough of furniture (the Hell-cat had ignored this room, too, at her husband's behest) to let a man pace. Edwin Stanton stalked the room like a caged lion, the white streaks livid in his flowing, unkempt beard.

"Nothing can prevent her destroying seriatim every naval vessel," the war secretary thundered, "laying Washington in ashes and then placing all of our seaport cities under her guns." He flung a fist at another map mounted over the sofa, of the Chesapeake Bay and the coastline to the north. "I have notified the governors to protect their cities—we can do nothing for them. Why, sir," Stanton blared to no one in particular, "it is not unlikely that we will have from one of her guns a cannonball in this very room before we leave it."

The rebels' latest threat—as Hay came to piece it together—had driven the emotional Stanton into an ecstasy of Armageddon. Desperate for warships, the Confederates had dredged up the USS *Merrimack*, a scuttled Union frigate, and covered it in iron plates. The telegrams had come in overnight, describing how the ironclad had sunk a Union warship off Hampton Roads, set another one ablaze, and was threatening a third. The worst naval defeat in the nation's history, more than two hundred sailors killed. A leviathan that could never be stopped—of this, Stanton was certain—as it lumbered through the Chesapeake Bay to the Potomac River and then upstream to Washington City. It could shell the Capitol and the Executive Mansion, then steam northward to Philadelphia, New York, Boston.

"The war is lost!" Stanton shouted—and who could say for sure he was wrong?

The eminences of the cabinet spouted their solutions, each sillier than the last. Pile rocks on barges and sink them to block the Potomac. String a huge net across the river to snare the ironclad. Move the capital to Pittsburgh. Seward looked as if a molar was being pulled without chloroform. The president pretended to pay attention, but his eye had shifted to the war map on the wall, and his mind was . . . Hay knew better than to guess. Not on the squabbling in the room.

"Surely, the *Merrimack* cannot come to Washington and New York at the same time," Gideon Welles piped up, earning Stanton's most menacing look. The navy secretary was either being a dullard or mocking his rival—probably both. Beneath the sycophant, Hay realized, was a bully.

This time, Gideon Welles knew his facts. General Burnside's forces, blockading the North Carolina coast, were safe from the *Merrimack*, "because her draft of water is such she could not approach them. And the *Monitor*, as perhaps you know"—or perhaps the war secretary did *not* know—"is steaming its way to Hampton Roads. Our own ironclad left the shipyard near New York on Thursday, and may have arrived in Hampton Roads already. When I get word from my men down there, I shall let you know. I have every confidence in the *Monitor*'s power to resist—and, I hope, to overcome—the *Merrimack*."

Calm amid the furor—or *because* of the furor—Lincoln pored

through the wires from the field. Then with a shake of his hand, he dismissed the cabinet's combatants and dispatched them to their respective churches, intending to leave no divine option untried. Seward stayed behind.

"Pittsburgh!" Lincoln sighed once the secretary of the interior was beyond earshot. "Why not Poughkeepsie?"

"Or Warsaw, Indiana," Seward said.

"Between the schoolhouse and the Turkish baths, the perfect spot for a Capitol," Hay said. "The barber would sell it for a song."

"Maybe you should buy it first," Seward said, "or I could. And turn a quick profit."

"Seward's folly, we could call it," Lincoln said, without an evident care in the world.

Seward, relighting his segar, issued a guttural laugh that caused him to choke. "And how . . . is the investi . . . investigation coming, my . . . dear Hay?" he managed between gasps.

Hay glanced warily at Lincoln, wondering how to describe the investigation he was supposed to have abandoned.

Lincoln said, "Well, John?"

"I think I know who it is, sir," Hay said. "Was."

Lincoln exclaimed, "Who *who* is?"

"Who mur . . ." He needed to be precise. "Who administered the toxic doses of calomel to Willie."

Lincoln seemed to sag. Then he said with a quaver, "And who is he?"

"She," Hay said. "That nurse, Eva. Eva Socrates. A fugitive slave." He told of matching the spikes of fever with the schedule of nurses and of finding *EJS* on duty during that shift or just before.

Seward said, "Always?"

"No. Two or three times she was off duty that day."

"Two *or* three?" said Lincoln.

"Let me check," Hay said.

"Do." That was Seward. "We need to know."

We?

"And this fugitive slave," Seward went on, "you say her name is . . ."

"Eva Socrates, Governor."

"Rather a whimsical—" Seward began.

Lincoln broke in, "E . . . *J* . . . S. John, what is the *J* for? It is rare, you know, for a slave to have a second Christian name."

Hay did not know. That, too, he would check.

He declined Lincoln's invitation to church. Seward accepted without being asked.

"Is Robert going?" said Hay.

"No," Lincoln replied, "he left last night. Back to college, where he belongs."

Without telling Hay good-bye.

Hay could not help but indulge in a round of self-congratulation. Anyone would. The case was closed, and Hay had solved it. He considered hunting up Pinkerton, to offer his own congratulations for capturing—and killing?—the perpetrator. But he recognized it was really to gloat. Better to refrain. More mature, anyway.

Still, something nagged at Hay. About Lincoln—he was acting oddly. Taking Hay off the case without explanation, then accepting Hay's solution without any show of interest. Simultaneously courtroom-sharp and disengaged. Even more remote than usual from the human race.

From habit and boredom, Hay gravitated to his desk and confronted the heap of correspondence. While penning a letter to Ohio's attorney general, setting his mind at ease about the Homestead Act that Congress was pondering in its own sweet time—no, sir, the president was not planning to give away the state's rich farmland—Hay found himself thinking about Eva. What possible reason could she have to poison a boy? A fugitive slave was not a secessionist. There could be no personal grudge. It was not the sort of crime one committed for pay or even as blackmail. It made no sense. Damn those Pinkerton men for killing her—now, Hay would never know her motive. Maybe Pinkerton himself wanted her dead, but Hay could think of no reason for that either.

A noise outside his door sent Hay looking for Nicolay, but the corner office was dark. The Sabbath quiet was creaky; it must be windy outside. Hay's own somber office seemed unappealing. He continued on through the double doors and into the central hallway, just as Elizabeth Keckly emerged from the Hell-cat's bedroom. She was carrying a silver tray with dishes jammed with napoleons and apple fritters—evidently ordered but not eaten.

"May I have a word, please?" he said.

Mrs. Keckly looked desperate to escape. "Of course," she said. "Where?"

Hay nodded toward the Prince of Wales Room. There, they would not be disturbed. And taking her to the scene of the crime could only amplify the power of his questions. Instead, it increased Hay's own unease. The gilt highlights on the opulently carved bedstead, the purple wallpaper, the heavy gold-and-purple drapes—Hay found the décor oppressive. Indeed, funereal. He kept thinking of the undersized body in the oversized bed.

Hay guided Mrs. Keckly into the less comfortable chair at the foot of the bed. He took the other, which left them sitting closer to each other than he wished.

She adjusted the folds in her billowing skirt and said, "How may I help you, Mister Hay?"

"An odd question first, if I might." He waited politely for a nod that did not come. "What is . . . was Eva's middle name?"

Mrs. Keckly visibly relaxed. "I am not aware she had one."

"You have her on the schedule as EJS, yes?"

"No, no. That is not Eva. She is not on this schedule at all. She came and went as she . . . could."

"So, she might have been here . . . here . . . in this room . . . anytime at all."

"That, I cannot say for certain."

"Then who is EJS?"

"You met her. More than once, I believe. You know her as Eugenia."

"Jenkins."

"Yes."

"What do you mean, 'I know her as'? Isn't that her name?"

"It is her confirmation name. After Sister Eugenia, her favorite teacher in Alexandria. Her family was Protestant, but they sent her to a Catholic school, and she converted. To her family's displeasure, I should add. She often calls herself Eugenia."

Hay pictured the pinch-faced woman with severe black hair. Efficient, businesslike, courteous in a mechanical way. With a glower. Not a lighthearted presence. In demeanor, rather dark.

Hay gasped. Then he whistled.

A dark lady.

"That explains the *E* and the *J,*" Hay said. "Eugenia Jenkins. What is the *S*?"

Jenkins was her maiden name. Her married name meant nothing to Hay.

Mrs. Keckly said, "I call her by her given name, her Christian"— she meant *Protestant*—"name. Which is Mary. Mary Elizabeth."

Mary Elizabeth Jenkins—Hay had seen this name before, within the past day or two. But where? Hay combed through his recent travels and his sources of information.

Then he remembered.

⊹⊱══⊰⊹

Hay shut the door to his office. From the top right drawer of his desk, he pulled the ledger that listed the Calvert plantation's resident staff. He leafed through the stiff pages until he found what he was looking for, from 1824:

> Jenkins, Archibald, 30, white, b. Md., farm manager
> Jenkins, Elizabeth Webster, 21, b. Md.
> Jenkins, John Zadoc, 2, white, b. Md.
> Jenkins, Mary Elizabeth, 1, white, b. Md.

All under the roof of *Webster, James.* The overseer Hay had met.

Mary Elizabeth Jenkins—Eugenia. EJS. On duty at the most incriminating times. More than likely, a murderess. And Hay knew where she lived.

He also knew this was something he should not handle alone. Lincoln might have returned from church by now, but Hay saw no reason to bother him with a suspect's arrest, not when a lethal threat to the Union was on his mind. Besides, Hay preferred to keep mum on his mistake—about Eva's guilt—until he knew he was not making another. That could wait until Eugenia—whatever her name—was in custody.

To call on Pinkerton, however—Hay saw no choice. Beyond his lack of legal authority, Hay could hardly arrest the woman by himself. He did not know *how*.

The detective was probably at his home, out on Sixteenth street, nearly to K. Hay stood to fetch his greatcoat. He was closing the ledger when the light from the window fell obliquely on an indentation in the thick scaly page. A furrow had been pressed into the paper. By a thumbnail, Hay guessed. Or a pencil. Hay picked up the open ledger and lifted it close to his face, then tilted it in every direction to make the most of the light. Yes, the line had been a pencil's marking, erased. Presumably by whoever had drawn it in the first place.

Hay could guess who that was, for the not-quite-obliterated line started at the end of

Webster, James, 45, white, b. Md., asst. overseer

and extended into the gutter between the facing pages. Hay knew what this kind of line meant in a genealogical listing—a liaison that clergy could never agree to bless. Only a family guileless enough, or unforgiving enough, would record it. And only when it produced a child.

Where the line ended, the indentations resembled hieroglyphics. Hay angled the book toward the window. He thought of shading the paper with the side of a pencil but feared concealing whatever it showed. Outside, a cloud must have moved, because the light brightened and nestled for an instant in the etchings.

Hay examined the crevices, as if made by a stylus without ink, and his stomach lurched.

AGNES H.

Agnes Hobbs.

The line ran from her name to . . . James Webster. Agnes Hobbs had borne his child, whose name was half-legible.

ELIZ.

Agnes and Elizabeth. *This* was Elizabeth Keckly's father. James Webster, the old overseer Hay had just met at Riversdale. The kinship Mrs. Keckly had not wanted known.

Hay glanced down at the names below Webster's. The last entry was as he remembered:

Jenkins, Mary Elizabeth, 1, white; b. Md.

Yes! That was Eugenia. Eugenia Jenkins—that is, Mary Elizabeth Jenkins. Tad's dark lady. Willie's murderess. Related to Mrs. Keckly by blood.

⊬⊷⊶⊣

"Asinine," Pinkerton sputtered. "Explain it again."

Hay tried. "The overseer out at the Calvert place, his name is James Webster, he is this Eugenia's grandfather, and he is also Missus Keckly's father. Which makes this Eugenia, or whatever her name is, Elizabeth Keckly's . . . aunt. No, niece. Anyway, blood kin."

Hay told Pinkerton about the house on H street, almost to Sixth, and described what he remembered of the floor plan. Pinkerton stared past Hay's shoulder, and his face took on an intelligent cast. This was Pinkerton at work, doing what he excelled at. After two or three minutes, he said, "Six men should be enough. Including myself."

"And me," Hay said.

"Oh no."

"Oh yes."

"This is a policin' operation. Armed."

"Plus me."

Pinkerton refused to tell Hay when the operation would begin.

⊬⊷⊶⊣

Hay was hungry but wary of arriving too late. He grabbed two hard rolls from the kitchen and left for the stables. He had nothing to give Hasheesh, who sulked.

"Please, be nice to me," Hay implored.

The mare paid no mind.

The daylight was fading when Hay concealed himself behind a blacksmith's shed on the northern side of H street. Across the way, the white-painted brick row house seemed to back away from the street, with a timidity Hay found affecting. It stood four stories high, counting the dormer windows. On the third story, four of the six shutters hung awry. An outside staircase was pressed diagonally against the front wall, rising from the sidewalk to the entrance on the second floor.

Hay sat on a barrel and looked over the fence. Nothing moved on the rutted road. He removed his fleece-lined gloves and gnawed on a roll, which tasted like hardtack, sandy and stale. Nothing like crumpets. Hay pitied the men in the field.

Hay felt in his greatcoat pocket for the comforting presence of his calfskin notebook and a stub of a pencil. The barrel top could serve as a desk.

> *In winter twilights, when the day has rolled . . .*

That was the opening line of his class poem at Brown, *winter* substituted for *summer*. Those 436 lines of poetry—on the subject of poetry— had said very little but said it . . . artfully.

> *In winter twilights, when the day has rolled,*
> *The biscuit is hard and the evening is cold . . .*

This new line, inspired by self-pity, an endless wellspring. *Keep going.*

> *In the middle of war, in the throes of a fight*
> *May we gird our loins in the darkening light . . . darkening*
> *night . . .*

No, oh no. He stared at the darkening sky as if its beauty were to blame for his poetic incapacity, his devotion to cliché. And so, he girded his own loins: *Try again.*

> *In winter twilights, when the day has rolled,*

Rolled? Well, leave it for now.

The biscuits are . . . biscuit is hard and the evening is cold . . .
Comes a moment of truth, not known to transpire

Perhaps.

Unless winter has fallen, and evil . . . goes . . . higher.

Not bad. Not entirely bad, anyway.

Hay returned his implements of creation to his pocket. His fingers were freezing; his gloves went back on. A rumbling was a carriage passing by. Across the street, a light flickered in the first-floor window. Could be the moonlight or a reflection from Hay's side of the street.

Then he heard the horses. Not the coordinated trot of a carriage but a jumble of rhythms that suddenly and simultaneously stopped. For suspenseful seconds, the night was silent. Hay peeked around the shed and saw men scurrying noiselessly in the moonlight. Pinkerton's men. One at each front corner of the house, two others on the staircase, and a short, stout—and yes, swaggering—man who was just reaching the top.

That was Pinkerton, who pounded on the door and shouted a word or two Hay could not comprehend—"Open up!" or something equally unpoetic. Although potentially effective, Hay had to admit. Pinkerton *knew* what he was doing. The man was a detective, not a dabbler like Hay.

Hay edged closer to his side of the street, into the shed's moon shadow. Pinkerton was calling to his men on the lower steps and pointing to the second-story door, miming an assault with a log. So Hay alone noticed the prick of light on the ground floor as it moved. Somebody was inside.

Hay crept across the road and circled around the operative at the corner. An alleyway ran along the side of the house, and Hay stole down it. He sidestepped the moonlit chunks of debris, although he kicked a rock, which skittered into the brick wall, just missing a window. The clatter was like an explosion. Hay froze. What if Pinkerton's men considered *him* . . . ? Hay thought of Eva. Shoot first and ask questions later—the Pinkerton way.

No one came running. A braying near the street gave Hay the cover to scuttle along to the rear of the house. He found a door and twisted the knob. It squeaked, and he stopped; then, hearing nothing, he turned the knob again. This time, it slid more easily. Hay pushed his weight against the door. No give.

He needed to break a glass pane in the door. Either that, or a window. He had seen the light on this floor, at the front of the house. Maybe the second-floor battering from Pinkerton and his men would distract the candle-bearer.

He had nothing to use but his fist. He wrapped his linen cambric handkerchief around the knuckles of his right hand and took aim at the pane on the lower-left. His professor of pugilism in Providence had taught him to snap his punches, not to push them, which increased their acceleration and the pain they caused. To a pane of glass as to a jaw.

Pushing with his legs, Hay twisted his hips and drove his fist through the glass. The shattering sounded like a hailstorm. He hardly felt any pain; he knew he would later. He slipped his hand through the hole and was thankful to touch a key in the lock. By contorting his wrist and jabbing himself with a shard, he grasped the key and tried to turn it. The lock was rusty and cold, and it took all the pressure he could apply with the base of his thumb—*that* hurt—to unfreeze it. When the lock clicked, Hay turned the knob and pressed his hip to the door. It gave way so easily he nearly fell through.

Because someone was pulling on the door.

And that someone held a gun. Six inches from Hay's right temple.

"Stop!" A man's voice, barely a growl.

And unnecessary. Hay had no plans to move.

Hay pivoted slowly toward his assailant. He could make out a silhouette, black against black, of a pointed chin and a triangular face. The shape of the face Hay had seen leaping into his carriage, then stalking the woods below Arlington House. The face of the young man who had tried twice to kill him. And who, Hay had every reason to assume, wanted to kill him still.

Now, the man had his chance, but so far he had not taken advantage.

Out of fear, probably, that a gunshot would alert the men who were barging in upstairs. This evened things up some.

"Go!" the man barked at Hay. He grabbed Hay's injured shoulder, snorting as he did, as if he knew which side was hurt. He turned Hay and shoved him into the blackness. Hay stretched both arms in front of his face, to ward off dangers unseen. At a dip in the floor, Hay stumbled, then stopped, and felt the gun poke at his back.

"Careful!" The man pushed at Hay's left shoulder—it hurt like hell, but Hay refused to show it. "To the left," the man said, steering Hay to a doorway. In the next room, a candle was lit, the one he had seen from outside. Someone was holding it, but the flame hid the face.

"You!" came the voice from behind the candle. A deep voice, a woman's.

"None other," Hay said, more jauntily than he felt. "At your service."

The woman who stepped toward him, candle in hand, he knew as Eugenia Jenkins. This was the opportunity Hay was waiting for. He grabbed for the candle as he spun to his right, elbowing the young man's gut and ramming the burning candle into his face. The man shrieked and toppled backward, and Hay snatched the gun.

Then fingernails scraped at Hay's cheek, and a knee slammed into his testicles. Hay started to crumple, but before he reached the floor, a feeling of rage overtook him, and he rose up through the pain and delivered a haymaker with his hand that held the gun.

Was it moral to strike a woman? That disputation would have to wait. His single punch put her on the ground.

⊣⊱═⊰⊢

"A ghastly looking thing, which is one of the beautiful things about it." Lincoln might have been talking about himself, Hay thought, and not about the USS *Monitor,* which wags described as a cheese-box on a raft. "The bullets rattled off the iron cladding like so many peas, they say. Until the *Merrimack* retired—*retired.* That was the beautiful word in the wire." Lincoln smacked the yellow flimsy in his lap. "This is a grand day, John, one of the rare ones."

Hay had made his report, and Lincoln was sitting by the telescope in his office, in a chair that was sized for Willie or Tad. The president had squeezed into it and looked as if he could never escape, nor wanted to. He had a delicate smile. The Confederates had abandoned Manassas; the weaponry McClellan had described as rebel cannons—based on Pinkerton's intelligence—turned out to be painted logs. Better still, the *Monitor* had withstood the *Merrimack*'s assault, and the Confederate ironclad had fled. Washington—indeed, the Union—was saved.

Chapter Nineteen

"So, you knocked down a woman of venerable age and a skinny fellow who had never sparred in his life. You have every reason to feel proud, Johnny."

"Well, he did have a gun, Nico."

"I will grant you that. But your brass is too big for your britches." Nicolay leaned over the porcelain bowl and expertly maneuvered a razor between his whiskers and right ear. His eyes met Hay's in the mirror, and he chortled. "So proud."

"I am, actually. Not bad for a night's work. Pinkerton would never admit it, of course. Nor you, apparently."

"Oh, I might, under duress."

⊹

Emerging from his room, stomach rumbling, Hay spotted Mrs. Keckly outside Mrs. Lincoln's bedchamber. He rushed through the double doors and called. She seemed not to hear him, but she must have, because at the sound of his voice she retreated into the Hell-cat's haven, where Hay could not—well, should not—follow.

But he did.

The door, swinging shut, smacked his palm, and Hay pushed it open again. The room smelled of camphor. Inside, Mrs. Keckly stood poised and calm, in a frilly black gown. As Hay passed through the door, she began to collapse. Her legs gave way first, followed by the swish of crinolines cascading into the floor. As her body fell forward, Hay caught it beneath the arms. He bent her back over his arm and looked for a resting place. If not on the floor, then the bed. Yes, the bed. Hay half carried, half dragged her over, pulling her head onto the pillows and then lifting her legs onto the bed. His shoulder did not hurt.

Royal-blue drapes shrouded three sides of the canopy bed. The entire bedchamber reminded Hay of a cavern at midnight, cut off from the everyday world. Only while Hay was gathering the folds of Mrs. Keckly's skirt did he notice the other body prone in the bed. It was motionless, like the guest of honor at a wake. Hay had known the Hellcat was here, of course—where else would she be?—but her presence made no demands. Even as Mrs. Keckly's eyes opened, the Hell-cat did not stir. Hay fetched a cup of water, passing up the piped Potomac water for the jug filled from Willard's sweet well. Mrs. Keckly sat up and sipped daintily.

"What happened?" she said. Water trickled from a corner of her mouth.

"You fainted."

"I know that. But why?"

"You tell me."

"I have no idea except . . ." She stopped—she did know why. "No idea at all."

"Let me ask you something, then." He did not wait for her consent. "How long have you known this Eugenia Jenkins—or whatever she calls herself?"

"Since we were girls."

"Did you know what she was trying to do—what she *did*—here?"

No reply, which Hay took as a yes. Hay felt his temper rise.

"How could you let her . . . ?" *That* was why Mrs. Keckly had wanted the slave ledger stolen, to conceal her connection to the Calvert plantation—to Eugenia. He told her of his discovery in the staff ledger, the erased line that connected Webster, James and Agnes H. "Your father," Hay said.

Mrs. Keckly stiffened, then started to tremble, until the pillows seemed to shake. Hay wondered if a person could collapse while lying down. He considered touching her forearm, to calm her, and looked across and saw a hand on her shoulder. The Hell-cat's, in a firm yet tender grip. She was whispering into Mrs. Keckly's ear, stroking her taut, graying hair. The dressmaker lay there and listened, eyes wide open, and eventually her trembling ceased.

Hay said, "Which makes Eugenia related to you by blood, does it not?"

No response.

"Your mother told you this when she was dying."

In a low voice, Mrs. Keckly said, "I promised I would take it to my grave."

"And you shall," Hay said. "Just not yet."

"Lizabeth, Lizabeth," Mrs. Lincoln murmured.

Out in the corridor, a child squealed. Mrs. Lincoln catapulted over Mrs. Keckly and leapt from the bed, her black satin dressing gown flowing behind her.

"Tad! Tad!" she shrieked, rushing through the doorway. "My darling, darling Tad!"

Hay heard the president's voice crackling with emotion, followed by the whoop of a boy smothered in loving arms.

Mrs. Keckly lay still, her eyes unfocused.

"When did you know?" said Hay.

She whispered, "Know what?"

"What she was doing."

The trembling resumed. Then: "She is a *good* nurse. Good at everything, is Mary."

Yes, everything, Hay thought. "So, when did you first understand her intentions?"

"Only when it was too late." A cry erupted from Mrs. Keckly's throat that belonged to a night-prowling animal, and then her voice lost all expression. "Not until . . . until Willie's fever started to rise. You could tell just by touching his forehead. And she said nothing about it. Acting unsurprised, like she expected it somehow. More than once this happened. After the third or fourth time, I got a feeling in my bones. I could neither prove it nor let it go."

"Nor tell anyone."

"What was there to tell? You would have laughed at me. Mister Lincoln would have smiled kindly. I knew nothing at all, really."

"Or tell Missus Lincoln."

Mrs. Keckly's passing look of amusement revealed more than she probably intended.

━━✦━━

The sugar maples were showing their first buds. Yet the Old Capitol Prison looked gray at midday. The ring of whitewash at ground level, meant to complicate prisoners' escapes, was ashen under the overcast sky. The prison's front door, on First street, just across from the Capitol, was made of the thickest oak.

At the entrance, a stocky soldier in blue flannel and a cape said, "State your business, sir."

"I am John Hay, of President Lincoln's staff, here to see a prisoner." He unfolded the note on Executive Mansion stationery.

The bearer of this letter, John M. Hay, is conducting business for the President of the United States of America. Please accord to him the same courtesies as you would accord to me.

—A. Lincoln

The soldier's rheumy eyes, inches away, peered accusingly into Hay's. He said, "Anyone might have written this."

"You are correct, Lieutenant. But only one anyone did."

The sentry cocked his head and said, "The prisoner's name?"

Hay glanced down at his calfskin notebook. "Mary Elizabeth Jenkins Surratt. Mary Surratt."

"Ah, our latest valued guest."

Hay wondered if the soldier was aware of the grounds for arrest; asking him would only pique his curiosity. The soldier pushed on the door and called to a guard with a scraggly red beard, "Missus Surratt." The guard grinned.

Hay managed to stay a half step behind as the guard hurried past the superintendent's office and turned into a short corridor. The guard mumbled something.

"Pardon?" said Hay.

"Treats her like a queen, he does."

"Who does?"

"*He* does"—gesturing at the office they had passed—"the new . . . man. Superintendent Wood is her friend. Her brother's friend. And so she merits our finest accommodations."

At the end of the corridor stood a Crusader archway and a door made of richly grained walnut. The guard detached the ungainliest key from a ring on his belt and guided it into the lock.

The room, modest in size though not in style, belonged in the pages of *Godey's Lady's Book*. Except no black-and-white lithograph would do justice to the furniture upholstered in reds and golds or to the brownish-red quilt that covered the wide bed. The rug showed a faded pattern of roses that were larger than any garden could know. Back when the building served as the temporary Capitol, after the British had burned the real one, this room must have hosted the Speaker of the House or the Senate president.

The prisoner sat in an armchair upholstered in magenta brocade. The light from the back windows threw her face into shadow, although Hay thought he saw bruises that darkened a cheek and her chin. Surely, there were worse things than hitting a woman. Although he was hard-pressed to name one. Well, murder. Damned if he would feel any guilt.

Severe black hair framed both sides of her face, like a nun's wimple. She wore the same black dress as the night before, with lace at the neck, now with splotches of dirt on the bodice. A tartan shawl was spread over her lap. Her thin lips, pressed into a line, reminded Hay of the prim ladies in Providence, until he took in her rough-hewn features and the eyes that glowed black with defiance.

"The last man I want to see," she said. There was steel in her voice.

"Our last meeting was all too brief, Missus . . . Surratt, is it?"

"It is."

"Then why did you use Jenkins?"

"That is also my name."

"And Eugenia."

"Also, that."

Actually, Hay knew why: because she had had murder in mind from the first and used a name—names—that would be harder to trace.

"Whatever you call yourself," he said, "it will go easier on you if you confess."

"Confess to what?"

Hay sighed; this would not be easy. "The murder of William Wallace Lincoln. And the attempted murder of Thomas 'Tad' Lincoln. As you know all too well."

"I trust you have compelling evidence of these . . . rather imaginative allegations."

Which was different, Hay thought, from saying they were untrue. "We have a witness, for one," Hay said, cringing at the thought of Tad in a courtroom. "Plus the correlation between your shifts on duty and the spikes in Willie's fever—that is what led us to you. And your use of a, shall we say, misleading name. And then the tin box of calomel found in your home, beneath the floorboards." All of this was true, but the more he talked, the weaker the evidence sounded. "So, how do you explain these things?"

"I am not aware that possessing calomel is against the law, or even a ground for suspicion."

"The quantity, and its being hidden away—those are grounds for suspicion." Hay had no doubts about Mrs. Surratt's guilt, but he feared she was right—that what he called evidence would be laughed out of court. "And that young man who was with you last night—I have seen him before, all too often."

"Where is he? I demand to see my son!"

Of course—Hay should have guessed. "Demand?" he said. "You are in no position to demand anything. No matter who you think you know"—Hay swept his hand in the air—"here. And even if I did know where he is, which I do not"—this was the truth, for the moment—"I would have no authority to tell you. Or any reason to. Unless, perhaps . . ."

Hay let the hint of an offer hang in the air, but she betrayed no interest in telling him anything to learn more about her son.

"Very well," Hay said.

"John would never kill anyone."

Hay had said nothing about the charges against John Surratt. "He tried to kill *me,* twice, you know. Three times, counting last night."

"I know nothing of the sort," Mrs. Surratt said. The shawl slipped a few inches; only now did Hay notice that her wrists were cuffed to the arms of the chair. "And if he did try, I can see with my own poor eyes that he failed. My son does not fail."

"Happily, he does. Did. Let me assure you, he tried. Tell me, how did you persuade Missus Keckly to hire you on as a nurse?"

"It took no persuasion at all, Mister Hay. I asked, and she agreed. She was looking for nurses. Besides, she would do anything I asked."

A bold assertion. "You have leverage over her?"

"I would not put it that way. It was her mother's dying wish—oh, she did not tell you that? Yes, when the sainted Agnes told poor Lizzy about the fortunes of her birth—and Lizzy told me, though of course I knew it already—Agnes asked her, begged her, to come to my assistance the instant I should need her. Related by blood. A Christian lady, Agnes was. Turn the other cheek to those who harm you."

"Such as yourself, you mean."

Hay suddenly remembered one of her answers. When he had asked whether Old Aunt Mary had administered medicine to Willie or Tad, *this* dark lady had replied that *that* dark lady would never hurt a cockroach. She had assumed—yes, assumed—that his inquiry about giving medicine was about doing harm. He should have noticed it at the time.

Hay said, "You knew Elizabeth Keckly—Hobbs—as a child, yes?"

"Oh yes. Very well. We spent part of every day together. Almost like sisters, you might say."

"Almost?"

"Almost."

Then it dawned on Hay—what kind of idiot was he? "You *owned* her. Your own flesh and blood."

"Oh my Lord, no. Mister Calvert owned her—the old Mister Calvert. I merely had the use of her. Seems I still do. Old habits do not change, Mister Hay, even when circumstances are new." Mrs. Surratt pulled at her restraints. "We were right to be worried about you."

" 'We'? You and your son?"

"You may believe that if you like."

Hay said, "There are others?"

"Others—for what?"

Hay's punches kept smiting air.

"You will tell us everything when your life is at stake," Hay said, for lack of a stronger argument. "Why not tell me now?"

"There is nothing to tell you. I have no cause for shame, Mister Hay. I am a patriot."

"You are under arrest for murder—you understand that?"

"I am a soldier for the South."

"So, you admit that you poisoned Willie Lincoln."

"I admit that I am a soldier for the South. Anything more, you will have to prove in court. Unless Mister Traitor Lincoln no longer believes in the courts."

That was the name on the second envelope. To Hay, more proof of her guilt. Yet judicially useless.

"I hope you enjoy this splendor," Hay said. "You may be enjoying it for a while. You are aware, are you not, that in wartime, the law is whatever the president says it is." That would never pass muster in front of a judge, but Hay hoped it might cow a laywoman. "He can have you held indefinitely."

"He would not dare to." A smile flitted across her face. "I have no fear of your president."

"And why is that, if I may ask?" Hay had not meant to be polite.

"He would not. He simply would not. Ask *him* why."

+=====+

Others.

In the hack on the way to the county jail, Hay considered the possibility of other conspirators. The rain had resumed, and the wheels of Hay's carriage along the Avenue splattered mud on a goose in the gutter.

Mrs. Keckly? Maybe she had learned of Mary Surratt's intentions earlier than she admitted. But could a mother whose son had died in battle conspire against another mother's son? Orphaned Nicolay's answer: maybe.

Or Thomas Stackpole. That his illicit trip to the enemy capital had been a matter of commerce, not betrayal—or so Pinkerton was convinced—did not prove he was innocent of murder. Always on the scene, facing Hay's office, able to slip a message into Hay's satchel whenever he liked. His father had left Calvert's plantation soon after James Webster arrived. Had they competed for the favors of Agnes Hobbs? For whatever the reason, there was no love lost between James Webster's illicit daughter and Henry Stackpole's son.

Or—and Hay shuddered at the thought, as much as he despised her—the Hell-cat. Possibly, just possibly, she was daft enough to murder her son, but surely she was too disorganized, too unreliable—too daft—to take part in a plot.

Before Hay raised any of this with the president, if he ever did, there was someone else he needed to question.

Superintendent Wood had told him where Mrs. Surratt's son was being held. (If the new superintendent had kept the information from her, maybe he *was* an honest man.) The county jail, on Fourth street near G, was known as the Blue Jug, for the paint that was a memory on its decaying walls. A defiled place, for common criminals. John Surratt Jr. was a common criminal, then.

Not *too* common, Hay hoped. Having just one man trying to kill him was more than enough. He felt a flutter of anticipation, like he was entering the ring. But this time, he had an advantage: His adversary could not punch back.

The stink of urine, stale and sharp, gut-punched him at the door. A runt of a guard with a bushy blond beard glanced up from his hard-backed chair, glaring at the day's latest bother.

"John Surratt Junior," Hay announced. The guard turned away, showing no sign of having heard. "John Su—"

"Ah hoid ya," the guard snapped. "Wait a Lord's minute, will ya?"

"Take all the time in the world," Hay said, his fists curling into balls.

At last, the guard pulled his nose out of the doorway and said, "All right, who are you?"

Hay gave his name and position with the president and got a yawn in return. "Papers?"

The note signed A. Lincoln was tattered by now and, indeed, could have been written by anyone.

"Come wit' me," the guard said.

In the dank basement, Hay preferred to breathe through his mouth. The guard left him by the barred cage, which was too small for all of its fifteen or twenty occupants to sleep or even sit at once. They milled around. Hay spotted his assailant at the back, leaning against the wall, staring at the ceiling blackened by decades of smoke. A slight and frightened boy, his goatee more a hint than a fact.

Hay wanted to beat his face in.

"Surratt!" Hay called. On his fourth cry, each louder than the one before, the boy-man seemed to stir. He lowered his eyes and, like a dazed dog, struggled to focus on the source of syllables so familiar.

"Over here," Hay said.

To his surprise, the young prisoner complied.

Surratt's triangular face looked blank, without a glint of recognition. His planed cheeks were covered with fuzz, and his sandy-brown hair was unkempt and grimy. *He* was grimy. Everything about him—his skin, his clothes, his slouch. The waistcoat was stained and ripped; his cravat hung from a collar that had come dislodged. Only his eyes had begun to show life, and they fastened on Hay's, and within moments they blazed into a molten and fiery hatred.

"You know who I am," Hay said. "And why I am here."

"I . . . do . . . not." The young Surratt had drawn close. His breath smelled of tobacco and last night's whiskey and too many hours without sleep.

"There is something I need to know. I can get you out of here"—Hay nodded at the filth and companionship—"if you will help me." He hoped this was true. More precisely, he hoped that Surratt believed it was true.

No response—a promising sign.

Hay had no time or patience to start at the edges and work his way in. "Why were you shooting at me?"

"Why do you think? I wanted you dead."

So, Hay *was* the target, not Robert.

The boy-man went on, "You were getting too close. Or she thought so."

"Your mother."

A nod.

How untrue. "You and your mother did not act alone," Hay said. "She told me this. That there were others."

Silence.

"She wants to see you, her darling boy," Hay said.

"And will she?"

"That is up to you."

"It is noisy here."

Two sinewy white men dressed in raggedy army blues hovered just behind, obviously trying to eavesdrop. Out of boredom, if nothing else.

"This will have to do," Hay said.

Hay fixed his eyes on Surratt's, with their wild expression. The prisoner's forearms rested on the vertical iron bars.

"Your mother has the fanciest accommodations any prison can offer. And here you are, in the filth of . . ."

Hay never saw Surratt's hands move, both at once, reaching through the bars and around Hay's slender neck. Thumbs pressed into his windpipe, and Hay could not breathe, much less scream. His face was pulled into the cold hard bar—blood spurted from his nose.

Yet his hands were free, and with his left fist he started to punch through the bars. Again and again he hit at Surratt's liver, propelling his leg into each punch, pummeling the abdomen while his right fist struck up at the undefended face. He kept punching, until the grip loosened around his neck. Hay clutched at a forearm and bent it crosswise and pressed it into the bars. When he whipped his right shin through the bars and kicked the boy-man in the groin, John Surratt was man enough to sink toward the rough concrete floor.

Except that Hay still had hold of a forearm, and he grabbed for the other wrist and pulled it out through the bars and trapped both of them with his chest. He reached his right hand through the bars and grasped the back of Surratt's neck and yanked. The boy-man's face slammed into the bars. Hay hissed into his ear: "Who helped?"

"I don't know, I don't know," Surratt whimpered.

"Tell me, you blackguard, tell me." Hay pushed the face away and then wrenched it back into the bars. He was dimly aware of other men gawking. Blood gushed from John Surratt's forehead. Hay was liking this, which disturbed him, though only mildly. As even Vidocq knew, violence worked.

Hay lifted the prisoner's shin from the floor and rammed it up into the horizontal bar, then rammed it again.

"I don't know, I tell you!" Surratt shrieked. " 'Twas somebody fed him puddin'—that be all I know, I swear to Jesus. She got 'im to help us—she never say who. Willin' enough, to mix calomel into the puddin'." The boy-man was gasping for breath. "Willie ate it down, and Tad, the little bugger, spit it out."

"Dang it to hell. He can go back to sleep when I'm done."

Hay regretted swearing at Rebecca Pomroy, but she refused to let him even look in on Tad. He was hoping loud voices might awaken the boy. This hope, unlike most of Hay's, came to pass.

"Papa-day, Papa-day!"

Mrs. Pomroy's width blocked the source of the yowl. She turned and said, " 'Tain't your daddy, sweet pea."

"Taddie, it's me, John." Hay tried to look around the nurse's waist and then over her shoulder.

"Johnny, Johnny!"

Hay shot Mrs. Pomroy a look of triumph. With a nod of warning, she stepped aside.

"Taddie, my boy, you like—"

"I am not your boy."

"No, you are your own boy," Hay said hastily. Tad sat up and beamed. "You like pudding, yes? What is your favorite kind of pudding? Ginger? Or . . ."

"Oh I do, I do. Yes, ginger. Or mowasses. Or . . ."

"Taddie, my . . . Tad, do you remember when you were sick, in your room here, when Willie was sick, do you remember the pudding you ate?"

Tad's face curled into a snarl.

"It tasted bad?" said Hay.

"Yes, bad. Bad."

"Did you eat any of it?"

Tad's oversized head bobbed. "Taddie is a good boy."

"Why, if it tasted so bad?"

"Because Wobert ask me so nice, and he look so cross if I say no."

· · ·

"What more can this woman do to me," Lincoln said, "than she has already done?"

"She could—"

"If it was my life she took, it would never be so painful."

Hay had intended to mention Tad.

"And something more," Hay said. He had wrestled with the question of telling the president what he had learned. Hay felt certain that Lincoln already knew, that this was why he had wanted Hay to stop the investigation. There was one way to find out. "Missus Surratt claims you will never press charges against her. Or against her son."

A hesitation. "She is correct, John."

"Because of what she knows—this is extortion. Because of what *you* know."

"I know nothing at all, John, nothing about anything. The older I get—and only the Lord knows how many years I have left—the more I understand how very little I know. I aspire, should I live long enough, to utter ignorance."

"About Bob, sir?"

Lincoln's gaze had returned from a place unknown to a sharp intelligent point. "He will not come back here for a while. I am the one at fault here, John. He lacked a father's love, and so he grew to hate the sons who lacked for nothing. He explained this to me the night he confessed what he had done. He told *me*. He bragged about it, killing his own . . ." Lincoln struggled to keep his composure, and he succeeded.

"He was only doing what Missus Surratt wanted."

"But he *did* it. *He* wanted it, too. This is my doing, John. My fault. I am the guilty party here. As a father, as a man. It is on my shoulders. In my most important job, to raise my sons to become hardy and capable men, I have failed utterly. And my failure with one son brought the . . . the . . ." His shoulders shook, then slumped. "Oh, John, John, John, this is worse, worse—*harder*—than the war."

Hay had never before seen anyone cry horizontal tears.

Oh, Robert! Hay marveled at his own ineptness, at never seeing the hatreds seething in his young friend's soul. Directed not so much at his younger brother, or brothers—of this, Hay felt unaccountably certain—but at the father who had never been a father to his eldest, the father who was a man of ambition and too rarely at home. Robert's shot had found its mark.

When Lincoln regained his control, he said, "Keeping this between ourselves, John, has nothing to do with Robert. It is for Mother. She could never survive another blow. For her it would mean losing another son—it would kill her. She must never know. Nor Tad. John, my dear, dear John, I would consider it the finest of favors—a blessing, really— if you would never mention this to another living soul. Including Robert. Never."

What blue-blasted choice did Hay have? He gave his word. "And you insist," he said, "on freeing this Mary Surratt, who vows to cause you harm? *And* her son."

"They may repent, John, you shall see. The power of mercy unstrained can touch the hardest heart."

Hay considered pleading the logic of deterrence and invoking the demands of justice. But who was he to judge? It was Lincoln who was the master of mercy and also the mind behind the war, the man who knew when to love and when to fight. What did Hay really know about any of this? He knew enough, at least, to keep his mouth shut. Besides, he knew beyond a doubt that any attempt to change Lincoln's mind was destined to fail.

Afterword

Around 5:00 P.M. on February 20, 1862, at the Executive Mansion, eleven-year-old William Wallace Lincoln died in the Prince of Wales Room, now known as the Lincoln Bedroom. The cause of death was thought to be typhoid fever. In my story, he was poisoned.

Almost everything else in this novel is true. John Hay and John George Nicolay shared a room upstairs in the Executive Mansion; they referred to the Lincolns as "the Ancient" and "the Hell-cat"; a House committee fingered secessionists throughout the government, in language I've borrowed; John Watt tried to blackmail Mrs. Lincoln for $20,000 and settled for $1,500; Lincoln lent $380 to Thomas Stackpole in November 1861; Tad swiped the gardener's strawberries and got a scolding; Elizabeth Keckly had worked for Mrs. Jefferson Davis (who invited her south) and for Mrs. Robert E. Lee before she made dresses for Mary Lincoln; Allan Pinkerton and his wife were once robbed in Warsaw, Illinois; the symptoms of mercury poisoning mimic those of typhoid fever, except for the spinach-like stool—all of this is true. Willie's embalming, funeral, and exhumation (which actually happened twice); Hay's spurned affections for Kate Chase; Mrs. Lincoln's séance at the Soldiers' Home (one of several); her slap across her husband's face; the Marsh and Smithson tests for, respectively, arsenic and mercury; Charles Calvert's octagonal cow barn; "Bowie Knife" Potter's nickname and ancestry; the Reverend Gurley's eulogy; the tussles with General McClellan; the cabinet's uproar over the *Merrimack*, with the dialogue drawn from navy secretary Gideon Welles's diary; each day's weather in Washington City—all fact. Where possible, I have used dialogue or observations taken from diaries, memoirs, and journalistic accounts. John Hay later became a published poet (occasional lines I've used were his), although there is no evidence he ever stepped into a boxing ring.

The biographical facts about Mary Surratt are accurate (her grandfather was the overseer of the Calvert estate; she often used her confirmation name, Eugenia; her brother's friend became Old Capitol Prison's superintendent in January 1862) but there is no reason to think she had any kinship to Elizabeth Keckly or any involvement in Willie Lincoln's death. Three years later, she was hanged as a coconspirator in the president's murder, for using her H Street house as a meeting place for John Wilkes Booth and the plotters. Her son John Jr. was tried but never convicted for his role in the assassination.

Every character in this novel is real except for Josiah, Hay's second in the boxing ring; Albert, the black butler at Riversdale; Sally Socrates, the slave woman there; and Sally's (offstage) escaped daughter, Eva. I have blended two slaves at Arlington House—James Parks, who lived from 1843 to 1929, and an older man known to Hay as "the African," born at Mount Vernon before George Washington died there in 1799. I've modeled Hay's professor of pugilism after Terrance Wood, my boxing instructor for the past seven years. The character of Dr. Jamie Hall conflates Dr. James C. Hall, a physician on Pennsylvania avenue in Washington at the time; Dr. Neal Hall, who consulted with Dr. Stone on Willie's case; and the (presumed) son of Lincoln's stepsister, Matilda, and her husband, Squire Hall. Little is known about John Watt (who was a Scotsman, not a Kentuckian), Thomas Stackpole, Edward McManus, Cornelia Mitchell, and some other minor characters, so I have invented their backgrounds, physical presence, and personalities. I've altered several facts about Elizabeth Keckly's life: She never lived at the Calvert estate; her mother disclosed on her deathbed (in 1857, not in 1862) that Elizabeth's real father was Armistead Burwell, their owner in Dinwiddie, Virginia. Otherwise, for the historically prominent characters and their relationships, I've hewed to what is known, with two exceptions. Historians generally see Robert Lincoln as a bland and dutiful Victorian, not a neurotic like the mother he otherwise resembled.

And I've kept John Hay's irreverence and his closeness to Lincoln and Nicolay, but his writing style (which was ornate and clever beyond compare) and inner life reflect more of my own.

A few other details have been changed for the sake of the story. I've made Dr. Stone handsomer than he was. The House Select Committee on the Loyalty of Government Clerks had already published its report, in January 1862; it described Thomas Stackpole as a messenger at the president's house (apparently because of an earlier post) instead of as a doorkeeper. Grant's army captured Fort Donelson, in Tennessee, five days earlier than I have it here. The soldier in Lincoln's anecdote was shot in the testicles at Antietam, six months after this story ends, not at Dranesville. Lincoln's tearful conversation in chapter 5 took place with Rebecca Pomroy, Tad's nurse, and not with Hay. His scolding of McClellan in chapter 9 was actually delivered to General Randolph Marcy, McClellan's son-in-law and chief of staff, and his jab at McClellan about borrowing his army happened a month later. I found no indication that Lincoln spoke from the White House window on the anniversary of his inauguration. The Calvert estate's slave ledger, which is real, lists "Negroes sold to Mr. Armfield," not to Armistead Burwell. I am not aware that the Calverts and Burwell were friends or that any staff ledger existed.

And, of course, many of the scenes and most of the dialogue are invented, but I hope they ring true.

Acknowledgments

One morning, while I was writing a book about FDR's attempt to pack the Supreme Court in 1937, I had Tommy Corcoran showing up at the White House. I wanted the brash aide to have a newspaper under his arm, but I couldn't do it. The book was nonfiction, and I'm a purist about the facts.

It was that day or the next, staring at my computer screen, that an idea came into my head: a murder mystery in the Lincoln White House. Then a second: John Hay as the detective. I didn't even know I knew who he was. But I love mysteries. I love Lincoln. This was a book I wanted to read. So I'd better write it.

It proved to be a labor of love, all the more because of the many people who helped me along. This is a work of fiction, but it was rooted in research. Librarians and curators were their usual wonderful selves, especially James M. Cornelius at the Abraham Lincoln Presidential Library and Museum, who kindly read the manuscript and saved me from many a mistake; Nancy Kervin at the US Senate Library; Stephen Greenberg at the US National Library of Medicine; Jerry McCoy and others at the D.C. Public Library's Washingtoniana Collection; and too many to mention at the Library of Congress. My thanks to National Park Service ranger Adam Gresek at Arlington House, director Erin Mast of the Lincoln cottage, historian Ann Wass at the Riversdale House Museum, boxing historian Elliott Gorn at Brown University, Wilson Golden of the New York Avenue Presbyterian Church, Scott Stephens at the National Weather Service, Isobel Ellis of *National Journal,* and Mathew Polowitz, my son-in-law's brother, for helping me learn the things I needed to know.

I am grateful to the editors at *National Journal* and *The Atlantic,* especially Charlie Green, Ron Brownstein, and Scott Stossel, for giving me chances to earn some dough while I was writing this.

Friends pitched in. Bill O'Brian masterminded a promotional video and, along with Steve Morgan and Joel Altschul, read early drafts. Jonathan Rauch proposed the title, Paul Golob suggested a detective series, and Monte Lorell thought Hay should compose bad poetry (which is way easier to write). Pat LoBrutto, as an editorial consultant, had astute ideas about how to sharpen the mystery and to deepen Hay as a character.

It's hard to sell fiction, and thanks to Jim Fallows and Jim Srodes, I've found literary agents willing to represent a first-time novelist. I am indebted to the late Wendy Weil, to Paul Bresnick and, above all, to Ron Goldfarb and Gerrie Sturman for taking on this book and finding a home for it. And such a good home. At Macmillan's Tom Doherty Associates, Claire Eddy's enthusiasm for this book and her deftness in editorial judgment have been a wonder.

The best home, of course, is my real home, with my unfathomably patient and ever-loving wife, Nancy Tuholski. After decades, I'm still smitten. If she had moments of doubt about what I was up to for five years, she was kind enough not to say so.